THE COMPLETE
OOM SCHALK LOURENS
STORIES

HERMAN CHARLES BOSMAN was born in Kuils River near Cape Town in 1905 but lived in the Transvaal for most of his life. Educated at Jeppe Boys' High and the University of the Witwatersrand, in 1926 he was sent as a novice teacher to the Marico District in what was then the Western Transvaal. There he encountered the spellbinding storytellers that he was later to immortalise in his Oom Schalk Lourens stories.

His spell in the Marico was cut short when, on a return home during the July holidays, he became involved in an argument with his step-brother and shot and killed him. Convicted of murder, he was initially sentenced to hang, but this sentence was later commuted to life imprisonment and he was eventually released after four years.

He embarked on a career as a journalist and began writing his Oom Schalk Lourens stories. They were eventually to number sixty in all, and are undoubtedly his best-known and best-loved works.

His first novel, *Jacaranda in the Night*, appeared in 1947, and was followed in the same year by a collection of Schalk Lourens stories, *Mafeking Road*, and, two years later, his prison memoir *Cold Stone Jug*.

He died of heart failure in 1951 at the age of forty-six.

The editor:

CRAIG MACKENZIE has edited nine volumes of Bosman's stories, seven of which were part of the fourteen-volume Anniversary Edition of Bosman's works, a project that he undertook with Stephen Gray between 1997 and 2005.

His doctoral study, *The Oral-style South African Short Story in English* (published in 1999), featured Bosman as its centrepiece. He is Professor and Chair of the English Department at the University of Johannesburg.

HERMAN CHARLES BOSMAN

THE COMPLETE OOM SCHALK LOURENS STORIES

Edited by
Craig MacKenzie

HUMAN & ROUSSEAU
Cape Town Pretoria

Acknowledgment: This volume draws substantially on the Anniversary Edition of Bosman's works that Stephen Gray and I undertook between 1997 and 2005, the centenary year of Bosman's birth. My grateful thanks are extended to my co-editor, both for his assistance with the Oom Schalk collections I edited for the Anniversary Edition and, more particularly, for advice here. – C. M.

Copyright © 2006 by the estate of Herman Charles Bosman
This selection, preface and notes © Craig MacKenzie, 2006
First published in this form in 2006 by Human & Rousseau,
an imprint of NB Publishers,
a division of Media24 Boeke (Pty) Ltd,
40 Heerengracht, Cape Town, 8001
Cover illustration by 'Flip', accompanying first publication of
"The Traitor's Wife" in *Spotlight*, February 1951.
Typography and cover design by Etienne van Duyker
Set in 11 on 12.75 pt Palatino by ALINEA STUDIO, Cape Town

FSC
www.fsc.org
MIX
Paper from
responsible sources
FSC® C105735

Printed in South Africa by Interpak Books, Pietermaritzburg

First hardcover edition, second impression 2007
First soft cover edition, first impression 2009
Third impression 2014

ISBN 978-0-7981-5073-6
ISBN 978-0-7981-5840-4 (epub)
ISBN 978-0-7981-6352-1 (mobi)

Contents

Unpublished in His Lifetime

PREFACE

Bosman's Oom Schalk Lourens is a literary creation without equal in South African literature. Precedents there are aplenty, to be sure (one thinks of Ernest Glanville's 'Uncle Abe Pike', Perceval Gibbon's 'Vrouw Grobelaar', Pauline Smith's 'Koenraad' or Jean Blignaut's 'Hottentot Ruiter'), but no storyteller figure looms as large in the popular imagination as Oom Schalk. His famous boast, ". . . I can tell the best stories of anybody in the Transvaal . . ." ("Mafeking Road", 1935), has gone unchallenged for the seventy years since it was first uttered.

Remarkably, Bosman got the formula right from the outset: his two earliest Oom Schalk stories – "Makapan's Caves" (1930) and "The Rooinek" (1931) – have remained classics despite the author's relative youth (25) and the many later gems that might well have eclipsed them. Subsequent refinements there certainly were: both early stories are somewhat overwritten, and "Makapan's Caves" even used the cumbersome and unnecessary device of inverted commas to denote Oom Schalk's narrative voice. But all of the characteristic irony, humour and pathos that were later to become so famous were present in these first efforts.

There were two main forms of influence on Bosman's creation, one literary and the other contextual. Bosman's liking for the American yarnsters in the Mark Twain and Bret Harte mould is well documented, and he also delighted in collecting tales by local practitioners of the 'tall tale' genre (some of which duly appeared in his *Veld-trails and Pavements* collection of 1949).

But these literary models found real-life equivalents in the Groot Marico District, to which Bosman was sent as a young and impressionable teacher in January 1926. The next six months in the young man's life were to prove momentous: he was exposed to a community poor in material wealth but rich in the art of storytelling. Sent out to convert the people of this region to the alphabet and literacy, he was instead won over by their own spell-binding mastery of oral narrative. Stories about the Anglo-Boer wars and tribal skirmishes, about life in the Boer Republics of Stellaland, Goshen and Ohrigstad, about local legend and lore were all eagerly absorbed by the young school-teacher over coffee on the farm stoep or in the voorkamer.

Later in life he was able to draw on this deep reservoir of material in over 150 stories spanning some twenty years, and this work established his reputation as one of South Africa's most popular and enduring writers. It also brought a unique region of the country to the public's attention: "There is no other place I know," Bosman later remarked ("Marico Revisited", November 1944), "that is so heavy with atmosphere, so strangely and darkly impregnated with that stuff of life that bears the authentic stamp of South Africa."

The first collection of Oom Schalks appeared under Bosman's own direction as *Mafeking Road* in 1947. It was rapturously received by the public and quickly established itself as a major South African classic, going into six editions and innumerable impressions in the years since its first appearance. For sixty years it has never been out of print. Bosman's premature death thwarted his intention to release a second Oom Schalk collection, which he apparently intended to title 'Seed-time and Harvest'. In 2001, a volume with this title appeared in the fourteen-volume Anniversary Edition of Bosman's works, and was followed in 2002 by *Unto Dust and Other Stories*, which completed the sequence.

Here between the covers of one volume for the first time, however, all sixty of these Oom Schalks are gathered, together with the illustrations that originally accompanied them. For, celebrated though Oom Schalk may be, the talented illustrators who contributed richly to the way his stories originally appeared have all but been forgotten. Here an attempt is made to recuperate this unique aspect of the Schalk Lourens story. H. E. Winder, A. E. Mason, Wilfrid Cross, Reginald Turvey, René Shapshak, Maurice van Essche and Abe Berry were giants of the magazine and art world of the period 1930 to 1960, and, as

10

any survey of periodicals from the 1930s through to the 1950s will show, Bosman was highly regarded by these men. No other writer of the period was able to attract such a range of creative talent – or, for that matter, induce editors to make available the extra space and cover the expense that illustrations involve.

As the notes on the illustrators reveal (see "Bosman's Illustrators"), Bosman either knew these men personally, or knew of and actually reviewed their work. He took local art very seriously, and made the time to view it in the various exhibitions that he enthusiastically attended both in Johannesburg and Cape Town. This aspect of Bosman is little known, and perhaps the present volume will restore it to the public's attention.

Two principles govern the sequencing of the stories here: publication chronology and publication venue. Fortunately, these dovetail neatly, because Bosman tended (until the last years, at least) to place his stories in one magazine until this was no longer viable and then move on to the next. So I was able to cluster the stories according to where they were published without significantly disrupting the publication sequence.

The Oom Schalk Lourens sequence as a whole can be divided into three broad phases: early stories (1930–31); those he wrote in London (1934–37); and those he wrote upon his return to South Africa in 1940 until his death in 1951. This last grouping has been further sub-divided for ease of reading – again, largely on the basis of where stories were first published. (A detailed contextualisation of the stories and the periodicals in which they appeared is offered in "Notes on the Stories.")

Bosman's achievement is to have created a character who has far outlived the time and place in which he is putatively situated. This is because Oom Schalk Lourens is only apparently simple, prejudiced and narrow-minded. He has endured as a much-loved South African literary figure because his humane vision extends to embrace all of South Africa, and all South Africans. He therefore speaks to us today as poignantly, beguilingly and movingly as he did when he made his first appearance seventy-six years ago.

On the dust-jacket of the first edition of *Mafeking Road* the following description of him appeared. Probably written by Bosman himself, it goes unrivalled to this day:

Each of the stories here presented is identified with the central character, Oom Schalk Lourens, an old Boer farmer, who has seen all the way into life, but whose experiences have not embittered him; and who retains, in spite of his Calvinistic outlook and background, and in spite of all his narrow backveld prejudices (and he has them in good measure), a warm kindliness of disposition, irradiating the stories he tells with a sincere and strangely moving humanity.

Craig MacKenzie
Johannesburg, 2006

The *Touleier* Years
(1930–31)

Makapan's Caves

Kaffirs? (said Oom Schalk Lourens). Yes, I know them. And they're all the same. I fear the Almighty, and I respect His works, but I could never understand why He made the kaffir and the rinderpest. The Hottentot is a little better. The Hottentot will only steal the biltong hanging out on the line to dry. He won't steal the line as well. That is where the kaffir is different.

Still, sometimes you come across a good kaffir, who is faithful and upright and a true Christian and doesn't let the wild-dogs catch the sheep. I always think that it isn't right to kill that kind of kaffir.

I remember about one kaffir we had, by the name of Nongaas. How we got him was after this fashion. It was in the year of the big drought, when there was no grass, and the water in the pan had dried up. Our cattle died like flies. It was terrible. Every day ten or twelve or twenty died. So my father said we must pack everything on the wagons and trek up to the Dwarsberge, where he heard there had been good rains. I was six years old, then, the youngest in the family. Most of the time I sat in the back of the wagon, with my mother and my two sisters. My brother Hendrik was seventeen, and he helped my father and the kaffirs to drive on our cattle. That was how we trekked. Many more of our cattle died along the way, but after about two months we got into the Lowveld and my father said that God had been good to us. For the grass was green along the Dwarsberge.

One morning we came to some kaffir huts, where my father bartered two sacks of mealies for a roll of tobacco. A piccanin of about my own age was standing in front of a hut, and he looked at us all the time and grinned. But mostly he looked at my brother Hendrik. And that was not a wonder, either. Even in those days my brother Hendrik was careful about his appearance, and he always tried to be fashionably dressed. On Sundays he even wore socks. When we had loaded up the mealies, my father cut off a plug of Boer tobacco and gave it to the piccanin, who grinned still more, so that we saw every one of his teeth, which were very white. He put the plug in his mouth and bit it. Then we all laughed. The piccanin looked just like a puppy that has swallowed a piece of meat, and turns his head sideways, to see how it tastes.

That was in the morning. We went right on until the afternoon, for my father wanted to reach Tweekoppiesfontein, where we were going to stand with our cattle for some time. It was late in the afternoon when we got there, and we started to outspan. Just as I was getting off the wagon, I looked round and saw something jumping quickly behind a bush. It looked like some animal, so I was afraid, and told my brother Hendrik, who took up his gun and walked slowly towards the bush. We saw, directly afterwards, that it was the piccanin whom we had seen that morning in front of the hut. He must have been following behind our wagons for about ten miles. He looked dirty and tired, but when my brother went up to him he began to grin again, and seemed very happy. We didn't know what to do with him, so Hendrik shouted to him to go home, and started throwing stones at him. But my father was a merciful man, and after he had heard Nongaas's story – for that was the name of the piccanin – he said he could stay with us, but he must be good, and not tell lies and steal, like the other kaffirs. Nongaas told us in the Sechuana language, which my father understood, that his father and mother had been killed by the lions, and that he was living with his uncle, whom he didn't like, but that he liked my brother Hendrik, and that was why he had followed our wagons.

Nongaas remained with us for many years. He grew up with us. He was a very good kaffir, and as time went by he became much attached to all of us. But he worshipped my brother Hendrik. As he grew older, my father sometimes spoke to Nongaas about his soul, and explained to him about God. But although he told my father that he understood, I could see that whenever Nongaas thought of God, he was really only thinking of Hendrik.

It was just after my twenty-first birthday that we got news that Hermanus Potgieter and his whole family had been killed by a kaffir tribe under Makapan. They also said that, after killing him, the

16

kaffirs stripped off old Potgieter's skin and made wallets out of it in which to carry their dagga. It was very wicked of the kaffirs to have done that, especially as dagga makes you mad and it is a sin to smoke it. A commando was called up from our district to go and attack the tribe and teach them to have respect for the white man's laws – and above all, to have more respect for the white man's skin. My mother and sisters baked a great deal of harde beskuit, which we packed up, together with mealie-meal and biltong. We also took out the lead mould and melted bullets. The next morning my brother and I set out on horseback for Makapan's kraal. We were accompanied by Nongaas, whom we took along with us to look after the horses and light the fires. My father stayed at home. He said that he was too old to go on commando, unless it was to fight the redcoats, if there were still any left.

But he gave us some good advice.

"Don't forget to read your Bible, my sons," he called out as we rode away. "Pray the Lord to help you, and when you shoot always aim for the stomach." These remarks were typical of my father's deeply religious nature, and he also knew that it was easier to hit a man in the stomach than in the head: and it is just as good, because no man can live long after his intestines have been shot away.

Well, we rode on, my brother and I, with Nongaas following a few yards behind us on the pack-horse. Now and again we fell in with other burghers, many of whom brought their wagons with them, until, on the third day, we reached Makapan's kraal, where the big commando had already gone into camp. We got there in the evening, and everywhere as far as we could see there were fires burning in a big circle. There were over two hundred wagons, and on their tents the fires shone red and yellow. We reported ourselves to the veldkornet, who showed us a place where we could camp, next to the four Van Rensburg brothers. Nongaas had just made the fire and boiled the coffee when one of the Van Rensburgs came up and invited us over to their wagon. They had shot a rietbok and were roasting pieces of it on the coals.

We all shook hands and said it was good weather for the mealies if only the ruspes didn't eat them, and that it was time we had another president, and that rietbok tasted very fine when roasted on the coals. Then they told us what had happened about the kaffirs. Makapan and his followers had seen the commandos coming from a distance, and after firing a few shots at them had all fled into the caves in the krantz. These caves stretched away underground very far and with many turnings. So, as the Boers could not storm the kaffirs without losing heavily, the kommandant gave instructions that the ridge was to be surrounded and the kaffirs starved out. They were all inside the caves, the whole tribe, men, women and children. They had already been there six days, and as they couldn't have much food left, and as there was only a small dam with brackish water, we were hopeful of being able to kill off most of the kaffirs without wasting ammunition.

Already, when the wind blew towards us from the mouth of the caves, the stink was terrible. We would have pitched our camp further back, only that we were afraid some of the kaffirs would escape between the fires.

The following morning I saw for the first time why we couldn't drive the kaffirs from their lairs, even though our commando was four hundred strong. All over, through the rocks and bushes, I could see black openings in the krantz that led right into the deep parts of the earth. Here and there we could see dead bodies lying. But there were still left a lot of kaffirs that were not dead, and them we could not see. But they had guns, which they had bought from the illicit traders and the missionaries, and they shot at us whenever we came within range. And all the time there was that stench of decaying bodies.

For another week the siege went on. Then we heard that our leaders, Marthinus Wessels Pretorius and Paul Kruger, had quarrelled. Kruger wanted to attack the kaffirs immediately and finish the affair, but Pretorius said it was too dangerous and he didn't want any more burghers killed. He said that already the hand of the Lord lay heavy upon Makapan, and in another few weeks the kaffirs would all be dead of starvation. But Paul Kruger said that it would even be better if the hand of the Lord lay still heavier upon the kaffirs. Eventually Paul Kruger obtained permission to take fifty volunteers and storm the caves from one side, while Kommandant Piet Potgieter was to advance from the other side with two hundred men, to distract the attention of the kaffirs. Kruger was popular with all of us, and nearly everyone volunteered to go with him. So he picked fifty men, among whom were the Van Rensburgs and my brother. Therefore, as I did not want to stay behind and guard the camp, I had to join Piet Potgieter's commando.

All the preparations were made, and the following morning we got ready to attack. My brother Hendrik was very proud and happy at having been chosen for the more dangerous part. He oiled his gun very carefully and polished up his veldskoens.

Then Nongaas came up and I noticed that he looked very miserable.

"My baas," he said to my brother Hendrik, "you mustn't go and fight. They'll shoot you dead."

My brother shook his head.

"Then let me go with you, baas," Nongaas said; "I will go in front and look after you."

Hendrik only laughed.

"Look here, Nongaas," he said, "you can stay behind and cook the dinner. I will get back in time to eat it."

The whole commando came together and we all knelt down and prayed. Then Marthinus Wessels Pretorius said we must sing Hymn Number 23, "Rest my soul, thy God is king." Furthermore, we sang another hymn and also a psalm. Most people would have thought that one hymn would be enough. But not so Pretorius. He always made quite sure of everything he did. Then we moved off to the attack. We fought bravely, but the kaffirs were many, and they lay in the darkness of the caves, and shot at us without our being able to see them. While the fighting lasted it was worse than the lyddite bombs at Paardeberg. And the stench was terrible. We tied handkerchiefs round the lower part of our face, but that did not help. Also, since we were not Englishmen, many of us had no handkerchiefs. Still we fought on, shooting at an enemy we could not see. We rushed right up to the mouth of one of the caves, and even got some distance into it, when our leader, Kommandant Piet Potgieter, flung up his hands and fell backwards, shot through the breast. We carried him out, but he was quite dead. So we lost heart and retired.

When we returned from the fight we found that the other attacking party had also been defeated. They had shot many kaffirs, but there were still hundreds of them left, who fought all the more fiercely with hunger gnawing at their bellies.

I went back to our camp. There was only Nongaas, sitting forward on a stone, with his face on his arms. An awful fear clutched me as I asked him what was wrong.

"Baas Hendrik," he replied, and as he looked at me in his eyes there was much sorrow, "Baas Hendrik did not come back."

I went out immediately and made enquiries, but nobody could tell me anything for sure. They remembered quite well seeing my brother Hendrik when they stormed the cave. He was right in amongst the foremost of the attackers. When I heard that, I felt a great pride in my brother, although I also knew that nothing else could be expected of the son of my father. But no man could tell me what had happened to him. All they knew was that when they got back he was not amongst them.

I spoke to Marthinus Wessels Pretorius and asked him to send out another party to seek for my brother. But Pretorius was angry.

"I will not allow one more man," he replied. "It was all Kruger's doing. I was against it from the start. Now Kommandant Potgieter has been killed, who was a better man than Kruger and all his Dopper clique put together. If any man goes back to the caves I shall discharge him from the commando."

But I don't think it was right of Pretorius. Because Paul Kruger was only trying to do his duty, and afterwards, when he was nominated for president, I voted for him.

It was eleven o'clock when I again reached our part of the laager. Nongaas was still sitting on the flat stone, and I saw that he had carried out my brother Hendrik's instructions, and that the pot was boiling on the fire. The dinner was ready, but my brother was not there. That sight was too much for me, and I went and lay down alone under the Van Rensburgs' wagon.

I looked up again, about half an hour later, and I saw Nongaas walking away with a water-bottle and a small sack strapped to his back. He said nothing to me, but I knew he was going to look for my brother Hendrik. Nongaas knew that if his baas was still alive he would need him. So he went to him. That was all. For a long while I watched Nongaas as he crept along through the rocks and bushes. I supposed it was his intention to lie in wait near one of the caves and then crawl inside when the night came. That was a very brave thing to do. If Makapan's kaffirs saw him they would be sure to kill him, because he was helping the Boers against them, and also because he was a Bechuana.

The evening came, but neither my brother Hendrik nor Nongaas. All that night I sat with my face to the caves and never slept. Then in the morning I got up and loaded my gun. I said to myself that if Nongaas had been killed in the attempt there was only one thing left for me to do. I myself must go to my brother.

I walked out first into the veld, in case one of the officers saw me and made me come back. Then I walked along the ridge and got under cover of the bushes. From there I crawled along, hiding in the long grass and behind the stones, so that I came to one part of Makapan's stronghold where things were more quiet. I got to within about two hundred yards of a cave. There I lay very still, behind a big rock, to find out if there were any kaffirs watching from that side. Occasionally I heard the sound of a shot being fired, but that was far away. Afterwards I fell asleep, for I was very weary with the anxiety and through not having slept the night before.

When I woke up the sun was right overhead. It was hot and there were no clouds in the sky. Only there were a few aasvoëls, which flew round and round very slowly, without ever seeming to flap their wings. Now and again one of them would fly down and settle on the ground, and it was very horrible. I thought of my brother Hendrik and shivered. I looked towards the cave. Inside it seemed as though there was something moving. A minute later I saw that it was a kaffir coming stealthily towards the entrance. He appeared to be looking in my direction, and for fear that he should see me and call the other kaffirs, I jumped up quickly and shot at him, aiming at the stomach. He fell over like a sack of potatoes and I was thankful for my father's advice. But I had to act quickly. If the other kaffirs had heard the shot they would all come running up at once. And I didn't want that to happen. I didn't like the look of those aasvoëls. So I decided to take a great risk. Accordingly I ran as fast as I could towards the cave and rushed right into it, so that, even if the kaffirs did come, they wouldn't see me amongst the shadows. For a long time I lay down and waited. But as no more kaffirs came, I got up and walked slowly down a dark passage, looking round every time to see that nobody followed me, and to make sure that I would find my way back. For there were many twists and turnings, and the whole krantz seemed to be hollowed out.

I knew that my search would be very difficult. But there was something that seemed to tell me that my brother was nearby. So I was strong in my faith, and I knew that the Lord would lead me aright. And I found my brother Hendrik, and he was alive. It was with a feeling of great joy that I came across him. I saw him in the dim light that came through a big split in the roof. He was lying against a boulder, holding his leg and groaning. I saw afterwards that his leg was sprained and much swollen, but that was all that was wrong. So great was my brother Hendrik's surprise at seeing me that at first he could not talk. He just held my hand and laughed softly, and when I touched his forehead I knew he was feverish. I gave him some brandy out of my flask, and in a few words he told me all that had happened. When they stormed the cave he was right in front and as the kaffirs retreated he followed them up. But they all ran in different ways, until my brother found himself alone. He tried to get back, but lost his way and fell down a dip. In that way he sprained his ankle so severely that he had been in agony all the time. He crawled into a far corner and remained there, with the danger and the darkness and his pain. But the worst of all was the stink of the rotting bodies.

"Then Nongaas came," my brother Hendrik said.

"Nongaas?" I asked him.

"Yes," he replied. "He found me and gave me food and water, and carried me on his back. Then the water gave out and I was very thirsty. So Nongaas took the bottle to go and fill it at the pan. But it is very dangerous to get there, and I am so frightened they may kill him."

"They will not kill him," I said. "Nongaas will come back." I said that, but in my heart I was afraid. For the caves were many and dark, and the kaffirs were blood-mad. It would not do to wait. So I lifted Hendrik on my shoulder and carried him towards the entrance. He was in much pain.

"You know," he whispered, "Nongaas was crying when he found me. He thought I was dead. He has been very good to me – so very good. Do you remember that day when he followed

22

behind our wagons? He looked so very trustful and so little, and yet I – I threw stones at him. I wish I did not do that. I only hope that he comes back safe. He was crying and stroking my hair."

As I said, my brother Hendrik was feverish.

"Of course he will come back," I answered him. But this time I knew that I lied. For as I came through the mouth of the cave I kicked against the kaffir I had shot there. The body sagged over to one side and I saw the face.

THE ROOINEK

Rooineks, said Oom Schalk Lourens, are queer.
For instance, there was that day when my
nephew Hannes and I had dealings with a couple
of Englishmen near Dewetsdorp. It was shortly
after Sanna's Post, and Hannes and I were lying
behind a rock watching the road. Hannes spent
odd moments like that in what he called a useful
way. He would file the points of his Mauser
cartridges on a piece of flat stone until the lead
showed through the steel, in that way making
them into dum-dum bullets.

I often spoke to my nephew Hannes about that.

"Hannes," I used to say. "That is a sin. The Lord
is looking at you."

"That's all right," Hannes replied. "The Lord knows that this
is the Boer War, and in war-time he will always forgive a little
foolishness like this, especially as the English are so many."

Anyway, as we lay behind that rock we saw, far down the road,
two horsemen come galloping up. We remained perfectly still and
let them approach to within four hundred paces. They were
English officers. They were mounted on first-rate horses and their
uniforms looked very fine and smart. They were the most stylish-
looking men I had seen for some time, and I felt quite ashamed of
my own ragged trousers and veldskoens. I was glad that I was
behind a rock and they couldn't see me. Especially as my jacket
was also torn all the way down the back, as a result of my having
had, three days before, to get through a barbed-wire fence rather
quickly. I just got through in time, too. The veldkornet, who was a
fat man and couldn't run so fast, was about twenty yards behind
me. And he remained on the wire with a bullet through him. All

through the Boer War I was pleased that I was thin and never troubled with corns. Hannes and I fired just about the same time. One of the officers fell off his horse. He struck the road with his shoulders and rolled over twice, kicking up the red dust as he turned. Then the other soldier did a queer thing. He drew up his horse and got off. He gave just one look in our direction. Then he led his horse up to where the other man was twisting and struggling on the ground. It took him a little while to lift him on to his horse, for it is no easy matter to pick up a man like that when he is helpless. And he did all this slowly and calmly, as though he was not concerned about the fact that the men who had shot his friend were lying only a few hundred yards away. He managed in some way to support the wounded man across the saddle, and walked on beside the horse. After going a few yards he stopped and seemed to remember something. He turned round and waved at the spot where he imagined we were hiding, as though inviting us to shoot. During all that time I had simply lain watching him, astonished at his coolness.

But when he waved his hand I thrust another cartridge into the breach of my Martini and aimed. At that distance I couldn't miss.

25

I aimed very carefully and was just on the point of pulling the trigger when Hannes put his hand on the barrel and pushed up my rifle.

"Don't shoot, Oom Schalk," he said. "That's a brave man."

I looked at Hannes in surprise. His face was very white. I said nothing, and allowed my rifle to sink down on to the grass, but I couldn't understand what had come over my nephew. It seemed that not only was that Englishman queer, but that Hannes was also queer. That's all nonsense not killing a man just because he's brave. If he's a brave man and he's fighting on the wrong side, that's all the more reason to shoot him.

I was with my nephew Hannes for another few months after that. Then one day, in a skirmish near the Vaal River, Hannes with a few dozen other burghers was cut off from the commando and had to surrender. That was the last I ever saw of him. I heard later on that, after taking him prisoner, the English searched Hannes and found dum-dum bullets in his possession. They shot him for that. I was very much grieved when I heard of Hannes's death. He had always been full of life and high spirits. Perhaps Hannes was right in saying that the Lord didn't mind about a little foolishness like dum-dum bullets. But the mistake he made was in forgetting that the English did mind.

I was in the veld until they made peace. Then we laid down our rifles and went home. What I knew my farm by was the hole under the koppie where I quarried slate-stones for the threshing-floor. That was about all that remained as I left it. Everything else was gone. My home was burnt down. My lands were laid waste. My cattle and sheep were slaughtered. Even the stones I had piled for the kraals were pulled down. My wife came out of the concentration camp, and we went together to look at our old farm. My wife had gone into the concentration camp with our two children, but she came out alone. And when I saw her again and noticed the way she had changed, I knew that I, who had been through all the fighting, had not seen the Boer War.

Neither Sannie nor I had the heart to go on farming again on that same place. It would be different without the children playing about the house and getting into mischief. We got paid out some money by the new Government for part of our losses. So I bought a wagon and oxen and left the Free State, which was not even the Free State any longer. It was now called the Orange River Colony.

We trekked right through the Transvaal into the northern part of the Marico Bushveld. Years ago, as a boy, I had trekked through that same country with my parents. Now that I went there again I felt that it was still a good country. It was on the far side of the Dwarsberge, near Derdepoort, that we got a Government farm. Afterwards other farmers trekked in there as well. One or two of them had also come from the Free State, and I knew them. There were also a few Cape rebels whom I had seen on commando. All of us had lost relatives in the war. Some had died in the concentration camps or on the battlefield. Others had been shot for going into rebellion. So, taken all in all, we who had trekked into that part of the Marico that lay nearest the Bechuanaland border were very bitter against the English.

Then it was that the rooinek came.

It was in the first year of our having settled around Derdepoort. We heard that an Englishman had bought a farm next to Gerhardus Grobbelaar. This was when we were sitting in the voorkamer of Willem Odendaal's house, which was used as a post office. Once a week the post-cart came up with letters from Zeerust, and we came together at Willem Odendaal's house and talked and smoked and drank coffee. Very few of us ever got letters, and then it was mostly demands to pay for the boreholes that had been drilled on our farms or for cement and fencing materials. But every week regularly we went for the post. Sometimes the post-cart didn't come, because the Groen River was in flood, and we would most of us have gone home without noticing it, if somebody didn't speak about it.

When Koos Steyn heard that an Englishman was coming to live amongst us he got up from the riempiesbank.

"No, kêrels," he said. "Always when the Englishman comes, it means that a little later the Boer has got to shift. I'll pack up my wagon and make coffee, and just trek first thing tomorrow morning."

Most of us laughed then. Koos Steyn often said funny things like that. But some didn't laugh. Somehow, there seemed to be too much truth in Koos Steyn's words.

We discussed the matter and decided that if we Boers in the

Marico could help it the rooinek would not stay amongst us too long. About half an hour later one of Willem Odendaal's children came in and said that there was a strange wagon coming along the big road. We went to the door and looked out. As the wagon came nearer we saw that it was piled up with all kinds of furniture and also sheets of iron and farming implements. There was so much stuff on the wagon that the tent had to be taken off to get everything on.

The wagon rolled along and came to a stop in front of the house. With the wagon there were one white man and two kaffirs. The white man shouted something to the kaffirs and threw down the whip. Then he walked up to where we were standing. He was dressed just as we were, in shirt and trousers and veldskoens, and he had dust all over him. But when he stepped over a thorn-bush we saw that he had got socks on. Therefore we knew that he was an Englishman.

Koos Steyn was standing in front of the door.

The Englishman went up to him and held out his hand.

"Good afternoon," he said in Afrikaans. "My name is Webber."

Koos shook hands with him.

"My name is Prince Lord Alfred Milner," Koos Steyn said.

That was when Lord Milner was Governor of the Transvaal, and we all laughed. The rooinek also laughed.

"Well, Lord Prince," he said, "I can speak your language a little, and I hope that later on I'll be able to speak it better. I'm coming to live here, and I hope that we'll all be friends."

He then came round to all of us, but the others turned away and refused to shake hands with him. He came up to me last of all; I felt sorry for him, and although his nation had dealt unjustly with my nation, and I had lost both my children in the concentration camp, still it was not so much the fault of this Englishman. It was the fault of the English Government, who wanted our gold mines. And it was also the fault of Queen Victoria, who didn't like Oom Paul Kruger, because they say that when he went over to London Oom Paul spoke to her only once for a few minutes. Oom Paul Kruger said that he was a married man and he was afraid of widows.

When the Englishman Webber went back to his wagon Koos

28

Steyn and I walked with him. He told us that he had bought the farm next to Gerhardus Grobbelaar and that he didn't know much about sheep and cattle and mealies, but he had bought a few books on farming, and he was going to learn all he could out of them. When he said that I looked away towards the poort. I didn't want him to see that I was laughing. But with Koos Steyn it was otherwise.

"Man," he said, "let me see those books."

Webber opened the box at the bottom of the wagon and took out about six big books with green covers.

"These are very good books," Koos Steyn said. "Yes, they are very good for the white ants. The white ants will eat them all in two nights."

As I have told you, Koos Steyn was a funny fellow, and no man could help laughing at the things he said.

Those were bad times. There was drought, and we could not sow mealies. The dams dried up, and there was only last year's grass on the veld. We had to pump water out of the borehole for weeks at a time. Then the rains came and for a while things were better.

Now and again I saw Webber. From what I heard about him it seemed that he was working hard. But of course no rooinek can make a living out of farming, unless they send him money every month from England. And we found out that almost all the money Webber had was what he had paid on the farm. He was always reading in those green books what he had to do. It's lucky that those books are written in English, and that the Boers can't read them. Otherwise many more farmers would be ruined every year. When his cattle had the heart-water, or his sheep had the blue-tongue, or there were cut-worms or stalk-borers in his mealies, Webber would look it all up in his books. I suppose that when the kaffirs stole his sheep he would look that up too.

Still, Koos Steyn helped Webber quite a lot and taught him a number of things, so that matters did not go as badly with him as they would have if he had only acted according to the lies that were printed in those green books. Webber and Koos Steyn became very friendly. Koos Steyn's wife had had a baby just a few weeks before Webber came. It was the first child they had after being married seven years, and they were very proud of it. It was a girl. Koos Steyn said that he would sooner it had been a boy; but that, even so, it was better than nothing. Right from the first Webber had taken a liking to that child, who was christened Jemima after her mother. Often when I passed Koos Steyn's house I saw the Englishman sitting on the front stoep with the child on his knees.

In the meantime the other farmers around there became annoyed on account of Koos Steyn's friendship with the rooinek. They said that Koos was a hendsopper and a traitor to his country. He was intimate with a man who had helped to bring about the downfall of the Afrikaner nation. Yet it was not fair to call Koos a hendsopper. Koos had lived in the Graaff-Reinet District when the war broke out, so that he was a Cape Boer and need not have fought. Nevertheless, he joined up with a Free State commando and remained until peace was made, and if at any time the English had caught him they would have shot him as a rebel, in the same way that they shot Scheepers and many others.

Gerhardus Grobbelaar spoke about this once when we were in Willem Odendaal's post office.

"You are not doing right," Gerhardus said; "Boer and Englishman have been enemies since before Slagtersnek. We've lost this war, but some day we'll win. It's the duty we owe to our children's children to stand against the rooineks. Remember the concentration camps."

There seemed to me to be truth in what Gerhardus said.

"But the English are here now, and we've got to live with them," Koos answered. "When we get to understand one another perhaps we won't need to fight anymore. This Englishman Webber is learning Afrikaans very well, and some day he might almost be one of us. The only thing I can't understand about him is that he has a bath every morning. But if he stops that and if he doesn't brush his teeth any more you will hardly be able to tell him from a Boer."

Although he made a joke about it, I felt that in what Koos Steyn said there was also truth.

Then, the year after the drought, the miltsiek broke out. The miltsiek seemed to be in the grass of the veld, and in the water of the dams, and even in the air the cattle breathed. All over the place I would find cows and oxen lying dead. We all became very discouraged. Nearly all of us in that part of the Marico had started farming again on what the Government had given us. Now that the stock died we had nothing. First the drought had put us back to where we were when we started. Now with the miltsiek we couldn't hope to do anything. We couldn't even sow mealies, because, at the rate at which the cattle were dying, in a short while we would have no oxen left to pull the plough. People talked of selling what they had and going to look for work on the gold mines. We sent a petition to the Government, but that did no good.

It was then that somebody got hold of the idea of trekking. In a few days we were talking of nothing else. But the question was where we could trek to. They would not allow us into Rhodesia for fear we might spread the miltsiek there as well. And it was useless going to any other part of the Transvaal. Somebody mentioned German West Africa. We had none of us been there before, and I suppose that really was the reason why, in the end, we decided to go there.

"The blight of the English is over South Africa," Gerhardus Grobbelaar said. "We'll remain here only to die. We must go away somewhere where there is not the Englishman's flag."

In a few weeks' time we arranged everything. We were going to trek across the Kalahari into German territory. Everything we had we loaded up. We drove the cattle ahead and followed behind on our wagons. There were five families: the Steyns, the Grobbelaars, the Odendaals, the Ferreiras and Sannie and I. Webber also came with us. I think it was not so much that he was anxious to leave as that he and Koos Steyn had become very much attached to one another, and the Englishman did not wish to remain alone behind.

The youngest person in our trek was Koos Steyn's daughter Jemima, who was then about eighteen months old. Being the baby, she was a favourite with all of us.

Webber sold his wagon and went with Koos Steyn's trek.

When at the end of the first day we outspanned several miles inside the Bechuanaland Protectorate, we were very pleased that we were done with the Transvaal, where we had had so much misfortune. Of course, the Protectorate was also British territory, but all the same we felt happier there than we had done in our country. We saw Webber every day now, and although he was a foreigner with strange ways, and would remain an Uitlander

31

until he died, yet we disliked him less than before for being a rooinek.

It was on the first Sunday that we reached Malopolole. For the first part of our way the country remained Bushveld. There were the same kind of thorn-trees that grew in the Marico, except that they became fewer the deeper into the Kalahari that we went. Also, the ground became more and more sandy, until even before we came to Malopolole it was all desert. But scattered thorn-bushes remained all the way. That Sunday we held a religious service. Gerhardus Grobbelaar read a chapter out of the Bible and offered up a prayer. We sang a number of psalms, after which Gerhardus prayed again. I shall always remember that Sunday and the way we sat on the ground beside one of the wagons, listening to Gerhardus. That was the last Sunday that we were all together.

The Englishman sat next to Koos Steyn and the baby Jemima lay down in front of him. She played with Webber's fingers and tried to bite them. It was funny to watch her. Several times Webber looked down at her and smiled. I thought then that although Webber was not one of us, yet Jemima certainly did not know it. Maybe in a thing like that the child was wiser than we were. To her it made no difference that the man whose fingers she bit was born in another country and did not speak the same language that she did.

There are many things that I remember about that trek into the Kalahari. But one thing that now seems strange to me is the way in which, right from the first day, we took Gerhardus Grobbelaar for our leader. Whatever he said we just seemed to do without talking very much about it. We all felt that it was right simply because Gerhardus wished it. That was a strange thing about our trek. It was not simply that we knew Gerhardus had got the Lord with him – for we did know that – but it was rather that we believed in Gerhardus as well as in the Lord. I think that even if Gerhardus Grobbelaar had been an ungodly man we would still have followed him in exactly the same way. For when you are in the desert and there is no water and the way back is long, then you feel that it is better to have with you a strong man who does not read the Book very much, than a man who is good and religious, and yet does not seem sure how far to trek each day and where to outspan.

But Gerhardus Grobbelaar was a man of God. At the same time there was something about him that made you feel that it was only by acting as he advised that you could succeed. There was only one other man I have ever known who found it so easy to get people to do as he wanted. And that was Paul Kruger. He was very much like Gerhardus Grobbelaar, except that Gerhardus was less quarrelsome. But of the two Paul Kruger was the bigger man.

Only once do I remember Gerhardus losing his temper. And that was with the Nagmaal at Elandsberg. It was on a Sunday, and we were camped out beside the Crocodile River. Gerhardus went round early in the morning from wagon to wagon and told us that he wanted everybody to come over to where his wagon stood. The Lord had been good to us at that time, so that we had had much rain and our cattle were fat. Gerhardus explained that he wanted to hold a service, to thank the Lord for all His good works, but more especially for what He had done for the farmers of the northern part of the Groot Marico District. This was a good plan, and we all came together with our Bibles and hymn-books. But one man, Karel Pieterse, remained behind at his wagon. Twice Gerhardus went to call him, but Karel Pieterse lay down on the grass and would not get up to come to the service. He said it was all right thanking the Lord now that there had been rains, but what about all those seasons when there had been drought and the cattle had died of thirst. Gerhardus Grobbelaar shook his head sadly, and said there was nothing he could do then, as it was Sunday. But he prayed that the Lord would soften Brother Pieterse's heart, and he finished off his prayer by saying that in any case, in the morning, he would help to soften the brother's heart himself.

The following morning Gerhardus walked over with a sjambok and an ox-riem to where Karel Pieterse sat before his fire, watching the kaffir making coffee. They were both of them men who were big in the body. But Gerhardus got the better of the struggle. In the end he won. He fastened Karel to the wheel of his own wagon with the ox-riem. Then he thrashed him with the sjambok while Karel's wife and children were looking on.

That had happened years before. But nobody had forgotten. And now, in the Kalahari, when Gerhardus summoned us to a service, it was noticed that no man stayed away.

Just outside Malopolole is a muddy stream that is dry part of the year and part of the year has a foot or so of brackish water. We were lucky in being there just at the time when it had water. Early the following morning we filled up the water-barrels that we had put on our wagons before leaving the Marico. We were going right into the desert, and we did not know where we would get water again. Even the Bakwena kaffirs could not tell us for sure.

"The Great Dorstland Trek," Koos Steyn shouted as we got ready to move off. "Anyway, we won't fare as badly as the Dorstland Trekkers. We'll lose less cattle than they did because we've got less to lose. And seeing that we are only five families, not more than about a dozen of us will die of thirst."

I thought it was bad luck for Koos Steyn to make jokes like that about the Dorstland Trek, and I think that others felt the same way about it. We trekked right through that day, and it was all desert. By sunset we had not come across a sign of water anywhere. Abraham Ferreira said towards evening that perhaps it would be better if we went back to Malopolole and tried to find out for sure which was the best way of getting through the Kalahari. But the rest said that there was no need to do that, since we would be sure to come across water the next day. And, anyway, we were Doppers and, having once set out, we were not going to turn back. But after we had given the cattle water our barrels did not have too much left in them.

By the middle of the following day all our water had given out except a little that we kept for the children. But still we pushed on. Now that we had gone so far we were afraid to go back because of the long way that we would have to go without water to get back to Malopolole. In the evening we were very anxious. We all knelt down in the sand and prayed. Gerhardus Grobbelaar's voice sounded very deep and earnest when he besought God to have mercy on us, especially for the sakes of the little ones. He mentioned the baby Jemima by name. The Englishman knelt down beside me, and I noticed that he shivered when Gerhardus mentioned Koos Steyn's child.

It was moonlight. All around us was the desert. Our wagons seemed very small and lonely; there was something about them that looked very mournful. The women and children put their

34

arms round one another and wept a long while. Our kaffirs stood some distance away and watched us. My wife Sannie put her hand in mine, and I thought of the concentration camp. Poor woman, she had suffered much. And I knew that her thoughts were the same as my own: that after all it was perhaps better that our children should have died then than now.

We had got so far into the desert that we began telling one another that we must be near the end. Although we knew that German West was far away, and that in the way we had been travelling we had got little more than into the beginning of the Kalahari, yet we tried to tell one another lies about how near water was likely to be. But, of course, we told those lies only to one another. Each man in his own heart knew what the real truth was. And later on we even stopped telling one another lies about what a good chance we had of getting out alive. You can understand how badly things had gone with us when you know that we no longer troubled about hiding our position from the women and children. They wept, some of them. But that made no difference then. Nobody tried to comfort the women and children who cried. We knew that tears were useless, and yet somehow at that hour we felt that the weeping of the women was not less useless than the courage of the men. After a while there was no more weeping in our camp. Some of the women who lived through the dreadful things of the days that came after, and got safely back to the Transvaal, never again wept. What they had seen appeared to have hardened them. In this respect they had become as men. I think that is the saddest thing that ever happens in this world, when women pass through great suffering that makes them become as men.

That night we hardly slept. Early the next morning the men went out to look for water. An hour after sun-up Ferreira came back and told us that he had found a muddy pool a few miles away. We all went there, but there wasn't much water. Still, we got a little, and that made us feel better. It was only when it came to driving our cattle towards the mudhole that we found our kaffirs had deserted us during the night. After we had gone to sleep they had stolen away. Some of the weaker cattle couldn't get up to go to the pool. So we left them. Some were trampled to death or got choked in the mud, and we had to pull them out to let the rest get to the hole. It was pitiful.

Just before we left one of Ferreira's daughters died. We scooped a hole in the sand and buried her.

So we decided to trek back.

After his daughter was dead Abraham Ferreira went up to Gerhardus and told him that if we had taken his advice earlier on and gone back, his daughter would not have died.

"Your daughter is dead now, Abraham," Gerhardus said. "It is no use talking about her any longer. We all have to die some day. I refused to go back earlier. I have decided to go back now."

Abraham Ferreira looked Gerhardus in the eyes and laughed. I shall always remember how that laughter sounded in the desert. In Abraham's voice there was the hoarseness of the sand and thirst. His voice was cracked with what the desert had done to him; his face was lined and his lips were blackened. But there was nothing about him that spoke of grief for his daughter's death.

"Your daughter is still alive, Oom Gerhardus," Abraham Ferreira said, pointing to the wagon wherein lay Gerhardus's wife, who was weak, and the child to whom she had given birth only a few months before. "Yes, she is still alive . . . so far."

Ferreira turned away laughing, and we heard him a little later explaining to his wife in cracked tones about the joke he had made.

Gerhardus Grobbelaar merely watched the other man walk away without saying anything. So far we had followed Gerhardus through all things, and our faith in him had been great. But now that we had decided to trek back we lost our belief in him. We lost it suddenly, too. We knew that it was best to turn back, and that to continue would mean that we would all die in the Kalahari. And yet, if Gerhardus had said we must still go on we would have done so. We would have gone through with him right to the end. But now that he as much as said he was beaten by the desert we had no more faith in Gerhardus. That is why I have said that Paul Kruger was a greater man than Gerhardus. Because Paul Kruger was that kind of man whom we still worshipped even when he decided to retreat. If it had been Paul Kruger who told us that we had to go back we would have returned with strong hearts. We would have retained exactly the same love for our leader, even if we knew that he was beaten. But from the moment that Gerhardus said we must go back we all knew that he was no longer our leader. Gerhardus knew that also.

We knew what lay between us and Malopolole and there was grave doubt in our hearts when we turned our wagons round. Our cattle were very weak, and we had to inspan all that could walk. We hadn't enough yokes, and therefore we cut poles from the scattered bushes and tied them to the trek-chains. As we were also without skeis we had to fasten the necks of the oxen straight on to the yokes with strops, and several of the oxen got strangled.

Then we saw that Koos Steyn had become mad. For he refused to return. He inspanned his oxen and got ready to trek on. His wife sat silent in the wagon with the baby; wherever her husband went she would go, too. That was only right, of course. Some women kissed her goodbye, and cried. But Koos Steyn's wife did not cry. We reasoned with Koos about it, but he said that he had made up his mind to cross the Kalahari, and he was not going to turn back just for nonsense.

"But, man," Gerhardus Grobbelaar said to him, "you've got no water to drink."

"I'll drink coffee then," Koos Steyn answered, laughing as always, and took up the whip and walked away beside the wagon. And Webber went off with him, just because Koos Steyn had been good to him, I suppose. That's why I have said that Englishmen are queer. Webber must have known that if Koos Steyn had not actually gone wrong in the head, still what he was doing now was madness, and yet he stayed with him.

We separated. Our wagons went slowly back to Malopolole. Koos Steyn's wagon went deeper into the desert. My wagon went last. I looked back at the Steyns. At that moment Webber also looked round. He saw me and waved his hand. It reminded me of that day in the Boer War when that other Englishman, whose companion we had shot, also turned round and waved.

Eventually we got back to Malopolole with two wagons and a handful of cattle. We abandoned the other wagons. Awful things happened on that desert. A number of children died. Gerhardus Grobbelaar's wagon was in front of me. Once I saw a bundle being dropped through the side of the wagon-tent. I knew what it was. Gerhardus would not trouble to bury his dead child, and his wife lay in the tent too weak to move. So I got off the wagon and scraped a small heap of sand over the body. All I remember of the rest of the journey to Malopolole is the sun and the sand. And the thirst. Although at one time we thought that we had lost our way, yet that did not matter much to us. We were past feeling. We could neither pray nor curse, our parched tongues cleaving to the roofs of our mouths.

Until today I am not sure how many days we were on our way back, unless I sit down and work it all out, and then I suppose I get it wrong. We got back to Malopolole and water. We said we would never go away from there again. I don't think that even those parents who had lost children grieved about them then. They were stunned with what they had gone through. But I knew that later on it would all come back again. Then they would remember things about shallow graves in the sand, and Gerhardus Grobbelaar and his wife would think of a little bundle lying out in the Kalahari. And I knew how they would feel.

Afterwards we fitted out a wagon with fresh oxen; we took an abundant supply of water and went back into the desert to look for the Steyn family. With the help of the Sechuana kaffirs, who could see tracks that we could not see, we found the wagon. The oxen had been outspanned; a few lay dead beside the wagon. The kaffirs pointed out to us footprints on the sand, which showed which way those two men and that woman had gone.

In the end we found them.

Koos Steyn and his wife lay side by side in the sand; the woman's head rested on the man's shoulder; her long hair had become loosened, and blew about softly in the wind. A great deal of fine sand had drifted over their bodies. Near them the Englishman lay, face downwards. We never found the baby Jemima. She must have died somewhere along the way and Koos Steyn must have buried her. But we agreed that the Englishman Webber must have passed through terrible things; he could not even have had

any understanding left as to what the Steyns had done with their baby. He probably thought, up to the moment when he died, that he was carrying the child. For, when we lifted his body, we found, still clasped in his dead and rigid arms, a few old rags and a child's clothes.

It seemed to us that the wind that always stirs in the Kalahari blew very quietly and softly that morning.

Yes, the wind blew very gently.

FRANCINA MALHERBE

After her father's death, Oom Schalk Lourens said, Francina Malherbe was left alone on the farm Maroelasdal. We all wondered then what she would do. She was close on to thirty, and in the Bushveld, when a girl is not married by twenty-five, you can be quite certain that she won't get a man anymore. Unless she has got money. And even then if she gets married at about thirty she is liable to be left afterwards with neither money nor husband. Look at what happened to Grieta Steyn.

But with Francina Malherbe it was different.

I remember Francina as a child. She was young when Flip first trekked into the Bushveld. There was an unlucky man for you. Just the year after he had settled on Maroelasdal the rinderpest broke out and killed off all his cattle. That was a bad time for all of us. But Flip Malherbe suffered most. Then, for the first time that anybody in the Marico District could remember, a pack of wolves came out of the Kalahari, driven into the Transvaal by the hunger. For in the Kalahari nearly all the game had died with the rinderpest. Maroelasdal was the nearest farm to the border, and in one night, as Flip told us, the wolves got into his kraal and tore the insides out of three hundred of his sheep. This was all the more remarkable, because Flip, to my knowledge, had never owned more than fifty sheep.

Then Flip Malherbe's wife died of the lung disease, and shortly afterwards also his two younger sons who were always delicate. That left only Francina, who was then about fifteen. All those troubles turned Flip's head a little. That year the Government voted money for the relief of farmers who had suffered from the rinderpest, and Flip put in a claim. He got paid quite a lot of money, but he spent most of it in Zeerust on drink. Then Flip went to the school-teacher and asked him if the Government would not give him compensation also because his wife and his sons had died, but the teacher, who did not know that Flip had become strange in the head, only laughed at him. Often after that, Flip told us that he was sorry his wife and children had died of the lung disease instead of the rinderpest, because otherwise he could have put in a claim for them.

Francina left school and set to work looking after the farm. With what was left out of the money Flip had got from the Government, she bought a few head of cattle. When the rains came she bought seed mealies and set the kaffir squatters ploughing in the vlakte. For three months in the year, by law, the kaffirs have to work for the white man on whose land they live. But you know what it is with kaffirs. As soon as they saw that there was no man on the farm who would see to it that they worked, the kaffirs ploughed only a little every day for Flip and spent the rest of the time in working for themselves. Francina spoke to her father about it, but it was no good. Flip just sat in front of the

house all day smoking his pipe. In the end, Francina wrote out all the trek-passes and made all the kaffirs clear off the farm, except old Mosigo, who had always been a good kaffir.

In those days, Francina was very pretty. She had dark eyes with long lashes that curled down on her red cheeks when her eyes were closed. I know, because I usually sat near her in church, and during prayers I sometimes looked sideways at her. That was sinful, but then I was not the only one who did it. Whenever I opened my eyes slightly to look at her, I saw that there were other men doing the same thing. Once a young minister, who had just finished his studies at Potchefstroom, came to preach to us, so that we could appoint him as our predikant if we wished. But we did not appoint him. The ouderlings and diakens in the church council said that perhaps they could permit a minister to look underneath his lids while he was praying, but it was only right that his eyes should be shut all the time when he pronounced the blessing.

For the next two years I don't know how Francina and her father managed to make a living on the farm. But they did it somehow. Also, after a while they got other kaffir families to squat on the farm, and to help Mosigo on the lands with the ploughing time. Once Flip left his place on the front stoep and got into the mule-cart and drove to Zeerust. After two days, the hotel proprietor sent him back to the farm on an Indian trader's wagon. Flip had sold the mules and cart and bought drink.

Shortly after that I saw Flip at the post office. The dining room of Hans Welman's house was the post office, and we all went there to talk and fetch our letters. Flip came in and shook hands with everybody in the way we all did, and said good morning. Then he went up to Hans Welman and held out his hand. Welman just looked Flip Malherbe up and down and walked away. But with all his nonsense, Flip was sane enough to know that he had been insulted.

"You go to hell, Hans Welman," he shouted.

Welman turned round at once.

"My house is the public post office," he said, "so I can't throw you out. But I can say what I think of you. You treat your daughter like a kaffir. You're a low, drunken mongrel."

We could see that Flip Malherbe was afraid, but he could do nothing else after what the other man had said to him. So he went up to Welman and hit him on the chest. Welman just laughed and grabbed Flip quickly by the collar. Then he ran with him to the door, spun him round and kicked him under the jacket.

"Filth," he said, when Flip fell in the dust.

We all felt that Hans Welman had no business to do that. After all, it was Flip's own affair as to how he treated his daughter.

After that we rarely saw Flip again. He hardly ever moved from his front stoep. At first young men still came to call on Francina. But later on they stopped coming, for she gave them no encouragement. She said she could not marry while her father was still alive as she had to look after him. That was usually enough for most young men. They had only to glance once at Flip, who of late had grown fat and hearty-looking, to be satisfied that it would still be many years before they could hope to get Francina. Accordingly, the young men stayed away.

By and by nobody went to the Malherbes' house. It was no use calling on Flip, because we all knew he was mad. Although, often, when I thought of it, it seemed to me that he was less insane than what people believed. After all, it is not every man who can so arrange his affairs that he has nothing more to do except to sit down all day smoking and drinking coffee.

But although Francina never visited anybody, yet she always went regularly to church. Only, as the years passed, she became faded and no more young men looked at her during prayers. There were other and younger girls whom they would look at now. She had become thinner and there were wrinkles under her eyes. Also, her cheeks were no longer red. And there are always enough fresh-looking girls in the Bushveld, without the young men having to trouble themselves overmuch about those who have grown old.

And so the years passed, as you read in the Book, summer and winter and seed-time and harvest.

Then one day Flip Malherbe died. The only people at the funeral were the Bekkers, the Van Vuurens, my family and Hendrik Oberholzer, the ouderling who conducted the service. We saw Francina scatter dust over her father's face and then we left.

That was the time when we began to wonder what Francina would do. It was fifteen years since her mother had died, so that Francina was now thirty, and during those fifteen years she had worked hard and in a careful way, so that the farm Maroelasdal was all paid and there were plenty of sheep and cattle, and every year they sowed many sacks of mealies. But Francina just went on exactly the same as she had done when her father was still alive. Only, now the best years of a woman's life were behind her, and during all that time she had had nothing but work. We all felt sorry for her, the womenfolk as well, but there was nothing we could do.

Francina came to church every Sunday, and that was about the only time that we saw her. Yet both before and after church she was always alone, and she seldom spoke to anybody. In her black mourning dress she began to look almost pretty again, but of what use was that at her age?

People who had trekked into the Marico District in the last four years and only knew her by sight said she must also be a little strange in the head, like her father was. They said it looked as though it was in the family. But we who saw her grow up knew better. We understood that it was her life that had made her lonely like that. On account of having to look after her father she had missed much.

One day an insurance agent came through the Bushveld. He called at all the houses, Francina's also. It did not seem as if he was doing much business in the district, and yet every time he came back. And people noticed that it was always to Francina's house that the insurance agent went first. They talked about it. The old people shook their heads in the way that old people do when, although they don't know for sure about a thing, yet all the same they would like to believe it is so.

But if Francina knew what was being said about her she never mentioned it to anybody, and she didn't try to act differently. Nevertheless, there came a Sunday when she missed going to church. At once everybody felt that what was being whispered about her was true. Especially when she did not come to church the next Sunday or the Sunday after. Of course, stories that are told in this way about women are always true. But there was one thing that they said that was a lie. They said that what the insurance agent wanted was Francina's farm and cattle. And they foretold that exactly the same thing would happen to Francina as had happened to Grieta Steyn: that in the end she would lose both her property and the man.

As I have told you, this last part of their stories did not come out in the way they had prophesied. If the insurance agent really had tried to get from her the farm and the cattle, nobody could say for sure. But what we did know was that he had gone back without them. He left quite suddenly, too, and he did not return anymore.

And Francina never again came to church. Yes, it's funny that women should get like that. For I did not imagine that anything could ever come across Francina's life that would make her go away from her religion. But, of course, you can't tell.

Sometimes when I ride past Maroelasdal in the evening, on my way home, I wonder about these things. When I pass that point near the aardvark mound, where the trees have been chopped down, and I see Francina in front of the house, I seem to remember her again as she was when she was fifteen. And if the sun is near to setting, and I see her playing with her child, I sometimes wish, somehow, that it was not a bastard.

THE RAMOUTSA ROAD

You'll see that grave by the side of the road as you go to Ramoutsa, Oom Schalk Lourens said.

It is under that clump of withaaks just before you get to the Protectorate border. The kaffirs are afraid to pass that place at night.

I knew Hendrik Oberholzer well. He was a good man. Unlike most of the farmers who lived here in those days, Hendrik Oberholzer was never caught smuggling cattle across the line. Perhaps it was because he was religious and would not break the law. Or else he chose only dark nights for the work. I don't know. I was rather good at bringing cattle over myself, and yet I was twice fined for it at Zeerust.

Hendrik Oberholzer lived on the farm Paradyskloof. When he first trekked in here he was already married and his son Paulus was about fourteen. Paulus was a lively youngster and full of spirits when there was drought in the land and there was no ploughing to be done. But when it rained, and they had to sow mealies, Paulus would be sulky for days. Once I went to Paradyskloof to borrow a sack of cement from Hendrik for a sheep-dip I was building. Paulus was on the lands, walking behind the plough. I went up and spoke to him, and told him about the cement for the sheep-dip. But he didn't stop the oxen or even turn his head to look at me. "To hell with you and your cement," he shouted.

Then he added, when he got about fifteen yards away, "And the sheep-dip."

For some time after that Hendrik Oberholzer and I were not on speaking terms. Hendrik said that he was not going to allow other men to thrash his son. But I had only flicked Paulus's bare leg with the sjambok. And that was after he had kicked me on the shin with his veldskoen, because I had caught him by the wrist and told him that he wasn't to abuse a man old enough to be his father. Anyway, I didn't get the cement.

Then, a few days before the minister came up to hold the Nagmaal, Hendrik called at my house and said we must shake hands and forgive one another. As he was the ouderling, the predikant stayed with him for three days, and if he was at enmity with anybody, Hendrik would not be allowed to share in the Nagmaal. I was pleased to have the quarrel settled. Hendrik Oberholzer was an upright man whom we all respected for his Christian ways, and he also regularly passed on to me the Pretoria newspapers after he had finished reading them himself.

Afterwards, as time went by, I could see that Hendrik was much worried on account of his son. Paulus was the only son of Hendrik and Lettie. I know that often Hendrik had sorrowed because the Lord had given him no more than one child, and yet this one had strange ways. Because of that, both Hendrik and his wife Lettie became saddened.

Paulus had had a good education. His father didn't take him out of school until he was in Standard Four. And for another thing he had been to Sunday school since he was seven. Also his uncle, who was a builder, had taught Paulus to lay flat stones for stoeps. So, taken all round, Paulus had more than enough learning for a farmer. But he was not content with that. He said he wanted to learn. Hendrik Oberholzer reasoned with him and, very fairly and justly, pointed out to him what had happened to Piet Slabberts. Piet Slabberts had gone to high school, and when he came back he didn't believe in God. So nobody was surprised when, two months later, Piet Slabberts fell off an ox-wagon and was killed by the wheels going over his head.

But Paulus only laughed.

"That is not so wonderful," he said. "If an ox-wagon goes over your head you always die, unless you've got a head like a Bushman's. If Piet Slabberts didn't die, only then would I say it was wonderful."

Yes, it was sinful of Paulus to talk like that when we could all see that in that happening was the hand of God. At the funeral the ouderling who conducted the service also spoke about it, and Piet

Slabberts's mother cried very much to think that the Lord had taken away her son because He was not satisfied with him.

Anyway, Paulus did less work on the farm. Even when the dam dried up, and for weeks they had to pump water for the cattle all day out of the borehole, Paulus just looked on and only helped when his father and the kaffirs could not do any more. And yet he was twenty and a strong, well-built young man. But there was something in him that was bad.

At first Hendrik Oberholzer had tried to make excuses for his son, saying that he was young and had still to learn wisdom, but later on he spoke no more about Paulus. Hendrik's wife Lettie also said nothing. But there was always sadness in her eyes. For Paulus was her only child and he was not like other sons. He would often take a piece of paper and a pencil with him and go away in the bush and write verses all day. Of course Hendrik tore up those bits of paper whenever he found them in the house. But that made no difference. Paulus just went on with his sinful, worldly things, even after the minister had spoken to him about it and told him that no good could come out of writing verses – unless they were hymns. But even then it was foolish. Because in the hymn-book there were more hymns than people could use.

Instead of starting to work for himself and finding some girl to whom he could get married, Paulus, as I have said, just loafed about. Yet he was not bad-looking and there were many girls who could have favoured him if he looked at them first. And from them he could have chosen a woman for himself. Only Paulus took no notice of girls and seemed shy in their company.

One afternoon I went over to Hendrik Oberholzer's farm to fetch back a saw that I had bought from him. But Hendrik and Paulus had gone to Zeerust with a load of mealies, so that when I got to the house only Hendrik's wife Lettie was there. I sat down and talked to her for a little while. By and by, after she had poured out the coffee, she started talking about Paulus. She was very grieved about him and I could see that she was not far off crying. Therefore I went and sat next to her on the riempiesbank, and did my best to comfort her.

"Poor woman. Poor woman," I said and patted her hand. But I couldn't comfort her much, because all the time I had to keep an eye on the door in case Hendrik came in suddenly.

Then Lettie showed me a few bits of paper that she had found under Paulus's pillow. It was the same kind of verses that he had been writing for a long time, all about mimosa trees and clouds and veld flowers and that sort of nonsense. When I read those things I felt sorry that I didn't hit him harder with the sjambok that day he kicked me on the shin.

"He does not work even as much as a piccanin," Hendrik's wife Lettie said. "All day he writes on these bits of paper. I can't understand what is wrong with him."

"A man who writes things like that will come to no good," I said to her. "And I am sorry for you. It is not good the way Paulus is treating you."

Immediately Lettie turned on me like one of those yellow-haired wild-cats, and told me I had no right to talk about her son. She said I ought to be ashamed of myself and that, no matter what Paulus was like, he was always a much better man than any impudent Dopper who dared to talk about him. She said a lot of other things besides, and I was pleased when Hendrik returned. But I saw then how much Lettie loved Paulus. Also, it just shows you that you never know where you are with a woman.

Then one day Paulus went away. He just left home without saying a word to anybody.

Hendrik Oberholzer was very much troubled. He rode about to all the farms around here and asked if anyone had seen his son. He also went to Zeerust and told the police, but the police did not do much. All they ever did was to get our people fined for bringing scraggy kaffir cattle across the line. The sergeant at the station was a raw Hollander who listened to everything Hendrik said, and then at the end told Hendrik, after he had written something in a book, that perhaps what had happened was that Paulus had gone away.

Of course, Hendrik came to me, and I did what I could to help him. I went up to the Marico River right to where it flows into the Limpopo, and from there I came back along the Bechuanaland Protectorate border. Everywhere I enquired for Paulus. I was many days away from the farm.

I had hardly got back home when Hendrik called for news.

From his lands he had seen me come through the poort and he had hastened over to see me.

We sat down in the voorkamer and filled our pipes.

"Well, Lourens," Hendrik said, and his eyes were on the floor, "have you heard anything about Paulus?"

It was early afternoon, with the sun shining in through the window, and in Hendrik's brown beard were white hairs that I had not noticed before.

I saw how Hendrik looked at the floor when he asked about his son. So I told him the truth, for I could see then that he already knew.

"The Lord will make all things right," I said.

"Yes, God knows what is best," Hendrik Oberholzer answered. "I heard about ——. They told me yesterday."

Hendrik could not bring himself to say that which we both knew about his son.

For, on my way back along the Bechuanaland border, I had come across Paulus. It was in some Mtosa huts outside Ramoutsa. There were about a dozen huts of red clay standing in a circle amongst the bushes. In front of each hut a kaffir lay stretched out in the sun with a blanket over him. All day long these kaffirs lie there in the sun, smoking dagga and drinking beer. Their wives and children sow the kaffir-corn and the mealies and look after the cattle. And with no clothes on, but just a blanket over him, Paulus also lay amongst those kaffirs. I looked at him only once and turned away, without knowing whether he had seen me.

Next to him a kaffir woman sat stringing white beads on to a piece of copper wire.

That was what I told Hendrik Oberholzer.

"It would be much better if he was dead," Hendrik said to me. "To think that a son of mine should turn kaffir."

That was very terrible. Hendrik Oberholzer was right when he said it would be better if Paulus was dead.

I had known before of low-class Uitlanders going to live in a kraal and marrying kaffir women and spending the rest of their lives sleeping in the sun and drinking bujali. But that was the first time I had heard of that being done by a decent Boer son.

Shortly afterwards Hendrik left. He said no more about

50

Paulus, except to let me know that he no longer had a son. After that I didn't speak about Paulus either.

In a little while all the farmers in the Groot Marico knew what had happened, and they talked much of the shame that had come to Hendrik Oberholzer's family. But Hendrik went on just the same as always, except that he looked a great deal older.

Things continued in that way for about six months. Or perhaps it was a little longer. I am not sure of the date, although I know that it was shortly after the second time that I had to pay ten pounds for cattle-smuggling.

One morning I was in the lands talking to Hendrik about putting some more wires on the fence, so that we wouldn't need herds for our sheep, when a young kaffir on a donkey came up to us with a note. He said that Baas Paulus had given him that note the night before, and had told him to bring it over in the morning. He also told us that Baas Paulus was dead.

Hendrik read the note. Then he tore it up. I never got to learn what Paulus had written to him.

"Will you come with me, Lourens?" he asked.

I went with him. He got the kaffirs to inspan the mule-cart, and also to put in a shovel and a pick-axe. All the way to the Mtosa huts Hendrik did not speak. It was a fresh, pleasant morning in spring. The grass everywhere was long and green, and when we got to the higher ground, where the road twists round the krantz, there was still a light mist hanging over the trees. The mules trotted steadily, so that it was a good while before midday when we reached the clump of withaaks that, with their tall, white trunks, stood high above the other thorn-trees. Hendrik stopped the cart. He jumped off and threw the reins to the kaffir in the back seat.

We left the road and followed one of the cow-paths through the bush. After we had gone a few yards we could see the red of the clay huts. But we also saw, on a branch overhanging the footpath, a length of ox-riem, the end of which had been cut. The ox-riem swayed in the wind, and at once, when I saw Hendrik Oberholzer's face, I knew what had happened. After writing the letter to his father Paulus had hanged himself on that branch and the kaffirs had afterwards found him there and had cut him down.

We walked into the circle of huts. The kaffirs lay on the ground under their blankets. But nobody lay in front of that hut where, on that last occasion, I had seen Paulus. Only in front of the door that same kaffir woman was sitting, still stringing white beads on to copper wires. She did not speak when we came up. She just shifted away from the door to let us pass in, and as she moved aside I saw that she was with child.

Inside there was something under a blanket. We knew that it was Paulus. So he lay the day I saw him for the first time with the Mtosas, with the exception that now the blanket was over his head as well. Only his bare toes stuck out underneath the blanket, and on them was red clay that seemed to be freshly dried. Apparently the kaffirs had not found him hanging from the tree until the morning.

Between us we carried the body to the mule-cart.

Then for the first time Hendrik spoke.

"I will not have him back on my farm," he said. "Let him stay out here with the kaffirs. Then he will be near later on, for his child by the kaffir woman to come to him."

But, although Hendrik's voice sounded bitter, there was also sadness in it.

So, by the side of the road to Ramoutsa, amongst the withaaks, we made a grave for Paulus Oberholzer. But the ground was hard. Therefore it was not until late in the afternoon that we had dug a grave deep enough to bury him.

"I knew the Lord would make it right," Hendrik said when we got into the mule-cart.

THE GRAMOPHONE

That was a terrible thing that happened with Krisjan Lemmer, Oom Schalk Lourens said. It was pretty bad for me, of course, but it was much worse for Krisjan.

I remember well when it happened, for that was the time when the first gramophone came into the Marico Bushveld. Krisjan bought the machine off a Jew trader from Pretoria. It's funny when you come to think of it. When there is anything that we Boers don't want you can be quite sure that the Jew traders will bring it to us, and that we'll buy it, too.

I remember how I laughed when a Jew came to my house once with a hollow piece of glass that had a lot of silver stuff in it. The Jew told me that the silver in the glass moved up and down to show you if it was hot or cold. Of course, I said that was all nonsense. I know when it is cold enough for me to put on my woollen shirt and jacket, without having first to go and look at that piece of glass. And I also know when it is too hot to work – which it is almost all the year round in this part of the Marico Bushveld. In the end I bought the thing. But it has never been the same since little Annie stirred her coffee with it.

Anyway, if the Jew traders could bring us the miltsiek, we would buy that off them as well, and pay them so much down, and the rest when all our cattle are dead.

Therefore, when a trader brought Krisjan Lemmer a second-hand gramophone, Krisjan sold some sheep and bought the thing. For many miles round the people came to hear the machine talk. Krisjan was very proud of his gramophone, and when he turned the handle and put in the little sharp pins, it was just like a child that has found something new to play with. The people who came to hear the gramophone said it was very wonderful what things man would think of making when once the devil had taken a hold on him properly. They said that, if nothing else, the devil has got good brains. I also thought it was wonderful, not that the gramophone could talk, but that people wanted to listen to it doing something that a child of seven could do as well. Most of the songs the gramophone played were in English. But there was one song in Afrikaans. It was "O Brandewyn laat my staan." Krisjan played that often; the man on the round plate sang it rather well. Only the way he pronounced the words made it seem as though he was a German trying to make "O Brandewyn laat my staan" sound English. It was just like the rooineks, I thought. First they took our country and governed it for us in a better way than we could do ourselves; now they wanted to make improvements in our language for us.

But if people spoke much about Krisjan Lemmer's gramophone, they spoke a great deal more about the unhappy way in which he and his wife lived together. Krisjan Lemmer was then about thirty-five. He was a big, strongly built man, and when he moved about you could see the muscles of his shoulders stand out under his shirt. He was also a surprisingly good-natured man who seldom became annoyed about anything. Even with the big drought, when he had to pump water for his cattle all day and the pump broke, so that he could get no water for his cattle, he just walked into the house and lit his pipe and said that it was the Lord's will. He said that perhaps it was as well that the pump broke, because, if the Lord wanted the cattle to get water, He wouldn't have sent the drought. That was the kind of man Krisjan Lemmer was. And he would never have set hand to the pump again, either, was it not that the next day rain fell, whereby Krisjan knew that the Lord meant him to understand that the drought was over. Yet, when anything angered him he was bad.

But the unfortunate part of Krisjan Lemmer was that he could not get on with his wife Susannah. Always they quarrelled. Susannah, as we knew, was a good deal younger than her husband, but often she didn't look so very much younger. She was small and fair. Her skin had not been much darkened by the Bushveld sun, for she always wore a very wide kappie, the folds of which she pinned down over the upper part of her face whenever she went out of the house. Her hair was the colour of the beard you

54

see on the yellow mealies just after they have ripened. She had very quiet ways. In company she hardly ever talked, unless it was to say that the Indian shopkeeper in Ramoutsa put roasted kreme-tart roots with the coffee he sold us, or that the spokes of the mule-cart came loose if you didn't pour water over them.

You see, what she said were things that everybody knew and that no one argued about. Even the Indian storekeeper didn't argue about the kremetart roots. He knew that was the best part of his cof-fee. And yet, although she was so quiet and unassuming, Susannah was always quarrelling with her husband. This, of course, was fool-ish of her, especially as Krisjan was a man with gentle ways until somebody purposely annoyed him. Then he was not quite so gen-tle. For instance, there was the time when the chief of the Mtosa kaffirs passed him in the veld and said "Good morning" without taking the leopard skin off his head and calling Krisjan baas. Krisjan was fined ten pounds by the magistrate and had to pay for the doctor during the three months that the Mtosa chief walked with a stick.

One day I went to Krisjan Lemmer's farm to borrow a roll of baling-wire for the teff. Krisjan had just left for the krantz to see if he could shoot a ribbok. Susannah was at home alone. I could see that she had been crying. So I went and sat next to her on the riempiesbank and took her hand.

"Don't cry, Susannah," I said, "everything will be all right. You must just learn to understand Krisjan a little better. He is not a bad fellow in his way."

At first she was angry with me for saying anything against Krisjan, and she told me to go home. But afterwards she became more reasonable about it, allowing me to move up a bit closer to her and to hold her hand a little tighter. In that way I comforted her. I would have comforted her even more, perhaps, only I couldn't be sure how long Krisjan would remain in the krantz; and I didn't like what happened to the Mtosa kaffir chief.

I asked her to play the gramophone for me, not because I wanted to hear it, but because you always pretend to take an interest in the things that your friends like, especially when you borrow a roll of baling-wire off them. When anybody visits me and gets my youngest son Willie to recite texts from the Bible, I know that before he leaves he is going to ask me if I will be using my mealie-planter this week.

So Susannah put the round plate on the thing, and turned the handle, and the gramophone played "O Brandewyn laat my staan." You couldn't hear too well what the man was singing, but I have said all that before.

Susannah laughed as she listened, and in that moment somehow she seemed very much younger than her husband. She looked very pretty, too. But I noticed also that when the music ended it was as though she was crying.

Then Krisjan came in. I left shortly afterwards. But I had heard his footsteps coming up the path, so there was no need for me to leave in a hurry.

But just before I went Susannah brought in coffee. It was weak coffee; but I didn't say anything about it. I am very much like an Englishman that way. It's what they call manners. When I am visiting strangers and they give me bad coffee I don't throw it out and say that the stuff isn't fit for a kaffir. I just drink it and then don't go back to that house again. But Krisjan spoke about it.

"Vrou," he said, "the coffee is weak."

"Yes," Susannah answered.

"It's very weak," he went on.

"Yes," she replied.

"Why do you always . . ." Krisjan began again.

"Oh, go to hell," Susannah said.

Then they went at it, swearing at one another, and they didn't even hear me when, on leaving, in the manner of the Bushveld, I said, "Goodbye and may the good Lord bless us all."

It was a dark night that time, about three months later, when I again went to Krisjan Lemmer's house by mule-cart. I was leaving early in the morning for Zeerust with a load of mealies and wanted to borrow Krisjan's wagon-sail. Before I was halfway to his house it started raining. Big drops fell on my face. There was something queer about the sound of the wind in the wet trees, and when I drove through the poort where the Government Road skirts the line of the Dwarsberge the place looked very dark to me. I thought of death and things like that. I thought of pale strange ghosts that come upon you from behind . . . suddenly. I felt sorry, then, that I had not brought a kaffir along. It was not that I was afraid of being alone; but it would have been useful, on the return, to have a kaffir sitting in the back of the mule-cart to look after the wagon-sail for me.

The rain stopped.

I came to the farm's graveyard, where had been buried members of the Lemmer family and of other families who had lived there before the Lemmers, and I knew that I was near the house. It seemed to me to be a very silly sort of thing to make a graveyard so close to the road. There's no sense in that. Some people, for instance, who are ignorant and a bit superstitious are liable, perhaps, to start shivering a little, especially if the night is dark and there is a wind and the mule-cart is bumpy.

There were no lights in the Lemmers' house when I got there. I knocked a long time before the door was opened, and then it was Krisjan Lemmer standing in the doorway with a lantern held above his head. He looked agitated at first, until he saw who it was and then he smiled.

"Come in, Neef Schalk," he said. "I am pleased you are here. I was beginning to feel lonely – you know, the rain and the wind and – "

"But you are not alone," I replied. "What about Susannah?"

"Oh, Susannah has gone back to her mother," Krisjan answered. "She went yesterday."

We went into the voorkamer and sat down. Krisjan Lemmer lit a candle and we talked and smoked. The window-panes looked black against the night. The wind blew noisily through openings between the wall and the thatched roof. The candle-flame flickered unsteadily. It could not be pleasant for Krisjan Lemmer alone in that house without his wife. He looked restless and uncomfortable. I tried to make a joke about it.

"What's the matter with you, Krisjan?" I asked. "You're looking so unhappy, anybody would think you've still got your wife here with you."

Krisjan laughed, and I wished he hadn't. His laughter did not sound natural; it was too loud. Somehow I got a cold kind of feeling in my blood. It was rather a frightening thing, the wind blowing incessantly outside the house, and inside the house a man laughing too loudly.

"Let us play the gramophone, Krisjan," I said.

By that time I knew how to work the thing myself. So I put in one of the little pins and started it off. But before doing that I had taken the gramophone off its table and placed it on the floor in front of my chair, where I could get at it more easily.

It seemed different without Susannah's being there. Also, it looked peculiar to me that she should leave so suddenly. And there was no doubt about it that Krisjan was acting in a strange way that I didn't like. He was restless. When he lit his pipe he had to strike quite a number of matches. And all that time round the house the wind blew very loudly.

The gramophone began to play.

The plate was "O Brandewyn laat my staan."

I thought of Susannah and of the way she had listened three months before to that same song. I glanced up quickly at Krisjan, and as soon as he caught my eye he looked away. I was glad when the gramophone finished playing. And there was something about Krisjan that made me feel that he was pleased also. He seemed very queer about Susannah.

Then an awful thought occurred to me.

You know sometimes you get a thought like that and you know that it is true.

I got up unsteadily and took my hat. I saw that all round the place where the gramophone stood the dung floor of the voor-kamer had been loosened and then stamped down again. The candle threw flickering shadows over the floor and over the clods of loose earth that had not been stamped down properly.

I drove back without the bucksail.

58

KAREL FLYSMAN

It was after the English had taken Pretoria that I first met Karel Flysman, Oom Schalk Lourens said.

Karel was about twenty-five. He was a very tall, well-built young man with a red face and curly hair. He was good-looking, and while I was satisfied with what the good Lord had done for me, yet I felt sometimes that if only He had given me a body like what Karel Flysman had got, I would go to church oftener and put more in the collection plate.

When the big commandos broke up, we separated into small companies, so that the English would not be able to catch all the Republican forces at the same time. If we were few and scattered the English would have to look harder to find us in the dongas and bushes and rante. And the English, at the beginning, moved slowly. When their scouts saw us making coffee under the trees by the side of the spruit, where it was cool and pleasant, they turned back to the main army and told their general about us. The general would look through his field-glasses and nod his head a few times.

"Yes," he would say, "that is the enemy. I can see them under those trees. There's that man with the long beard eating out of a pot with his hands. Why doesn't he use a knife and fork? I don't think he can be a gentleman. Bring out the maps and we'll attack them."

Then the general and a few of his kommandants would get together and work it all out.

"This cross I put here will be those trees," the general would say. "This crooked line I am drawing here is the spruit, and this circle will stand for the pot that that man is eating out of with his fingers . . . No, that's no good, now. They've moved the pot. Wonderful how crafty these Boers are."

Anyway, they would work out the plans of our position for half an hour, and at the end of that time they would find out that they

59

had got it all wrong. Because they had been using a map of the Rustenburg District, and actually they were halfway into the Marico. So by the time they had everything ready to attack us, we had already moved off and were making coffee under some other trees.

How do I know all these things? Well, I went right through the Boer War, and I was only once caught. And that was when our kommandant, Apie Terblanche, led us through the Bushveld by following some maps that he had captured from the British. But Apie Terblanche never was much use. He couldn't even hang a Hottentot properly.

As I was saying, Karel Flysman first joined up with our commando when we were trekking through the Bushveld north of the railway line from Mafeking to Bulawayo. It seemed that he had got separated from his commando and that he had been wandering about through the bush for some days before he came across us. He was mounted on a big black horse and, as he rode well, even for a Boer, he was certainly the finest-looking burgher I had seen for a long time.

One afternoon, when we had been in the saddle since before sunrise, and had also been riding hard the day before, we off-saddled at the foot of a koppie, where the bush was high and thick. We were very tired. A British column had come across us near the Molopo River. The meeting was a surprise for the British as well as for us. We fought for about an hour, but the fire was so heavy that we had to retreat, leaving behind us close on a dozen men, including the veldkornet. Karel Flysman displayed great promptitude and decision. As soon as the first shot was fired he jumped off his horse and threw down his rifle; he crawled away from the enemy on his hands and knees. He crawled very quickly too. An hour later, when we had ourselves given up resisting the English, we came across him in some long grass about a mile away from where the fighting had been. He was still crawling.

Karel Flysman's horse had remained with the rest of the horses, and it was just by good luck that Karel was able to get into the saddle and take to flight with us before the English got too close. We were pursued for a considerable distance. It didn't seem as though we would ever be able to shake off the enemy. I suppose that the reason they followed us so well was because that column could not have been in the charge of a general; their leader must have been only a captain or a kommandant, who probably did not understand how to use a map.

It was towards the afternoon that we discovered that the English were no longer hanging on to our rear. When we dismounted in the thick bush at the foot of the koppie, it was all we could do to unsaddle our horses. Then we lay down on the grass and stretched out our limbs and turned round to get comfortable, but we were so fatigued that it was a long time before we could get into restful positions.

Even then we couldn't get to sleep. The kommandant called us together and selected a number of burghers who were to form a committee to try Karel Flysman for running away. There wasn't much to be said about it. Karel Flysman was young, but at the same time he was old enough to know better. An ordinary burgher has got no right to run away from a fight at the head of the commando. It was the general's place to run away first. As a member of this committee I was at pains to point all this out to the prisoner.

We were seated in a circle on the grass. Karel Flysman stood in the centre. He was bare-headed. His Mauser and bandolier had

been taken away from him. His trousers were muddy and broken at the knees from the way in which he had crawled that long distance through the grass. There was also mud on his face. But in spite of all that, there was a fine, manly look about him, and I am sure that others besides myself felt sorry that Karel Flysman should be so much of a coward.

We were sorry for him, in a way. We were also tired, so that we didn't feel like getting up and doing any more shooting. Accordingly we decided that if the kommandant warned him about it we would give him one more chance.

"You have heard what your fellow burghers have decided about you," the kommandant said. "Let this be a lesson to you. A burgher of the Republic who runs away quickly may rise to be kommandant. But a burgher of the Republic must also know that there is a time to fight. And it is better to be shot by the English than by your own people, even though," the kommandant added, "the English can't shoot straight."

So we gave Karel Flysman back his rifle and bandolier, and we went to sleep. We didn't even trouble to put out guards round the camp. It would not have been any use putting out pickets, for they would have been sure to fall asleep, and if the English did come during the night they would know of our whereabouts by falling over our pickets.

As it happened, that night the English came.

The first thing I knew about it was when a man put his foot on my face. He put it on heavily, too, and by the feel of it I could tell that his veldskoens were made of unusually hard ox-hide. In those days, through always being on the alert for the enemy, I was a light sleeper, and that man's boot on my face woke me up without any difficulty. In the darkness I swore at him and he cursed back at me, saying something about the English. So we carried on for a few moments; he spoke about the English; I spoke about my face.

Then I heard the kommandant's voice, shouting out orders for us to stand to arms. I got my rifle and found my way to a sloot where our men were gathering for the fight. Up to that moment it had been too dark for me to distinguish anything that was more than a few feet away from me. But just then the clouds drifted away, and the moon shone down on us. It happened so quickly that for a brief while I was almost afraid. Everything that had been black before suddenly stood out pale and ghostly. The trees became silver with dark shadows in them, and it was amongst these shadows that we strove to see the English. Wherever a branch rustled in the wind or a twig moved, we thought we could see soldiers. Then somebody fired a shot. At once the firing became general.

I had been in many fights before, so that there was nothing new to me in the rattle of Mausers and Lee-Metfords, and in the red spurts of flame that suddenly broke out all round us. We could see little of the English. That meant that they could see even less of us. All we had to aim at were those spurts of flame. We realised quickly that it was only an advance party of the English that we had up against us; it was all rifle fire; the artillery would be coming along behind the main body. What we had to do was to go on shooting a little longer and then slip away before the rest of the English came. Near me a man shouted that he was hit. Many more were hit that night.

I bent down to put another cartridge-clip into my magazine, when I noticed a man lying flat in the sloot, with his arms about his head. His gun lay on the grass in front of him. By his dress and the size of his body I knew it was Karel Flysman. I didn't know whether it was a bullet or cowardice that had brought him down in that way. Therefore, to find out, I trod on his face. He shouted out something about the English, whereupon (as he used the same words), I was satisfied that he was the man who had awakened me with his boot before the fight started. I put some more of my weight on to the foot that was on his face.

"Don't do that. Oh, don't," Karel Flysman shouted. "I am dying. Oh, I am sure I am dying. The English . . ."

I stooped down and examined him. He was unwounded. All that was wrong with him was his spirit.

"God," I said, "why can't you try to be a man, Karel? If you've got to be shot nothing can stop the bullet, whether you are afraid or whether you're not. To see the way you're lying down there anybody would think that you are at least the kommandant-general."

He blurted out a lot of things, but he spoke so rapidly and his lips trembled so much that I couldn't understand much of what he said. And I didn't want to understand him, either. I kicked him in the ribs and told him to take his rifle and fight, or I would shoot him as he lay. But of course all that was of no use. He was actually so afraid of the enemy that even if he knew for sure that I was going to shoot him he would just have lain down where he was and have waited for the bullet.

In the meantime the fire of the enemy had grown steadier, so that we knew that at any moment we could expect the order to retreat.

"In a few minutes you can get back to your old game of running," I shouted to Karel Flysman, but I don't think he heard much of what I said, on account of the continuous rattle of the rifles.

But he must have heard the word 'running.'

"I can't," he cried. "My legs are too weak. I am dying."

He went on like that some more. He also mentioned a girl's name. He repeated it several times. I think the name was Francina. He shouted out the name and cried out that he didn't want to die. Then a whistle blew, and shortly afterwards we got the order to prepare for the retreat.

I did my best to help Karel out of the sloot. The Englishmen would have laughed if they could have seen that struggle in the moonlight. But the affair didn't last too long. Karel suddenly collapsed back into the sloot and lay still. That time it was a bullet. Karel Flysman was dead.

Often after I have thought of Karel Flysman and of the way he died. I have also thought of that girl he spoke about. Perhaps she thinks of her lover as a hero who laid down his life for his country. And perhaps it is as well that she should think that.

London Stories

The South African Opinion

(1934–37)

VELD MAIDEN

I know what it is – Oom Schalk Lourens said – when you talk that way about the veld. I have known people who sit like you do and dream about the veld, and talk strange things, and start believing in what they call the soul of the veld, until in the end the veld means a different thing to them from what it does to me.

I only know that the veld can be used for growing mealies on, and it isn't very good for that, either. Also, it means very hard work for me, growing mealies. There is the ploughing, for instance. I used to get aches in my back and shoulders from sitting on a stone all day long on the edge of the lands, watching the kaffirs and the oxen and the plough going up and down, making furrows. Hans Coetzee, who was a Boer War prisoner at St. Helena, told me how he got sick at sea from watching the ship going up and down, up and down, all the time.

And it's the same with ploughing. The only real cure for this ploughing sickness is to sit quietly on a riempies bench on the stoep, with one's legs raised slightly, drinking coffee until the ploughing season is over. Most of the farmers in the Marico Bushveld have adopted this remedy, as you have no doubt observed by this time.

But there the veld is. And it is not good to think too much about it. For then it can lead you in strange ways. And sometimes – sometimes when the veld has led you very far – there comes into your eyes a look that God did not put there.

It was in the early summer, shortly after the rains, that I first came across John de Swardt. He was sitting next to a tent that he had pitched behind the maroelas at the far end of my farm, where it adjoins Frans Welman's lands. He had been there several days and I had not known about it, because I sat much on my stoep then, on account of what I have already explained to you about the ploughing.

He was a young fellow with long black hair. When I got nearer I saw what he was doing. He had a piece of white bucksail on a stand in front of him and he was painting my farm. He seemed to have picked out all the useless bits for his picture – a krantz and a few stones and some clumps of kakiebos.

"Young man," I said to him, after we had introduced ourselves, "when people in Johannesburg see that picture they will laugh and say that Schalk Lourens lives on a barren piece of rock, like a lizard does. Why don't you rather paint the fertile parts? Look at that vlei there, and the dam. And put in that new cattle-dip that I have just built up with reinforced concrete. Then, if Piet Grobler or General Kemp sees this picture, he will know at once that Schalk Lourens has been making improvements on the farm."

The young painter shook his head.

"No," he said, "I want to paint only the veld. I hate the idea of painting boreholes and cattle-dips and houses and concrete – especially concrete. I want only the veld. Its loneliness. Its mystery. When this picture is finished I'll be proud to put my name to it."

"Oh, well, that is different," I replied, "as long as you don't put my name to it. Better still," I said, "put Frans Welman's name to it. Write underneath that this is Frans Welman's farm."

I said that because I still remembered that Frans Welman had voted against me at the last election of the Drogekop School Committee.

John de Swardt then took me into his tent and showed me some other pictures he had painted at different places along the Dwarsberge. They were all the same sort of picture, barren and stony. I thought it would be a good idea if the Government put up a lot of pictures like that on the Kalahari border for the locusts to see. Because that would keep the locusts out of the Marico.

Then John de Swardt showed me another picture he had painted and when I saw that I got a different opinion about this thing that he said was Art. I looked from De Swardt to the picture and then back again to De Swardt.

"I'd never have thought it of you," I said, "and you look such a quiet sort, too."

"I call it the 'Veld Maiden'," John de Swardt said.

"If the predikant saw it he'd call it by other names," I replied. "But I am a broad-minded man. I have been once in the bar in Zeerust and twice in the bioscope when I should have been attending Nagmaal. So I don't hold it against a young man for having ideas like this. But you mustn't let anybody here see this Veld Maiden unless you paint a few more clothes on her."

"I couldn't," De Swardt answered, "that's just how I see her. That's just how I dream about her. For many years now she has come to me so in my dreams."

"With her arms stretched out like that?" I asked.

"Yes."

"And with –"

"Yes, yes, just like that," De Swardt said very quickly. Then he blushed and I could see how very young he was. It seemed a pity that a nice young fellow like that should be so mad.

"Anyway, if ever you want a painting job," I said when I left, "you can come and whitewash the back of my sheep-kraal."

I often say funny things like that to people.

I saw a good deal of John de Swardt after that, and I grew to like him. I was satisfied – in spite of his wasting his time in painting bare stones and weeds – that there was no real evil in him. I was sure that he only talked silly things about visions and the spirit of the veld because of what they had done to him at the school in Johannesburg where they taught him all that nonsense about art, and I felt sorry for him. Afterwards I wondered for a little while if I shouldn't rather have felt sorry for the art school. But when I had thought it all out carefully I knew that John de Swardt was only very young and innocent, and that what happened to him later on was the sort of thing that does happen to those who are simple of heart.

On several Sundays in succession I took De Swardt over the rant to the house of Frans Welman. I hadn't a very high regard for Frans's judgment since the time he voted for the wrong man at the School Committee. But I had no other neighbour within walking distance, and I had to go somewhere on a Sunday.

We talked of all sorts of things. Frans's wife Sannie was young and pretty, but very shy. She wasn't naturally like that. It was only

69

that she was afraid to talk in case she said something of which her husband might disapprove. So most of the time Sannie sat silent in the corner, getting up now and again to make more coffee for us.

Frans Welman was in some respects what people might call a hard man. For instance, it was something of a mild scandal the way he treated his wife and the kaffirs on his farm. But then, on the other hand, he looked very well after his cattle and pigs. And I have always believed that this is more important in a farmer than that he should be kind to his wife and the kaffirs.

Well, we talked about the mealies and the drought of the year before last and the subsidies, and I could see that in a short while the conversation would come round to the Volksraad, and as I wasn't anxious to hear how Frans was going to vote at the General Election – believing that so irresponsible a person should not be allowed to vote at all – I quickly asked John de Swardt to tell us about his paintings.

Immediately he started off about his Veld Maiden.

"Not that one," I said, kicking his shin, "I meant your other paintings. The kind that frighten the locusts."

I felt that this Veld Maiden thing was not a fit subject to talk about, especially with a woman present. Moreover, it was Sunday.

Nevertheless, that kick came too late. De Swardt rubbed his shin a few times and started on his subject, and although Frans and I cleared our throats awkwardly at different parts, and Sannie looked on the floor with her pretty cheeks very red, the young painter explained everything about that picture and what it meant to him.

"It's a dream I have had for a long time, now," he said at the end, "and always she comes to me, and when I put out my arms to clasp her to me she vanishes, and I am left with only her memory in my heart. But when she comes the whole world is clothed in a terrible beauty."

"That's more than she is clothed in, anyway," Frans said, "judging from what you have told us about her."

"She's a spirit. She's the spirit of the veld," De Swardt murmured, "she whispers strange and enchanting things. Her coming is like the whisper of the wind. She's not of the earth at all."

70

"Oh, well," Frans said shortly, "you can keep these Uitlander ghost-women of yours. A Boer girl is good enough for ordinary fellows like me and Schalk Lourens."

So the days passed.

John de Swardt finished a few more bits of rock and drought-stricken kakiebos, and I had got so far as to persuade him to label the worst-looking one "Frans Welman's Farm."

Then one morning he came to me in great excitement.

"I saw her again, Oom Schalk," he said, "I saw her last night. In a surpassing loveliness. Just at midnight. She came softly across the veld towards my tent. The night was warm and lovely, and the stars were mad and singing. And there was low music where her white feet touched the grass. And sometimes her mouth seemed to be laughing, and sometimes it was sad. And her lips were very red, Oom Schalk. And when I reached out with my arms she went away. She disappeared in the maroelas, like the whispering of the wind. And there was a ringing in my ears. And in my heart there was a green fragrance, and I thought of the pale asphodel that grows in the fields of paradise."

"I don't know about paradise," I said, "but if a thing like that grew in my mealie-lands I would see to it at once that the kaffirs pulled it up. I don't like this spook nonsense."

I then gave him some good advice. I told him to beware of the moon, which was almost full at the time. Because the moon can do strange things to you in the Bushveld, especially if you live in a tent and the full moon is overhead and there are weird shadows amongst the maroelas.

But I knew he wouldn't take any notice of what I told him.

Several times after that he came with the same story about the Veld Maiden. I started getting tired of it.

Then, one morning when he came again, I knew everything by the look he had in his eyes. I have already told you about that look.

"Oom Schalk," he began.

"John de Swardt," I said to him, "don't tell me anything. All I ask of you is to pack up your things and leave my farm at once."

"I'll leave tonight," he said. "I promise you that by tomorrow morning I will be gone. Only let me stay here one more day and night."

His voice trembled when he spoke, and his knees were very unsteady. But it was not for these reasons or for his sake that I relented. I spoke to him civilly for the sake of the look he had in his eyes.

"Very well, then," I said, "but you must go straight back to Johannesburg. If you walk down the road you will be able to catch the Government lorry to Zeerust."

He thanked me and left. I never saw him again.

Next day his tent was still there behind the maroelas, but John de Swardt was gone, and he had taken with him all his pictures. All, that is, except the Veld Maiden one. I suppose he had no more need for it.

And, in any case, the white ants had already started on it. So that's why I can hang the remains of it openly on the wall in my voorhuis, and the predikant does not raise any objection to it. For the white ants have eaten away practically all of it except the face.

As for Frans Welman, it was quite a long time before he gave up searching the Marico for his young wife, Sannie.

Yellow Moepels

If ever you spoke to my father about witch-doctors (Oom Schalk Lourens said), he would always relate one story. And at the end of it he would explain that, while a witch-doctor could foretell the future for you from the bones, at the same time he could only tell you the things that didn't matter. My father used to say that the important things were as much hidden from the witch-doctor as from the man who listened to his prophecy.

My father said that when he was sixteen he went with his friend, Paul, a stripling of about his own age, to a kaffir witch-doctor. They had heard that this witch-doctor was very good at throwing the bones.

This witch-doctor lived alone in a mud hut. While they were still on the way to the hut the two youths laughed and jested, but as soon as they got inside they felt different. They were impressed. The witch-doctor was very old and very wrinkled. He had on a queer head-dress made up from the tails of different wild animals.

You could tell that the boys were overawed as they sat there on the floor in the dark. Because my father, who had meant to hand the witch-doctor only a plug of Boer tobacco, gave him a whole roll. And Paul, who had said, when they were outside, that he was going to give him nothing at all, actually handed over his hunting knife.

Then he threw the bones. He threw first for my father. He told him many things. He told him that he would grow up to be a good burgher, and that he would one day be very prosperous. He would have a big farm and many cattle and two ox-wagons.

But what the witch-doctor did not tell my father was that in years to come he would have a son, Schalk, who could tell better stories than any man in the Marico.

Then the witch-doctor threw the bones for Paul. For a long while he was silent. He looked from the bones to Paul, and back to the bones, in a strange way. Then he spoke.

"I can see you go far away, my kleinbaas," he said, "very far away over the great waters. Away from your own land, my kleinbaas."

"And the veld," Paul asked, "and the krantzes and the vlaktes?"

"And away from your own people," the witch-doctor said.

"And will I – will I –"

"No, my kleinbasie," the witch-doctor answered, "you will not come back. You will die there."

My father said that when they came out of that hut Paul Kruger's face was very white. That was why my father used to say that, while a witch-doctor could tell you true things, he could not tell you the things that really mattered.

And my father was right.

Take the case of Neels Potgieter and Martha Rossouw, for instance. They became engaged to be married just before the affair at Paardekraal. There, on the hoogte, our leaders pointed out to us that, although the Transvaal had been annexed by Sir Theophilus Shepstone, it nevertheless meant that we would have to go on paying taxes just the same. Everybody knew then that it was war.

Neels Potgieter and I were in the same commando.

It was arranged that the burghers of the neighbourhood should assemble at the veldkornet's house. Instructions had also been given that no women were to be present. There was much fighting to be done, and this final leave-taking was likely to be an embarrassing thing.

Nevertheless, as always, the women came. And among them was Neels's sweetheart, Martha Rossouw. And also there was my sister, Annie.

I shall never forget that scene in front of the veldkornet's house, in the early morning, when there were still shadows on the rante, and a thin wind blew through the grass. We had no predikant there; but an ouderling, with two bandoliers slung across his body, and a Martini in his hand, said a few words. He was a

74

strong and simple man, with no great gifts of oratory. But when he spoke about the Transvaal we could feel what was in his heart, and we took off our hats in silence.

And it was not long afterwards that I again took off my hat in much the same way. Then it was at Majuba Hill. It was after the battle, and the ouderling still had his two bandoliers around him when we buried him at the foot of the koppie.

But what impressed me most was the prayer that followed the ouderling's brief address. In front of the veldkornet's house we knelt, each burgher with his rifle at his side. And the womenfolk knelt down with us. And the wind seemed very gentle as it stirred the tall grass-blades; very gentle as it swept over the bared heads of the men and fluttered the kappies and skirts of the women; very gentle as it carried the prayers of our nation over the veld.

After that we stood up and sang a hymn. The ceremony was over. The agterryers brought us our horses. And, dry-eyed and tight-lipped, each woman sent her man forth to war. There was no weeping.

Then, in accordance with Boer custom, we fired a volley into the air.

"Voorwaarts, burghers," came the veldkornet's order, and we cantered down the road in twos. But before we left I had over-heard Neels Potgieter say something to Martha Rossouw as he leant out of the saddle and kissed her. My sister Annie, standing beside my horse, also heard.

"When the moepels are ripe, Martha," Neels said, "I will come to you again."

Annie and I looked at each other and smiled. It was a pretty thing that Neels had said. But then Martha was also pretty. More pretty than the veld-trees that bore those yellow moepels, I re-flected – and more wild.

I was still thinking of this when our commando had passed over the bult, in a long line, on our way to the south, where Natal was, and the other commandos, and Majuba.

This was the war of Bronkhorstspruit and General Colley and Laing's Nek. You have no doubt heard many accounts of this war, some of them truthful, perhaps. For it is a singular thing that, as

75

a man grows older, and looks back on fights that he has been in, he keeps on remembering, each year, more and more of the enemy that he has shot.

Klaas Uys was a man like that. Each year, on his birthday, he remembered one or two more redcoats that he had shot, whereupon he got up straight away and put another few notches in the wood part of his rifle, along the barrel. And he said his memory was getting better every year.

All the time I was on commando, I received only one letter. That came from Annie, my sister. She said I was not to take any risks, and that I must keep far away from the English, especially if they had guns. She also said I was to remember that I was a white man, and that if there was any dangerous work to be done, I had to send a kaffir out to do it.

There were more things like that in Annie's letter. But I had no need of her advice. Our kommandant was a God-fearing and wily man, and he knew even better ways than Annie did for keeping out of range of the enemy's fire.

But Annie also said, at the end of her letter, that she and Martha Rossouw had gone to a witch-doctor. They had gone to find out about Neels Potgieter and me. Now, if I had been at home, I would not have permitted Annie to indulge in this nonsense.

Especially as the witch-doctor said to her, "Yes, missus, I can see Baas Schalk Lourens. He will come back safe. He is very clever, Baas Schalk. He lies behind a big stone, with a dirty brown blanket pulled over his head. And he stays behind that stone until the fighting is finished – quite finished."

According to Annie's letter, the witch-doctor told her a few other things about me, too. But I won't bother to repeat them now. I think I have said enough to show you what sort of a scoundrel that old kaffir was. He not only took advantage of the credulity of a simple girl, but he also tried to be funny at the expense of a young man who was fighting for his country's freedom.

What was more, Annie said that she had recognised it was me right away, just from the kaffir's description of that blanket.

To Martha Rossouw the witch-doctor said, "Baas Neels Potgieter will come back to you, missus, when the moepels are ripe again. At sun-under he will come."

That was all he said about Neels, and there wasn't very much in that, anyway, seeing that Neels himself – except for the bit about the sunset – had made the very same prophecy the day the commando set out. I suppose that witch-doctor had been too busy thinking out foolish and spiteful things about me to be able to give any attention to Neels Potgieter's affairs.

But I didn't mention Annie's letter to Neels. He might have wanted to know more than I was willing to tell him. More, even, perhaps, than Martha was willing to tell him – Martha of the wild heart.

Then, at last, the war ended, and over the Transvaal the Vierkleur waved again. And the commandos went home by their different ways. And our leaders revived their old quarrels as to who should be president. And, everywhere, except for a number of lonely graves on hillside and vlakte, things were as they had been before Shepstone came.

It was getting on towards evening when our small band rode over the bult again, and once more came to a halt at the veldkor-net's house. A messenger had been sent on in advance to an-nounce our coming, and from far around the women and children and old men had gathered to welcome their victorious burghers back from the war. And there were tears in many eyes when we sang, "Hef, Burghers, Hef."

And the moepels were ripe and yellow on the trees.

And in the dusk Neels Potgieter found Martha Rossouw and kissed her. At sundown, as the witch-doctor had said. But there was one important thing that the witch-doctor had not told. It was something that Neels Potgieter did not know, either, just then. And that was that Martha did not want him anymore.

THE LOVE POTION

You mention the juba-plant (Oom Schalk Lourens said). Oh, yes, everybody in the Marico knows about the juba-plant. It grows high up on the krantzes, and they say you must pick off one of its little red berries at midnight, under the full moon. Then, if you are a young man, and you are anxious for a girl to fall in love with you, all you have to do is to squeeze the juice of the juba-berry into her coffee.

They say that after the girl has drunk the juba-juice she begins to forget all sorts of things. She forgets that your forehead is rather low, and that your ears stick out, and that your mouth is too big. She even forgets having told you, the week before last, that she wouldn't marry you if you were the only man in the Transvaal.

All she knows is that the man she gazes at, over her empty coffee-cup, has grown remarkably handsome. You can see from this that the plant must be very potent in its effects. I mean, if you consider what some of the men in the Marico look like.

One young man I knew, however, was not very enthusiastic about juba-juice. In fact, he always said that before he climbed up the krantz one night, to pick one of those red berries, he was more popular with the girls than he was afterwards. This young man said that his decline in favour with the girls of the neighbourhood might perhaps be due to the fact that, shortly after he had picked the juba-berry, he lost most of his front teeth.

This happened when the girl's father, who was an irascible sort of fellow, caught the young man in the act of squeezing juba-juice into his daughter's cup.

And afterwards, while others talked of the magic properties of this love potion, the young man would listen in silence, and his lip would curl in a sneer over the place where his front teeth used to be.

"Yes, kêrels," he would lisp at the end, "I suppose I must have picked that juba-berry at the wrong time. Perhaps the moon wasn't full enough, or something. Or perhaps it wasn't just exactly midnight. I am only glad now that I didn't pick off two of those red berries while I was about it."

We all felt it was a sad thing that the juba-plant had done to that young man.

But with Gideon van der Merwe it was different.

One night I was out shooting in the veld with a lamp fastened on my hat. You know that kind of shooting: in the glare of the lamp-light you can see only the eyes of the thing you are aiming at, and you get three months if you are caught. They made it illegal to hunt by lamp-light since the time a policeman got shot in the foot, this way, when he was out tracking cattle-smugglers on the Bechuanaland border.

The magistrate at Zeerust, who did not know the ways of the cattle-smugglers, found that the shooting was an accident. This verdict satisfied everybody except the policeman, whose foot was still bandaged when he came into court. But the men in the Volksraad, some of whom had been cattle-smugglers themselves, knew better than the magistrate did as to how the policeman came to have a couple of buckshot in the soft part of his foot, and accordingly they brought in this new law.

Therefore I walked very quietly that night on the krantz.

Frequently I put out my light and stood very still amongst the trees, and waited long moments to make sure I was not being followed. Ordinarily, there would have been little to fear, but a couple of days before two policemen had been seen disappearing into the bush. By their looks they seemed young policemen, who were anxious for promotion, and who didn't know that it is more becoming for a policeman to drink an honest farmer's peach brandy than to arrest him for hunting by lamp-light.

I was walking along, turning the light from side to side, when suddenly, about a hundred paces from me, in the full brightness of the lamp, I saw a pair of eyes. When I also saw, above the eyes, a policeman's khaki helmet, I remembered that a moonlight night, such as that was, was not good for finding buck.

So I went home.

I took the shortest way, too, which was over the side of the krantz – the steep side – and on my way down I clutched at a variety of branches, tree-roots, stone ledges and tufts of grass. Later on, at the foot of the krantz, when I came to and was able to sit up, there was that policeman bending over me.

"Oom Schalk," he said, "I was wondering if you would lend me your lamp."

I looked up. It was Gideon van der Merwe, the young policeman who had been stationed for some time at Derdepoort. I had met him on several occasions and had found him very likeable.

"You can have my lamp," I answered, "but you must be careful. It's worse for a policeman to get caught breaking the law than for an ordinary man."

Gideon van der Merwe shook his head.

"No, I don't want to go shooting with the lamp," he said, "I want to –"

And then he paused.

He laughed nervously.

"It seems silly to say it, Oom Schalk," he said, "but perhaps you'll understand. I have come to look for a juba-plant. I need it for my studies. For my third-class sergeant's examination. And it will soon be midnight, and I can't find one of those plants anywhere."

I felt sorry for Gideon. It struck me that he would never make a good policeman. If he couldn't find a juba-plant, of which there were thousands on the krantz, it would be much harder for him to find the spoor of a cattle-smuggler.

So I handed him my lamp and explained where he had to go and look. Gideon thanked me and walked off.

About half an hour later he was back.

He took a red berry out of his tunic pocket and showed it to me. For fear he should tell any more lies about needing that juba-berry for his studies, I spoke first.

"Lettie Cordier?" I asked.

Gideon nodded. He was very shy, though, and wouldn't talk much at the start. But I had guessed long ago that Gideon van der Merwe was not calling at Krisjan Cordier's house so often just to hear Krisjan relate the story of his life.

Nevertheless, I mentioned Krisjan Cordier's life-story.

"Yes," Gideon replied, "Lettie's father has got up to what he was like at the age of seven. It has taken him a month, so far."

"He must be glad to get you to listen," I said, "the only other man who listened for any length of time was an insurance agent. But he left after a fortnight. By that time Krisjan had reached to only a little beyond his fifth birthday."

"But Lettie is wonderful, Oom Schalk," Gideon went on. "I have never spoken more than a dozen words to her. And, of course, it is ridiculous to expect her even to look at a policeman. But to sit there, in the voorkamer, with her father talking about all the things he could do before he was six – and Lettie coming in now and again with more coffee – that is love, Oom Schalk."

I agreed with him that it must be.

"I have worked it out," Gideon explained, "that at the rate he is going now, Lettie's father will have come to the end of his life-story in two years' time, and after that I won't have any excuse for going there. That worries me."

I said that no doubt it was disconcerting.

"I have tried often to tell Lettie how much I think of her," Gideon said, "but every time, as soon as I start, I get a foolish feeling. My uniform begins to look shabby. My boots seem to curl up at the toes. And my voice gets shaky, and all I can say to her is that I will come round again, soon, as I have simply got to hear the rest of her father's life-story."

"Then what is your idea with the juba-juice?" I asked.

"The juba-juice," Gideon van der Merwe said, wistfully, "might make her say something first."

We parted shortly afterwards. I took up my lamp and gun, and as I saw Gideon's figure disappear among the trees I thought of what a good fellow he was. And very simple. Still, he was best off as a policeman, I reflected. For if he was a cattle-smuggler it seemed to me that he would get arrested every time he tried to cross the border.

Next morning I rode over to Krisjan Cordier's farm to remind him about the tin of sheep-dip that he still owed me from the last dipping season.

As I stayed for only about an hour, I wasn't able to get in a word about the sheep-dip, but Krisjan managed to tell me quite a lot about the things he did at the age of nine. When Lettie came in with the coffee I made a casual remark to her father about Gideon van der Merwe.

"Oh, yes, he's an interesting young man," Krisjan Cordier said, "and very intelligent. It is a pleasure for me to relate to him the story of my life. He says the incidents I describe to him are not only thrilling, but very helpful. I can quite understand that. I wouldn't be surprised if he is made a sergeant one of these days. For these reasons I always dwell on the more helpful parts of my story."

I didn't take much notice of Krisjan's remarks, however. Instead, I looked carefully at Lettie when I mentioned Gideon's name. She didn't give much away, but I am quick at these things, and I saw enough. The colour that crept into her cheeks. The light that came in her eyes.

On my way back I encountered Lettie. She was standing under a thorn-tree. With her brown arms and her sweet, quiet face and her full bosom, she was a very pretty picture. There was no doubt that Lettie Cordier would make a fine wife for any man. It wasn't hard to understand Gideon's feelings about her.

"Lettie," I asked, "do you love him?"

"I love him, Oom Schalk," she answered.

It was as simple as that.

Lettie guessed I meant Gideon van der Merwe, without my having spoken his name. Accordingly, it was easy for me to acquaint Lettie with what had happened the night before, on the krantz, in the moonlight. At least, I only told her the parts that mattered to her, such as the way I explained to Gideon where the juba-plant grew. Another man might have wearied her with a long and unnecessary description of the way he fell down the krantz, clutching at branches and tree-roots. But I am different. I told her that it was Gideon who fell down the krantz.

After all, it was Lettie's and Gideon's love affair, and I didn't want to bring myself into it too much.

"Now you'll know what to do, Lettie," I said. "Put your coffee on the table within easy reach of Gideon. Then give him what you think is long enough to squeeze the juba-juice into your cup."

82

"Perhaps it will be even better," Lettie said, "if I watch through a crack in the door."

I patted her head approvingly.

"After that you come into the voorkamer and drink your coffee," I said.

"Yes, Oom Schalk," she answered simply.

"And when you have drunk the coffee," I concluded, "you'll know what to do next. Only don't go too far."

It was pleasant to see the warm blood mount to her face. As I rode off I said to myself that Gideon van der Merwe was a lucky fellow.

There isn't much more to tell about Lettie and Gideon.

When I saw Gideon some time afterwards, he was very elated, as I had expected he would be.

"So the juba-plant worked?" I enquired.

"It was wonderful, Oom Schalk," Gideon answered, "and the funny part of it was that Lettie's father was not there, either, when I put the juba-juice into her coffee. Lettie had brought him a message, just before then, that he was wanted in the mealie-lands."

"And was the juba-juice all they claim for it?" I asked.

"You'd be surprised how quickly it acted," he said. "Lettie just took one sip at the coffee and then jumped straight on to my lap."

But then Gideon van der Merwe winked in a way that made me believe that he was not so very simple, after all.

"I was pretty certain that the juba-juice would work, Oom Schalk," he said, "after Lettie's father told me that you had been there that morning."

In the Withaak's Shade

Leopards? – Oom Schalk Lourens said – Oh, yes, there are two varieties on this side of the Limpopo. The chief difference between them is that the one kind of leopard has got a few more spots on it than the other kind. But when you meet a leopard in the veld, unexpectedly, you seldom trouble to count his spots to find out what kind he belongs to. That is unnecessary. Because, whatever kind of leopard it is that you come across in this way, you only do one kind of running. And that is the fastest kind.

I remember the occasion that I came across a leopard unexpectedly, and to this day I couldn't tell you how many spots he had, even though I had all the time I needed for studying him. It happened about midday, when I was out on the far end of my farm, behind a koppie, looking for some strayed cattle. I thought the cattle might be there because it is shady under those withaak trees, and there is soft grass that is very pleasant to sit on. After I had looked for the cattle for about an hour in this manner, sitting up against a tree-trunk, it occurred to me that I could look for them just as well, or perhaps even better, if I lay down flat. For even a child knows that cattle aren't so small that you have got to get on to stilts and things to see them properly.

So I lay on my back, with my hat tilted over my face, and my legs crossed, and when I closed my eyes slightly the tip of my boot, sticking up into the air, looked just like the peak of Abjaterskop.

Overhead a lone aasvoël wheeled, circling slowly round and round without flapping his wings, and I knew that not even a calf could pass in any part of the sky between the tip of my toe and that aasvoël without my observing it immediately. What was more, I could go on lying there under the withaak and looking for

84

the cattle like that all day, if necessary. As you know, I am not the sort of farmer to loaf about the house when there is man's work to be done.

The more I screwed up my eyes and gazed at the toe of my boot, the more it looked like Abjaterskop. By and by it seemed that it actually was Abjaterskop, and I could see the stones on top of it, and the bush trying to grow up its sides, and in my ears there was a far-off, humming sound, like bees in an orchard on a still day. As I have said, it was very pleasant.

Then a strange thing happened. It was as though a huge cloud, shaped like an animal's head and with spots on it, had settled on top of Abjaterskop. It seemed so funny that I wanted to laugh. But I didn't. Instead, I opened my eyes a little more and felt glad to think that I was only dreaming. Because otherwise I would have to believe that the spotted cloud on Abjaterskop was actually a leopard, and that he was gazing at my boot. Again I wanted to laugh. But then, suddenly, I knew.

And I didn't feel so glad. For it was a leopard, all right – a large-sized, hungry-looking leopard, and he was sniffing suspiciously at my feet. I was uncomfortable. I knew that nothing I could do would ever convince that leopard that my toe was Abjaterskop. He was not that sort of leopard: I knew that without even counting the number of his spots. Instead, having finished with my feet, he started sniffing higher up. It was the most terrifying moment of my life. I wanted to get up and run for it. But I couldn't. My legs wouldn't work.

Every big-game hunter I have come across has told me the same story about how, at one time or another, he has owed his escape from lions and other wild animals to his cunning in lying down and pretending to be dead, so that the beast of prey loses interest in him and walks off. Now, as I lay there on the grass, with the leopard trying to make up his mind about me, I understood why, in such a situation, the hunter doesn't move. It's simply that he can't move. That's all. It's not his cunning that keeps him down. It's his legs.

In the meantime, the leopard had got up as far as my knees. He was studying my trousers very carefully, and I started getting embarrassed. My trousers were old and rather unfashionable.

Also, at the knee, there was a torn place, from where I had climbed through a barbed-wire fence, into the thick bush, the time I saw the Government tax-collector coming over the bult before he saw me. The leopard stared at that rent in my trousers for quite a while, and my embarrassment grew. I felt I wanted to explain about the Government tax-collector and the barbed wire. I didn't want the leopard to get the impression that Schalk Lourens was the sort of man who didn't care about his personal appearance.

When the leopard got as far as my shirt, however, I felt better. It was a good blue flannel shirt that I had bought only a few weeks ago from the Indian store at Ramoutsa, and I didn't care how many strange leopards saw it. Nevertheless, I made up my mind that next time I went to lie on the grass under the withaak, looking for strayed cattle, I would first polish up my veldskoens with sheep's fat, and I would put on my black hat that I only wear to Nagmaal. I could not permit the wild animals of the neighbourhood to sneer at me.

But when the leopard reached my face I got frightened again. I knew he couldn't take exception to my shirt. But I wasn't so sure about my face. Those were terrible moments. I lay very still, afraid

to open my eyes and afraid to breathe. Sniff-sniff, the huge creature went, and his breath swept over my face in hot gasps. You
hear of many frightening experiences that a man has in a lifetime.
I have also been in quite a few perilous situations. But if you want
something to make you suddenly old and to turn your hair white
in a few moments, there is nothing to beat a leopard – especially
when he is standing over you, with his jaws at your throat, trying
to find a good place to bite.

The leopard gave a deep growl, stepped right over my body,
knocking off my hat, and growled again. I opened my eyes and
saw the animal moving away clumsily. But my relief didn't last
long. The leopard didn't move far. Instead, he turned over and lay
down next to me.

Yes, there on the grass, in the shade of the withaak, the leopard
and I lay down together. The leopard lay half-curled up, on his
side, with his forelegs crossed, like a dog, and whenever I tried to
move away he grunted. I am sure that in the whole history of the
Groot Marico there have never been two stranger companions
engaged in the thankless task of looking for strayed cattle.

Next day, in Fanie Snyman's voorkamer, which was used as a
post office, I told my story to the farmers of the neighbourhood,
while they were drinking coffee and waiting for the motor-lorry
from Zeerust.

"And how did you get away from that leopard in the end?"
Koos van Tonder asked, trying to be funny. "I suppose you crawled
through the grass and frightened the leopard off by pretending to
be a python."

"No, I just got up and walked home," I said. "I remembered
that the cattle I was looking for might have gone the other way
and strayed into your kraal. I thought they would be safer with
the leopard."

"Did the leopard tell you what he thought of General Pienaar's
last speech in the Volksraad?" Frans Welman asked, and they all
laughed.

I told my story over several times before the lorry came with
our letters, and although the dozen odd men present didn't say
much while I was talking, I could see that they listened to me in
the same way that they listened when Krisjan Lemmer talked.

And everybody knew that Krisjan Lemmer was the biggest liar in the Bushveld.

To make matters worse, Krisjan Lemmer was there, too, and when I got to the part of my story where the leopard lay down beside me, Krisjan Lemmer winked at me. You know that kind of wink. It was to let me know that there was now a new understanding between us, and that we could speak in future as one Marico liar to another.

I didn't like that.

"Kêrels," I said in the end, "I know just what you are thinking. You don't believe me, and you don't want to say so."

"But we do believe you," Krisjan Lemmer interrupted me, "very wonderful things happen in the Bushveld. I once had a twenty-foot mamba that I named Hans. This snake was so attached to me that I couldn't go anywhere without him. He would even follow me to church on a Sunday, and because he didn't care much for some of the sermons, he would wait for me outside under a tree. Not that Hans was irreligious. But he had a sensitive nature, and the strong line that the predikant took against the serpent in the Garden of Eden always made Hans feel awkward. Yet he didn't go and look for a withaak to lie under, like your leopard. He wasn't stand-offish in that way. An ordinary thorn-tree's shade was good enough for Hans. He knew he was only a mamba, and didn't try to give himself airs."

I didn't take any notice of Krisjan Lemmer's stupid lies, but the upshot of this whole affair was that I also began to have doubts about the existence of that leopard. I recalled queer stories I had heard of human beings that could turn themselves into animals, and although I am not a superstitious man I could not shake off the feeling that it was a spook thing that had happened. But when, a few days later, a huge leopard had been seen from the roadside near the poort, and then again by Mtosas on the way to Nietverdiend, and again in the turf-lands near the Molopo, matters took a different turn.

At first people jested about this leopard. They said it wasn't a real leopard, but a spotted animal that had walked away out of Schalk Lourens's dream. They also said that the leopard had come to the Dwarsberge to have a look at Krisjan Lemmer's twenty-foot mamba. But afterwards, when they had found his spoor at several waterholes, they had no more doubt about the leopard.

It was dangerous to walk about in the veld, they said. Exciting times followed. There was a great deal of shooting at the leopard and a great deal of running away from him. The amount of Martini and Mauser fire I heard in the krantzes reminded me of nothing so much as the First Boer War. And the amount of running away reminded me of nothing so much as the Second Boer War.

But always the leopard escaped unharmed. Somehow, I felt sorry for him. The way he had first sniffed at me and then lain down beside me that day under the withaak was a strange thing that I couldn't understand. I thought of the Bible, where it is written that the lion shall lie down with the lamb.

But I also wondered if I hadn't dreamt it all. The manner in which those things had befallen me was all so unearthly. The leopard began to take up a lot of my thoughts. And there was no man to whom I could talk about it who would be able to help me in any way. Even now, as I am telling you this story, I am expecting you to wink at me, like Krisjan Lemmer did.

Still, I can only tell you the things that happened as I saw them, and what the rest was about only Africa knows.

It was some time before I again walked along the path that leads through the bush to where the withaaks are. But I didn't lie down on the grass again. Because when I reached the place, I found that the leopard had got there before me. He was lying on the same spot, half-curled up in the withaak's shade, and his forepaws were folded as a dog's are, sometimes. But he lay very still. And even from the distance where I stood I could see the red splash on his breast where a Mauser bullet had gone.

THE WIDOW

There had been no rain in the Potchefstroom District for many months, and so the ground was very hard that morning, and the picks and shovels of the kaffirs rang on the gravel, by the side of the mud hut that had been used as a courthouse.

I was a boy then. It was at the time when the Transvaal was divided into four separate republics, and Potchefstroom, which was a small village, was the capital of the southern republic.

For several days there had been much activity in the court-house. From distant parts the farmers had come to attend the trial of Tjaart van Rensburg. Only a few could get inside the court. The rest watched at the door, crowding forward eagerly after each witness had stepped down from the stand; those inside told them what evidence had been given.

Naturally there was much excitement over these court proceedings, and in Potchefstroom people talked of little else but the Transvaal's first murder trial.

The whole thing started when Andries Theron was found beside the borehole on his farm. He had been pumping water for his cattle. One Rossouw, a neighbour of Andries Theron's, passing by in his ox-wagon, saw a man lying next to the pump-handle.

Thus it was that Francina Theron saw her husband arrive home in a stranger's ox-wagon, with a piece of bucksail pulled over his body, and a Martini bullet in his heart. The landdrost's men came from Potchefstroom and proceeded to investigate the murder, spending much of their time, as landdrosts' men always do, in trying to frighten the wrong people into confessing.

But afterwards they got their information.

They say there was a large crowd at the funeral of Andries Theron, which took place at the foot of a koppie on the far end of his farm. They came, the women in black clothes and the men in their Sunday hats; and in that sad procession that wound slowly over the veld, following the wagon with the coffin on it, there were also two landdrost's men.

Among the mourners was the dead man's cousin, Tjaart van Rensburg. The minister did not take long over the funeral service. He said a few simple words about the tragic way in which Andries Theron had died, adding that no man knew when his hour was come. He then spoke a brief message of comfort to the widow, Francina, and offered up a prayer for the dead man's soul.

The last notes of the Boer hymn had died on the veld, and the crowd had already begun to move away from the graveside, when one of the landdrost's men put his hand on Tjaart van Rensburg's shoulder. With an officer of the law on each side of him, the fetters on his wrists, Tjaart van Rensburg led the procession down the stony road.

The prisoner had turned very pale. But they all noticed that his head was erect and his step firm, when he walked to the bluegum trees on the other side of the hill, where the Government Cape-cart waited.

A month later the trial commenced in Potchefstroom.

Andries Theron's widow, Francina, was a slenderly built woman, still in her early twenties. She had been very pretty at one time, with light-hearted ways and a merry laugh. But the shock of her husband's death had changed her in an hour. She did not weep when Rossouw, who had a good heart but blunt ways, informed her that he had found her husband lying dead on the veld.

"I was lucky," Rossouw said, "to have found him before the vultures did."

"Where is he?" Francina asked.

"On my wagon," Rossouw answered, "under the first bucksail you come to. Next to the sacks of potatoes."

In some respects Rossouw did not have what you would call a real delicacy of feeling. But he possessed a sombre thing of the veld, which told him that he must not follow Francina to the wagon, because it was right that, at her first meeting with her dead husband, a wife should be alone.

Francina was at the wagon a long time.

When she came back she was sadly changed. The colour had left her cheeks and her lips. Her mouth sagged at the corners. But in her tearless eyes there was a lost and hopeless look, a dreadful desolation that frightened Rossouw when he saw it, so that he made no effort to comfort her.

It was the same with the women who came to console Francina. If a woman wanted to take Francina in her arms, so that she could weep on her bosom, there was that look in her eyes that spoke of a sorrow that must be for always.

You can't do much, if all you have to offer a widow is human sympathy, and she looks back at you with wide eyes that seem to want nothing more from this world or the world to come. You get uneasy, then, and feel that you have no right to trespass on this sort of sorrow.

That was what happened to the women who knew Francina. They were kind to her in little ways. When the time for the murder trial came, and it seemed likely that Francina would be called as a witness, a woman accompanied her to Potchefstroom and stayed with her there. But even to this woman, in her grief, Francina remained a stranger.

In fact, this woman always said, afterwards, that during all the time she was with her, Francina spoke to her only once; and that was when they were at the Mooi River, which flows through Potchefstroom, and Francina said how pretty the yellow flowers grew on the banks of the river.

So the trial began. Every morning, at nine o'clock, Tjaart van Rensburg was led from the gaol to the courthouse with the mud walls. There were always many people standing around to see him pass. I saw him quite often. The impression I get, when I look back to that time, is that Tjaart van Rensburg was a broad-shouldered man of about thirty, taller than the guards who escorted him, and rather good-looking.

I remember the way he walked, with his head up, and his hat on a slant, and his wrists close together in front of him. On each side of him was a burgher with a bandolier and a rifle.

The landdrost looked important, as a landdrost should look at his first murder trial. The jurymen also looked very dignified. But the most pompous of all was Rossouw. Over and over again, to anyone who would listen, he told the story of how he discovered the body before the vultures did. He told everybody just what evidence he was going to give, and what theories he was going to put forward as to how the murder was committed.

He even brought his ox-wagon along to the courthouse and drew it up on the sidewalk, so that the landdrost and the jurymen had difficulty in getting in at the door. He said he was willing to demonstrate to the court just at what pace he drove the body from the borehole to Andries Theron's house.

Afterwards, Rossouw was the most disappointed man I ever saw. For he was only kept in the witness-box for about five minutes, and they wouldn't listen to any of his theories.

On the other hand, a kaffir, who saw Tjaart van Rensburg arguing with the deceased in front of the borehole, gave evidence for over three hours. And another kaffir, who heard a shot and thought he saw Tjaart van Rensburg running down the road with a gun, was in the witness-box for the best part of a day.

"What do you think of this for a piece of nonsense?" Rossouw asked of a group standing about the courthouse. "I am a white man. I have borne arms for the Transvaal in three kaffir wars. And I am only in the witness-box for five minutes, when they tell me to step down and move my ox-wagon away from the door. And yet a raw kaffir, who can't even sign his name, but has got to put a cross at the foot of the things he has said – this raw kaffir is allowed to stand there wasting the time of the court for ten hours on end.

"What's more," Rossouw went on, "Tjaart van Rensburg's lawyer never once cross-questioned me or called me a liar. Whereas he spent half a day in calling that kaffir names. Doesn't that lawyer think that my evidence is of any value to the court?"

Rossouw said a lot more things like that. Some of the burghers laughed at his remarks, but others took him seriously, and agreed with him, and said it was a shame that such things should be allowed, and that it all proved that the president did not have the interests of the nation at heart.

You can see, from this, that it must have been a difficult task to govern the Transvaal in those days.

The case lasted almost a week, what with all the witnesses, and the long speeches made by the prosecution and the defence. Also, the landdrost said a great many learned things about the Roman-Dutch law. During all this time Francina sat in court with that same unearthly look in her eyes. They say that she never once wept. Even when the doctor, a Hollander, explained how he cut open Andries Theron's body, and found that the bullet had gone through his heart, the expression on Francina's face did not change.

People who knew her grew anxious about her state. They said it was impossible for her to continue in this way, with that stony grief inside her. They said that if she did not break down and weep she could not go on living much longer.

Anyway, Francina was not called as a witness. Perhaps they felt that there was nothing of importance that she could say.

So the days passed.

And Rossouw was still complaining about the unfair way he had been treated in the witness-box, when Tjaart van Rensburg, his hat tilted over the eye and his wrists close together in front of him, strode into the courthouse for the last time.

The landdrost looked less important on that morning. And the jurymen did not seem very happy. But they were not the kind of men to shirk a duty they had sworn to carry out.

Tjaart van Rensburg was asked if he had anything to say before sentence was passed on him.

"Yes, I am guilty," he answered. "I shot Andries Theron."

His voice was steady, and as he spoke he twirled the brim of his hat slowly round and round between his fingers.

And that was how it came about that, early one winter's morning, a number of kaffirs were swinging their picks into the hard gravel, digging a hole by the side of the courthouse.

A small group had gathered at the graveside. Some were kneeling in prayer. Among the spectators was Francina Theron, looking very frail and slender in her widow's weeds. When the grave was deep enough a roughly constructed coffin was lifted out of a cart that bore, painted on its side, the arms of the republic.

The grave was filled in. The newly made mound of gravel and red earth was patted smooth with the shovels.

Then, for the first time since her husband's death, Francina wept.

She flung herself at full-length on the mound, and trailed her fingers through the pebbles and fresh earth. And calling out tender and passionate endearments, Francina sobbed noisily on the grave of her lover.

WILLEM PRINSLOO'S PEACH BRANDY

No (Oom Schalk Lourens said) you don't get flowers in the Groot Marico. It is not a bad district for mealies, and I once grew quite good onions in a small garden I made next to the dam. But what you can really call flowers are rare things here. Perhaps it's the heat. Or the drought.

Yet whenever I talk about flowers, I think of Willem Prinsloo's farm on Abjaterskop, where the dance was, and I think of Fritz Pretorius, sitting pale and sick by the roadside, and I think of the white rose that I wore in my hat, jauntily. But most of all I think of Grieta.

If you walk over my farm to the hoogte, and look towards the north-west, you can see Abjaterskop behind the ridge of the Dwarsberge. People will tell you that there are ghosts on Abjaterskop, and that it was once the home of witches. I can believe that. I was at Abjaterskop only once. That was many years ago. And I never went there again. Still, it wasn't the ghosts that kept me away; nor was it the witches.

Grieta Prinsloo was due to come back from the finishing school at Zeerust, where she had gone to learn English manners and dictation and other high-class subjects. Therefore Willem Prinsloo, her father, arranged a big dance on his farm at Abjaterskop to celebrate Grieta's return.

I was invited to the party. So was Fritz Pretorius. So was every white person in the district, from Derdepoort to Ramoutsa. What was more, practically everybody went. Of course, we were all somewhat nervous about meeting Grieta. With all the superior things she had learnt at the finishing school, we wouldn't be able to talk to her in a chatty sort of way, just as though she were an ordinary Boer girl. But what fetched us all to Abjaterskop in the end was our knowledge

96

that Willem Prinsloo made the best peach brandy in the district.

Fritz Pretorius spoke to me of the difficulty brought about by Grieta's learning.

"Yes, jong," he said, "I am feeling pretty shaky about talking to her, I can tell you. I have been rubbing up my education a bit, though. Yesterday I took out my old slate that I last used when I left school seventeen years ago, and I did a few sums. I did some addition and subtraction. I tried a little multiplication, too. But I have forgotten how it is done."

I told Fritz that I would have liked to have helped him, but I had never learnt as far as multiplication.

The day of the dance arrived. The post-cart bearing Grieta to her father's house passed through Drogedal in the morning. In the afternoon I got dressed. I wore a black jacket, fawn trousers, and a pink shirt. I also put on the brown boots that I had bought about a year before, and that I had never had occasion to wear. For I would have looked silly walking about the farm in a pair of shop boots when everybody else wore homemade veldskoens.

I believed, as I got on my horse, and set off down the Government Road, with my hat rakishly on one side, that I would be easily the best-dressed young man at that dance.

It was getting on towards sunset when I arrived at the foot of Abjaterskop, which I had to skirt in order to reach Willem Prinsloo's farm, nestling in a hollow behind the hills. I felt, as I rode, that it was stupid for a man to live in a part that was reputed to be haunted. The trees grew taller and denser, as they always do on rising ground. And they also got a lot darker.

All over the place were queer, heavy shadows. I didn't like the look of them. I remembered stories I had heard of the witches of Abjaterskop, and what they did to travellers who lost their way in the dark. It seemed an easy thing to lose your way among those tall trees. Accordingly, I spurred my horse on to a gallop, to get out of this gloomy region as quickly as possible. After all, a horse is sensitive about things like ghosts and witches, and it was my duty to see my horse was not frightened unnecessarily. Especially as a cold wind suddenly sprang up through the poort, and once or twice it sounded as though an evil voice were calling my name. I started riding fast then. But a few moments later I looked round and realised the position. It was Fritz Pretorius galloping along behind me.

"What was your hurry?" Fritz asked when I had slowed down to allow his overtaking me.

"I wished to get through those trees before it was too dark," I answered, "I didn't want my horse to get frightened."

"I suppose that's why you were riding with your arms round his neck," Fritz observed, "to soothe him."

I did not reply. But what I did notice was that Fritz was also very stylishly dressed. True, I beat him as far as shirt and boots went, but he was dressed in a new grey suit, with his socks pulled up over the bottoms of his trousers. He also had a handkerchief which he ostentatiously took out of his pocket several times.

Of course, I couldn't be jealous of a person like Fritz Pretorius. I was only annoyed at the thought that he was making himself ridiculous by going to a party with an outlandish thing like a handkerchief.

We arrived at Willem Prinsloo's house. There were so many ox-wagons drawn up on the veld that the place looked like a laager. Prinsloo met us at the door.

"Go right through, kêrels," he said, "the dancing is in the voorhuis. The peach brandy is in the kitchen."

Although the voorhuis was big it was so crowded as to make it almost impossible to dance. But it was not as crowded as the kitchen. Nor was the music in the voorhuis – which was provided by a number of men with guitars and concertinas – as loud as the music in the kitchen, where there was no band, but each man sang for himself.

We knew from these signs that the party was a success.

When I had been in the kitchen for about half an hour I decided to go into the voorhuis. It seemed a long way, now, from the kitchen to the voorhuis, and I had to lean against the wall several times to think. I passed a number of other men who were also leaning against the wall like that, thinking. One man even found that he could think best by sitting on the floor with his head in his arms.

You could see that Willem Prinsloo made good peach brandy.

Then I saw Fritz Pretorius, and the sight of him brought me to my senses right away. Airily flapping his white handkerchief in time with the music, he was talking to a girl who smiled up at him with bright eyes and red lips and small white teeth.

I knew at once that it was Grieta.

She was tall and slender and very pretty, and her dark hair was braided with a wreath of white roses that you could see had been picked that same morning in Zeerust. And she didn't look the sort of girl, either, in whose presence you had to appear clever and educated. In fact, I felt I wouldn't really need the twelve times table which I had torn off the back of a school writing book and had thrust into my jacket pocket before leaving home.

You can imagine that it was not too easy for me to get a word in with Grieta while Fritz was hanging around. But I managed it eventually, and while I was talking to her I had the satisfaction of seeing, out of the corner of my eye, the direction Fritz took. He went into the kitchen, flapping his handkerchief behind him – into the kitchen, where the laughter was, and the singing, and Willem Prinsloo's peach brandy.

I told Grieta that I was Schalk Lourens.

"Oh, yes, I have heard of you," she answered, "from Fritz Pretorius."

I knew what that meant. So I told her that Fritz was known all over the Marico for his lies. I told her other things about Fritz. Ten minutes later, when I was still talking about him, Grieta smiled and said that I could tell her the rest some other night.

"But I must tell you one more thing now," I insisted. "When he knew that he would be meeting you here at the dance, Fritz started doing homework."

I told her about the slate and the sums, and Grieta laughed softly. It struck me again how pretty she was. And her eyes were radiant in the candlelight. And the roses looked very white against her dark hair. And all this time the dancers whirled around us, and the band in the voorhuis played lively dance tunes, and from the kitchen there issued weird sounds of jubilation.

The rest happened very quickly.

I can't even remember how it all came about. But what I do know is that when we were outside, under the tall trees, with the stars over us, I could easily believe that Grieta was not a girl at all, but one of the witches of Abjaterskop who wove strange spells.

Yet to listen to my talking nobody would have guessed the wild, thrilling things that were in my heart.

I told Grieta about last year's drought, and about the difficulty of keeping the white ants from eating through the door and window-frames, and about the way my new brown boots tended to take the skin off my toe if I walked quickly.

Then I moved close up to her.

"Grieta," I said, taking her hand, "Grieta, there is something I want to tell you."

She pulled away her hand. She did it very gently, though. Sorrowfully, almost.

"I know what you want to say," she answered.

I was surprised at that.

"How do you know, Grieta?" I asked.

"Oh, I know lots of things," she replied, laughing again, "I haven't been to finishing school for nothing."

"I don't mean that," I answered at once, "I wasn't going to talk about spelling or arithmetic. I was going to tell you that –"

"Please don't say it, Schalk," Grieta interrupted me. "I – I don't know whether I am worthy of hearing it. I don't know, even –"

"But you are so lovely," I exclaimed. "I have got to tell you how lovely you are."

But at the very moment I stepped forward she retreated swiftly, eluding me. I couldn't understand how she had timed it so well. For, try as I might, I couldn't catch her. She sped lightly and gracefully amongst the trees, and I followed as best I could.

Yet it was not only my want of learning that handicapped me. There were also my new boots. And Willem Prinsloo's peach brandy. And the shaft of a mule-cart – the lower end of the shaft, where it rests in the grass.

I didn't fall very hard, though. The grass was long and thick there. But even as I fell a great happiness came into my heart. And I didn't care about anything else in the world.

Grieta had stopped running. She turned round. For an instant her body, slender and misty in the shadows, swayed towards me. Then her hand flew to her hair. Her finger pulled at the wreath. And the next thing I knew was that there lay, within reach of my hand, a small white rose.

I shall always remember the thrill with which I picked up that rose, and how I trembled when I stuck it in my hat. I shall always remember the stir I caused when I walked into the kitchen. Everybody stopped drinking to look at the rose in my hat. The young men made jokes about it. The older men winked slyly and patted me on the back.

Although Fritz Pretorius was not in the kitchen to witness my triumph, I knew he would get to hear of it somehow. That would make him realise that it was impudence for a fellow like him to set up as Schalk Lourens's rival.

During the rest of the night I was a hero.

The men in the kitchen made me sit on the table. They plied me with brandy and drank to my health. And afterwards, when a dozen of them carried me outside, on to an ox-wagon, for fresh air, they fell with me only once.

At daybreak I was still on that wagon.

I woke up feeling very sick – until I remembered about Grieta's rose. There was that white rose still stuck in my hat, for the whole world to know that Grieta Prinsloo had chosen me before all other men.

But what I didn't want people to know was that I had remained asleep on that ox-wagon hours after the other guests had gone. So I rode away very quietly, glad that nobody was astir to see me go.

My head was dizzy as I rode, but in my heart it felt like green wings beating; and although it was day now, there was the same soft wind in the grass that had been there when Grieta flung the rose at me, standing under the stars.

I rode slowly through the trees on the slope of Abjaterskop, and had reached the place where the path turns south again, when I saw something that made me wonder if, at these fashionable finishing schools, they did not perhaps teach the girls too much.

First I saw Fritz Pretorius's horse by the roadside.

Then I saw Fritz. He was sitting up against a thorn-tree, with his chin resting on his knees. He looked very pale and sick. But what made me wonder much about those finishing schools was that in Fritz's hat, which had fallen on the ground some distance away from him, there was a small white rose.

101

Ox-wagons on Trek

When I see the rain beating white on the thorn-trees, as it does now (Oom Schalk Lourens said), I remember another time when it rained. And there was a girl in an ox-wagon who dreamed. And in answer to her dreaming a lover came, galloping to her side from out of the veld. But he tarried only a short while, this lover who had come to her from the mist of the rain and the warmth of her dreams.

And yet when he had gone there was a slow look in her eyes that must have puzzled her lover very much, for it was a look of satisfaction, almost.

There had been rain all the way up from Sephton's Nek, that time. And the five ox-wagons on the road to the north rolled heavily through the mud. We had been to Zeerust for the Nagmaal church service, which we attended once a year.

You know what it is with these Nagmaals.

The Lord spreads these festivities over so many days that you have not only got time to go to church, but you also get a chance of going to the bioscope. Sometimes you even get a chance of going to the bar. But then you must go in the back way, through the dark passage next to the draper's shop.

Because Zeerust is a small place, and if you are seen going into the bar during Nagmaal people are liable to talk. I can still remember how surprised I was one morning when I went into that dark passage next to the draper's shop and found the predikant there, wiping his mouth. The predikant looked at me and shook his head solemnly, and I felt very guilty.

So I went to the bioscope instead.

The house was very crowded. I couldn't follow much of the picture at the beginning, but afterwards a little boy who sat next to me and understood English explained to me what it was all about.

There was a young man who had the job of what he called tak-ing people for a ride. Afterwards he got into trouble with the police. But he was a good-looking young man, and his sweetheart was very sorry for him when they took him into a small room and fastened him down on to a sort of chair.

I can't tell what they did that for. All I know is that I have been a Boer War prisoner at St. Helena, and they never gave me a chair to sit on. Only a long wooden bench that I had to scrub once a week.

Anyway, I don't know what happened to the young man after that, because he was still sitting in that chair when the band start-ed playing an English hymn about King George, and everybody stood up.

And a few days later five ox-wagons, full of people who had been to the Zeerust Nagmaal, were trekking along the road that led back to the Groot Marico. Inside the wagon-tents sat the women and children, listening to the rain pelting against the canvas. By the side of the oxen the drivers walked, cracking their long whips while the rain beat in their faces.

Overhead everything was black, except for the frequent flashes of lightning that tore across the sky.

After I had walked in this manner for some time, I began to get lonely. So I handed my whip to the kaffir voorloper and went on ahead to Adriaan Brand's wagon. For some distance I walked in silence beside Adriaan, who had his trousers rolled up to his knees, and had much trouble to brandish his whip and at the same time keep the rain out of his pipe.

"It's Minnie," Adriaan Brand said suddenly, referring to his nineteen-year-old daughter. "There is one place in Zeerust that Minnie should not go to. And every Nagmaal, to my sorrow, I find she has been there. And it all goes to her head."

"Oh, yes," I answered. "It always does."

All the same, I was somewhat startled at Adriaan's remarks. Minnie didn't strike me as the sort of girl who would go and spend her father's money drinking peach brandy in the bar. I started wondering if she had seen me in that draper's passage. Then Adriaan went on talking and I felt more at ease.

"The place where they show those moving pictures," he explained. "Every time Minnie goes there, she comes back with ideas that are useless for a farmer's daughter. But this last time has made her quite impossible. For one thing, she says she won't marry Frans du Toit anymore. She says Frans is too honest."

"Well, that needn't be a difficulty, Adriaan," I said. "You can teach Frans du Toit a few of the things you have done. That will make him dishonest enough. Like the way you put your brand on those oxen that strayed into your kraal. Or the way you altered the figures on the compensation forms after the rinderpest. Or the way –"

Adriaan looked at me with some disfavour.

"It isn't that," he interrupted me, while I was still trying to call to mind a lot of the things that he was able to teach Frans du Toit, "Minnie wants a mysterious sort of man. She wants a man who is dishonest, but who has got foreign manners and a good heart. She saw a man like that at the picture place she went to, and since then –"

We both looked round together.

Through the mist of the white rain a horseman came galloping up towards our wagons. He rode fast. Adriaan Brand and I stood and watched him.

By this time our wagons were some distance behind the others.

The horseman came thundering along at full gallop until he was abreast of us. Then he pulled up sharply, jerking the horse on to his hind legs.

The stranger told us that his name was Koos Fichardt and that he was on his way to the Bechuanaland Protectorate. Adriaan Brand and I introduced ourselves, and shortly afterwards Fichardt accepted our invitation to spend the night with us.

We outspanned a mile or so farther on, drawing the five wagons up close together and getting what shelter we could by spreading bucksails.

Next morning there was no more rain. By that time Koos Fichardt had seen Adriaan Brand's daughter Minnie. So he decided to stay with us longer.

We trekked on again, and from where I walked beside my oxen I could see Koos Fichardt and Minnie. They sat at the back of Adriaan Brand's wagon, hatless, with their legs hanging down and the morning breeze blowing through their hair, and it was evident that Minnie was fascinated by the stranger. Also, he seemed to be very much interested in her.

You do get like that, when there is suddenly a bright morning after long rains, and a low wind stirs the wet grass, and you feel, for a little while, that you know the same things that the veld knows, and in your heart are whisperings.

Most of the time they sat holding hands, Fichardt talking a great deal and Minnie nodding her pretty head at intervals and encouraging him to continue. And they were all lies he told her, I suppose, as only a young man in love really can tell lies.

I remembered what Adriaan had told me about the ideas Minnie had got after she had been to the bioscope. And when I looked carefully at Fichardt I perceived that in many respects he was like that man I saw in the picture who was being fastened on to a chair.

Fichardt was tall and dark and well dressed. He walked with a swagger. He had easy and engaging manners, and we all liked him.

But I noticed one or two peculiar things about Koos Fichardt. For instance, shortly after our wagons had entered a clump of tall camel-thorn trees, we heard horses galloping towards us. It turned out that the riders were a couple of farmers living in the neighbourhood. But as soon as he heard the hoof-beats, Koos Fichardt let go of Minnie's hand and crept under a bucksail.

It would be more correct to say that he dived under – he was so quick.

I said to myself that Fichardt's action might have no meaning, of course. After all, it is quite permissible for a man to feel that he would suddenly like to take a look at what is underneath the bucksail he is sitting on. Also, if he wants to, there is no harm in his spending quite a while on this task. And it is only natural, after he has had a bucksail on top of him, that he should come out with his hair rather ruffled, and that his face should be pale.

That night, when we outspanned next to the Groen River, it was very pleasant. We all gathered round the camp-fire and roasted meat and cooked crushed mealies. We sang songs and told ghost stories. And I wondered what Frans du Toit – the honest youth whom Minnie had discarded in Zeerust – would have thought if he could see Minnie Brand and Koos Fichardt, sitting unashamedly in each other's arms, for all the world to see their love, while the light of the camp-fire cast a rich glow over the thrill that was on their faces.

And although I knew how wonderful were the passing moments for those two, yet somehow, somehow, because I had seen so much of the world, I also felt sorry for them.

The next day we did not trek.

The Groen River was in flood from the heavy rains, and Oupa van Tonder, who had lived a long time in the Cape and was well

versed in the ways of rivers, and knew how to swim, even, told us that it would not be safe to cross the drift for another twenty-four hours. Accordingly, we decided to remain camped out where we were until next morning.

At first Koos Fichardt was much disturbed by this news, explaining how necessary it was for him to get into the Bechuana-land Protectorate by a certain day. After a while, however, he seemed to grow more reconciled to the necessity of waiting until the river had gone down.

But I noticed that he frequently gazed out over the veld in the direction from which we had come. He gazed out rather anxiously, I thought.

Some of the men went shooting. Others remained at their wagons, doing odd jobs to the yokes or the trek-chains. Koos Fichardt made himself useful in various little ways, amongst other things, helping Minnie with the cooking. They laughed and romped a good deal.

Night came, and the occupants of the five wagons again gathered round the blazing fire. In some ways, that night was even grander than the one before. The songs we sang were more rousing. The stories we told seemed to have more power in them.

There was much excitement the following morning by the time the wagons were ready to go through the drift. And the excitement did not lie only in the bustle of inspanning the oxen.

For when we crossed the river it was without Koos Fichardt, and there was a slow look in Minnie's eyes.

The wagons creaked and splashed into the water, and we saw Koos Fichardt for the last time, sitting on his horse, with a horseman in uniform on each side of him. And when he took off his hat in farewell he had to use both hands, because of the cuffs that held his wrists together.

But always what I will remember is that slow look in Minnie's eyes. It was a kind of satisfaction, almost, at the thought that all the things that came to the girl she saw in the picture had now come to her, too.

THE MUSIC MAKER

Of course, I know about history – Oom Schalk Lourens said – it's the stuff children learn in school. Only the other day, at Thys Lemmer's post office, Thys's little son Stoffel started reading out of his history book about a man called Vasco da Gama, who visited the Cape. At once Dirk Snyman started telling young Stoffel about the time when he himself visited the Cape, but young Stoffel didn't take much notice of him. So Dirk Snyman said that that showed you.

Anyway, Dirk Snyman said that what he wanted to tell young Stoffel was that the last time he went down to the Cape a kaffir came and sat down right next to him in a tram. What was more, Dirk Snyman said, was that people seemed to think nothing of it.

Yes, it's a queer thing about wanting to get into history.

Take the case of Manie Kruger, for instance.

Manie Kruger was one of the best farmers in the Marico. He knew just how much peach brandy to pour out for the tax-collector to make sure that he would nod dreamily at everything Manie said. And at a time of drought Manie Kruger could run to the Government for help much quicker than any man I ever knew.

Then one day Manie Kruger read an article in the *Kerkbode* about a musician who said that he knew more about music than Napoleon did. After that – having first read another article to find out who Napoleon was – Manie Kruger was a changed man. He could talk of nothing but his place in history and of his musical career.

Of course, everybody knew that no man in the Marico could be counted in the same class with Manie Kruger when it came to playing the concertina.

No Bushveld dance was complete without Manie Kruger's

concertina. When he played a vastrap you couldn't keep your feet still. But after he had decided to become the sort of musician that gets into history books, it was strange the way that Manie Kruger altered. For one thing, he said he would never again play at a dance. We all felt sad about that. It was not easy to think of the Bushveld dances of the future. There would be the peach brandy in the kitchen; in the voorkamer the feet of the dancers would go through the steps of the schottische and the polka and the waltz and the mazurka, but on the riempies bench in the corner, where the musicians sat, there would be no Manie Kruger. And they would play "Die Vaal Hare en die Blou Oge" and "Vat Jou Goed en Trek, Ferreira," but it would be another's fingers that swept over the concertina keys. And when, with the dancing and the peach brandy, the young men called out "Dagbreek toe!" it would not be Manie Kruger's head that bowed down to the applause.

It was sad to think about all this.

For so long, at the Bushveld dances, Manie Kruger had been the chief musician.

And of all those who mourned this change that had come over Manie, we could see that there was no one more grieved than Letta Steyn.

And Manie said such queer things at times. Once he said that what he had to do to get into history was to die of consumption in the arms of a princess, like another musician he had read about. Only it was hard to get consumption in the Marico, because the climate was so healthy.

Although Manie stopped playing his concertina at dances, he played a great deal in another way. He started giving what he called recitals. I went to several of them. They were very impressive.

At the first recital I went to, I found that the front part of Manie's voorkamer was taken up by rows of benches and chairs that he had borrowed from those of his neighbours who didn't mind having to eat their meals on candle-boxes and upturned buckets. At the far end of the voorkamer a wide green curtain was hung on a piece of string. When I came in the place was full. I managed to squeeze in on a bench between Jan Terreblanche and

a young woman in a blue kappie. Jan Terreblanche had been trying to hold this young woman's hand.

Manie Kruger was sitting behind the green curtain. He was
already there when I came in. I knew it was Manie by his veldskoens, which were sticking out from underneath the curtain.
Letta Steyn sat in front of me. Now and again, when she turned
round, I saw that there was a flush on her face and a look of dark
excitement in her eyes.

At last everything was ready, and Joel, the farm kaffir to whom
Manie had given this job, slowly drew the green curtain aside. A
few of the younger men called out "Middag, ou Manie," and Jan
Terreblanche asked if it wasn't very close and suffocating, sitting
there like that behind that piece of green curtain.

Then he started to play.

And we all knew that it was the most wonderful concertina
music we had ever listened to. It was Manie Kruger at his best. He
had practised a long time for that recital; his fingers flew over the
keys; the notes of the concertina swept into our hearts; the music
of Manie Kruger lifted us right out of that voorkamer into a
strange and rich and dazzling world.

It was fine.

The applause right through was terrific. At the end of each piece
the kaffir closed the curtains in front of Manie, and we sat waiting for
a few minutes until the curtains were drawn aside again. But after
that first time there was no more laughter about this procedure. The
recital lasted for about an hour and a half, and the applause at the
end was even greater than at the start. And during those ninety
minutes Manie left his seat only once. That was when there was
some trouble with the curtain and he got up to kick the kaffir.

At the end of the recital Manie did not come forward and
shake hands with us, as we had expected. Instead, he slipped
through behind the green curtain into the kitchen, and sent word
that we could come and see him round the back. At first we
thought this a bit queer, but Letta Steyn said it was all right. She
explained that in other countries the great musicians and stage
performers all received their admirers at the back. Jan Terreblanche said that if these actors used their kitchens for entertaining their visitors in, he wondered where they did their cooking.

110

Nevertheless, most of us went round to the kitchen, and we had a good time congratulating Manie Kruger and shaking hands with him; and Manie spoke much of his musical future, and of the triumphs that would come to him in the great cities of the world, when he would stand before the curtain and bow to the applause.

Manie gave a number of other recitals after that. They were all equally fine. Only, as he had to practise all day, he couldn't pay much attention to his farming. The result was that his farm went to pieces and he got into debt. The court messengers came and attached half his cattle while he was busy practising for his fourth recital. And he was practising for his seventh recital when they took away his ox-wagon and mule-cart.

Eventually, when Manie Kruger's musical career reached that stage when they took away his plough and the last of his oxen, he sold up what remained of his possessions and left the Bushveld, on his way to those great cities that he had so often talked about. It was very grand, the send-off that the Marico gave him. The predikant and the Volksraad member both made speeches about how proud the Transvaal was of her great son. Then Manie replied. Instead of thanking his audience, however, he started abusing us left and right, calling us a mob of hooligans and soulless Philistines, and saying how much he despised us.

Naturally, we were very much surprised at this outburst, as we had always been kind to Manie Kruger and had encouraged him all we could. But Letta Steyn explained that Manie didn't really mean the things he said. She said it was just that every great artist was expected to talk in that way about the place he came from.

So we knew it was all right, and the more offensive the things were that Manie said about us, the louder we shouted "Hoor, hoor vir Manie." There was a particularly enthusiastic round of applause when he said that we knew as much about art as a boomslang. His language was hotter than anything I had ever heard – except once. And that was when De Wet said what he thought of Cronje's surrender to the English at Paardeberg. We could feel that Manie's speech was the real thing. We cheered ourselves hoarse, that day.

And so Manie Kruger went. We received one letter to say that he had reached Pretoria. But after that we heard no more from him.

Yet always, when Letta Steyn spoke of Manie, it was as a child speaks of a dream, half wistfully, and always, with the voice of a wistful child, she would tell me how one day, one day he would return. And often, when it was dusk, I would see her sitting on the stoep, gazing out across the veld into the evening, down the dusty road that led between the thorn-trees and beyond the Dwarsberg, waiting for the lover who would come to her no more.

It was a long time before I again saw Manie Kruger. And then it was in Pretoria. I had gone there to interview the Volksraad member about an election promise. It was quite by accident that I saw Manie. And he was playing the concertina – playing as well as ever, I thought. I went away quickly. But what affected me very strangely was just that one glimpse I had of the green curtain of the bar in front of which Manie Kruger played.

DRIEKA AND THE MOON

There is a queer witchery about the moon when it is full – Oom Schalk Lourens remarked – especially the moon that hangs over the valley of the Dwarsberge in the summer-time. It does strange things to your mind, the Marico moon, and in your heart are wild and fragrant fancies, and your thoughts go very far away. Then, if you have been sitting on your front stoep, thinking these thoughts, you sigh and murmur something about the way of the world, and carry your chair inside.

I have seen the moon in other places besides the Marico. But it is not the same, there.

Braam Venter, the man who fell off the Government lorry once, near Nietverdiend, says that the Marico moon is like a woman laying green flowers on a grave. Braam Venter often says things like that. Particularly since the time he fell off the lorry. He fell on his head, they say.

Always when the moon shines full like that it does something to our hearts that we wonder very much about and that we never understand. Always it awakens memories. And it is singular how different these memories are with each one of us.

Johannes Oberholzer says that the full moon always reminds him of one occasion when he was smuggling cattle over the Bech-uanaland border. He says he never sees a full moon without thinking of the way it shone on the steel wire-cutters that he was holding in his hand when two mounted policemen rode up to him. And the next night Johannes Oberholzer again had a good view of the full moon; he saw it through the window of the place he was in. He says the moon was very large and very yellow, except for the black stripes in front of it.

And it was in the light of the full moon that hung over the thorn-trees that I saw Drieka Breytenbach.

Drieka was tall and slender. She had fair hair and blue eyes, and lots of people considered that she was the prettiest woman in the Marico. I thought so, too, that night I met her under the full moon by the thorn-trees. She had not been in the Bushveld very long. Her husband, Petrus Breytenbach, had met her and married her in the Schweizer-Reneke district, where he had trekked with his cattle for a while during the big drought.

Afterwards, when Petrus Breytenbach was shot dead with his own Mauser by a kaffir working on his farm, Drieka went back to Schweizer-Reneke, leaving the Marico as strangely and as silently as she had come to it.

And it seemed to me that the Marico was a different place because Drieka Breytenbach had gone. And I thought of the moon, and the tricks it plays with your senses, and the stormy witchery that it flings at your soul. And I remembered what Braam Venter said, that the full moon is like a woman laying green flowers on a grave. And it seemed to me that Braam Venter's words were not so much nonsense, after all, and that worse things could happen to a man than that he should fall off a lorry on his head. And I thought of other matters.

But all this happened only afterwards.

When I saw Drieka that night she was leaning against a thorn-tree beside the road where it goes down to the drift. But I didn't recognise her at first. All I saw was a figure dressed in white with long hair hanging down loose over its shoulders. It seemed very unusual that a figure should be there like that at such a time of night. I remembered certain stories I had heard about white ghosts. I also remembered that a few miles back I had seen a boulder lying in the middle of the road. It was a fair-sized boulder and it might be dangerous for passing mule-carts. So I decided to turn back at once and move it out of the way.

I decided very quickly about the boulder. And I made up my mind so firmly that the saddle-girth broke from the sudden way in which I jerked my horse back on his haunches. Then the figure came forward and spoke, and I saw it was Drieka Breytenbach.

"Good evening," I said in answer to her greeting, "I was just going back because I had remembered about something."

"About ghosts?" she asked.

114

"No," I replied truthfully, "about a stone in the road."

Drieka laughed at that. So I laughed, too. And then Drieka laughed again. And then I laughed. In fact, we did quite a lot of laughing between us. I got off my horse and stood beside Drieka in the moonlight. And if somebody had come along at that moment and said that the predikant's mule-cart had been capsized by the boulder in the road I would have laughed still more.

That is the sort of thing the moon in the Marico does to you when it is full.

I didn't think of asking Drieka how she came to be there, or why her hair was hanging down loose, or who it was that she had been waiting for under the thorn-tree. It was enough that the moon was there, big and yellow across the veld, and that the wind blew softly through the trees and across the grass and against Drieka's white dress and against the mad singing of the stars.

Before I knew what was happening we were seated on the grass under the thorn-tree whose branches leant over the road. And I remember that for quite a while we remained there without talk-

115

ing, sitting side by side on the grass with our feet in the soft sand. And Drieka smiled at me with a misty sort of look in her eyes, and I saw that she was lovely.

I felt that it was not enough that we should go on sitting there in silence. I knew that a woman – even a moon-woman like Drieka – expected a man to be more than just good-humoured and honest. I knew that a woman wanted a man also to be an entertaining companion for her. So I beguiled the passing moments for Drieka with interesting conversation.

I explained to her how a few days before a pebble had worked itself into my veldskoen and had rubbed some skin off the top of one of my toes. I took off my veldskoen and showed her the place. I also told her about the rinderpest and about the way two of my cows had died of the miltsiek. I also knew a lot about blue-tongue in sheep, and about gallamsiekte and the haarwurm, and I talked to her airily about these things, just as easily as I am talking to you.

But, of course, it was the moonlight that did it. I never knew before that I was so good in this idle, butterfly kind of talk. And the whole thing was so innocent, too. I felt that if Drieka Breytenbach's husband, Petrus, were to come along and find us sitting there side by side, he would not be able to say much about it. At least, not very much.

After a while I stopped talking.

Drieka put her hand in mine.

"Oh, Schalk," she whispered, and the moon and that misty look were in her blue eyes. "Do tell me some more."

I shook my head.

"I am sorry, Drieka," I answered, "I don't know any more."

"But you must, Schalk," she said softly. "Talk to me about – about other things."

I thought steadily for some moments.

"Yes, Drieka," I said at length, "I have remembered something. There is one more thing I haven't told you about the blue-tongue in sheep –"

"No, no, not that," she interrupted, "talk to me about other things. About the moon, say."

So I told her two things that Braam Venter had said about the moon. I told her the green flower one and the other one.

"Braam Venter knows lots more things like that about the moon," I explained, "you'll see him next time you go to Zeerust for the Nagmaal. He is a short fellow with a bump on his head from where he fell –"

"Oh, no, Schalk," Drieka said again, shaking her head, so that a wisp of her fair hair brushed against my face, "I don't want to know about Braam Venter. Only about you. You think out something on your own about the moon and tell it to me."

I understood what she meant.

"Well, Drieka," I said thoughtfully. "The moon – the moon is all right."

"Oh, Schalk," Drieka cried. "That's much finer than anything Braam Venter could ever say – even with that bump on his head."

Of course, I told her that it was nothing and that I could perhaps say something even better if I tried. But I was very proud, all the same. And somehow it seemed that my words brought us close together. I felt that that handful of words, spoken under the full moon, had made a new and witch thing come into the life of Drieka and me.

We were holding hands then, sitting on the grass with our feet in the road, and Drieka leant her head on my shoulder, and her long hair stirred softly against my face, but I looked only at her feet. And I thought for a moment that I loved her. And I did not love her because her body was beautiful, or because she had red lips, or because her eyes were blue. In that moment I did not understand about her body or her lips or her eyes. I loved her for her feet; and because her feet were in the road next to mine.

And yet all the time I felt, far away at the back of my mind, that it was the moon that was doing these things to me.

"You have got good feet for walking on," I said to Drieka.

"Braam Venter would have said that I have got good feet for dancing on," Drieka answered, laughing. And I began to grow jealous of Braam Venter.

The next thing I knew was that Drieka had thrown herself into my arms.

"Do you think I am very beautiful, Schalk?" Drieka asked.

"You are very beautiful, Drieka," I answered slowly, "very beautiful."

"Will you do something for me, Schalk?" Drieka asked again, and her red lips were very close to my cheek. "Will you do something for me if I love you very much?"

"What do you want me to do, Drieka?"

She drew my head down to her lips and whispered hot words in my ear.

And so it came about that I thrust her from me, suddenly. I jumped unsteadily to my feet; I found my horse and rode away. I left Drieka Breytenbach where I had found her, under the thorn-tree by the roadside, with her hot whisperings still ringing in my ears, and before I reached home the moon had set behind the Dwarsberge.

Well, there is not much left for me to tell you. In the days that followed, Drieka Breytenbach was always in my thoughts. Her long, loose hair and her red lips and her feet that had been in the road-side sand with mine. But if she really was the ghost that I had at first taken her to be, I could not have been more afraid of her.

And it seemed singular that, while it had been my words, spoken in the moonlight, that helped to bring Drieka and me closer together, it was Drieka's hot breath, whispering wild words in my ear, that sent me so suddenly from her side.

Once or twice I even felt sorry for having left in that fashion.

And later on when I heard that Drieka Breytenbach had gone back to Schweizer-Reneke, and that her husband had been shot dead with his own Mauser by one of the farm kaffirs, I was not surprised. In fact, I had expected it.

Only it did not seem right, somehow, that Drieka should have got a kaffir to do the thing that I had refused to do.

MAFEKING ROAD

When people ask me – as they often do – how it is that I can tell the best stories of anybody in the Transvaal (Oom Schalk Lourens said, modestly), then I explain to them that I just learn through observing the way that the world has with men and women. When I say this they nod their heads wisely, and say that they understand, and I nod my head wisely also, and that seems to satisfy them. But the thing I say to them is a lie, of course.

For it is not the story that counts. What matters is the way you tell it. The important thing is to know just at what moment you must knock out your pipe on your veldskoen, and at what stage of the story you must start talking about the School Committee at Drogevlei. Another necessary thing is to know what part of the story to leave out.

And you can never learn these things.

Look at Floris, the last of the Van Barnevelts. There is no doubt that he had a good story, and he should have been able to get people to listen to it. And yet nobody took any notice of him or of the things he had to say. Just because he couldn't tell the story properly.

Accordingly, it made me sad whenever I listened to him talk. For I could tell just where he went wrong. He never knew the moment at which to knock the ash out of his pipe. He always mentioned his opinion of the Drogevlei School Committee in the wrong place. And, what was still worse, he didn't know what part of the story to leave out.

And it was no use my trying to teach him, because as I have said, this is the thing that you can never learn. And so, each time he had told his story, I would see him turn away from me, with a look of doom on his face, and walk slowly down the road, stoop-shouldered, the last of the Van Barnevelts.

On the wall of Floris's voorkamer is a long family tree of the Van Barnevelts. You can see it there for yourself. It goes back for over two hundred years, to the Van Barnevelts of Amsterdam. At one time it went even further back, but that was before the white ants started on the top part of it and ate away quite a lot of Van Barnevelts. Nevertheless, if you look at this list, you will notice that at the bottom, under Floris's own name, there is the last entry, "Stephanus." And behind the name, "Stephanus," between two bent strokes, you will read the words: "Obiit Mafeking."

At the outbreak of the Second Boer War Floris van Barnevelt was a widower, with one son, Stephanus, who was aged seventeen. The commando from our part of the Transvaal set off very cheerfully. We made a fine show, with our horses and our wide hats and our bandoliers, and with the sun shining on the barrels of our Mausers.

Young Stephanus van Barnevelt was the gayest of us all. But he said there was one thing he didn't like about the war, and that was that, in the end, we would have to go over the sea. He said that, after we had invaded the whole of the Cape, our commando would have to go on a ship and invade England also.

But we didn't go overseas, just then. Instead, our veldkornet told us that the burghers from our part had been ordered to join the big commando that was lying at Mafeking. We had to go and shoot a man there called Baden-Powell.

We rode steadily on into the west. After a while we noticed that our veldkornet frequently got off his horse and engaged in conversation with passing kaffirs, leading them some distance from the roadside and speaking earnestly to them. Of course, it was right that our veldkornet should explain to the kaffirs that it was war-time, now, and that the Republic expected every kaffir to stop smoking so much dagga and to think seriously about what was going on. But we noticed that each time at the end of the conversation the kaffir would point towards something, and that our veldkornet would take much pains to follow the direction of the kaffir's finger.

Of course, we understood, then, what it was all about. Our veldkornet was a young fellow, and he was shy to let us see that he didn't know the way to Mafeking.

Somehow, after that, we did not have so much confidence in our veldkornet.

After a few days we got to Mafeking. We stayed there a long while, until the English troops came up and relieved the place. We left, then. We left quickly. The English troops had brought a lot of artillery with them. And if we had difficulty in finding the road to Mafeking, we had no difficulty in finding the road away from Mafeking. And this time our veldkornet did not need kaffirs, either, to point with their fingers where we had to go. Even though we did a lot of travelling in the night.

Long afterwards I spoke to an Englishman about this. He said it gave him a queer feeling to hear about the other side of the story of Mafeking. He said there had been very great rejoicings in England when Mafeking was relieved, and it was strange to think of the other aspect of it – of a defeated country and of broken columns blundering through the dark.

I remember many things that happened on the way back from Mafeking. There was no moon. And the stars shone down fitfully on the road that was full of guns and frightened horses and desperate men. The veld throbbed with the hoof-beats of baffled commandos. The stars looked down on scenes that told sombrely of a nation's ruin; they looked on the muzzles of the Mausers that had failed the Transvaal for the first time.

Of course, as a burgher of the Republic, I knew what my duty was. And that was to get as far away as I could from the place where, in the sunset, I had last seen English artillery. The other burghers knew their duty also. Our kommandants and veldkornets had to give very few orders. Nevertheless, though I rode very fast, there was one young man who rode still faster. He kept ahead of me all the time. He rode, as a burgher should ride when there may be stray bullets flying, with his head well down and with his arms almost round the horse's neck.

He was Stephanus, the young son of Floris van Barnevelt.

There was much grumbling and dissatisfaction, some time afterwards, when our leaders started making an effort to get the commandos in order again. In the end they managed to get us to halt. But most of us felt that this was a foolish thing to do. Especially as there was still a lot of firing going on, all over the place, in haphazard fashion, and we couldn't tell how far the English had followed us in the dark. Furthermore, the commandos had scattered in so many different directions that it seemed hopeless to try and get them together again until after the war. Stephanus and I dismounted and stood by our horses. Soon there was a large body of men around us. Their figures looked strange and shadowy in the starlight. Some of them stood by their horses. Others sat on the grass by the roadside. "Vas staan, burghers, vas staan," came the commands of our officers. And all the time we could still hear what sounded a lot like lyddite. It seemed foolish to be waiting there.

"The next they'll want," Stephanus van Barnevelt said, "is for us to go back to Mafeking. Perhaps our kommandant has left his tobacco pouch behind, there."

Some of us laughed at this remark, but Floris, who had not dis-

mounted, said that Stephanus ought to be ashamed of himself for talking like that. From what we could see of Floris in the gloom, he looked quite impressive, sitting very straight in the saddle, with the stars shining on his beard and rifle.

"If the veldkornet told me to go back to Mafeking," Floris said, "I would go back."

"That's how a burgher should talk," the veldkornet said, feeling flattered. For he had had little authority since the time we found out what he was talking to the kaffirs for.

"I wouldn't go back to Mafeking for anybody," Stephanus replied, "unless, maybe, it's to hand myself over to the English."

"We can shoot you for doing that," the veldkornet said. "It's contrary to military law."

"I wish I knew something about military law," Stephanus answered. "Then I would draw up a peace treaty between Stephanus van Barnevelt and England."

Some of the men laughed again. But Floris shook his head sadly. He said the Van Barnevelts had fought bravely against Spain in a war that lasted eighty years.

Suddenly, out of the darkness there came a sharp rattle of musketry, and our men started getting uneasy again. But the sound of the firing decided Stephanus. He jumped on his horse quickly.

"I am turning back," he said, "I am going to hands-up to the English."

"No, don't go," the veldkornet called to him lamely, "or at least, wait until the morning. They may shoot you in the dark by mistake." As I have said, the veldkornet had very little authority.

Two days passed before we again saw Floris van Barnevelt. He was in a very worn and troubled state, and he said that it had been very hard for him to find his way back to us.

"You should have asked the kaffirs," one of our number said with a laugh. "All the kaffirs know our veldkornet."

But Floris did not speak about what happened that night, when we saw him riding out under the starlight, following after his son and shouting to him to be a man and to fight for his country. Also, Floris did not mention Stephanus again, his son who was not worthy to be a Van Barnevelt.

After that we got separated. Our veldkornet was the first to be taken prisoner. And I often felt that he must feel very lonely on St. Helena. Because there were no kaffirs from whom he could ask the way out of the barbed-wire camp.

Then, at last our leaders came together at Vereeniging, and peace was made. And we returned to our farms, relieved that the war was over, but with heavy hearts at the thought that it had all been for nothing and that over the Transvaal the Vierkleur would not wave again.

And Floris van Barnevelt put back in its place, on the wall of the voorkamer, the copy of his family tree that had been carried with him in his knapsack throughout the war. Then a new schoolmaster came to this part of the Marico, and after a long talk with Floris, the schoolmaster wrote behind Stephanus's name, between two curved lines, the two words that you can still read there: "Obiit Mafeking."

Consequently, if you ask any person hereabouts what "obiit" means, he is able to tell you, right away, that it is a foreign word, and that it means to ride up to the English, holding your Mauser in the air, with a white flag tied to it, near the muzzle.

But it was long afterwards that Floris van Barnevelt started telling his story.

And then they took no notice of him. And they wouldn't allow him to be nominated for the Drogevlei School Committee on the grounds that a man must be wrong in the head to talk in such an irresponsible fashion.

But I knew that Floris had a good story, and that its only fault was that he told it badly. He mentioned the Drogevlei School Committee too soon. And he knocked the ash out of his pipe in the wrong place. And he always insisted on telling that part of the story that he should have left out.

MARICO SCANDAL

When I passed young Gawie Erasmus by the wall of the new dam (Oom Schalk Lourens said) I could see clearly that he had had another disagreement with his employer, Koos Deventer. Because, as Gawie walked away from me, I saw, on the seat of his trousers, the still damp imprint of a muddy boot. The dried mud of another footprint, higher up on his trousers, told of a similar disagreement that Gawie had had with his employer on the previous day. I thought that Gawie must be a high-spirited young man to disagree so frequently with his employer.

Nevertheless, I felt it my duty to speak to Koos Deventer about this matter when I sat with him in his voorkamer, drinking coffee.

"I see that Gawie Erasmus still lays the stones unevenly on the wall of the new dam you are building," I said to Koos Deventer.

"Indeed," Koos answered, "have you been looking at the front part of the wall?"

"No," I said, "I have been looking at Gawie's trousers. The back part of the trousers."

"The trouble with Gawie Erasmus," Koos said, "is that he is not really a white man. It doesn't show in his hair or his fingernails, of course. He is not as coloured as all that. But you can tell it easily in other ways. Yes, that is what's wrong with Gawie. His Hottentot forebears."

At that moment Koos Deventer's eldest daughter, Francina, brought us in more coffee.

"It is not true, father, what you said about Gawie Erasmus," Francina said. "Gawie is white. He is as white as I am."

Francina was eighteen. She was tall and slender. She had a neat figure. And she looked very pretty in that voorkamer, with the yellow hair falling on to her cheeks from underneath a blue ribbon.

126

Another thing I noticed about Francina, as she moved daintily towards me with the tray, was the scent that she bought in Zeerust at the last Nagmaal. The perfume lay on her strangely, like the night.

Koos Deventer made no reply to Francina. And only after she had gone back into the kitchen, and the door was closed, did he return to the subject of Gawie Erasmus.

"He is so coloured," Koos said, "that he even sleeps with a blanket over his head, like a kaffir does."

It struck me that Koos Deventer's statements were rather peculiar. For, according to Koos, you couldn't tell that Gawie Erasmus was coloured, just by looking at his hair and fingernails. You had to wait until Gawie lay underneath a blanket, so that you saw nothing of him at all.

But I remembered the way that Francina had walked out of the voorkamer with her head very high and her red lips closed. And it seemed to me, then, that Gawie's disagreements with his employer were not all due to the unevenness of the wall of the new dam. I did not see Gawie Erasmus again until the meeting of the Drogevlei Debating Society.

127

But in the meantime the story that Gawie was coloured gained much ground. Paulus Welman said that he knew a man once in Vryburg who had known Gawie's grandfather. And this man said that Gawie's grandfather had a big belly and wore a copper ring through his nose. At other times, again, Paulus Welman said that it was Gawie's father whom this man in Vryburg had known, and that Gawie's father did not wear the copper ring in his nose, but in his one ear. It was hard to know which story to believe. So most of the farmers in the Marico believed both.

The meeting of the Drogevlei Debating Society was held in the schoolroom. There was a good attendance. For the debate was to be on the Native Question. And that was always a popular subject in the Marico. You could say much about it without having to think hard.

I was standing under the thorn-trees talking to Paulus Welman and some others, when Koos Deventer arrived with his wife and Francina and Gawie. They got off the mule-cart, and the two women walked on towards the schoolroom. Koos and Gawie stayed behind, hitching the reins on to a tree. Several of the men with me shook their heads gravely at what they saw. For Gawie, while stooping for a riem, had another hurried disagreement with his employer.

Francina, walking with her mother towards the school, sensed that something was amiss. But when she turned round she was too late to see anything.

Francina and her mother greeted us as they passed. Paulus Welman said that Francina was a pretty girl, but rather stand-off-ish. He said her understanding was a bit slow, too. He said that when he had told her that joke about the copper ring in the one ear of Gawie's father, Francina looked at him as though he had said there was a copper ring in his own ear. She didn't seem to be quite all there, Paulus Welman said.

But I didn't take much notice of Paulus.

I stood there, under the thorn-tree, where Francina had passed, and I breathed in stray breaths of that scent which Francina had bought in Zeerust. It was a sweet and strange fragrance. But it was sad, also, like youth that has gone.

I waited in the shadows. Gawie Erasmus came by. I scrutinised him carefully, but except that his hair was black and his skin rather dark, there seemed to be no justification for Koos Deventer to say that he was coloured. It looked like some kind of joke that Koos Deventer and Paulus Welman had got up between them. Gawie seemed to be just an ordinary and rather good-looking youth of about twenty.

By this time it was dark. Oupa van Tonder, an old farmer who was very keen on debates, lit an oil-lamp that he had brought with him and put it on the table.

The schoolmaster took the chair, as usual. He said that, as we all knew, the subject was that the Bantu should be allowed to develop along his own lines. He said he had got the idea for this debate from an article he had read in the *Kerkbode*.

Oupa van Tonder then got up and said that, the way the schoolmaster put it, the subject was too hard to understand. He proposed, for the sake of the older debaters, who had not gone to school much, that they should just be allowed to talk about how the kaffirs in the Marico were getting cheekier every day. The older debaters cheered Oupa van Tonder for putting the schoolmaster in his place.

Oupa van Tonder was still talking when the schoolmaster banged the table with a ruler and said that he was out of order. Oupa van Tonder got really annoyed then. He said he had lived in the Transvaal for eighty-eight years, and this was the first time in his life that he had been insulted. "Anybody would think that I am the steam machine that threshes the mealies at Nietverdiend, that I can get out of order," Oupa van Tonder said.

Some of the men started pulling Oupa van Tonder by his jacket to get him to sit down, but others shouted out that he was quite right, and that they should pull the schoolmaster's jacket instead.

The schoolmaster explained that if some people were talking on the *Kerkbode* subject, and others were talking on Oupa van Tonder's subject, it would mean that there were two different debates going on at the same time. Oupa van Tonder said that that was quite all right. It suited him, he said. And he told a long story about a kaffir who had stolen his trek-chain. He also said that if the schoolmaster kept on banging the table like that, while he was talking, he would go home and take his oil-lamp with him.

In the end the schoolmaster said that we could talk about anything we liked. Only, he asked us not to use any of that coarse language that had spoilt the last three debates. "Try to remember that there are ladies present," he said in a weak sort of way.

The older debaters, who had not been to school much, spoke at great length.

Afterwards the schoolmaster suggested that perhaps some of our younger members would like to debate a little, and he called on Gawie Erasmus to say a few words on behalf of the kaffirs. The schoolmaster spoke playfully.

Koos Deventer guffawed behind his hand. Some of the women tittered. On account of his unpopularity the schoolmaster heard little of what went on in the Marico. The only news he got was what he could glean from reading the compositions of the children in the higher classes. And we could see that the children had not yet mentioned, in their compositions, that Gawie Erasmus was supposed to be coloured.

You know how it is with a scandalous story. The last one to hear it is always that person that the scandal is about.

That crowd in the schoolroom realised quickly what the situation was. And there was much laughter all the time that Gawie spoke. I can still remember that half-perplexed look on his dark face, as though he had meant to make a funny speech, but had not expected quite that amount of appreciation. And I noticed that Francina's face was very red, and that her eyes were fixed steadily on the floor.

There was so much laughter, finally, that Gawie had to sit down, still looking slightly puzzled.

After that Paulus Welman got up and told funny stories about so-called white people whose grandfathers had big bellies and wore copper rings in their ears. I don't know at what stage of the debate Gawie Erasmus found out at whom these funny remarks were being directed. Or when it was that he slipped out of the schoolroom, to leave Drogevlei and the Groot Marico for ever.

130

And some months later, when I again went to visit Koos De-venter, he did not once mention Gawie Erasmus to me. He seemed to have grown tired of Marico scandals. But when Francina brought in the coffee, it was as though she thought that Koos had again spoken about Gawie. For she looked at him in a disapproving sort of way and said: "Gawie is white, father. He is as white as I am."

I could not at first make out what the change was that had come over Francina. She was as good-looking as ever, but in a different sort of way. I began to think that perhaps it was because she no longer wore that strange perfume that she bought in Zeerust.

But at that moment she brought me my coffee.

And I saw then, when she came towards me from behind the table, with the tray, why it was that Francina Deventer moved so heavily.

BECHUANA INTERLUDE

When I last saw Lenie Venter – Oom Schalk Lourens said – she was sitting in the voorkamer of her parents' farmhouse at Koedoesrand, drawing small circles on the blotting-paper. And I didn't know whether I had to be sorry for Lenie. Or for Johnny de Clerk. Or for Gert Oosthuizen. Or perhaps for the kaffir schoolmaster at Ramoutsa.

Of course, Lenie had learnt this trick of drawing circles from Johnny de Clerk, the young insurance agent. She had watched him, very intently, the first time he had called on Piet Venter. He had been in the Marico for some time, but this was his first visit to Koedoesrand. Johnny de Clerk looked very elegant, in his blue suit with the short jacket and the wide trousers, and while he sat with a lot of printed documents in front of him, talking about the advantages of being insured, he drew lots of small circles on the blotting-paper.

I was going by mule-cart to the Bechuanaland Protectorate, and on my way I had stopped at Piet Venter's house for a cup of coffee, and to ask him if there was anything I could order for him from the Indian store at Ramoutsa. But he said there wasn't.

"What about a drum of cattle-dip?" I hinted, remembering that Piet still owed me five gallons of dip.

"No," he answered. "I don't need cattle-dip now."

"Perhaps I can order you a few rolls of barbed wire," I suggested. This time I was thinking of the wire he had borrowed from me for his new sheep-camp.

"No, thank you," he said politely, "I don't need barbed wire, either."

Piet Venter was funny, that way.

I was on the point of leaving, when Johnny de Clerk came in, very smart in his blue suit and his light felt hat and his pointed shoes. He introduced himself, and we all sat down and chatted very affably for a while. Afterwards Johnny took out a number of insurance forms, and said things to Piet Venter about a thousand pound policy, speaking very fast. From the way Johnny de Clerk kept on looking sideways at me, while he talked, I gathered that my presence was disturbing him, and that he couldn't talk his best while there was a third party listening.

So I lit my pipe and stayed longer.

I noticed that Lenie kept flitting in and out of the voorkamer, with bright eyes and red cheeks. I also noticed that, soon after Johnny de Clerk's arrival, she had gone into the bedroom for a few minutes and had come out wearing a new pink frock. Lenie was pretty enough to make any man feel flattered if he knew that she had gone into the bedroom and put on a new pink frock just because he was there. She had dark hair and dark eyes, and when she smiled you could see that her teeth were very white.

Her sudden interest in this young insurance agent struck me as being all the more singular, because everybody in the Marico knew that Lenie was being courted by Gert Oosthuizen.

But it seemed that Johnny de Clerk had not noticed Lenie's blushes and her new frock. He appeared very unobservant about these things. It did not seem right that a young girl's efforts at attracting a man should be wasted in that fashion. That was another reason why I went on sitting there while the insurance agent talked to Piet Venter. I even went so far as to cough, once or twice, when Johnny de Clerk mentioned the amount of the policy that he thought Piet Venter should take out.

When he had filled the whole sheet of blotting-paper with small circles, Johnny de Clerk stopped talking and put the printed documents in order.

"I have proved to you why you should be insured for a thousand pounds, Oom Piet," he said, "so just sign your name here."

Piet Venter shook his head.

"Oh no," he replied, "I don't want to."

"But you must," Johnny de Clerk went on, waving his hand towards Lenie, without looking up, "for the sake of your wife, here, you must."

"That is not my wife," Piet Venter replied, "that's my daughter, Lenie. My wife has gone to Zeerust to visit her sister."

"Well, then, for the sake of your wife and daughter, Lenie," Johnny de Clerk said, "and what's more, I've already spent an hour talking to you. If I spend another hour I shall have to insure you for two thousand pounds."

Piet Venter got frightened then, and took off his jacket and signed the application form without any more fuss. By the way he passed his hand over his forehead I could see he was pleased to have got out of it so easily. I thought it was very considerate of Johnny de Clerk to have warned him in time. A more dishonest insurance agent, I felt, would just have gone on sitting there for the full two hours, and would then have filled in the documents, very coolly, for two thousand pounds. It was a pleasure for me to see an honest insurance agent at work, after I had come across so many of what you can call the dishonest kind.

Johnny de Clerk went out then, with the papers, saying that he would call again.

I left shortly afterwards.

"By the way," I said to Piet Venter, as I took up my hat, "perhaps I could order another trek-chain for you at Ramoutsa. It's always useful to have two trek-chains."

Piet Venter thought deeply for a few moments.

"No, Schalk, it's no good," he said, slowly. "If a man has got a spare trek-chain, people always want to borrow it."

I wondered much about Piet Venter as I walked out to the mule-cart.

I had just unfastened the reins from the front wheel, and was getting ready to drive away, when I heard light footsteps running across the grass. I looked round. It was Lenie. She looked very pretty running like that, with her eyes shining and her dark hair flying in the wind.

She had been running fast. The breath came in short gasps from between her parted lips. The sun shone very white on her small teeth.

Lenie was too excited at first to talk. She leant against the side of the cart, panting. I was glad she hadn't taken it into her mind to lean up against one of the mules, instead.

At last she found her voice.

"I have just remembered, Oom Schalk," she said, "we have run out of blotting-paper. Will you please get me a few sheets from Ramoutsa?"

"Yes, certainly, Lenie," I replied, "yes, of course. Blotting-paper. Oh, yes, for sure. Blotting-paper."

I spoke to her in that way, tactfully, to make it appear as though it was quite an ordinary thing she had asked me to get. And I said other things that were even more tactful.

She smiled when I spoke like that. And I remembered her smile for most of the way to Ramoutsa. It was an uneasy sort of smile.

The usual small crowd of farmers from different parts of the Marico were hanging around the Indian store when I got there. After making their purchases they whiled away the time in discussing politics and the mealie-crops and the miltsiekte. They stood there, talking, to give their mules a chance to rest. Sometimes a mule got sunstroke, from resting for such a long time in the sun, while his owner was talking.

I ordered the things I wanted. The Indian wrote them all down in a book, and then got one of his kaffirs to carry them out to my mule-cart.

"By the way," I said, clearing my throat, and trying to speak as though I had just remembered something, "I also want blotting-paper. Six sheets will do."

The Indian looked in my eyes and nodded his head up and down, several times, very solemnly. I understood, from that, that the Indian didn't know what blotting-paper was. It took me about half an hour to explain it to him, and in the end he said that he hadn't any in his store, but that if I liked he could order some for me from England. But by that time several of the thoughtful farmers, who were allowing their mules to rest, had heard what I was asking for. And they made remarks which were considered, in the Protectorate, to be funny.

One farmer said that Schalk Lourens was beginning to get very up-to-date, and that the next thing he would be ordering was a collar and tie.

"The last Boer who used blotting-paper," another man said, "was Piet Retief. When he signed that treaty with Dingaan."

They were still laughing in their meaningless way when I drove off, feeling very bitter at the thought that a nice girl like Lenie, who was so sensible in other respects, should have got me into that unpleasant situation.

On my way back over the border I had to pass the Bechuana school. And that was where, in the end, I obtained the blotting-paper. I got a few sheets from the kaffir schoolmaster. In exchange for the blotting-paper I gave him half a can of black axle-grease, which he explained that he wanted for rubbing on his hair. I did not think that he was a very highly-educated kaffir schoolmaster.

And when I took the blotting-paper back to Koedoesrand, I did not mention where I had obtained it. Consequently, I did not tell them, either, that the kaffir schoolmaster at Ramoutsa had made many enquiries of me in regard to a Baas Johnny de Clerk. There was no need for me to enlighten them. For I knew that the school-master had told me only the truth, and that, therefore, it would all be found out in time.

In the weeks that followed I saw very little of Piet Venter and Lenie. But I heard that Johnny de Clerk was still travelling about the neighbourhood, selling insurance. I also heard that he was in the habit of calling rather frequently at Piet Venter's house, to the annoyance of Gert Oosthuizen, the young farmer who was betrothed to Lenie.

And so the days passed by, as they do in the Marico, quietly.

Now and again vague stories reached me to the effect that Johnny de Clerk was seeing more and more of Lenie Venter, and that Gert Oosthuizen was viewing the matter with growing dissatisfaction. For these reasons I couldn't go to Koedoesrand. I realised that if I saw Piet Venter it would be my duty to tell him all I knew. And, somehow, there was something that prevented me.

The dry season passed and the rains came, and the dams were

full. Then, one day, the whole Marico knew this thing about Johnny de Clerk. And, shortly afterwards, I went again to see Piet Venter at Koedoesrand.

But, in the meantime, Johnny de Clerk had had rather an unpleasant time. For, when they found out that, in his ignorant way, the kaffir schoolmaster was right to look upon the insurance agent as his son-in-law, a number of farmers waited until Johnny de Clerk again went to call on Lenie Venter. And they threw him into the dam, which was full with the rains, and when he came out his blue suit was very bedraggled, and his light hat was still in the water.

And so Johnny de Clerk left the Marico. But nobody could say for sure whether he went back to Pretoria, where he had come from, or to the Bechuana hut in Ramoutsa, where one of the farmers told him to go, when he kicked him.

The last time I saw Lenie Venter in her father's voorkamer was just before she married Gert Oosthuizen. And Gert was talking sentimental words to her, in a heavy fashion. But most of the time Lenie's face was turned away from Gert's, as she sat, with a far-off look in her dark eyes, drawing small circles on a piece of blotting-paper.

VISITORS TO PLATRAND

When Koenrad Wium rode back to his farm at Platrand, in the evening, with fever in his body and blood on his face (Oom Schalk Lourens said), nobody could guess about the sombre thing that was in his heart.

It was easy to guess about the fever, though. For, that night, when he lay on his bed, and the moon shone in through the window, Lettie Wium, his sister, had to shut out the moonlight with a curtain, because of the way that Koenrad kept on trying to rise from the bed in order to blow out the moon.

Koenrad Wium had gone off with Frik Engelbrecht into the Protectorate. They took with them rolls of tobacco and strings of coloured beads, which they were going to barter with the kaffirs for cattle. When he packed his last box of coloured beads on the wagon, Koenrad Wium told me that he and Frik Engelbrecht expected to be away a long time. And I said I supposed they would. That was after I had seen some of the beads.

I knew, then, that Koenrad Wium and Frik Engelbrecht would have to go into the furthest parts of the Protectorate, where only the more ignorant kind of kaffirs are.

Koenrad was very enthusiastic when they set out. But I could see that Frik Engelbrecht was less keen. Frik was courting Koenrad's sister, Lettie. And Lettie's looks were not of the sort that would make a man regard a box of beads as a good enough excuse for departing on a long journey out of the Marico. I felt that his chief reason for going was that he wanted to oblige his future brother-in-law. And this was quite a strange reason.

"The only trouble," Koenrad said, "is that when I get back I'll have to go and live in a bigger district than the Marico. Otherwise I won't have enough space for all my cattle to move about in. The Dwarsberge take up too much room."

But Frik Engelbrecht did not laugh at Koenrad's joke. He only looked sullen.

And I still remember what Lettie answered, when her brother asked her what she would like him to give her for a wedding present, when he had made all that money.

"I would like," Lettie said, after thinking for a few moments, "some beads."

It was singular, therefore, that when Koenrad came back it was without the cattle. And without Frik Engelbrecht. And without the beads.

And he said strange things with the fever on him. He was sick for a long while. And with wasted cheeks, and a hollow look about his eyes, and his forehead bandaged with a white rag, Koenrad Wium lay in bed and talked mad words in his delirium. Consequently, on the days that the lorry from Zeerust came to the post office, there was not the usual crowd of Bushveld farmers discussing the crops and politics. They did not come to the post office anymore: they went, instead, to the farmhouse at Platrand, where they smoked and drank coffee in the bedroom, and listened to Koenrad's babblings.

When the ouderling got to hear about these goings-on, he said it was very scandalous. He said it was a sad thing for the Dopper Church that some of its members could derive amusement from listening to the ravings of a delirious man. The ouderling had a keen sense of duty, and he was not content with merely reprimanding those of his neighbours whom he happened to meet casually. He went straight up to Koenrad's house in Platrand, right into the bedroom, where he found a lot of men sitting around the wall; they were smoking their pipes and occasionally winking at one another.

The ouderling remained there for several hours. He sat very stiffly on a chair near the bed. He glared a good deal at the

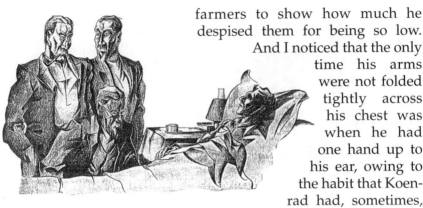

farmers to show how much he despised them for being so low. And I noticed that the only time his arms were not folded tightly across his chest was when he had one hand up to his ear, owing to the habit that Koenrad had, sometimes, of mumbling. The ouderling was a bit deaf.

And all this time Lettie would pass in and out of the room, silently. She greeted us when we came, and brought us coffee, and said goodbye to us again when we left. But it was hard to gather just exactly what Lettie thought of the daily visits of ours. For she said so little. Just those cool words when we left. And those words, when we came, that we noticed were cooler.

In fact, during the whole period of Koenrad's illness, she spoke on only one other occasion. That was on the third day the ouderling called. And it was to me that she spoke, then.

"I think, Oom Schalk, it is bad for my brother," Lettie said, "if you sit right on top of him, like that. If you can't hear too well what he is saying, you can bend your ear over with your hand, like the ouderling does."

It was hard to follow the drift of Koenrad's remarks. For he kept on bringing in things that he did as a boy. He spoke very much about his childhood days. He told us quite instructive things, too. For instance, we never knew, until then, that Koenrad's father stole. Several times he spoke about his father, and each time he ended up by saying, in a thin sort of voice: "No, father, you must not steal so much. It is not right." He would also say: "You may laugh now, father. But one day you will not laugh."

It was on these occasions that we would look at one another and wink. Sometimes Lettie would come into the room while Koenrad was saying these things about their father. But you could not tell by her face that she heard. There was just that calm and distant look in her eyes.

140

But we listened most attentively when Koenrad spoke about his trek into the Protectorate with Frik Engelbrecht. He said awful things about thirst and sin and fever, and we held our breath in fear that we should miss a word. It gave me a queer sort of feeling, more than once, to be sitting in that room of sickness, looking at a man with wasted cheeks, whose cracked lips were mumbling dark words. And in the midst of these frightening things he would suddenly talk about little red flowers that lay on the grass. He spoke about the foot of a hill where shadows were. And about small red flowers on the grass. He spoke as though these flowers were the most dreadful part of the story.

It was always at this stage that the argument started amongst the men sitting in the room.

Piet Snyman said it was all nonsense, the first time that Koenrad mentioned the flowers. Piet said that he had never seen any red flowers in the Protectorate, and he had been there often.

Stephanus Naudé agreed with him, and said that Koenrad was just trying to be funny with us, now, and was wasting our time. He said he didn't get up early every morning and ride sixteen miles to hear Koenrad Wium discuss flowers. Piet Snyman sympathised with Stephanus Naudé, and said that he himself had almost as far to ride. "While Koenrad tells us about himself and Engelbrecht, or about his father's dishonesty, we can listen to him," Piet added.

The ouderling held up his hand.

"Broeders," he said. "Let us not judge Koenrad Wium too harshly. Maybe he already had the fever, then, when he thought he saw the red flowers."

Piet Snyman said that was all very well, but then why couldn't Koenrad tell us so, straight out? "After all, we are his guests," Piet explained. "We sit here and drink his coffee, and then he tries to be funny."

There was much that was reasonable in what Piet Snyman said.

We said that Koenrad was not being honest with us, and that it looked as though he had inherited that dishonesty from his father. We said, further, that he wasn't grateful for the trouble we were taking over him. He seemed to forget that it didn't happen to just any sick person to have half the able-bodied men in the Marico watching at his bedside. Practically day and night, you could say. And sitting as near the bed as Lettie would allow us.

Gradually Koenrad began to get better.

But before that happened a kaffir brought a message to us from the man in charge of the Drogevlei post office. The man wanted to know if we would like to have our letters re-addressed to Koenrad Wium's house at Platrand. We realised that it was a sarcastic message, and when we pointed this out to the ouderling, he went to the back of the house and kicked the kaffir for bringing it.

Koenrad's recovery was slow. But when he regained consciousness he did not talk much. Furthermore, he seemed to have no recollection of the things he had said in his days of delirium. He seemed to remember nothing of his mumblings about his boyhood, and about Engelbrecht and the Bechuanaland Protectorate. And although the ouderling questioned him, subtly, when Lettie was in the kitchen and the bedroom door was closed, there was not much that we could learn from his replies.

"Take your father, for instance," the ouderling said – and we looked significantly at one another – "can you remember him in the old days, when you were living in the Cape?"

"Yes," Koenrad answered.

"And did they ever – I mean," the ouderling corrected himself, "did your father ever go away from the house for, say, six months?"

"No," Koenrad replied.

"Twelve months, then?"

"No," Koenrad said.

"Did you ever see him walking about," the ouderling asked, "with a red handkerchief fastened over the lower part of his face?" We could see, from this question, that the ouderling had more exciting ideas than we had about the sort of things that a thief does.

"No," Koenrad said again, looking surprised.

All Koenrad's replies were like that – unsatisfactory. Still, it wasn't the ouderling's fault. We knew that the ouderling had done his best. Piet Snyman's methods, however, were not the same as the ouderling's. His words were not so well thought out.

"You don't seem to remember much about your father – huh?" Piet Snyman said. "But what about all those small red flowers lying around on the grass?"

The change that came over Koenrad Wium's face at this question was astonishing. But he didn't answer. Instead, he drew the

142

blanket over his head and lay very still. Piet Snyman was still try-ing to pull the blanket off his face, again, when Lettie walked into the bedroom.

"Your brother has had a relapse," the ouderling said to Lettie.

Lettie looked at the ouderling without speaking. She picked up the quinine bottle and knelt at Koenrad's bedside.

Koenrad relapsed quite often after that, when Lettie was in the kitchen. He relapsed four times over questions that the ouderling asked him, and seven times over things that Piet Snyman wanted to know. It was noticeable that Koenrad's condition did not im-prove very fast.

Nevertheless, his periods of delirium grew fewer, and the number of his visitors dwindled. Towards the end only the ou-derling and I were left. And we began discussing, cautiously, the mystery of Frik Engelbrecht's disappearance.

"It's funny about those red flowers on the grass," the ouder-ling said in a whisper, when Koenrad was asleep. "I wonder if he meant that there was blood on the grass?"

We also said that Lettie seemed to be acting strangely, and I said I wondered how she felt about the fact that her lover had not returned.

"Perhaps she has already got her eye on some other man," the ouderling said, and he pushed out his chest and stroked his beard. "Perhaps what she wants now is an older man, with more understanding. A man who has been married before."

The ouderling was a widower.

I thought he was talking very foolishly. For it was easy to see – from the look of patient dignity that passed over her face when-ever she glanced at me – that Lettie preferred the kind of man that I was.

Then, one day, when Koenrad Wium was well enough to be able to move about the room, two men came for him. One wore a policeman's uniform. The other was in plain clothes, and walked with a brisk step. And Lettie opened the door for them and led them into the bedroom, very calmly, as though she had been expecting them.

STARLIGHT ON THE VELD

It was a cold night (Oom Schalk Lourens said), the stars shone with that frosty sort of light that you see on the wet grass some mornings, when you forget that it is winter, and you get up early, by mistake. The wind was like a girl sobbing out her story of betrayal to the stars.

Jan Ockerse and I had been to Derdepoort by donkey-cart. We came back in the evening. And Jan Ockerse told me of a road round the foot of a koppie that would be a short cut back to Drogevlei. Thus it was that we were sitting on the veld, close to the fire, waiting for the morning. We would then be able to ask a kaffir to tell us a short cut back to the foot of that koppie.

"But I know that it was the right road," Jan Ockerse insisted, flinging another armful of wood on the fire.

"Then it must have been the wrong koppie," I answered, "or the wrong donkey-cart. Unless you also want me to believe that I am at this moment sitting at home, in my voorkamer."

The light from the flames danced frostily on the spokes of a cartwheel, and I was glad to think that Jan Ockerse must be feeling as cold as I was.

"It is a funny sort of night," Jan Ockerse said, "and I am very miserable and hungry."

I was glad of that, too. I had begun to fear that he was enjoying himself.

"Do you know how high up the stars are?" Jan asked me next.

"No, not from here," I said, "but I worked it all out once, when I had a pencil. That was on the Highveld, though. But from where we are now, in the Lowveld, the stars are further away. You can see that they look smaller, too."

"Yes, I expect so," Jan Ockerse answered, "but a school-teacher told me a different thing in the bar at Zeerust. He said that the stargazers work out how far away a star is by the number of years that it takes them to find it in their telescopes. This school-teacher dipped his finger in the brandy and drew a lot of pictures and things on the bar counter, to show me how it was done. But one part of his drawings always dried up on the counter before he had finished doing the other part with his finger. He said that was the worst of that dry sort of brandy. Yet he didn't finish his explanations, because the barmaid came and wiped it all off with a rag. Then the school-teacher told me to come with him and he would use the blackboard in the other classroom. But the barmaid wouldn't allow us to take our glasses into the private bar, and the school-teacher fell down just about then, too."

"He seems to be one of that new kind of school-teacher," I said, "the kind that teaches the children that the earth turns round the sun. I am surprised they didn't sack him."

"Yes," Jan Ockerse answered, "they did."

I was glad to hear that also.

It seemed that there was a waterhole near where we were outspanned. For a couple of jackals started howling mournfully. Jan Ockerse jumped up and piled more wood on the fire.

"I don't like those wild animal noises," he said.

"They are only jackals, Jan," I said.

"I know," he answered, "but I was thinking of our donkeys. I don't want our donkeys to get frightened."

Suddenly a deep growl came to us from out of the dark bush. And it didn't sound a particularly mournful growl, either. Jan Ockerse worked very fast then with the wood.

"Perhaps it will be even better if we make two fires, and lie down between them," Jan Ockerse said, "our donkeys will feel less frightened if they see that you and I are safe. You know how a donkey's mind works."

The light of the fire shone dimly on the skeletons of the tall trees that the white ants had eaten, and we soon had two fires going. By the time that the second deep roar from the bush reached us, I had made an even bigger fire than Jan Ockerse, for the sake of the donkeys.

Afterwards it got quiet again. There was only the stirring of the wind in the thorn branches, and the rustling movement of things that you hear in the Bushveld at night.

Jan Ockerse lay on his back and put his hands under his head, and once more looked up at the stars.

"I have heard that these stars are worlds, just like ours," he said, "and that they have got people living on them, even."

"I don't think they would be good for growing mealies on, though," I answered, "they look too high up. Like the rante of the Sneeuberge, in the Cape. But I suppose they would make quite a good horse and cattle country. That's the trouble with these low-lying districts, like the Marico and the Waterberg: there is too much horse-sickness and tsetse-fly here."

"And butterflies," Jan Ockerse said sleepily, "with gold wings."

I also fell asleep shortly afterwards. And when I woke up again the fires were almost dead. I got up and fetched more wood. It took me quite a while to wake Jan Ockerse, though. Because the veldskoens I was wearing were the wrong kind, and had soft toes. Eventually he sat up and rubbed his eyes; and he said, of course, that he had been lying awake all night. What made him so certain that he had not been asleep, he said, was that he was imagining all the time that he was chasing bluebottles amongst the stars.

"And I would have caught up with them, too," he added,

"only a queer sort of thing happened to me, while I was jumping from one star to another. It was almost as though somebody was kicking me."

Jan Ockerse looked at me in a suspicious kind of way.

So I told him that it was easy to see that he had been dreaming.

When the fires were piled high with wood, Jan Ockerse again said that it was a funny night, and once more started talking about the stars.

"What do you think sailors do at sea, Schalk," he said, "if they don't know the way and there aren't any other ships around from whom they can ask?"

"They have got it all written down on a piece of paper with a lot of red and blue on it," I answered, "and there are black lines that show you the way from Cape Town to St. Helena. And figures to tell you how many miles down the ship will go if it sinks. I went to St. Helena during the Boer War. You can live in a ship just like an ox-wagon. Only, a ship isn't so comfortable, of course. And it is further between outspans."

"I heard, somewhere, that sailors find their way by the stars," Jan Ockerse said, "I wonder what people want to tell me things like that for."

He lay silent for a while, looking up at the stars and thinking.

"I remember one night when I stood on Annie Steyn's stoep and spoke to her about the stars," Jan Ockerse said, later. "I was going to trek with the cattle to the Limpopo because of the drought. I told Annie that I would be away until the rains came, and I told her that every night, when I was gone, she had to look at a certain star and think of me. I showed her which star. Those three stars there, that are close together in a straight line. She had to remember me by the middle one, I said. But Annie explained that Willem Mostert, who had trekked to the Limpopo about a week before, had already picked that middle star for her to remember him by. So I said, all right, the top star would do. But Annie said that one already belonged to Stoffel Brink. In the end I agreed that she could remember me by the bottom star, and Annie was still saying that she would look at the lower one of those three stars every night and think of me, when her father, who seemed to have been listening behind the door, came on to the stoep and said: 'What about cloudy nights?' in what he supposed was a clever sort of way."

"What happened then?" I asked Jan Ockerse.

"Annie was very annoyed," he replied, "she told her father that he was always spoiling things. She told him that he wasn't a bit funny, really, especially as I was the third young man to whom he had said the same thing. She said that no matter how foolish a young man might be, her father had no right to make jokes like that in front of him. It was good to hear the way that Annie stood up for me. Anyway, what followed was a long story. I came across Willem Mostert and Stoffel Brink by the Limpopo.

And we remained together there for several months. And it must have been an unusual sight for a stranger to see three young men sitting round the camp-fire, every night, looking up at the stars. We got friendly, after a while, and when the rains came the three of us trekked back to the Marico. And I found, then, that Annie's father had been right. About the cloudy nights, I mean. For I understood that it was on just such a sort of night that Annie had run off to Johannesburg with a bywoner who was going to look for work on the mines."

Jan Ockerse sighed and returned to his thinking.

But with all the time that we had spent in talking and sleeping, most of the night had slipped away. We kept only one fire going now, and Jan Ockerse and I took turns in putting on the wood. It gets very cold just before dawn, and we were both shivering.

"Anyway," Jan Ockerse said after a while, "now you know

why I am interested in stars. I was a young man when this happened. And I have told very few people about it. About seventeen
people, I should say. The others wouldn't listen. But always, on a
clear night, when I see those three bright stars in a row, I look for
a long time at that lowest star, and there seems to be something
very friendly about the way it shines. It seems to be my star, and
its light is different from the light of the other stars . . . and you
know, Schalk, Annie Steyn had such red lips. And such long, soft
hair, Schalk. And there was that smile of hers."

Afterwards the stars grew pale and we started rounding up the
donkeys and got ready to go. And I wondered what Annie Steyn
would have thought of it, if she had known that during all those
years there was this man, looking up at the stars on nights when
the sky was clear, and dreaming about her lips and her hair and
her smile. But as soon as I reflected about it, I knew what the
answer was, also. Of course, Annie Steyn would think nothing of
Jan Ockerse. Nothing at all.

And, no doubt, Annie Steyn was right.

But it was strange to think that we had passed a whole night
in talking about the stars. And I did not know, until then, that it
was all on account of a love story of long ago.

We climbed on to the cart and set off to look for the way home.

"I know that school-teacher in the Zeerust bar was all wrong,"
Jan Ockerse said, finally, "when he tried to explain how far away
the stars are. The lower one of those three stars – ah, it has just
faded – is very near to me. Yes, it is very near."

MARICO MOON

I buttoned up my jacket because of the night wind that came whistling through the thorn-trees (Oom Schalk Lourens said); my fingers on the reins were stiff with the cold.

There were four of us in the mule-cart, driving along the Government Road on our way back from the dance at Withaak. I sat in front with Dirk Prinsloo, a young school-teacher. In the back were Petrus Lemmer and his sister's step-daughter, Annie.

Petrus Lemmer was an elder in the Dutch Reformed Church. He told us that he was very strongly opposed to parties, because people got drunk at parties, and all sorts of improper things happened. He had only gone to the dance at Withaak, he said, because of Annie. He explained that he had to be present to make quite sure that nothing unseemly took place at a dance that his sister's step-daughter went to.

We all thought that it was very fine of Petrus Lemmer to sacrifice his own comfort in that way. And we were very glad when he said that this was one of the most respectable dances he had ever attended.

He said that at two o'clock in the morning. But before that he had said a few other things of so unusual a character that all the women walked out. And they only came back a little later on, after a number of young men had helped Petrus Lemmer out through the front door. One of the young men was Dirk Prinsloo, the school-teacher, and I noticed that there was quite a lot of peach brandy on his clothes. The peach brandy had come out of a big glass that Petrus Lemmer had in his hand, and when he went out of the door he was still saying how glad he was that this was not an improper party, like others he had seen.

Shortly afterwards Petrus Lemmer fell into the dam, backwards. And when they pulled him out he was still holding on to the big glass, very tightly. But when he put the glass to his mouth he said that what was in it tasted to him a lot like water. He threw the glass away, then.

So it came about that, in the early hours of the morning, there were four of us driving along the road back from Withaak. Petrus Lemmer had wanted to stay longer at the dance, after they had pulled him out of the dam and given him a dry pair of trousers and a shirt. But they said, no, it wasn't right that he should go on sacrificing himself like that. Petrus Lemmer said that was nothing. He was willing to sacrifice himself a lot more. He said he would go on sacrificing himself until the morning, if necessary, to make quite sure that nothing disgraceful took place at the dance. But the people said there was no need for him to stay any longer. Nothing more disgraceful could happen than what had already happened, they said.

At first, Petrus Lemmer seemed pleased at what they said. But afterwards he grew a bit more thoughtful. He still appeared to be thinking about it when a number of young men, including Dirk Prinsloo, helped him on to my mule-cart, heavily. His sister's step-daughter, Annie, got into the back seat beside him. Dirk Prinsloo came and sat next to me.

It was a cold night, and the road through the bush was very long. The house where Dirk Prinsloo boarded was the first that we would come to. It was a long way ahead. Then came Petrus Lemmer's farm, several miles further on. I had the longest distance to go of us all.

In between shivering, Petrus Lemmer said how pleased he was that nobody at the dance had used really bad language.

"Nobody except you, Uncle," Annie said then.

Petrus Lemmer explained that anybody was entitled to forget himself a little, after having been thrown into the dam, like he was.

"You weren't thrown, Uncle," Annie said. "You fell in."

"Thrown," Petrus persisted.

"Fell," Annie repeated firmly.

Petrus said that she could have it her way, if she liked. It was no use arguing with a woman, he explained. Women couldn't under-

151

stand reason, anyway. But what he maintained strongly was that, if you were wet right through, and standing in the cold, you might perhaps say a few things that you wouldn't say ordinarily.

"But even before you fell in the dam, Uncle," Annie went on, "you used bad language. The time all the women walked out. It was awful language. And you said it just for nothing, too. You ought to be ashamed of yourself, Uncle. And you an elder in the Reformed Church."

But Petrus Lemmer said that was different. He said that if he hadn't been at the dance he would like to know what would have happened. That was all he wanted to know. Young girls of today had no sense of gratitude. It was only for Annie's sake that he had come to the dance in the first place. And then they went and threw him into the water.

The moon was big and full above the Dwarsberge; and the wind grew colder; and the stars shone dimly through the thorn-trees that overhung the road.

Then Petrus Lemmer started telling us about other dances he had attended in the Bushveld, long ago. He was a young man, then, he said. And whenever he went to a dance there was a certain amount of trouble. "Just like tonight," he said. He went to lots of dances, and it was always the same thing. They were the scandal of the Marico, those dances he went to. And he said it was no use his exercising his influence, either; people just wouldn't listen to him.

"Influence," Annie said, and I could hear her laughter above the rattling of the mule-cart.

"But there was one dance I went to," Petrus Lemmer continued, "on a farm near Abjaterskop. That was very different. It was a quiet sort of dance. And it was different in every way."

Annie said that perhaps it was different because they didn't have a dam on that farm. But Petrus Lemmer replied, in a cold kind of voice, that he didn't know what Annie was hinting at, and that, anyway, she was old enough to have more sense.

"It was mainly because of Grieta," Petrus Lemmer said, "that I went to that dance at Abjaterskop. And I believed that it was because she hoped to see me there that Grieta went."

152

Annie said something about this, also. I couldn't hear what it was. But this time Petrus Lemmer ignored her.

"There were not very many people at this dance," he went on. "A large number who had been invited stayed away."

"It seems that other people besides Grieta knew you were going to that dance, Uncle," Annie remarked then.

"It was because of the cold," Petrus Lemmer said shortly. "It was a cold night, just like it is tonight. I wore a new shirt with stripes and I rubbed sheep-fat on my veldskoens, to make them shine. At first I thought it was rather foolish, my taking all this trouble over my appearance, for the sake of a girl whom I had seen only a couple of times. But when I got to the farmhouse at Abjaterskop, where the dance was, and I saw Grieta in the voorkamer, I no longer thought it was foolish of me to get all dressed up like that."

Petrus Lemmer fell silent for a few moments, as though waiting for one of us to say what an interesting story it was, and would he tell us what happened next. But none of us said anything. So Petrus just coughed and went on with his story without being asked. That was the sort of man Petrus Lemmer was.

"I saw Grieta in the voorkamer," Petrus Lemmer repeated, "and she had on a pink frock. She was very pretty. Even now, after all these years, when I look back on it, I can still picture to myself how pretty she was. For a long time I stood at the far end of the room and just watched her. Another young man was wasting her time, talking to her. Afterwards he wasted still more of her time by dancing with her. If it wasn't that I knew that I was the only one in that voorkamer that Grieta cared for, I would have got jealous of the way in which that young fellow carried on. And he kept getting more and more foolish. But afterwards I got tired of standing up against that wall and watching Grieta from a distance. So I sat down on a chair, next to the two men with the guitar and the concertina. For some time I sat and watched Grieta from the chair. By then that fellow was actually wasting her time to the extent of tickling her under the chin with a piece of grass."

Petrus Lemmer stopped talking again, and we listened to the bumping of the mule-cart and the wind in the thorn-trees. The moon was large and full above the Dwarsberge.

"But how did you know that this girl liked you, Oom Petrus?" Dirk Prinsloo asked. It seemed as though the young school-teacher was getting interested in the story.

"Oh, I just knew," Petrus Lemmer replied. "She never said anything to me about it, but with these things you can always tell."

"Yes, I expect you can," Annie said softly, in a faraway sort of voice. And she asked Petrus Lemmer to tell us what happened next.

"It was just like I said it was," Petrus Lemmer continued. "And shortly afterwards Grieta left that foolish young man, with his piece of grass and all, and came past the chair where I was sitting, next to the musicians. She walked past me quickly, and what she said wasn't much above a whisper. But I heard all right. And I didn't even bother to look up and see whether that other fellow had observed anything. I felt so superior to him, at that moment."

Once again Petrus Lemmer paused. But it was obvious that Annie wanted him to get to the end of the story quickly.

"Then did you go and meet Grieta, Oom Petrus?" she asked.

"Oh, yes," Petrus answered. "I was there at the time she said."

"By the third withaak?" Annie asked again. "Under the moon?"

"By the third withaak," Petrus Lemmer replied. "Under the moon."

I wondered how Annie knew all that. In some ways there seemed little that a woman didn't know.

"There's not much more to tell," Petrus Lemmer said. "And I could never understand how it happened, either. It was just that, when I met Grieta there, under the thorn-tree, it suddenly seemed that there was nothing I wanted to say to her. And I could see that she felt the same way about it. She seemed just an ordinary woman, like lots of other women. And I felt rather foolish, standing there beside her, wearing a new striped shirt, and with sheep-fat on my veldskoens. And I knew just how she felt, also. At first I tried to pretend to myself that it was the fault of the moon. Then I blamed that fellow with the piece of grass. But I knew all the time that it was nobody's fault. It just happened like that.

"As I have said," Petrus Lemmer concluded sombrely, "I don't know how it came about. And I don't think Grieta knew, either.

We stood there wondering – each of us – what it was that had been, a little while before, so attractive about the other. But whatever it was, it had gone. And we both knew that it had gone for good. Then I said that it was getting cold. And Grieta said that perhaps we had better go inside. So we went back to the voorkamer. It seemed an awfully quiet party, and I didn't stay much longer. And I remember how, on my way home, I looked at the moon under which Grieta and I had stood by the thorn-tree. I watched the moon until it went down behind the Dwarsberge."

Petrus Lemmer finished his story, and none of us spoke.

Some distance further on we arrived at the place where Dirk Prinsloo stayed. Dirk got off the mule-cart and said good night. Then he turned to Annie.

"It's funny," he said, "this story of your uncle's. It's queer how things like that happen."

"He's not my uncle," Annie replied. "He's only my stepmother's brother. And I never listen to his stories, anyway."

So we drove on again, the three of us, down the road, through the thorn-trees, with the night wind blowing into our faces. And a little later, when the moon was going down behind the Dwarsberge, it sounded to me as though Annie was crying.

Splendours from Ramoutsa

No – Oom Schalk Lourens said – no, I don't know why it is that people always ask me to tell them stories. Even though they all know that I can tell better stories than anybody else. Much better. What I mean is, I wonder why people listen to stories. Of course, it is easy to understand why a man should ask me to tell him a story when there is drought in the Marico. Because then he can sit on the stoep and smoke his pipe and drink coffee, while I am talking, so that my story keeps him from having to go to the borehole, in the hot sun, to pump water for his cattle.

By the earnest manner in which the farmers of the Marico ask me for stories at certain periods, I am always able to tell that there is no breeze to drive the windmill, and the pump-handle is heavy, and the water is very far down. And at such times I have often observed the look of sorrow that comes into a man's eyes, when he knows that I am near the end of my story and that he will shortly have to reach for his hat.

And when I have finished the story he says, "Yes, Oom Schalk. That is the way of the world. Yes, that story is very deep."

But I know that all the time he is really thinking of how deep the water is in the borehole.

As I have said, it is when people have other reasons for asking me to tell them a story that I start wondering as I do now. When they ask me at those times when there is no ploughing to be done and there are no barbed-wire fences to be put up in the heat of the day. And I think that these reasons are deeper than any stories and deeper than the water in the boreholes when there is drought.

There was young Krisjan Geel, for instance. He once listened to a story. It was foolish of him to have listened, of course, especially as I hadn't told it to him. He had heard it from the Indian behind the counter of the shop in Ramoutsa. Krisjan Geel related this story

156

to me, and I told him straight out that I didn't think much of it. I said anybody could guess, right from the start, why the princess was sitting beside the well. Anybody could see that she hadn't come there just because she was thirsty. I also said that the story was too long, and that even if I was thinking of something else I would still have told it in such a way that people would have wanted to hear it to the end. I pointed out lots of other details like that.

Krisjan Geel said he had no doubt that I was right, but that the man who told him the story was only an Indian, after all, and that for an Indian, perhaps, it wasn't too bad. He also said that there were quite a number of customers in the place, and that made it more difficult for the Indian to tell the story properly, because he had to stand at such an awkward angle, all the time, weighing out things with his foot on the scale.

By his tone it sounded as though Krisjan Geel was quite sorry for the Indian.

So I spoke to him very firmly.

"The Indian in the store at Ramoutsa," I said, "has told me much better stories than that before today. He once told me that there were no burnt mealies mixed with the coffee-beans he sold me. Another one that was almost as good was when he said –"

"And to think that the princess went and waited by the well," Krisjan Geel interrupted me, "just because once she had seen the young man there."

"– Another good one," I insisted, "was when he said that there was no Kalahari sand in the sack of yellow sugar I bought from him."

"And she had only seen him once," Krisjan Geel went on, "and she was a princess."

"– And I had to give most of that sugar to the pigs," I said, "it didn't melt or sweeten the coffee. It just stayed like mud at the bottom of the cup."

"She waited by the well because she was in love with him," Krisjan Geel ended up, lamely.

"– I just mixed it in with the pigs' mealie-meal," I said, "they ate it very fast. It's funny how fast a pig eats."

Krisjan Geel didn't say any more after that one. No doubt he realised that I wasn't going to allow him to impress me with a story told by an Indian; and not very well told either. I could see what the Indian's idea was. Just because I had stopped buying from his shop after that unpleasantness about the coffee-beans and the sugar – which were only burnt mealies and Kalahari sand, as I explained to a number of my neighbours – he had hit on this uncalled-for way of paying me back. He was setting up as my rival. He was also going to tell stories.

And on account of the long start I had on him he was using all sorts of unfair methods. Like putting princesses in his stories. And palaces. And elephants that were all dressed up with yellow and red hangings and that were trained to trample on the king's enemies at the word of command. Whereas the only kind of elephants I could talk about were those that didn't wear red hangings or gold bangles and that didn't worry about whether or not you were the king's enemy: they just trampled on you first, anyhow, and without any sort of training either.

At first I felt it was very unfair of the Indian to come along with stories like that. I couldn't compete. And I began to think that there was much reason in what some of the speakers said at election meetings about the Indian problem.

But when I had thought it over carefully, I knew it didn't matter. The Indian could tell all the stories he wanted to about a princess riding around on an elephant. For there was one thing that I knew I could always do better than the Indian. Just in a few words, and without even talking about the princess, I would be able to let people know, subtly, what was in her heart. And this was more important than the palaces and the temples and the elephants with gold ornaments on their feet.

Perhaps the Indian realised the truth of what I am saying now. At all events, after a while he stopped wasting the time of his customers with stories of emperors. In between telling them that the price of sheep-dip and axle-grease had gone up. Or perhaps his customers got tired of listening to him.

But before that happened several of the farmers had hinted to me, in what they thought was a pleasantly amusing manner, that I would have to start putting more excitement into my stories if I wanted to keep in the fashion. They said I would have to bring in at least a king and a couple of princes, somehow, and also a string of elephants with Namaqualand diamonds in their ears.

158

I said they were talking very foolishly. I pointed out that there was no sense in my trying to tell people about kings and princes and trained elephants, and so on, when I didn't know anything about them or what they were supposed to do even.

"They don't need to do anything," Frik Snyman explained, "you can just mention that there was a procession like that nearby when whatever you are talking about happened. You can just mention them quickly, Oom Schalk, and you needn't say anything about them until you are in the middle of your next story. You can explain that the people in the procession had nothing to do with the story, because they were only passing through to some other place."

Of course, I said that that was nonsense. I said that if I had to keep on using that same procession over and over again, the people in it would be very travel-stained after they had passed through a number of stories. It would be a ragged and dust-laden procession.

"And the next time you tell us about a girl going to Nagmaal in Zeerust, Oom Schalk," Frik Snyman went on, "you can say that two men held up a red umbrella for her and that she had jewels in her hair, and she was doing a snake-dance."

I knew that Frik Snyman was only speaking like that, thoughtlessly, because of things he had seen in the bioscope that had gone to his head.

Nevertheless, I had to listen to many unreasonable remarks of this description before the Indian at Ramoutsa gave up trying to entertain his customers with empty discourse.

The days passed, and the drought came, and the farmers of the Marico put in much of their time at the boreholes, pushing the heavy pump-handles up and down. So that the Indian's brief period of story-telling was almost forgotten. Even Krisjan Geel came to admit that there was such a thing as overdoing these stories of magnificence.

"All these things he says about temples, and so on," Krisjan Geel said, "with white floors and shining red stones in them. And rajahs. Do you know what a rajah is, Oom Schalk? No, I don't know, either. You can have too much of that. It was only that one story of his that was any good. That one about the princess. She had rich stones in her hair, and pearls sewn on to her dress. And so the young man never guessed why she had come there. He didn't guess that she loved him. But perhaps I didn't tell you the story properly the first time, Oom Schalk. Perhaps I should just tell it to you again. I have already told it to many people."

But I declined his offer hurriedly. I replied that there was no need for him to go over all that again. I said that I remembered the story very well and that if it was all the same to him I should prefer not to hear it a second time. He might just spoil it in telling it again.

But it was only because he was young and inexperienced, I said, that he had allowed the Indian's story to carry him away like that. I told him about other young men whom I had known at various times, in the Marico, who had formed wrong judgments about things and who had afterwards come along and told me so.

"Why you are so interested in that story," I said, "is because you like to imagine yourself as that young man."

Krisjan Geel agreed with me that this was the reason why the Indian's story had appealed to him so much. And he went on to say that a young man had no chance, really, in the Marico. What with the droughts, and the cattle getting the miltsiek, and the mosquitoes buzzing around so that you couldn't sleep at night.

And when Krisjan Geel left me I could see, very clearly, how much he envied the young man in the Indian's story.

As I have said before, there are some strange things about stories and about people who listen to them. I thought so particularly on a hot afternoon, a few weeks later, when I saw Lettie Viljoen. The sun shone on her upturned face and on her bright yellow hair. She sat with one hand pressed in the dry grass of last summer, and I thought of what a graceful figure she was, and of how slender her wrists were.

And because Lettie Viljoen hadn't come there riding on an elephant with orange trappings and gold bangles, and because she wasn't wearing a string of red stones at her throat, Krisjan Geel knew, of course, that she wasn't a princess.

And I suppose that this was the reason why, during all the time in which he was talking to her, telling her that story about the princess at the well, Krisjan Geel never guessed about Lettie Viljoen, and what it was that had brought her there, in the heat of the sun, to the borehole.

160

BUSHVELD ROMANCE

It's a queer thing – Oom Schalk Lourens observed – how much trouble people will take to hide their weaknesses from the world. Often, of course, they aren't weaknesses at all; only the people who have these peculiarities don't know that. Another thing they don't know is that the world is aware all the time of these things that they imagine they are concealing. I remember a story my grandfather used to tell of something that happened when he was a boy.

Of course, that was a long time ago. It was before the Great Trek. But it seems that even in those days there was a lot of trouble between the Boers and English. It had a lot to do with slaves. The English Government wanted to free the slaves, my grandfather said, and one man who was very prominent at the meetings that were held to protest against this was Gert van Tonder.

Now, Gert van Tonder was a very able man and a good speaker; he was at his best, too, when dealing with a subject that he knew nothing at all about. He always spoke very loudly then. You can see that he was a fine leader. So, when the slaves were freed and a manifesto was drawn up to be sent to the King of England, the farmers of Graaff-Reinet took it first to Gert van Tonder for his signature.

You can imagine how surprised everybody was when he refused to sign. They didn't know until long afterwards that it was because he couldn't write. He sat with the manifesto in front of him, and the pen in his hand, and said that he had changed his mind. He said that perhaps they were a bit hasty in writing to the King of England about so trivial a matter.

"Even though the slaves are free, now," he said, "it doesn't make a difference. Just let one of my slaves try to act as though he's a free slave, and I'll show him. That's all, just let him try."

The farmers told Gert van Tonder that he was quite right. It didn't really make any difference whether the slaves were free or whether they weren't. But they said that they knew that already. There were a lot of other grievances on the manifesto, they explained, and they were sending it to let the King of England know that unless the Boers got their wrongs redressed they would trek out of the Cape Colony.

My grandfather used to say that everybody was still more surprised when Gert van Tonder put down the pen, very firmly, and told the farmers that they could trek right to the other end of Africa, for all he cared. He was quite satisfied with the way the King of England did things, Gert said, and there was a lot about English rule for which they had to be thankful. He said that when he was in Cape Town, some months back, at the Castle, he saw an English soldier leave his post to go and kick a coloured man; he said this gave him a respect for the English that he had never had before. He said that, for somebody who couldn't have been in the country very long, that soldier made an extraordinarily good job of assaulting a coloured person.

The upshot of it all was that, when the farmers of the Cape Colony trekked into the north, with their heavily laden wagons and their long spans of oxen and their guns, Gert van Tonder did not go with them. By that time he was saying that another thing they had to be thankful for was the British navy.

My grandfather often spoke about how small a thing it was that kept Gert van Tonder from being remembered in history as one of the leaders of the nation. And it was all just on account of that one weakness of his – of not wanting people to know that he couldn't read or write.

When I talk of people and their peculiarities it always makes me think of Stoffel Lemmer. He had a weakness that was altogether of a different sort. What was peculiar about Stoffel Lemmer was that if a girl or a woman so much as looked at him he was quite certain that she was in love with him. And what made it worse was that he never had the courage to go up and talk to the girl that he thought was making eyes at him.

Another queer thing about Stoffel Lemmer was that he was

just as much in love with the girl as he imagined she was with him. There was that time when that new school-teacher arrived from somewhere in the Cape. The school-teacher we had before that had to leave because he was soft in the head. He was always talking about co-operation between parent and teacher, and he used to encourage the parents to call round at the school building just so that everybody could feel friendly.

At first nobody accepted the invitation: the farmers of Drogevlei were diffident about it, and suspicious. But afterwards one or two of them went, and then more of them, until in the end things got very disgraceful. That was when some of the parents, including Piet Terblans, who had never been to school in his life, started fighting in the classroom over what they should tell the teacher he had to do. Piet Terblans said he had his own ideas about how children should be taught, and he couldn't do his work properly if the other parents kept on interrupting him. He used to drive in to school with the children every morning in the donkey-wagon and he took his lunch with him.

Then one day shortly after the inspector had called the teacher left. Because when the inspector walked into the classroom he found that the teacher wasn't there at all: he had been pulled out into the passage by several of the rougher parents, who were arguing with him about sums. Instead, when the inspector entered the place, two of the parents were busy drawing on the board with coloured chalk, and Piet Terblans was sitting at the desk, looking very solemn and pretending to write things in the register.

They all said that the teacher was quite well educated and gentlemanly, but soft.

So this time the Education Department sent us a woman schoolteacher. Stoffel Lemmer had been at the post office when she arrived. He told me, talking rapidly, that her name was Minnie Bonthuys, and that she had come up from the Cape, and that she had large dark eyes, and that she was in love with him.

"I was standing in the doorway," Stoffel Lemmer explained, "and so it wasn't easy for her to get into the voorkamer. As you know, it is only a small door. She stopped and looked at me without speaking. It was almost as though she looked right through me. She looked me up and down, from my head to my feet, I

163

might say. And then she held her chin up very high. And for that reason I knew that she was in love with me. Every girl that's in love with me looks at me like that. Then she went into the voorkamer sideways, because I was standing in the door; and as she passed she drew her skirts close about her. I expect she was afraid that some of the dust she had on her frock from the motor-lorry might shake off on to my khaki trousers. She was very polite. And the first thing she said when she got inside was that she had heard, in Zeerust, that the Groot Marico is a very good district for pigs."

Stoffel Lemmer went on to say that Piet Terblans, who, out of habit, had again brought his lunch with him, was also there. He said that just before then Piet Terblans had been very busy explaining to the others that he was going to co-operate even more with the new school-teacher than he had done with the last one.

Nevertheless, when the new school-teacher walked into the post office – Stoffel Lemmer said – Piet Terblans didn't mention anything to her about his ideas on education. Stoffel Lemmer said he didn't know why. It appears that Piet Terblans got as far as clearing his throat several times, as though preparing to introduce himself and his plan to Minnie Bonthuys. But after that he gave it up and ate his lunch instead.

Later on, when I saw the new school-teacher, I was able to understand quite easily why Stoffel Lemmer had fallen in love with her. I could also understand why Piet Terblans didn't manage to interest her very much in the co-operation scheme that had ended up with the previous teacher having to leave the Bushveld. There was no doubt about Minnie Bonthuys being very good-looking, with a lot of black hair that was done up in ringlets. But she had a determined mouth. And in her big dark eyes there was an expression whose meaning was perfectly clear to me. I could see that Minnie Bonthuys knew her own mind and that she was very sure of herself.

As the days passed, Stoffel Lemmer's infatuation for the young school-teacher increased, and he came and spoke to me about it, as was his custom whenever he fancied himself in love with a girl. So I didn't take much notice of the things he said. I had heard them all so often before.

"I saw her again this morning, Oom Schalk," he said to me on one occasion. "I was passing the schoolroom and I was saying her name over to myself, softly. I know I'll never have the courage to go up to her and tell her how I – how I think about her. It's always like that with me, Oom Schalk. I can never bring myself to the point of telling a girl that I love her. Or even saying anything at all to her. I get too frightened somehow. But I saw her this morning, Oom Schalk. I went and leant over the barbed-wire fence, and I saw her standing in front of the window looking out. I saw her quite a while before she saw me, so that by the time she turned her gaze towards me I was leaning more than halfway over the barbed-wire fence."

Stoffel Lemmer shook his head sadly.

"And I could see by that look in her eyes that she loved me, Oom Schalk," he went on, "and by the firm way that her mouth

165

shut when she caught sight of me. In fact, I can hardly even say that she looked at me. It all happened so quickly. She just gave one glance in my direction and then slammed down the window. All girls who are in love with me do just that."

For some moments Stoffel Lemmer remained silent. He seemed to be thinking.

"I would have gone on standing there, Oom Schalk," he ended up in a faraway sort of voice. "Only I couldn't see her anymore, because of the way that the sun was shining on the window-panes. And I only noticed afterwards how much of the barbed wire had been sticking into me."

This is just one example of the sort of thing that Stoffel Lemmer would relate to me, sitting on my stoep. Mostly it was in the evening. And he would look out into the dusk and say that the shadows that lay on the thorn-trees were in his heart also. As I have told you, I had so frequently heard him say exactly the same thing. About other girls.

And always he would end up in the same way – saying what a sorrowful thing it was that he would never be able to tell her how much he loved her. He also said how grateful he was to have somebody who could listen to his sad story with understanding. That one, too, I had heard before. Often.

What's that? Did he ever tell her? Well, I don't know. The last time I saw Stoffel Lemmer was in Zeerust. It was in front of the church, after the ceremony. And by the determined expression that Minnie still had on her face when the wedding guests threw rice and confetti over Stoffel and herself – no, I don't think he ever got up the courage to tell her.

DREAM BY THE BLUEGUMS

In the heat of the midday – Oom Schalk Lourens said – Adriaan Naudé and I were glad to be resting there, shaded by the tall bluegums that stood in a clump by the side of the road.

I sat on the grass, with my head and shoulders supported against a large stone. Adriaan Naudé, who had begun by leaning against a tree-trunk with his legs crossed and his fingers inter-laced behind his head and his elbows out, lowered himself to the ground by degrees; for a short while he remained seated on his haunches; then he sighed and slid forward, very carefully, until he was lying stretched out at full length, with his face in the grass.

And all this while Adriaan Naudé was murmuring about how lazy kaffirs are, and about the fact that the kaffir Jonas should already have returned with the mule-cart, and about how, if you wanted a job done properly, you had to do it yourself. I agreed with Adriaan Naudé that Jonas had been away rather long with the mule-cart; he ought to be back quite soon, now, I said.

"The curse of the Transvaal," Adriaan Naudé explained, stretching himself out further along the grass, and yawning, "the curse of the Transvaal is the indolence of the kaffirs."

"Yes, Neef Adriaan," I replied. "You are quite correct. It would perhaps have been better if one of us had gone along in the mule-cart with Jonas."

"It's not so bad for you, Neef Schalk," Adriaan Naudé went on, yawning again. "You have got a big comfortable stone to rest your head and shoulders against. Whereas I have got to lie flat down on the dry grass with all the sharp points sticking into me. You are always like that, Neef Schalk. You always pick the best for yourself."

By the unreasonable nature of his remarks I could tell that Adriaan Naudé was being overtaken by a spell of drowsiness.

"You are always like that," Adriaan went on. "It's one of the low traits of your character. Always picking the best for yourself. There was that time in Zeerust, for instance. People always mention that – when they want to talk about how low a man can be . . ."

I could see that the heat of the day and his condition of being half-asleep might lead Adriaan Naudé to say things that he would no doubt be sorry for afterwards. So I interrupted him, speaking very earnestly for his own good.

"It's quite true, Neef Adriaan," I said, "that this stone against which I am lying is the only one in the vicinity. But I can't help that any more than I can help this clump of bluegums being here. It's funny about these bluegums, now, growing like this by the side of the road, when the rest of the veld around here is bare. I wonder who planted them. As for this stone, Neef Adriaan, it is not my fault that I saw it first. It was just luck. But you can knock out your pipe against it whenever you want to."

This offer seemed to satisfy Adriaan. At all events, he didn't pursue the argument. I noticed that his breathing had become very slow and deep and regular; and the last remark that he made was so muffled as to be almost unintelligible. It was: "To think that a white man can fall so low."

From that I judged that Adriaan Naudé was dreaming about something.

It was very pleasant, there, on the yellow grass, by the roadside, underneath the bluegums, whose shadows slowly lengthened as midday passed into afternoon. Nowhere was there sound or movement. The whole world was at rest, with the silence of the dust on the deserted road, with the peace of the bluegums' shadows. My companion's measured breathing seemed to come from very far away.

Then it was that a strange thing happened.

What is in the first place remarkable about the circumstance that I am now going to relate to you is that it shows you clearly how short a dream is. And how much you can dream in just a few moments. In the second place, as you'll see when I get to the end of it, this story proves how right in broad daylight a queer thing can take place – almost in front of your eyes, as it were – and you may wonder about it for ever afterwards, and you will never understand it.

Well, as I was saying, what with Adriaan Naudé lying asleep within a few feet of me, and everything being so still, I was on the point of also dropping off to sleep, when, in the distance – so small that I could barely distinguish its outlines – I caught sight of the mule-cart whose return Adriaan and I were awaiting. From where I lay, with my head on the stone, I had a clear view of the road all the way up to where it disappeared over the bult.

For a while I lay watching the approach of the mule-cart. As I have said, it was still very far away. But gradually it drew nearer and I made out more of the details. The dark forms of the mules. The shadowy figure of Jonas, the driver.

But as I gazed I felt my eyelids getting heavy. I told myself that with the glare of the sun on the road I would not be able to keep my eyes open much longer. I remember thinking how foolish it would be to fall asleep, then, with the mule-cart only a short distance away. It would pull up almost immediately, and I would have to wake up again. I told myself I was being foolish – and, of course, I fell asleep.

It was while I was still telling myself that in a few moments the mule-cart would be coming to a stop in the shadow of the bluegums that my eyes closed and I fell asleep. And I started to dream. And from this you can tell how swift a thing a dream is, and how much you can dream in a few moments.

For I know the exact moment in which I started to dream. It was when I was looking very intently at the driver of the mule-cart and I suddenly saw, to my amazement, that the driver was no longer Jonas, the kaffir, but Adriaan Naudé. And seated beside Adriaan Naudé was a girl in a white frock. She had yellow hair that hung far down over her shoulders and her name was Francina. The next minute the mule-cart drew up and Jonas jumped off and tied the reins to a wheel.

So it was in between those flying moments that I dreamt about Adriaan Naudé and Francina.

"It is difficult to believe, Francina," Adriaan Naudé was saying, nodding his head in my direction, "it is difficult to believe that a white man can sink so low. If I tell you what happened in Zeerust –"

I was getting annoyed, now. After all, Francina was a complete stranger, and Adriaan had no right to slander me in that fashion. What was more, I had a very simple explanation of the Zeerust incident. I felt that if only I could be alone with Francina for a few minutes I would be able to convince her that what had happened in Zeerust was not to my discredit at all.

Furthermore, I would be able to tell her one or two things about Adriaan; things of so unfortunate a character that even if she believed about the Zeerust affair it would not matter much. Because, compared with Adriaan Naudé, the most inferior kind of man would still look as noble and heroic as Wolraad Woltemade that you read about in the school books.

But even as I started to talk to Francina I realised that there was no need for me to say anything. She put her hand on my arm and looked at me; and the sun was on her hair and the shadows of the bluegums were in her eyes; and by the way she smiled at me I knew that nothing Adriaan could say about me would ever make any difference to her.

Moreover, Adriaan Naudé had gone. You know how it is in a dream. He had completely disappeared, leaving Francina and me alone by the roadside. And I knew that Adriaan Naudé would not trouble us any more. All he had come there for was to bring Francina along to me. Yet I regretted his departure, somehow. It seemed too easy, almost. There were a couple of things about Adriaan Naudé that I felt Francina really ought to know.

Then it all changed, suddenly. I seemed to know that it was only a dream and that I wasn't really standing up under the trees with Francina. I seemed to know that I was actually resting on the grass, with my head and shoulders resting against a stone. I even heard the mule-cart jolting over the rough part of the road.

But in the next instant I was dreaming again.

I dreamt that Francina was explaining to me, in gentle and sorrowful tones, that she couldn't stay any longer; and that she had put her hand on my arm for the last time, in farewell; she said I was not to follow her, but that I had to close my eyes when she turned away; for no one was to know where she had come from.

While she was saying these things my eyes lighted on her frock, which was brilliant in the sunshine. But it seemed an old-fashioned sort of frock; the kind that was worn many years before. Then, in the same moment, I saw her face, and it seemed to me that her smile was old-fashioned, somehow. It was a sweet smile, and her face, turned upwards, was strangely beautiful; but I felt in some queer way that women had smiled like that very long ago.

It was a vivid dream. Part of it seemed more real than life; as is frequently the case with a dream on the veld, fleetingly, in the heat of the noonday.

I asked Francina where she lived.

"Not far from here," she answered, "no, not far. But you may not follow me. None may go back with me."

She still smiled, in that way in which women smiled long ago; but as she spoke there came into her eyes a look of such intense sorrow that I was afraid to ask why I could not accompany her. And when she told me to close my eyes I had no power to protest.

And, of course, I didn't close my eyes. Instead, I opened them. Just as Jonas was jumping down from the mule-cart to fasten the reins on to a wheel.

Adriaan Naudé woke up about the same time that I did, and asked Jonas why he had been away so long, and spoke more about the indolence of the kaffirs. And I got up from the grass and stretched my limbs and wondered about dreams. It seemed in-credible that I could have dreamt so much in such a few moments.

And there was a strange sadness in my heart because the dream had gone. My mind was filled with a deep sense of loss. I told myself that it was foolish to have feelings like that about a dream: even though it was a particularly vivid dream, and part of it seemed more real than life.

Then, when we were ready to go, Adriaan Naudé took out his pipe; before filling it he stooped down as though to knock the ash out of it, as I had invited him to do before we fell asleep. But it so happened that Adriaan Naudé did not ever knock his pipe out against that stone.

"That's funny," I heard Adriaan say as he bent forward.

I saw what he was about; so I knelt down and helped him. When we had cleared away the accumulation of yellow grass and dead leaves at the foot of the stone we found that the inscription on it, though battered, was quite legible. It was very simply word-ed. Just a date chiselled on to the stone. And below the date a name: Francina Malherbe.

ON TO FREEDOM

How we could tell that Gawie Prinsloo had been changed by his experiences on the diggings – Oom Schalk Lourens said – was when he came back from the diamond fields wearing a tie.

It was sad to see a young man altered so much by a few months of pick and shovel work on a claim. We came to the conclusion, however, that it wasn't the time he had spent on his claim with the pick and shovel that had changed Gawie Prinsloo: he must have got changed like that during those periods in which he didn't have a shovel in his hand, and the sweat wasn't dripping off him, and when he wasn't on his claim, even.

And judging by the way he had altered, it would seem that during much of Gawie Prinsloo's stay on the diggings he was not on the claim.

Of course, it was not a new thing in the Bushveld for a young man to go to the diggings, fresh and unspoilt and God-fearing, and to come back different. Often at the Nagmaal the predikant would utter warnings about the dangers of the diamond fields; he would speak in solemn tones about what he called the false glitter of the alluvial diggings, and about the vanity of its carnal shows and sinful worldly riches. But it is just the unfortunate way of the world that many young men, who in the ordinary course would never have thought of leaving the Marico, packed up and went to the diggings after they heard about some of the things the predikant said: about the wild sort of life that was led there, and about the evils of suddenly acquired wealth.

The predikant was on occasion very outspoken in dealing with the shameful things that took place on the diggings, and it was noticeable that at such times certain members of his congregation would shuffle their feet and get restless at his language. And only afterwards the predikant would discover that the reason they were restless was because they wanted to be off to the diggings.

I can still remember a remark that Wynand Oosthuizen once made in regard to this matter. It was when we were preparing to leave Zeerust after the Nagmaal.

"As you all know," Wynand Oosthuizen said, "my farm is situated right up against the Limpopo, and I live there alone. Consequently, I have much time in which to think. And I have thought about this question of the predikant and the young men and the diamond diggings. Yes, I have given it much thought. And I perceive that there is only one way in which the predikant will be able to get people to stay away from the diamond fields: he must say that the diamond fields are a lot like heaven."

We looked at Wynand Oosthuizen, wondering. It seemed to do queer things to a man, living alone like that beside the Limpopo.

Because we made no answer, Wynand Oosthuizen thought, apparently, that we hadn't understood what he was saying.

"You see," he went on, "after every Nagmaal I have observed that there is a big rush to the diamond diggings. That is because the predikant talks so much about the wickedness of the life on the diggings; how the diamond fields are like Babylon, and how vice and evil flourish there, and how people make money there and then forget all about their duty to the church. Now, if the predikant were to say that the diggings are exactly like the Kingdom of Heaven, nobody would want to go. No, nobody at all."

Wynand Oosthuizen winked, then, and set his hat at a slant and strode across to his ox-wagon. In silence, shaking our heads, we watched him getting ready to trek back to the Limpopo.

To do some more thinking, no doubt.

Then there was this matter of Gawie Prinsloo. As I have said, he was more changed than any other man that I had ever seen come back from the diggings. And I had seen many of them come back. Some came back with money that they didn't quite know what to do with: there seemed so much of it. Others came back penniless. One man whom I knew very well was reduced to selling his wagon and oxen on the diggings; and he returned to the Marico on foot, singing.

But Gawie Prinsloo was the only man who had ever come back

from the diggings wearing a tie. What was more, it was a red tie; and Gawie Prinsloo said that he was wearing it for a political reason.

It was some time before I realised what Gawie Prinsloo meant by this. Then I proceeded to tell him about politics in the old days. Things were much better then, I said, and much simpler. Politics was concerned only with the question as to which man was going to be president.

"And if the wrong man got elected," I said to Gawie, very pointedly, "you merely inspanned and trekked out of the country. You didn't put on a red tie and walk about talking the sort of thing that you are talking now."

Gawie thought that over for a little while. Then he said that it was cowardly to inspan and trek away from a difficulty. He explained that the right thing to do was to face a problem and to find a solution to it. It was easy to see, he said, how this spirit of trekking away had produced a race of men with weak characters and unenlightened minds.

Naturally, I asked him what he meant by a statement like that. I told him that in the past I had on several occasions trekked out of both the Transvaal and the Free State because I disapproved of the presidents.

"Yes, Oom Schalk," Gawie said, "and look at you."

From that remark, thoughtlessly uttered on a summer afternoon, you can see how much the diggings had altered Gawie Prinsloo.

Afterwards we found out that there were other points about Gawie's new politics besides the wearing of a red tie. For instance, he held views about kaffirs that nobody in the Bushveld had ever heard of before. He spoke a great deal about freedom, and in between mentioning what a good thing freedom was he would mumble something to the effect that in the Marico the kaffirs weren't being treated right.

But, of course, it was quite a while before we discovered the extent to which Gawie Prinsloo's mind had been influenced by this kind of politics. He introduced us to it gradually, as though he was afraid of the shock it might give us if he acquainted us with all his opinions right away.

174

One day, however, in the home of Jasper Steyn, the ouderling, a number of farmers questioned Gawie Prinsloo closely on his beliefs, and you can imagine the sensation that was caused when he admitted that, in his view, a kaffir was just as good as a white man.

"Do you really mean to say," Jasper Steyn, the ouderling, asked, choosing his words very carefully, "that you can't see any important difference between a kaffir and a white man?"

"No," Gawie Prinsloo answered. "There is only a difference of colour, and that doesn't count."

Several of us burst out laughing at that; the ouderling rocked in his chair from side to side; you could hear him laughing right across in the next district, almost.

"Would you say," the ouderling went on, wiping the tears out of his eyes, "would you say that there was no difference between me and a kaffir? Would you say, for instance, that I am just a white kaffir?"

"Yes," Gawie Prinsloo responded, promptly, "but that's what I thought about you even before I went to the diggings."

Subsequently, others took up the task of questioning Gawie Prinsloo. After he had got over his first sort of diffidence, however, there was no stopping him; he embarked on a long speech about justice and human rights and liberty; and what he kept on stressing all the time was what he called the wrongs to the kaffirs.

It was easy to see that Gawie Prinsloo had been associating with a very questionable type of person on the diggings.

And because we knew that it was the diamond diggings that had led him astray we extended a great deal of tolerance towards his unusual utterances. We treated him as somebody who was not altogether responsible for what he said. In this way it became quite a fashionable pastime in the Marico for people to listen to Gawie Prinsloo talk. And he would talk by the hour about the way the kaffirs were being oppressed.

"Look, Gawie," I said to him once. "Why do you tell only the white people about the injustice that is being inflicted on the kaffirs? Why don't you go and tell the kaffirs about what is being done to them?"

Gawie told me that he had already done so.

"I have gone among the kaffirs," he said, "and I have told them about their wrongs."

But he admitted that his talks didn't seem to do much good, somehow; because the kaffirs just went on smoking dagga – inhaling it through water, he said.

"And when I have told them about their wrongs and about freedom they have laughed," Gawie explained, looking very puzzled. "Loudly."

So the months passed, and Gawie Prinsloo's red tie got crinkled and faded-looking, and when Nagmaal came round again he was still in exactly the same position in regard to his politics; he still spoke fervently about justice for the kaffirs, and he had not yet brought anybody round to his way of thinking. Moreover, he was no longer considered to be amusing. People began to remark that it was annoying to have to listen to his saying the same thing over and over again; they also hinted that it was about time he left the Bushveld.

It was then that Wynand Oosthuizen, once more coming to Zeerust for the Nagmaal, encountered Gawie Prinsloo and his faded red tie and his politics. Several of us were present at this meeting. By this time Gawie Prinsloo was slightly desperate with his message. He had grown so used to people not taking him seriously anymore that he had given up reasoning with them in a calm way. So it was in a markedly aggressive manner that he approached Wynand Oosthuizen.

"The kaffirs," Gawie Prinsloo called out to Wynand, "the kaffirs aren't getting justice in the Marico. And a kaffir is just as good as you are."

Gawie Prinsloo started to walk away, then; but Wynand Oosthuizen pulled him back – by his neck tie.

"Say that again," Wynand demanded.

Nothing if not fearless, Gawie repeated what he had said, and a lot more besides.

Contrary to what we had expected, Wynand Oosthuizen did not get annoyed. Nor did he laugh. Instead, he pushed back his hat and looked intently at the young man with the washed-out red tie.

"This is something new," he said slowly. "I haven't heard that point of view before. And I can't tell whether you are right or wrong. But I have got an idea. My farm is in the far north, on the Limpopo, and I live there alone. I do a lot of thinking there. You come and stay with me until the next Nagmaal, and we will think this question out together."

We were accustomed to Wynand Oosthuizen acting, on occasion, in a singular fashion; it was well known that the loneliness of his life by the Limpopo made his outlook different from that of most people. So we were not surprised at the nature of the invitation that he extended to Gawie Prinsloo. Nor were we surprised at Gawie Prinsloo's acceptance. For that matter, Gawie could not very well have done anything else: Wynand Oosthuizen was holding him so firmly by the tie.

"I will come with you," Gawie Prinsloo said, "but I know that I am right."

Thus it was that they met in Zeerust and arranged to travel together to the Limpopo, to study the new politics about freedom and about equal rights for the kaffirs – Wynand Oosthuizen, the lonely thinker, and Gawie Prinsloo, the young firebrand.

They agreed to meet again in church, at the Nagmaal, and to trek away as soon as possible after the service was over.

And I often wondered, subsequently, to what extent it was the predikant's sermon that had influenced two men who had planned to sojourn by the Limpopo and think of freedom. Because, in the morning, after the Nagmaal service, when Wynand Oosthuizen trekked away in his ox-wagon, Gawie Prinsloo was with him, and together they travelled the long and dusty road that led south, away from the thorn-trees of the Lowveld, to the diggings.

MARTHA AND THE SNAKE

Yes, Roderick Guise was his name.

I remember the time he first came to live on this side of the Dwarsberge. He came in a donkey-cart and in the back, along with a pile of blankets and things, he had a thick bundle of white paper. We found out at once that he was a man who wrote animal stories. It wasn't difficult for us to find this out, either. For that was the first thing he said to us when he stopped at Kris Lemmer's post office.

"I am Roderick Guise, kêrels," he said. "I am the man who writes the animal stories in the *Huisgenoot* and the *Boereweekblad* and so on. I suppose you have all heard of me."

I could see he was disappointed when we all said that we hadn't heard of him. One man, Martinus Snyman, nearly brought the whole of Drogevlei into disgrace in front of a stranger by thinking that animal stories were stories written by animals. He had seen a horse once in a circus at Zeerust adding up figures, and he thought that perhaps the Englishman had also trained animals to write stories.

Martinus Snyman was easily the most ignorant man I had ever come across.

But afterwards we felt more intimate with this Roderick Guise. By that I mean that we felt less contempt for him. That was after we had found out that Guise was perhaps the Johannesburg way of saying Gous. And at that time Koos Gous was in gaol for smuggling cattle over the Bechuanaland border. So we forgave Roderick Guise for a lot of his nonsense because he had the same name as the biggest cattle-smuggler in the Marico.

Later on, whenever he found two or three of us together, Roderick Guise would take a roll of papers out of his pocket and read us some of his stories. There was one story about a jackal and another one about a lion and quite a few about snakes – mostly rinkhalses and mambas.

What he wrote was all silly stuff. I mean, it might have been true enough for animals that you read about in other countries. Animals like polar bears and whales. But I know that any sensible South African animals would laugh at the nonsense Roderick Guise wrote about what he called Wild Life.

For instance, Guise wrote one story about a leopard chasing him for half a mile across the veld. Now, you know as well as I do that no leopard has ever yet chased a white man, except for fun. And I am sure that particular leopard only chased Roderick so that he could have a story written about him. We, who understand animals, know how vain they can be in that way. And it is just little things like this that people who write about Wild Life will never believe.

But I am sorry that that leopard chased Roderick Guise for only half a mile. While he felt in that playful mood, he should have chased him right out of the Marico District.

One day, when we were sitting in Kris Lemmer's dining room, waiting for the post-cart to bring the letters, a little kaffir-boy came running into the house, shouting that there was a mamba in the Government Road. Lemmer laughed and said that it must be a mamba that had got loose out of one of Roderick Guise's stories.

But we went to have a look.

It was a mamba, all right. When we got into the road we were just in time to see that last few feet of the snake's tail disappearing in the yellow grass.

Kris said that the mamba had come from the direction of the kraal. He suspected that this snake was in the habit of milking one of his cows. Of course, we all know that certain snakes have the habit of getting friendly with a cow and draining her milk. So we told him that was the best way of lying in wait for the snake. Then the post-cart came and we forgot all about it.

Only, I am mentioning this thing about the snake now, because of what happened afterwards. You'll see then that this is a strange story. People who don't know the Marico won't believe this, I suppose. But then, they don't matter. There are always persons like Roderick Guise who tell them lies that they can believe. But I have told you that this is a strange story.

When the predikant came here some years ago, and the ouderling took him aside and told him the whole thing on behalf of the Dwarsberg congregation – for we all decided that it wasn't right for the predikant to hold Nagmaal unless he knew everything – then the predikant turned very pale and trembled a little, and said that the Evil Spirit knows what to make of it.

What we did know was that when he got on to the post-cart, Roderick Guise, the man who wrote animal stories and the man who had vaunted his powers in a cheap and silly way, was the most pitiful spectacle in the whole of the Marico District.

We were all pleased that the arrogance had been taken out of Roderick Guise, and in that way we felt grateful to Martha. By whatever means she had set about making Roderick look the poor creature he really was, she had succeeded remarkably well.

We remembered that in addition to her madness there was another ugly thing about Martha. And that was about the way her mother had died. We wondered how much there was about this that Roderick Guise knew. But, of course, it was useless trying to ask him. He was not in a fit state to talk about that or about anything else. I wonder if he has ever been able to talk again.

Afterwards the kaffirs told us that the Mad White Missus had had a baby. We were surprised about this, in a way. Somehow, from the stories that had grown up around Martha, it did not seem natural to think of her and a baby. In a way, that was about the most terrible thing we had heard about her, so far. You know what I mean. The thought of her baby actually seemed a lot more frightening than her madness, even. We felt that we really had to do something about this.

Then, one morning, a kaffir told us that the baby had died. He didn't know for sure what it had died of, but he believed it was from a snakebite. We all agreed that it was absurd to imagine that a snake would bite a baby that was only a few days old.

It was then that the veldkornet decided that we had to take action.

"This is where the law comes in," he said. "It doesn't matter what else Martha does. But if she has murdered her child the law must have its way."

We agreed with the veldkornet that it was his duty to go over to Martha's farm and make enquiries about the baby's death. But we also made it clear to him that we considered it was his duty to go alone. We could see what he hinted at. He meant that three or four of us should volunteer to go with him. But if he was veldkornet, he should also carry out the duties that went with it, and not drag other people into his affairs.

"If you won't come with me willingly," the veldkornet said, "I shall have to commandeer you."

Accordingly he commandeered four men to go with him. We cleaned and loaded our rifles and early the next morning the five of us set off on horseback. I am sure I never felt more uncomfortable in all my life than I did that morning. And I have been right through the Boer War and I fought with De Wet at Sanna's Post. Yet all those things seemed like nothing at all compared with the heavy feeling I had in my stomach that morning when the five of us were riding down the road together.

By their silence and the expressions on their faces, I could see that my companions felt the same.

Anyway, I'll say no more about this part of the affair, except that we rode twice round the farmyard before going in and we could have gone round a third time if the veldkornet didn't slip off his horse sideways, so that he had to dismount completely to save face. Of course, he said afterwards that he had intended getting off there, anyway, and he had just slipped like that on purpose to dismount more quickly.

Piet Steyn gasped at what we saw then. On the table by the side of the house, in the shade of a big camel-thorn tree, lay the body of a naked baby. I remember the queer, frightened way in which all five of us took off our hats. It must have looked strange to a stranger passing by then to see five armed burghers standing hat in hand and afraid to talk in front of a madwoman's dead baby.

But, of course, nobody could tell from its looks that the mother was mad. It looked just like an ordinary baby, and rather pretty, I thought. And there was no doubt as to how it had died. We had all seen the effects of a mamba's bite and we knew.

The veldkornet whispered to us to return. And we were on the point of going back as noiselessly as we had come, when a queer kind of curiosity made us look through the window. It was what

we saw then that made the predikant pray fervently when we told him about it.

What we saw then made us understand a great deal more about what the Bible says of Evil and Sin.

On the bed in front of the window the madwoman Martha was lying. She was awake. Her eyes stared at the ceiling. A long brown mamba lay on her bosom. In what looked like a sweet and soft and very tender way, Martha's hand stroked the head of the snake.

Back Home

The South African Opinion (new series)
(1944–46)

Concertinas and Confetti

Hendrik Uys and I were boys together (Oom Schalk Lourens said). At school we were also classmates. That is, if you can call it being classmates, seeing that our relationship was that we sat together at the same desk, and that Hendrik Uys, who was three years older than I, used to sit almost on top of me so as to make it easier for him to copy off me. And whenever I got an answer wrong Hendrik Uys used to get very annoyed, because it meant that he also got caned for doing bad work, and after we got caned he always used to kick me after we got outside the school.

"This will teach you to pay attention to the teacher when he is talking," Hendrik Uys used to say to me when we were on our way home. "You ought to be ashamed of yourself, when your father is making all these sacrifices to keep you at school. You got two sums wrong, and you made three mistakes in spelling to-day." And after that he would start kicking me.

And the strange thing is that what he said really made me feel sad, and I felt that in making mistakes in spelling and sums I was throwing away my opportunities; and when he spoke about my father's sacrifices to give me an education I felt that Hendrik Uys was a good son who had fine feelings towards his parents; and it never occurred to me at the time that in not doing any work of his own, but just copying down everything I wrote – that in that respect Hendrik Uys was a lot more ungrateful than I was. In fact, it was only years later that it struck me that in carrying on in the way he was Hendrik Uys was displaying a most unpraiseworthy kind of contempt for his own parents' sacrifices.

And because he spoke so touchingly about my father I had a deep respect for Hendrik Uys. There were no limits to my admiration for him.

Yet afterwards, when I grew up, I found that real life amongst grown-up people was not so very different from what went on in that little schoolroom with the whitewashed walls, and the wooden step that had been worn hollow by the passage of hundreds of little feet – including the somewhat larger veldskoened feet of Hendrik Uys. And the delicate green of the rosyntjie bush that grew just to the side of the school building, within convenient reach of the penknife of the Hollander schoolmaster, who went out and cut a number of thick but supple canes every morning just after the Bible lesson, before the more strenuous work of the day started.

And I remember how always, after we had been caned for getting wrong answers, Hendrik Uys would walk down the road with me, rubbing the places where the rosyntjie-bush cane had fallen, and calling the schoolmaster a useless, fat-faced, squint-eyed Hollander. But shortly afterwards he would turn on me and upbraid me, and he would say he could not understand how I could have the heart, through my slothfulness, to bring such sorrow to the grey hairs of a poor schoolmaster who already had one foot in the grave.

And as if to emphasise this last statement about its being the schoolmaster's foot that was in the grave, Hendrik Uys would proceed, with each foot alternately, to kick me.

Yes, I suppose you could say that Hendrik was a school-friend of mine.

And once when my father asked him how we got on in school, Hendrik said that it was all right. Only there was rather a lot of copying going on. And he looked meaningly in my direction. Hendrik Uys was so convincing that it was impossible for me to try and tell my father the truth. Instead, I just kept silent and felt very much ashamed of myself. I suppose it is because of what the term 'school-friend' implies that I am glad that our schooling did not last very long in those days.

If he had continued in that way after he had grown up, and had applied to practical life the knowledge of the world which he had acquired in the classroom, there is no doubt that Hendrik Uys would have gone far. I feel sure that he would at least have got elected to the Volksraad.

But when he was a young man something happened to Hendrik Uys that changed him completely. He fell in love with Marie Snyman, and his whole life became different.

I don't think I have ever witnessed so amazing a change in any person as what came over Hendrik Uys in his late twenties when he first discovered that he was in love with Marie Snyman, a dark-haired girl with a low, soft voice and quiet eyes that never seemed to look at you, but that appeared to gaze inwards, always, as though she was looking at frail things. There was a disturbing sort of wisdom in her eyes, shadowy, something like the knowledge that the past has of a future that is made of dust.

"I can't understand how I could have been such a fool," Hendrik Uys said to us one day while we were drinking coffee in the dining room of the new post office. "To think that Marie Snyman was at school with me, and that I never saw her, even, if you know what I mean. She seemed just an ordinary girl to me, with thin legs and her hair in plaits. And she has been living here, in these parts, all these years, and it is only now that I have found her. I wasted all these years when the one woman in my life has been living here, right amongst us, all the time. It seems so foolish, I feel like kicking myself."

When Hendrik Uys spoke those last words about kicking, I moved uneasily on my chair for a moment. Although my schooldays were far in the past, there were still certain painful memories that lingered.

"But I must have been in love with her even then, without knowing it," Hendrik Uys went on, "otherwise I wouldn't have remembered her plaits. Ordinary-looking plaits they seemed, too. Stringy."

"The post-cart with the letters is late," Theunis Bekker said, yawning.

"And her thin legs," Hendrik Uys continued.

"Perhaps the post-cart had trouble getting through the Groen River," Adriaan Schoeman said. "I hear it has been raining in Zeerust."

"Maybe love is like that," Hendrik Uys went on. "It's there a long time, but you don't always know it."

"The post-cart may be stuck in the mud," Theunis Bekker said, yawning again. "The turf beyond Sephton's Nek is all thick, slimy mud when it rains."

"But her eyes weren't like that then, when she was at school," Hendrik Uys finished up lamely. "You know what her eyes are like – quiet, sort of."

His voice trailed off into silence.

And if a great change had come over Hendrik Uys when he fell in love with Marie Snyman, it was nothing compared with the way in which he changed after they were married. For up to that time Hendrik Uys had abundantly fulfilled the promise of his schooldays. He had been appointed a diaken of the Dutch Reformed Church and he was a prominent committee member of the Farmers' Association and the part he was playing in politics was already of such a character as to make more than one person regard him as a prospective candidate for the Volksraad in a few years' time.

And then, I suppose, like every other Volksraad member, he would pay a visit to his old school some day, and he would talk to the teacher and the children and he would tell them that in that same classroom, where the teacher had been a kindly old Hollander, long since dead, the foundation of his public career had been laid. And that he had got into the Volksraad simply through having applied the sound knowledge which he had acquired in the school.

Which would no doubt have been true enough.

But after he had fallen in love with Marie Snyman, Hendrik Uys changed altogether. For one thing, he resigned his position as diaken of the Dutch Reformed Church. This was a shock to everybody, because it was a very honoured position, and many envied him for having received the appointment at so early an age. Then, when he explained the reason for his resignation, the farmers in the neighbourhood were still more shocked.

What Hendrik Uys said was that since he had found Marie Snyman he had been so altered by the purity of her love for him that from now on he wanted to do only honest things. He wanted to be worthy of her love, he said.

"And I used unfair means to get the appointment as diaken," Hendrik Uys explained. "I got it through having induced the predikant to use his influence on my behalf. I had made the predikant a present of two trek-oxen just at that time, when it was uncertain whether the appointment would go to me or to Hans van Tonder."

They were married in the church in Zeerust, Hendrik Uys and Marie Snyman, and that part of the wedding made us feel very uncomfortable, for it was obvious by the sneer that the predikant wore on his face throughout the religious ceremony that he had certain secret reservations about how he thought the marriage was going to turn out. It was obvious that the predikant had been told the reason for Hendrik's resignation as diaken.

But the reception afterwards made up for a lot of the unhappier features of the church ceremony. The guests were seated at long tables in the grounds of the hotel, and when one of the waiters shouted "Aan die brand!" as a signal to the band leader, and the strains of the concertina and the guitars swept across our hearts, thrillingly, like a sudden wind through the grass, and the bride and bridegroom entered, the bride wearing a white satin dress with a long train, and there was confetti in Marie's hair and on Hendrik's shoulders – oh, well, it was all so very beautiful. And it seemed sad that life could not always be like that. It seemed a pity that life was not satisfied to let us always bear on our shoulders things only as light as confetti.

And as a kind of gesture to Hendrik, to let him sort of see that I was prepared to let schooldays be bygones, when the bride and bridegroom drove off on their honeymoon I was the one that flung the old veldskoen after them.

Afterwards, when I was inspanning to go back to the Bushveld, I saw the predikant. I was still thinking about life. By that time I was wondering why it was that we always had to carry in our hearts things that were so much heavier than concertina music borne on the wind. The predikant was talking to a number of Marico farmers grouped around him. And because that sneer was still on his face I could see that the predikant was talking about Hendrik Uys. So I walked nearer.

"He resigned as diaken because he said he bribed me with a couple of trek-oxen," I heard the predikant say. "I wonder what does he take me for? Does he think I am an Evangelist or an Apostolic pastor that I can be bribed with a couple of trek-oxen? And those beasts were as thin as crows. Man, they went for next to nothing on the Johannesburg market."

The men listening to the predikant nodded gravely.

This was the beginning of Hendrik Uys's unpopularity in the Marico Bushveld. It wasn't that Hendrik and Marie were avoided by people, or anything like that: it was just that it came to be recognised that the two of them seemed to prefer to live alone as much as possible. And, of course, there was nothing unfriendly about it all. Only, it seemed strange to me that as long as Hendrik Uys had been cunning and active in pushing his own interests, without being much concerned as to whether the means he employed were right or wrong, he appeared to be generally liked. But when he started becoming honest and over-scrupulous in his dealings with others, then it seemed that people did not have the same kind of affection for him.

I saw less and less of Hendrik and Marie as the years went by. They had a daughter whom they christened Annette. And after that they had no more children. Hendrik made one or two further attempts to get reappointed as a diaken. He also spoke vaguely of having political ambitions. But it was clear that his heart was no longer in public or social activities. And on those occasions on which I saw him he spoke mostly of his love for his wife, Marie.

And he spoke much of how the years had not changed their love. And he said that his greatest desire in life was that his daughter, Annette, should grow up like her mother and make a loyal and gentle and loving wife to a man who would be worthy of her love.

I remembered how Hendrik had spoken about Marie, years before in the post office, when they were first thinking of getting married. And I remembered how he spoke of that stillness that seemed to be so deep a part of her nature. And Hendrik's wife Marie did not seem to change with the passage of the years. She always moved about the house very quietly, and when she spoke it was usually with downcast eyes, and whether she was working, or sitting at rest on the riempies bench, what seemed to come all the time out of her whole personality was a strange and very deep kind of stillness. And the quiet that flowed out of her body did not appear to be like that calmness that comes to one after grief, that tranquillity of the spirit that follows on weeping, but it had in it more of the quality of that other stillness, like when at high noon the veld is still.

I knew that it was this quiet that Hendrik loved above all in his wife Marie, and when he spoke of his daughter Annette – and he spoke of her in such a way that it was clear that he was devoting his whole life to the vision of his daughter growing up to be exactly like her mother – I always knew what that quality was that he looked to find in his daughter, Annette. Even when he never mentioned it in actual words.

Annette grew up to be a very pretty girl, a lot like her mother in looks, and when it came to her turn to be married, it was to Koos de Bruyn, a wealthy farmer from Rustenburg. For her wedding in the church in Zeerust Annette wore the same wedding dress of white satin that her mother had worn twenty years before, and I was surprised to see how little the material had yellowed. It was pleasing to think that there were things that throughout those many years remained unchanged.

And when Annette came out of the church after the ceremony, leaning on her husband's arm, and there was confetti in her hair and on his shoulder, I knew then that it was not only in respect of the white satin dress that there was similarity between the marriage of Annette and that of her mother twenty years before. And

193

I knew that that depth of stillness that Hendrik had loved in his wife would form a part of his daughter's nature, also. And of her life. And for ever. I saw just in a single moment what it was that would bring that stillness of the body and the spirit to Annette for the rest of her married life. And in that way I guessed what had caused it as well in the case of her mother, Marie, the wife of Hendrik. And I wondered whether Annette's husband would love that quality in her, also.

It was a very slight thing. And it was so very quick that one would hardly have noticed it, even. It was just that something that came into her eyes – so apparently insignificant that it might had been no more than the trembling of an eyelash, almost – when Annette tripped out of the church, leaning on her husband's arm, and she glanced swiftly at a young man with broad shoulders whose very white face was half turned away.

THE STORY OF HESTER VAN WYK

When I think of the story of Hester van Wyk I often wonder what it is about some stories that I have wanted to tell (Oom Schalk Lourens said). About things that have happened and about people that I have known – and that I still know, some of them; if you can call it knowing a person when your mule-carts pass each other on the Government Road, and you wave your hat cheerfully and call out that it will be a good season for the crops, if only the stalk-borers and other pests keep away, and the other person just nods at you, with a distant sort of a look in his eyes, and says, yes, the Marico Bushveld has unfortunately got more than one kind of pest.

That was what Gawie Steyn said to me one afternoon on the Government Road, when I was on my way to the Drogedal post office for letters and he was on his way home. And it was because of the sorrowful sort of way in which he uttered the word 'unfortunately' that I knew that Gawie Steyn had heard what I had said about him to Frik Prinsloo three weeks before, after the meeting of the Dwarsberg debating society in the schoolroom next to the poort.

In any case, I never finished that story that I told Frik Prinsloo about Gawie Steyn, although I began telling it colourfully enough that night after the meeting of the debating society was over and the farmers and their wives and children had all gone home, and Frik Prinsloo and I were sitting alone on two desks in the middle of the schoolroom, with our feet up, and our pipes pleasantly filled with strong plug-cut tobacco whose thick blue fumes made the school-teacher cough violently at intervals.

The schoolmaster was seated at the table, with his head in his hands, and his face looking very pale in the light of the one paraffin lamp. And he was waiting for us to leave so that he could blow out his lamp and lock up the schoolroom and go home.

The schoolmaster did not interrupt us only with his coughing but also in other ways. For instance, he told us on several occasions that he had a weak chest, and if we had made up our minds to stay on like this in the classroom, talking, after the meeting was over, would we mind very much, he asked, if he opened one of the windows to let out some of the blue clouds of tobacco smoke.

But Frik Prinsloo said that we would mind very much. Not for our sakes, Frik said, but for the schoolmaster's sake. There was nothing worse, Frik explained, than for a man with a weak chest to sit in a room with a window open.

"It is nothing for us," Frik Prinsloo said, "for Schalk Lourens and myself to sit in a room with an open window. We are two Bushveld farmers with sturdy physiques who have been through the Boer War and through the anthrax pestilence. We have survived not only human hardships, but also cattle and sheep and pig diseases. At Magersfontein I even slept in an aardvark hole that was half-full of water with a piece of newspaper tied around my left ankle for the rheumatism. And even so neither Schalk Lourens nor I will be so foolish as to be in a room that has got a window open."

"No," I agreed. "Never."

"And you have to take greater care of your health than any of us," Frik Prinsloo said to the school-teacher. "With your weak chest it would be dangerous for you to have a window open in

here. Why, you can't even stand our tobacco smoke. Look at the way you are coughing right now."

After he had knocked the ash out of his pipe into an inkwell that was let into a little round hole in one of the desks, an action which he had performed just in order to show how familiar, for an uneducated man, he was with the ways of a schoolroom, Frik started telling the school-teacher about other places he had slept in, both during the Boer War and at another time when he was doing transport driving.

Frik Prinsloo embarked on a description of the hardships of a transport driver's life in the old days. It was a story that seemed longer than the most ambitious journey ever undertaken by ox-wagon, and much heavier, and more roundabout. And there was one place where Frik Prinsloo's story got stuck much more hopelessly than any of his ox-wagons had ever got stuck in a drift.

Then the schoolmaster said, please, gentlemen, he could not stand it anymore. His health was bad, and while he could perhaps arrange to let us have the use of the schoolroom on some other night, so that I could finish the story that I appeared to be telling to Mr Prinsloo, and he would even provide the paraffin for the lamp himself, he really had to go home and get some sleep.

But Frik Prinsloo said the schoolmaster did not need to worry about the paraffin. We could sit just as comfortably in the dark and talk, he said. For that matter, the schoolmaster could go to sleep in the classroom, if he liked. Just like that, sitting at the table.

"You already look half asleep," Frik told him, winking at me, "and sleeping in a schoolroom is a lot better than what happened to me during the English advance on Bloemfontein, when I slept in a donga with a lot of slime and mud and slippery tadpoles at the bottom . . ."

"In a donga half-full of water with a piece of mealie sacking fastened around your stomach because of the colic," the school-teacher said, speaking with his head still between his hands. "And for heaven's sake, if you have got to sleep out on the veld, why don't you sleep on top of it? Why must you go and lie inside a hole full of water or inside a slimy donga? If you farmers have had hard lives, it seems to me that you yourselves did quite a lot to make them like that."

We ignored this remark of the schoolmaster's, which we both realised was based on his lack of worldly experience, and I went on to relate to Frik Prinsloo those incidents from the life of Gawie Steyn that were responsible for Gawie's talking about Marico pests, some weeks later, in gloomy tones, on the road winding between the thorn-trees to the post office.

And this was one of those stories that I never finished. Because the schoolmaster fell asleep at his table, with the result that he didn't cough anymore, and I could see that because of this Frik Prinsloo could not derive the same amount of amusement from my story. And what is even more strange is that I also found that the funny parts in the story did not sound so funny anymore, now that the schoolmaster was no longer in discomfort. The story seemed to have had much more life in it, somehow, in the earlier stages, when the schoolmaster was anxiously waiting for us to go home, and coughing at intervals through the blue haze of our tobacco smoke.

"And so that man came round again the next night and sang some more songs to Gawie Steyn's wife," I said, "and they were old songs that he sang."

"It sounds to me as though he is even snoring," Frik Prinsloo said. "Imagine that for ill-bred. Here are you telling a story that teaches one all about the true and deep things of life and the schoolmaster is lying with his head on the table, snoring."

"And when Gawie Steyn started objecting after a while," I continued, with a certain amount of difficulty, "the man said the excuse he had to offer was that they were all old songs, anyway, and they didn't mean very much. Old songs had no meaning. They were only dead things from the past. They were yellowed and dust-laden, the man said."

"I've got a good mind to wake him," Frik Prinsloo went on. "First he disturbs us with his coughing and now I can't hear what you're saying because of his snoring. It will be a good thing if we just go home now and leave him. He seems so attached to his old schoolroom. Even staying behind at night to sleep in it. What would people say if I liked ploughing so much that I didn't go home at night, but just lay down and slept on a strip of grass next to a furrow?"

"Then Gawie Steyn said to this man," I continued, with greater difficulty than ever before, "he said that it wasn't so much the old songs he objected to. The old songs might be well enough. But the way his wife listened to the songs, he said, seemed to him to be not so much like an old song as like an old story."

"Not that I don't sleep out on the lands sometimes," Frik Prinsloo explained, "and even in the ploughing season. But then it is the early afternoon of a hot day. And the kaffirs go on with the ploughing all the same. And it is very refreshing, then, to sleep under a withaak tree knowing that the kaffirs are at work in the sun. Sleeping on a strip of green grass next to a furrow . . ."

"Or inside the furrow," the schoolmaster said, and we only noticed then that he was no longer snoring. "Inside a furrow half filled with wet fertiliser and with a turnip fastened on your head because of the blue tongue."

As I have said, this story about Gawie Steyn and his wife is one of those stories that I never finished telling. And I would never have known, either, that Frik Prinsloo had listened to as much of it as I had told him, if it wasn't for Gawie Steyn's manner of greeting me on the Government Road, three weeks later, with sorrowful politeness, like an Englishman.

There is always something unusual about a story that does not come to an end on its own. It is as though that story keeps going on, getting told in a different way each time, as though the story itself is trying to find out what happened next.

It was like the way life came to Hester van Wyk.

Hester was a very pretty girl, with black hair and a way of smiling that seemed very childlike, until you were close enough to her to see what was in her eyes, and then you realised, in that same moment, that no child had ever smiled like that. And whether it was for her black hair or whether it was because of her smile, it so happened that Hester van Wyk was hardly ever without a lover. They came to her, the young men from the neighbourhood. But they also went away again. They tarried for a while, like birds in their passage, and they paid court to her, and sometimes the period in which they wooed her was quite long, and at other times again she would have a lover whose ardour seemed to last for no longer than a few brief weeks before he also went his way.

And it seemed that the story of Hester van Wyk and her lovers was also one of those stories that I have mentioned to you, whose end never gets told.

And Gert van Wyk, Hester's father, would talk to me about these young men that came into his daughter's life. He talked to me both as a neighbour and as a relative on his wife's side, and while what he said to me about Hester and her lovers were mostly words spoken lightly, in the way that you flick a pebble into a dam, and watch the yellow ripples widening, there were also times when he spoke differently. And then what he said was like the way a footsore wanderer flings his pack on to the ground.

"She's a pretty girl," Gert said to me. "Yes, she is pretty enough. But her trouble is that she is too soft-hearted. These young men come to her, and they tell her stories. Sad stories about their lives. And she listens to their stories. And she feels sorry for them. And she says that they must be very nice young men for life to have treated them so badly. She even tries to tell me some of these stories, so that I should also feel sorry for them. But, of course, I have got too much sense to listen. I simply tell her –"

"Yes," I answered, nodding, "you tell her that what the young man says is a lot of lies. And by the time you have convinced her about one lover's lies you find that he has already departed, and that some other young man has got into the habit of coming to your house three times a week, and that he is busy telling her a totally new and different story."

"That's what he imagines," Gert van Wyk replied, "that it's new. But it's always the same old story. Only, instead of telling of his unhappy childhood the new young man will talk about his aged mother, or about how life has been cruel to him, so that he has got to help on the farm, for which he isn't suited at all, because it makes him dizzy to have to pump water out of the borehole for the cattle – up and down, up and down, like that, with the pump-handle – when all the time his real ambition is to have the job of wearing a blue and gold uniform outside of a bioscope in Johannesburg. And my daughter Hester is so soft-hearted that she goes on listening to these same stupid stories day after day, year in and year out."

"Yes," I said, "they are the same old stories."

And I thought of what Gawie Steyn said about the man who sang old songs to his wife. And it seemed that Hester van Wyk's was also an old story, and that for that reason it would never end.

"Did she also have a young man who said that he was not wor-

200

thy of her because he was not educated?" I asked Gert. "And did she take pity on him because he said people looked down on him because of his table manners?"

"Yes," Gert answered with alacrity, "he said he was badly brought up and always forgot to take the teaspoon out of the cup before drinking his coffee."

"Did she also have a young man who got her sympathy by telling her that he had fallen in love years ago, and that he had lost that girl, because her parents had objected to him, and that he could never fall in love again?"

"Quite right," Gert said. "This young man said that his first girl's parents refused to let her marry him because his forehead was too low. Even though he tried to make it look higher by training his eyebrows down and shaving the hair off most of the top of his head. But how do you know all these things?"

"There are only a few stories that young men tell girls in order to get their sympathy," I said to Gert. "There are only a handful of stories like that. But it seems to me that your daughter Hester has been told them all. And more than once, too, sometimes, by the look of it."

"And you can imagine how awful that young man with the low forehead looked," Gert continued. "He must have been unattractive enough before. But with his eyebrows trained down and the top of his head shaved clean off, he looked more like a –"

"And for that very reason, of course," I explained, "your daughter Hester fell in love with him. After she had heard his story."

And it seemed to me that the oldest story of all must be the story of a woman's heart.

It was some years after this, when Gert van Wyk and his family had moved out of the Marico into the Waterberg, that I heard that Hester van Wyk had married. And I knew then what had happened, of course. And I knew it even without Gert having had to tell me.

I knew then that some young man must have come to Hester van Wyk from out of some far-lying part of the Waterberg. He came to her and found her. And in finding her he had no story to tell.

But what I have no means of telling, now that I have related to you all that I know, is whether this is the end of the story about Hester van Wyk.

THE WIND IN THE TREE

There were dark patches on the washed-out blue of Gerrit van Biljon's shirt (Oom Schalk Lourens said), when I saw him on that forenoon, kneeling before a hole that he had been chopping out of the stony ground in front of his house. Those patches were damp marks of sweat. Gerrit van Biljon was kneeling down in front of the hole, on that forenoon of a summer's day when I saw him, and he was scraping out fragments of loosened earth and stones with his hands.

The ground was very hard, and Gerrit was digging the hole with a long cold chisel and a heavy hammer, which were more serviceable than the pick-axe with which he had evidently commenced digging, and which was now lying some distance away from the hole. About twenty yards away, to be exact. It was apparent to me that that was how far Gerrit van Biljon had thrown the pick at the moment when he had decided to go to the tool-shed for the hammer and cold chisel.

"You are digging, Neef Gerrit," I observed.

I was curious why a farmer of the Marico Bushveld should be down on his hands and knees, like the way Gerrit was, in the heat of the forenoon, with the sweat coming out through his shirt in dark patches, and the sun striking on to the back of his neck, in the space between the wide brim of his hat and the top of his faded shirt-collar.

Gerrit van Biljon did not answer. Instead, he reached still deeper into the hole and started feeling for more bits of loose ground. The sun beat full on to the back of his neck, which would have been very red by now if he had been an Englishman. As it was, no amount of sun could do much more to the colour of the back of Gerrit's neck, which was already almost as brown as the earth lying beside the hole. The worst that could happen to Gerrit

202

would be sunstroke. And as you know, the most suitable conditions under which you can get sunstroke in the Marico are when the rays of the midday sun strike on the back of your neck through a thin haze of cloud.

Therefore, when for the second time Gerrit van Biljon had not answered my question, I looked hopefully upwards. But from one horizon to the other the heavens were a deep and intense blue. Bush and koppie, withaak and kremetart and kameeldoring were dreaming languidly under a cloudless sky. I realised that there was not much prospect of Gerrit getting sunstroke, but I nevertheless consoled myself with the thought that having the full blaze on his neck like that must be very unpleasant for him.

I also realised that it was no use my asking Gerrit van Biljon any more direct questions. So I tried sideways, in the manner in which De Wet, after studying the ground, brought his commando round to that part of Sanna's Post where the English general did not want any Mauser bullets to come from.

"Have the Bechuanas on your farm trekked somewhere else, Neef Gerrit?" I asked, casually. "Back to the Protectorate, perhaps?"

Thus I succeeded, for the first time, in getting Gerrit van Biljon to talk.

"No, they have not left," he replied. And then, a little later, after he had struck the cold chisel about another half-dozen times, he asked, very reluctantly, "Why?"

"Because, if the Bechuanas have not left," I answered, "why is it that you, a Marico Boer, should so far have forgotten about farming, as to be here, on your hands and knees, digging a hole in the ground and in the hot sun, with the sweat making all those damp patches on your shirt?"

And after I had looked the back of Gerrit van Biljon over carefully, from his battered hat to his patched veldskoens, I added, "Like a kaffir."

When Gerrit stood up, at that point, and dusted some of the worst pieces of loose earth from the knees of his khaki trousers, I noticed that his digging the hole had not done his hands much good. I don't mean the scraping-out portion of the digging. That part had been all right: his hands were tough enough for that. But

I could see that there had been a few occasions when Gerrit had missed the head of the cold chisel. I could see that from his left hand. And it also seemed that he had swung his hammer quite powerfully on those occasions when he had missed.

"I am digging," Gerrit van Biljon said to me, and he spoke with a grave thoughtfulness, as though he wanted to make quite sure that he used the right words, "a hole."

I said that I had thought as much. I told him that I believed that he had first used the pick and had found that it was not much good. And that he had then gone to fetch the cold chisel.

"It doesn't look as though that is much good, either," I added.

Gerrit van Biljon put his left hand behind his back with what he apparently thought was an unobtrusive gesture.

"No," he said, "I am getting on all right."

"And after you have finished digging the hole?" I enquired, trying to sound unconcerned, and as though I was really thinking about something else.

"Then," Gerrit said solemnly, "I am going to dig another hole."

That was how difficult it was for me to find out, on that hot forenoon that was already lengthening into midday, why Gerrit van Biljon was digging holes in the stony ground in front of his house.

So I sat down on the grass under a nearby thorn-tree. I lit my pipe, and while the blue smoke curled away among the green foliage I reflected on the strange way in which the mind of the human being works, and how the human being can always distinguish, very readily, between what is important and what is unimportant. Thus, I had set out from my farm early that morning on foot to search for my mules that had strayed out of the

204

camp two days before. And when in the course of my wanderings through the bush I had at various times come across four kaffirs, each of whom had, in reply to my questionings, pointed in a different direction, I knew that the mules could not be far off. Mules are like that.

But my search for the mules had led me as far as Gerrit van Biljon's homestead, and the moment I saw Gerrit crouched over that hole in the ground I knew right away, without having to think, even, that it was more important for me to satisfy my curiosity in regard to what Gerrit van Biljon was doing than to find the mules. And so I decided to stay.

When the sun was directly overhead Gerrit's wife Sarie came and called us for dinner. Gerrit and Sarie had several young children who would not be back from school until the afternoon. Accordingly, the three of us arranged ourselves about the table in the voorkamer. While we ate we talked at first only of trivial things. I said that what had brought me there was that I was looking for my mules, which had strayed.

"It seems to me that it is not only your mules that have strayed," Gerrit van Biljon said, without looking up from his plate. "If you stay away from your farm much longer it will be your mules that will be starting to look for you."

This remark of Gerrit's made me feel rather uncomfortable. Therefore, to relieve the tension, I began relating what I thought was an amusing little story about Koos Venter, who had at one time farmed at Derdepoort, and who had started digging holes on his farm because of something a kaffir witch-doctor had told him about buried treasure.

"His pick was very blunt by the time they took it away from him," I said. "And when they put him on the lorry for Pretoria, and he was singing, nobody knew for sure whether he was mad before he started digging those holes, or whether he went mad, at a later stage, from sunstroke. But next time you go near Derdepoort you must have a look at that farm where Koos Venter stayed. It has got so many holes in it that the man who is on it now says that he is wondering if he can't use it as some sort of sieve. He thinks the Government might be able to make use of his farm for sifting something in a big way. But he can't think what, exactly. Yes, it is lucky that it does not rain very often in this part of the Marico. Because in wet weather that farm leaks very badly.

"You'll probably be able to see that farm quite soon, now, Neef Gerrit," I finished up significantly. "The lorry for Pretoria passes that way."

I would have said still more. But at that moment I caught Sarie's eye. Gerrit van Biljon's wife Sarie was a pleasant-looking woman. When she smiled her eyes had a pretty trick of getting long and narrow, so that she looked like a little girl, and there came with her smile a soft and alluring curve to her lips. But Sarie's eyes got narrow now in a manner I did not like. And what curves there were on her lips went all the wrong way.

So I said that I was only joking. And that I had best be going. And that I didn't think I would really wait for coffee. And that perhaps the mules were quite near, somewhere, waiting for me, maybe, and that if I didn't leave at once I might miss them.

And so it came about, just because I no longer had any curiosity in that direction, that Gerrit van Biljon explained to me what it was that he was doing. While he talked, his wife Sarie came into the voorkamer several times with coffee. Sometimes she lingered a little while, and I noticed that whenever she glanced in her husband's direction, while he talked, there was a look in her eyes which made me realise what risks I had been running in jesting about Gerrit. And when she walked about the room, driving out the flies with quick little movements, I knew that the cloth she was waving around was not a piece of wedding-dress.

It was a simple story that Gerrit van Biljon told me, and he took a long time over it, and when he had finished with the telling it was no story at all. And that was one of the reasons why I liked his story.

"I am planting bluegum trees," Gerrit van Biljon said, "in those holes that I am digging. For shade."

I was speechless. For a moment I wondered if Gerrit van Biljon's condition was not perhaps even worse than the state of mind of Koos Venter, the other man who had dug holes on his farm.

"But trees," I said, "Neef Gerrit, trees. Surely the whole Marico

206

is full of trees. I mean, there is nothing here but trees. We can't even grow mealies. Why, you had to chop down hundreds of trees to clear a space for your homestead and the cattle-kraal. And they are all shady trees, too."

Gerrit van Biljon shook his head. And he told me the story of how he met his wife Sarie on her father's farm in Schweizer-Reneke, in front of the farmhouse, under a tall bluegum. It was a simple story of a boy and girl who fell in love. Of initials carved on a white tree-trunk. Of a smile in the dusk. And hands touching and a quick kiss. And tears. Oh, it was a very simple story that Gerrit van Biljon told me. And as he spoke I could see that it was a story that would go on for ever. Two lovers in the evening and a pale wind in a tall tree. And Sarie's red lips. And two hearts haunted for ever by the fragrance of the bluegum trees. No, there was nothing at all in that story. It was the sort of thing that happens every day. It was just something foolish about the human heart.

"And if it had been any other but a bluegum tree," Gerrit van Biljon said, "it would not have been the same thing."

I knew better, of course, but I did not tell him so.

Then Gerrit explained that he was going to plant a row of bluegums in front of his house.

"I have ordered the plants from the Government Test Station in Potchefstroom," he went on. "I am getting only the best plants. It takes a bluegum only twelve years to grow to its full height. For the first couple of years the trees will grow hardly at all, because of the stones. But after a few years, when the roots have found their way into the deeper parts of the soil, the trunks will shoot up very quickly. And in the late afternoons I shall sit under the tallest bluegum, with my wife beside me and our children playing about. The wind stirring through a bluegum makes a different sound from when it blows through any other tree. And a bluegum's shadow on the ground has an altogether different feeling from any other kind of shadow. At least, that is how it is for me."

Gerrit van Biljon said he didn't even care if a pig occasionally wandered away from the trough at the back of the house, at feeding time, and scratched himself on the trunk of one of the trees. That was how tolerant the thought of the bluegums made him feel.

"Only," he added, rather quickly, "I only hope the pig doesn't overdo it. I don't want him to make a habit of it, of course.

"Perhaps I will even read a book under one of the trees, some day," Gerrit said, finally. "You see, outside of the Bible I have never read a book. Just bits of newspaper and things. Yes, perhaps I will even read a book. But mostly – well, mostly I will just rest."

So that was Gerrit van Biljon's story.

As he had prophesied, the bluegums, after not seeming to want to grow at all, at first, suddenly started to shoot up, and they grew almost to their full height in something over eight years. And I often saw Sarie sitting under the tallest tree, with her youngest child playing on the grass beside her, and I was sure that Gerrit van Biljon rested as peacefully under the withaak by the foot of the koppie at the far end of the farm as he would have done in the bluegum's shade.

CAMP-FIRES AT NAGMAAL

Of course, the old days were best (Oom Schalk Lourens said), I mean the really old days. Those times when we still used to pray, "Lord give us food and clothes. The veldskoens we make ourselves."

There was faith in the land in those days. And when things went wrong we used to rely on our own hands and wills, and when we asked for the help of the Lord we also knew the strength of our trek-chains. It was quite a few years before the Boer War that what I can call the old days came to an end. That was when the Boers in these parts stopped making the soles of their veldskoens out of strips of raw leather that they cut from quagga skins. Instead, they started using the new kind of blue sole that came up from the Cape in big square pieces, and that they bought at the Indian store.

I remember the first time I made myself a pair of veldskoens out of that blue sole. The stuff was easy to work with, and smooth. And all the time I was making the veldskoens I knew it was very wrong. And I was still more disappointed when I found that the blue sole wore well. If anything, it was even better than raw quagga hide. This circumstance was very regrettable to me. And there remained something foreign to me about those veldskoens, even after they had served me through two kaffir wars.

It was in the early days, also, that a strange set of circumstances unfolded, in which the lives of three people, Maans Prinsloo and Stoffelina Lemmer and Petrus Steyn, became intertwined like the strands of the grass covers that native women weave for their beer-pots: in some places your eye can separate the various strands of plaited grass, the one from the other; in other places the weaving is all of one piece.

And the story of the lives of these three people, two men and a girl, is something that could only have happened long ago, when there was still faith in the Transvaal, and the stars in the sky were constant, and only the wind changed.

Maans Prinsloo and I were young men together, and I knew Stoffelina Lemmer well, also. But because Petrus Steyn, who was a few years older than we were, lived some distance away, to the north, on the borders of the Bechuanaland Protectorate, I did not see him very often. We met mostly at Nagmaals, and then Petrus Steyn would recount to us, at great length, the things he had seen and the events that had befallen him on his periodic treks into the further parts of the Kalahari Desert.

You can imagine that these stories of Petrus Steyn's were very tedious to listen to. They were empty as the desert is, and as unending. And as flat.

After all, it is easy to understand that Petrus Steyn's visits to the Kalahari Desert would not give him very much to talk about that would be of interest to the listener – no matter how far he trekked. Simply because a desert is a desert. One part of it is exactly like another part. Thousands of square miles of sand dotted with occasional thorn-trees. And a stray buck or two. And, now and again, a few Bushmen who have also strayed – but who don't know it, of course.

I have noticed that Bushmen are always in a hurry. But they have nowhere to go to. Where they are running to is all just desert, like where they came from. So they never know where they are, either. But because they don't care where they are it doesn't matter to them that they are lost. They just don't know any better. All they are concerned about is to keep on hurrying.

Consequently, the stories that Petrus Steyn had to tell of his experiences in the Kalahari Desert were as fatiguing to listen to as if you were actually trekking along with him. And the further he trekked into the desert the more wearisome his narrative became, on account of the interludes getting fewer, there being less buck and less Bushmen the deeper he got into the interior. Even so, we felt that he was keeping on using the same Bushmen over and over again. There was also a small herd of springbok that we were suspicious about in the same way.

210

You can picture to yourself the scene around one of the fires on the church square in Zeerust. It happened at many Nagmaals. A number of young men and women seated around the fire, and Petrus Steyn, a few years older than the members of his audience, would be talking. And when you saw people's mouths going open, it wasn't in astonishment. They were just yawning.

But there was one reason why the young men and women came to Petrus Steyn, and this reason had nothing to do with his Kalahari stories. But it is one of the things I was thinking about when I spoke about the old days and about the faith that was in the land then. For Petrus Steyn was regarded as a prophet. Sometimes people believed in his prognostications, and sometimes they didn't. But, of course, this made no difference to Petrus Steyn. He didn't care whether or not his prophecies came out. He believed

in them just the same. More, even. You would understand what I mean by this if you knew Petrus Steyn.

And Petrus Steyn said that why he went into the Kalahari periodically was in order to get fresh inspiration and guidance in regard to the future. He also said it was written in the Bible that a prophet had to go into the desert.

"I wonder what the Bushmen thought of Zephaniah, when he was in the desert," Maans Prinsloo asked. "I suppose they painted portraits of him, on rocks."

Maans Prinsloo knew that Zephaniah was Petrus Steyn's favourite prophet.

"I don't know whether Ekron was rooted up, like Zephaniah said would happen," Petrus Steyn replied. "I read the Bible right through to Revelations, once, to find out. But I couldn't be sure if Zephaniah was right or not. That's where my prophecies are different. When I see a thing in the Kalahari Desert, that thing comes out, no matter who gets struck down by it" – and Petrus Steyn looked sternly at Maans Prinsloo – "and no matter how long it takes."

That was how Petrus Steyn always talked about his prophecies. And maybe that was the reason why they believed in him, even when they should not have done so.

Anyway, I can still recall, very clearly, that particular Nagmaal at Zeerust when I first understood in which way Stoffelina Lemmer came into the story. And I also knew why Maans Prinsloo and Petrus Steyn were on unfriendly terms. Stoffelina Lemmer had dark hair, and eyes that had a far-off light in them when she smiled, and that were strangely shadowed when she looked at you without smiling. And she had red lips.

Stoffelina Lemmer was much in Maans Prinsloo's company at this Nagmaal. But she was also a great deal with Petrus Steyn. She was nearly always one of the little group that listened to Petrus Steyn's Kalahari stories, and even if Maans Prinsloo was with her, holding her hand, even, it still seemed that she listened to Petrus Steyn's talk. That is, she appeared, unlike anybody else, actually to listen, and with an interest that was not simulated.

Once or twice, also, after the rest of Petrus Steyn's audience had departed, it was observed that Stoffelina Lemmer remained behind, talking to the prophet. And to judge by the animation of Stoffelina Lemmer's lips and eyes, if they were talking about the future it was not in terms of Petrus Steyn's desert prophecies. Beside the burnt-out camp-fire they lingered thus, once or twice, Stoffelina and Petrus, with the dull glow of the dying embers on their faces.

It was only reasonable, therefore, that Maans Prinsloo should want to know where he stood with Stoffelina Lemmer. That he was in love with her, everybody knew by this time. It was also known, shortly afterwards, that Maans had asked Stoffelina to marry him. And from the way that Maans Prinsloo walked about, looking disconsolate and making remarks of a slighting nature about the whole of the Kalahari, and not just the parts that Petrus Steyn went into, it was clear to us that Stoffelina Lemmer had not accepted Maans Prinsloo just out of hand.

Then, when it was becoming very tense, this situation that involved two men and a girl, Stoffelina Lemmer found a way out.

"Let Petrus Steyn go into the desert again, after this Nagmaal," Stoffelina said. "And let him then come back and tell us what he has seen. He will learn in the Kalahari what is to happen. When he comes back he will tell us."

Although he believed in Petrus Steyn's prophecies, in spite of his pretence to the contrary, Maans Prinsloo nevertheless seemed doubtful.

"But, look," he began, "Petrus Steyn is sure to go in just a little distance. And then he will come out and say that Stoffelina Lemmer is going to marry Petrus Steyn, and that . . ."

Petrus Steyn silenced Maans Prinsloo with a look.

"I shall trek into the Kalahari Desert," he said. "It will be the longest journey I have ever made into the desert. And whatever I see will be prophecy. And just as I see it I shall come back and announce it. Zephaniah may prophesy wrongly, dishonestly, even . . . Petrus Steyn, never! I am still not satisfied about what Zephaniah spoke against Ekron."

Maans Prinsloo was convinced. And so the matter was decided. We inspanned on the Nagmaal plein at Zeerust and journeyed back to our farms by ox-wagon, and shortly afterwards we heard that Petrus Steyn had set out on a long trek into the Kalahari Desert.

Nothing remained to be told after that Nagmaal at which it was decided that Petrus Steyn should trek into the Kalahari once more. The story ended when the last red ember turned to ashes in that camp-fire on the Nagmaal plein.

Maans Prinsloo remained nervous for a very considerable period.

Because this time Petrus Steyn went on a trip that was longer than anything he had ever undertaken before. In fact, he trekked right across the Kalahari, right through to the other side, and far into Portuguese Angola. Indeed, it was more than fifteen years before we again heard of him, and then it was indirectly, through some Boers who had trekked into Portuguese territory in order to get away from British rule.

I often wondered if those Boers had ever asked Petrus Steyn what it was that he had trekked away from.

But before that time there were many Nagmaals, one succeeding the other, when Stoffelina Lemmer and Maans Prinsloo sat near each other, in front of the same camp-fire, each one waiting, and each one's heart crowded with different emotions, for the return of Petrus Steyn from the desert.

No, Stoffelina Lemmer never married Maans Prinsloo.

THE PROPHET

No, I never came across the Prophet van Rensburg, the man who told General Kemp that it was the right time to rebel against the English. As you know, General Kemp followed his advice and they say that General Kemp still believed in Van Rensburg's prophecies, even after the two of them were locked up in the Pretoria Gaol.

But I knew another prophet. His name was Erasmus. Stephanus Erasmus. Van Rensburg could only foretell that so and so was going to happen, and then he was wrong, sometimes. But with Stephanus Erasmus it was different. Erasmus used to make things come true just by prophesying them.

You can see what that means. And yet, in the end I wondered about Stephanus Erasmus.

There are lots of people like Van Rensburg who can just foretell the future, but when a man comes along who can actually make the future, then you feel that you can't make jokes about him. All the farmers in Droëdal talked about Stephanus Erasmus with respect. Even when he wasn't present to hear what was being said about him. Because there would always be somebody to go along and tell him if you happened to make some slighting remark about him.

I know, because once in Piet Fourie's house I said that if I was a great prophet like Stephanus Erasmus I would try and prophesy myself a new pair of veldskoens, seeing that his were all broken on top and you could see two corns and part of an ingrowing toenail. After that things went all wrong on my farm for six months. So I knew that Piet Fourie had told the prophet what I had said. Amongst other things six of my best trek-oxen died of the miltsiekte.

After that, whenever I wanted to think anything unflattering about Stephanus Erasmus I went right out into the veld and did it all there. You can imagine that round that time I went into the veld alone very often. It wasn't easy to forget about the six trek-oxen.

More than once I hoped that Stephanus Erasmus would also take it into his head to tell General Kemp that it was the right time to go into rebellion. But Erasmus was too wise for that. I remember once when we were all together just before a meeting of the Dwarsberg School Committee I asked Stephanus about this.

"What do you think of this new wheel-tax, Oom Stephanus?" I said. "Don't you think the people should go along with their rifles and hoist the Vierkleur over the magistrates' court at Zeerust?"

Erasmus looked at me and I lowered my eyes. I felt sorry in a way that I had spoken. His eyes seemed to look right through me. I felt that to him I looked like a springbok that has been shot and cut open, and you can see his heart and his ribs and his liver and his stomach and all the rest of his insides. It was not very pleasant to be sitting talking to a man who regards you as nothing more than a cut-open springbok.

But Stephanus Erasmus went on looking at me. I became frightened. If he had said to me then, "You know you are just a cut-open springbok," I would have said, "Yes, Oom Stephanus, I know." I could see then that he had a great power. He was just an ordinary sort of farmer on the outside, with a black beard and dark eyes and a pair of old shoes that were broken on top. But inside he was terrible. I began to be afraid for my remaining trek-oxen.

Then he spoke, slowly and with wisdom.

"There are also magistrates' courts at Mafeking and Zwartruggens and Rysmierbult," he said. "In fact there is a magistrates' court in every town I have been in along the railway line. And all these magistrates' courts collect wheel-tax," Oom Stephanus said.

I could see then that he not only had great power inside him, but that he was also very cunning. He never went in for any wild guessing, like saying to a stranger, "You are a married man with five children and in your inside jacket-pocket is a letter from the

Kerkraad asking you to become an ouderling." I have seen some so-called fortune-tellers say that to a man they had never seen in their lives before in the hope that they might be right.

You know, it is a wonderful thing this, about being a prophet. I have thought much about it, and what I know about it I can't explain. But I know it has got something to do with death. This is one of the things I have learnt in the Marico, and I don't think you could learn it anywhere else. It is only when you have had a great deal of time in which to do nothing but think and look at the veld and at the sky where there have been no rain-clouds for many months, that you grow to an understanding of these things.

Then you know that being a prophet and having power is very simple. But it is also something very terrible. And you know then that there are men and women who are unearthly, and it is this that makes them greater than kings. For a king can lose his power when people take it away from him, but a prophet can never lose his power – if he is a real prophet.

It was the schoolchildren who first began talking about this. I have noticed how often things like this start with the stories of kaffirs and children.

Anyway, a very old kaffir had come to live at the outspan on the road to Ramoutsa. Nobody knew where he had come from, except that when questioned he would lift up his arm very slowly and point towards the west. There is nothing in the west. There is only the Kalahari Desert. And from his looks you could easily believe that this old kaffir had lived in the desert all his life. There was something about his withered body that reminded you of the Great Drought.

We found out that this kaffir's name was Mosiko. He had made himself a rough shelter of thorn-bushes and old mealie bags. And there he lived alone. The kaffirs round about brought him mealies and beer, and from what they told us it appeared that he was not very grateful for these gifts, and when the beer was weak he swore vilely at the persons who brought it.

As I have said, it was the kaffirs who first took notice of him. They said he was a great witch-doctor. But later on white people also starting taking him presents. And they asked him questions about what was going to happen. Sometimes Mosiko told them what they wanted to know. At other times he was impudent and told them to go and ask Baas Stephanus Erasmus.

You can imagine what a stir this created.

"Yes," Frans Steyn said to us one afternoon, "and when I asked this kaffir whether my daughter Anna should get married to Gert right away or whether she should go to High School to learn English, Mosiko said that I had to ask Baas Stephanus. 'Ask him,' he said, 'that one is too easy for me'."

Then the people said that this Mosiko was an impertinent kaffir, and that the only thing Stephanus could do was not to take any notice of him.

I watched closely to see what Erasmus was going to do about it. I could see that the kaffir's impudence was making him mad. And when people said to him, "Do not take any notice of Mosiko, Oom Stephanus, he is a lazy old kaffir," anyone could see that this annoyed him more than anything else. He suspected that they said this out of politeness. And there is nothing that angers you more than when those who used to fear you start being polite to you.

The upshot of the business was that Stephanus Erasmus went to the outspan where Mosiko lived. He said he was going to boot him back into the Kalahari, where he came from. Now, it was a mistake for Stephanus to have gone out to see Mosiko. For Mosiko looked really important to have the prophet coming to visit him. The right thing always is for the servant to visit the master.

All of us went along with Stephanus.

On the way down he said, "I'll kick him all the way out of Zeerust. It is bad enough when kaffirs wear collars and ties in Johannesburg and walk on the pavements reading newspapers. But we can't allow this sort of thing in the Marico."

But I could see that for some reason Stephanus was growing angry as we tried to pretend that we were determined to have Mosiko shown up. And this was not the truth. It was only Erasmus's quarrel. It was not our affair at all.

We got to the outspan.

Mosiko had hardly any clothes on. He sat up against a bush with his back bent and his head forward near his knees. He had many wrinkles. Hundreds of them. He looked to be the oldest man in the world. And yet there was a kind of strength about the curve of his back and I knew the meaning of it. It seemed to me that with his back curved in that way, and the sun shining on him and his head bent forward, Mosiko could be much greater and do more things just by sitting down than other men could do by working hard and using cunning. I felt that Mosiko could sit down and do nothing and yet be more powerful than the Kommandant-General.

He seemed to have nothing but what the sun and the sand and the grass had given him, and yet that was more than what all the men in the world could give him.

I was glad that I was there that day, at the meeting of the wizards.

Stephanus Erasmus knew who Mosiko was, of course. But I wasn't sure if Mosiko knew Stephanus. So I introduced them. On another day people would have laughed at the way I did it. But at that moment it didn't seem so funny, somehow.

"Mosiko," I said, "this is Baas Prophet Stephanus Erasmus.

"And, Oom Stephanus," I said, "this is Witch-doctor Mosiko."

Mosiko raised his eyes slightly and glanced at Erasmus. Erasmus looked straight back at Mosiko and tried to stare him out of countenance. I knew the power with which Stephanus Erasmus could look at you. So I wondered what was going to happen. But Mosiko looked down again, and kept his eyes down on the sand.

Now, I remembered how I felt that day when Stephanus Erasmus had looked at me and I was ready to believe that I was a cut-open springbok. So I was not surprised at Mosiko's turning away his eyes. But in the same moment I realised that Mosiko looked down in the way that seemed to mean that he didn't think that Stephanus was a man of enough importance for him to want to stare out of countenance. It was as though he thought there were other things for him to do but look at Stephanus.

Then Mosiko spoke.

"Tell me what you want to know, Baas Stephanus," he said, "and I'll prophesy for you."

I saw the grass and the veld and the stones. I saw a long splash of sunlight on Mosiko's naked back. But for a little while I neither saw nor heard anything else. For it was a deadly thing that the kaffir had said to the white man. And I knew that the others also felt it was a deadly thing. We stood there, waiting. I was not sure whether to be glad or sorry that I had come. The time seemed so very long in passing.

"Kaffir," Stephanus said at last, "you have no right to be here on a white man's outspan. We have come to throw you off it. I am going to kick you, kaffir. Right now I am going to kick you. You'll see what a white man's boot is like."

Mosiko did not move. It did not seem as though he had heard anything Stephanus had said to him. He appeared to be thinking of something else – something very old and very far away.

Then Stephanus took a step forward. He paused for a moment. We all looked down.

220

Frans Steyn was the first to laugh. It was strange and unnatural at first to hear Frans Steyn's laughter. Everything up till then had been so tense and even frightening. But immediately afterwards we all burst out laughing together. We laughed loudly and uproariously. You could have heard us right at the other side of the bult.

I have told you about Stephanus Erasmus's veldskoens, and that they were broken on top. Well, now, in walking to the outspan, the last riem had burst loose, and Stephanus Erasmus stood there with his right foot raised from the ground and a broken shoe dangling from his instep.

Stephanus never kicked Mosiko. When we had finished laughing we got him to come back home. Stephanus walked slowly, carrying the broken shoe in his hand and picking the soft places to walk on, where the burnt grass wouldn't stick into his bare foot.

Stephanus Erasmus had lost his power.

But I knew that even if his shoe hadn't broken, Stephanus would never have kicked Mosiko. I could see by that look in his eyes that, when he took the step forward and Mosiko didn't move, Stephanus had been beaten for always.

MAMPOER

The berries of the kareeboom (Oom Schalk Lourens said, nodding his head in the direction of the tall tree whose shadows were creeping towards the edge of the stoep) may not make the best kind of mampoer that there is. What I mean is that karee brandy is not as potent as the brandy you distil from moepels or maroelas. Even peach brandy, they say, can make you forget the rust in the corn quicker than the mampoer you make from karee-berries.

But karee mampoer is white and soft to look at, and the smoke that comes from it when you pull the cork out of the bottle is pale and rises up in slow curves. And in time of drought, when you have been standing at the borehole all day, pumping water for the cattle, so that by the evening water has got a bitter taste for you, then it is very soothing to sit on the front stoep, like now, and to get somebody to pull the cork out of a bottle of this kind of mampoer. Your hands will be sore and stiff from the pump-handle, so that if you try and pull it out yourself the cork will seem as deep down in the bottle as the water is in the borehole.

Many years ago, when I was a young man, and I sat here, on the front stoep, and I saw that white smoke floating away slowly and gracefully from the mouth of the bottle, and with a far-off fragrance, I used to think that the smoke looked like a young girl walking veiled under the stars. And now that I have grown old, and I look at that white smoke, I imagine that it is a young girl walking under the stars, and still veiled. I have never found out who she is.

Hans Kriel and I were in the same party that had gone from this section of the Groot Marico to Zeerust for the Nagmaal. And it was a few evenings after our arrival, when we were on a visit to Kris Wilman's house on the outskirts of the town, that I learnt something of the first half of Hans Kriel's love story – that half at

222

which I laughed. The knowledge of the second half came a little later, and I didn't laugh then.

We were sitting on Krisjan Wilman's stoep and looking out in the direction of Sephton's Nek. In the setting sun the koppies were red on one side; on the other side their shadows were lengthening rapidly over the vlakte. Krisjan Wilman had already poured out the mampoer, and the glasses were going round.

"That big shadow there is rushing through the thorn-trees just like a black elephant," Adriaan Bekker said. "In a few minutes' time it will be at Groot Marico station."

"The shorter the days are, the longer the shadows get," Frikkie Marais said. "I learnt that at school. There are also lucky and un-lucky shadows."

"You are talking about ghosts, now, and not shadows," Adriaan Bekker interrupted him, learnedly. "Ghosts are all the same length, I think, more or less."

"No, it is the ghost stories that are all the same length," Krisjan Wilman said. "The kind you tell."

It was good mampoer, made from karee-berries that were

plucked when they were still green and full of thick sap, just before they had begun to whiten, and we said things that contained much wisdom.

"It was like the shadow of a flower on her left cheek," I heard Hans Kriel say, and immediately I sat up to listen, for I could guess of what it was that he was talking.

"Is it on the lower part of her cheek?" I asked. "Two small purple marks?"

Because in that case I would know for sure that he was talking about the new waitress in the Zeerust café. I had seen her only once, through the plate-glass window, and because I had liked her looks I had gone up to the counter and asked her for a roll of Boer tobacco, which she said they did not stock. When she said they didn't stock koedoe biltong, either, I had felt too embarrassed to ask for anything else. Only afterwards I remembered that I could have gone in and sat down and ordered a cup of coffee and some harde beskuit. But it was too late then. By that time I felt that she could see that I came from this part of the Marico, even though I was wearing my hat well back on my head.

"Did you – did you speak to her?" I asked Hans Kriel after a while.

"Yes," he said, "I went in and asked her for a roll of Boer tobacco. But she said they didn't sell tobacco by the roll, or koedoe biltong, either. She said this last with a sort of a sneer. I thought it was funny, seeing that I hadn't asked her for koedoe biltong. So I sat down in front of a little table and ordered some harde beskuit and a cup of coffee. She brought me a number of little dry, flat cakes with letters on them that I couldn't read very well. Her name is Marie Rossouw."

"You must have said quite a lot to her to have found out her name," I said, with something in my voice that must have made Hans Kriel suspicious.

"How do you know who I am talking about?" he demanded suddenly.

"Oh, never mind," I answered. "Let us ask Krisjan Wilman to refill our glasses."

I winked at the others and we all laughed, because by that time Hans Kriel was sitting half-sideways on the riempies bench, with his shoulders drawn up very high and his whole body seeming to be

224

kept up by one elbow. It wasn't long after that he moved his elbow, so that we had to pick him up from the floor and carry him into the voorkamer, where we laid him in a corner on some leopard skins.

But before that he had spoken more about Marie Rossouw, the new waitress in the café. He said he had passed by and had seen her through the plate-glass window and there had been a vase of purple flowers on the counter, and he had noticed those two marks on her cheek, and those marks had looked very pretty to him, like two small shadows from those purple flowers.

"She is very beautiful," Hans Kriel said. "Her eyes have got deep things in them, like those dark pools behind Abjaterskop. And when she smiled at me once – by mistake, I think – I felt as though my heart was rushing over the vlaktes like that shadow we saw in the sunset."

"You must be careful of those dark pools behind Abjaterskop," I warned him. "We know those pools have got witches in them."

I felt it was a pity that we had to carry him inside, shortly afterwards. For the mampoer had begun to make Hans Kriel talk rather well.

As it happened, Hans Kriel was not the only one, that night, who encountered difficulties with the riempies bench. Several more of us were carried inside. And when I look back on that Nagmaal my most vivid memories are not of what the predikant said at the church service, or of Krisjan Wilman's mampoer, even, but of how very round the black spots were on the pale yellow of the leopard skin. They were so round that every time I looked at them they were turning.

In the morning Krisjan Wilman's wife woke us up and brought us coffee. Hans Kriel and I sat up side by side on the leopard skins, and in between drinking his coffee Hans Kriel said strange things. He was still talking about Marie Rossouw.

"Just after dark I got up from the front stoep and went to see her in the café," Hans Kriel said.

"You may have got up from the front stoep," I answered, "but you never got up from these leopard skins. Not from the moment we carried you here. That's the truth."

"I went to the café," Hans Kriel said, ignoring my interruption,

225

"and it was very dark. She was there alone. I wanted to find out how she got those marks on her cheek. I think she is very pretty even without them. But with those marks Marie Rossouw is the most wild and beautiful thing in the whole world."

"I suppose her cheek got cut there when she was a child," I suggested. "Perhaps when a bottle of her father's mampoer exploded."

"No," Hans Kriel replied, very earnestly. "No. It was something else. I asked her where the marks came from. I asked her there, in the café, where we were alone together, and it suddenly seemed as though the whole place was washed with moonlight, and there was no counter between us anymore, and there was a strange laughter in her eyes when she brought her face very close to mine. And she said, 'I know you won't believe me. But that is where the devil kissed me. Satan kissed me there when we were behind Abjaterskop. Shall I show you?'

"That was what she said to me," Hans Kriel continued, "and I knew, then, that she was a witch. And that it was a very sinful thing to be in love with a witch. And so I caught her up in my arms, and I whispered, trembling all the time, 'Show me,' and our heads rose up very tall through the shadows. And everything moved very fast, faster than the shadows move from Abjaterskop in the setting of the sun. And I knew that we were behind Abjaterskop, and that her eyes were indeed the dark pools there, with the tall reeds growing on the edges. And then I saw Satan come in between us. And he had hooves and a forked tail. And there were flames coming out of him. And he stooped down and kissed Marie Rossouw, on her cheek, where those marks were. And she laughed. And her eyes danced with merriment. And I found that it was all the time I who was kissing her. Now, what do you make of this, Schalk?"

I said, of course, that it was the mampoer. And that I knew, now, why I had been sleeping in such discomfort. It wasn't because the spots on the leopard skin were turning like round wheels; but because I had Satan sleeping next to me all night. And I said that this discovery wasn't new, either. I had always suspected something like that about him.

But I got an idea. And while the others were at breakfast I went out, on the pretext that I had to go and help Manie Burgers with his oxen at the church square outspan. But, instead, I went into the café, and because I knew her name was Marie Rossouw, when the waitress came for my order I could ask her whether she was related to the Rossouws of Rysmierbult, and I could tell her that I was distantly related to that family, also. In the daylight there was about that café none of the queerness that Hans Kriel had spoken about. It was all very ordinary. Even those purple flowers were still on the counter. They looked slightly faded.

And then, suddenly, while we were talking, I asked her the thing that I was burning to know.

"That mark on your cheek, juffrou," I said, "will you tell me where you got it from?"

Marie Rossouw brought her face very close to mine, and her eyes were like dark pools with dancing lights in them.

"I know you won't believe me," she said, "but that is where Satan kissed me. When we were at the back of Abjaterskop together. Shall I show you?"

It was broad daylight. The morning lay yellow on the world and the sun shone in brightly through the plate-glass window, and there were quite a number of people in the street. And yet as I walked out of the café quickly, and along the pavement, I was shivering.

With one thing and another, I did not come across Hans Kriel again until three or four days later, when the Nagmaal was over and we were trekking to the other side of the Dwarsberge once more.

We spoke of a number of things, and then, trying to make my voice sound natural, I made mention of Marie Rossouw.

"That was a queer sort of dream you had," I said.

"Yes," he answered, "it was queer."

"And did you find out," I asked, again trying to sound casual, "about those marks on her cheek?"

"Yes," Hans Kriel answered, "I asked Marie and she told me. She said that when she was a child a bottle of mampoer burst in the voorkamer. Her cheek got cut by a splinter of glass. She is an unusual kind of girl, Marie Rossouw."

"Yes," I agreed, moving away. "Oh, yes."

But I also thought that there are things about mampoer that you can't understand very easily.

Seed-time and Harvest

At the time of the big drought (Oom Schalk Lourens said) Jurie Steyn trekked with what was left of his cattle to the Schweizer-Reneke District. His wife, Martha, remained behind on the farm. After a while an ouderling from near Vleisfontein started visiting Jurie Steyn's farm to comfort Martha. And as time went on everybody in the Marico began talking about the ouderling's visits, and they said that the ouderling must be neglecting his own affairs quite a lot, coming to Jurie Steyn's farm so often, especially since Vleisfontein was so far away. Other people, again, said that Vleisfontein couldn't be far enough away for the ouderling: not when Jurie Steyn got back, they said.

The ouderling was a peculiar sort of man, too. When some neighbour called at Jurie Steyn's farm, and Martha was there alone with the ouderling, and the neighbour would drop a hint about the drought breaking some time, meaning that Jurie Steyn would then be coming back to the Marico from the Schweizer-Reneke District with his cattle, then the ouderling would just look very solemn, and he would say that it must be the Lord's will that this drought had descended on the Marico, and that he himself had been as badly stricken by the hand of the Lord as anybody and that the windmill pumped hardly enough water even for his prize Large Whites, and that in spite of what people might think he would be as pleased as anybody else when the rains came again.

228

That was a long drought. It was a very bitter period. But a good while before the drought broke the ouderling's visits to Martha Steyn had ceased. And the grass was already turning green in the heavy rains that followed on the great drought when Jurie Steyn got back to his farmhouse with his wagon and his red Afrikaner cattle. And by that time the ouderling's visits to Martha were hardly even a memory any longer.

But a while later, when Martha Steyn had a child, again, there was once more a lot of talk, especially among the women. But there was no way of telling how much Jurie Steyn knew or guessed about what was being said about himself and Martha and the ouderling, and about his youngest child, whom they had christened Kobus.

It only seemed that for a good while thereafter Jurie Steyn seemed to be like a man lost in thought. And it would appear that he had grown absent-minded in a way that we hadn't noticed about him before. And it would seem, also, that his absent-mindedness was of a sort that did not make him very reliable in his dealings with his neighbours. It was almost as though what had been happening between the ouderling and Martha Steyn – whatever had been happening – had served to undermine not Martha's moral character but Jurie Steyn's.

This change that had taken place in Jurie Steyn was brought home to me most forcibly some years later in connection with some fence-poles that he had gone to fetch for me from Ramoutsa station. There was a time when I had regarded Jurie Steyn as somebody strong and upright, like a withaak tree, but it seemed that his character had gradually grown flat and twisted along the ground, like the tendrils of a pumpkin that has been planted in the cool side of a manure-pile at the back of the house. And that is a queer thing, too, that I have noticed about pumpkins. They thrive better if you plant them at the back of the house than in the front. Something like that seemed to be the case with Jurie Steyn, too, somehow.

Anyway, it was when the child Kobus was about nine years old, and Jurie Steyn's mind seemed to have grown all curved like a green mamba asleep in the sun, that the incident of the fence-poles occurred.

But I must first tell you about the school-teacher that we had at Drogevlei then. This school-teacher started doing a lot of farming in his spare time. Then he began taking his pupils round to his farm, some afternoons, and he showed them how to plant mealies as part of their school subjects. We all said that that was nonsense, because there was nothing that we couldn't teach the children ourselves, when it came to matters like growing mealies. But the teacher said, no, the children had to learn the theory of what nature did to the seeds, and it was part of natural science studies, and he said our methods of farming were all out of date, anyway.

We didn't know whether our methods of farming were out of date, but we certainly thought that there were things about the teacher's methods of education that were altogether different from anything we had come across so far. Because the school hours got shorter and shorter as the months went by, and the children spent more and more time on the teacher's farm, on their hands and knees, learning how to put things into the ground to make them grow. And when the mealies were about a foot high the teacher made the whole school learn how to pull up the weeds that grew between the mealies. This lesson took about a week: the teacher had planted so large an area. The children would get home from school very tired and stained from their lessons on the red, clayey sort of soil that was on that part of the teacher's farm.

And near the end of the school term, when the dams were drying up, the children were given an examination in pumping water out of the borehole for the teacher's cattle.

But afterwards, when the teacher showed the children how to make a door for his pigsty out of the school blackboard, and how to wrap up his eggs for the Zeerust market in the pages torn from their exercise books, we began wondering whether the more old-fashioned kind of school-teacher was not perhaps better – the kind of schoolmaster who only taught the children to read and write and to do sums, and left the nature-science job of cooking the mangolds for the pigs' supper to the kaffirs.

And then there came that afternoon when I went to see Jurie Steyn about some fence-poles that he had gone to fetch for me from Ramoutsa station, and I found that Jurie was too concerned about something that the teacher had said to be able to pay much attention to my questions. I have mentioned how the deterioration in his moral character took the form of making him absent-minded, at times, in a funny sort of way.

"You can have the next lot I fetch," Jurie said. "I have been so worried about what the school-teacher said that I have already planted all your fence-poles – look, along there – by mistake. I planted them without thinking. I was so concerned about the schoolmaster's impudence that I had got the kaffirs to dig the holes and plant in the poles before I realised what I was doing. But I'll pay you for them, some time – when I get my cheque from the creamery, maybe. And while we are about it, I may as well use up the roll of barbed wire that is also lying at Ramoutsa station, consigned to you. You won't need that barbed wire, now."

"No," I said, looking at my fence-poles planted in a long line. "No, Jurie, I won't need that barbed wire now. And another thing, if you stand here, just to the left of this ant-hill, and you look all along the tops of the poles, you will see that they are not planted in a straight line. You can see the line bends in two places."

But Jurie said, no, he was satisfied with the way he had planted in my fence-poles. The line was straight enough for him, he said. And I felt that this was quite true, and that anything would be straight enough for him – even if it was something as twisted as a raw ox-hide thong that you brei with a stick and a heavy stone slung from a tree.

"What did the school-teacher say about you?" I asked Jurie eventually, doing my best not to let him see how eager I was to hear if what had been said about him was really low enough.

"He said I was dishonest," Jurie answered. "He said . . ."

"How does he know?" I interrupted him quickly. "He's so busy on his farm there, with the harvesting, I didn't think he would have time to hear what is going on among us farmers. Did he make any mention of my fence-poles at all?"

"He didn't mean it that way," Jurie answered, standing to the side of the ant-hill and gazing into the distance with one eye shut. "No, I think those poles are planted in all right. When the school-master told me I was dishonest he meant it in a different sense. But what he said was bad enough. He said that my youngest son,

Kobus, was dishonest, and that he feared that in that respect Kobus took after me."

I thought this was very singular. Did not the school-teacher know the story of the ouderling's visits to Jurie Steyn's wife, Martha, in the time of the big drought? Had Jurie Steyn no suspicions, either, about the boy, Kobus, not being his own child? But I did not let on to Jurie Steyn, of course, what my real thoughts were.

"So he said Kobus is dishonest?" I continued, trying to make my voice sound disarming. "Why, did Kobus go along to Ramoutsa station with you, for my poles?"

"No," Jurie Steyn answered. "The schoolmaster won't allow Kobus to stay away from school for a day – not until the harvesting is over. But I am sending Kobus and a kaffir to Ramoutsa on Saturday, by donkey-cart. I am sending him for that roll of barbed wire. And, oh, by the way, Schalk, while Kobus is in Ramoutsa, is there anything you would like him to get for you?"

I thanked Jurie and said, no, there was nothing for me at Ramoutsa that had not already been fetched. Then I asked him another question.

"Did the schoolmaster perhaps say that you and Kobus were a couple of aardvarks?" I asked. "I daresay he used pretty rough language. Snakes, too, he must have said. I mean to say . . ."

"You are quite right," Jurie interrupted me. "That fourth pole from the end must come out. It's not in line."

"The whole lot must come out," I said, "and be planted on my farm. That's what I ordered those poles for."

"That fourth pole of yours, Oom Schalk," Jurie repeated, "must be taken out and planted further to the left – I planted it in crooked because I was so upset by the schoolmaster. It was only when I got home that I realised the cheek of the whole thing. I have got a good mind to report the schoolmaster to the Education Department for writing private letters with school ink. I'd like to see him get out of that one."

If the Education Department did not take any action after the schoolmaster had used the front part of the school building to store his sweet-potatoes in, I did not think they would worry much about this complaint of Jurie Steyn's. By way of explanation the school-teacher told the parents that why he had to store the sweet-potatoes in that part of the school building for a while was because the prices on the Johannesburg market were so low, it was sheer robbery. He also complained that the Johannesburg produce agents had no sense of responsibility in regard to the interests of the farmers.

"If I had so little sense of responsibility about my duties as a school-teacher," he said, "the Education Department would have sacked me long ago."

When the schoolmaster made this remark several of the parents looked at him with a good deal of amazement.

These were the things that were passing through my mind while Jurie Steyn was telling me about the way the school-teacher had insulted him. I was anxious to learn more about it. I tried another way of getting Jurie to talk. I wanted to find out how much the schoolmaster knew, and how much Jurie himself suspected, of the facts of Kobus's paternity. I felt almost as inquisitive as a woman, then.

"I once heard the schoolmaster using very strong expressions, Jurie," I said, "and that was when he spoke to a Pondo kaffir whom he had caught stealing one of the back wheels of his ox-wagon. I have never been able to understand how that kaffir got the wheel off so quickly, because he didn't have a jack, as far as I know, and they say that the wagon had not been outspanned for more than two hours. But that was only a Pondo kaffir without much understanding of the white man's language of abuse. No doubt what the school-teacher said about you and your son Kobus was . . ."

"It's possible to get a back wheel off an ox-wagon even if you haven't got a jack, so long as the wagon isn't too heavily loaded," Jurie said, without giving me a chance to finish, "and as long as you have got two other men to help you. Still, it would be interesting to know how the Pondo did it. Was it dark at the time, do you know?"

I couldn't tell him. But it was getting dark on Jurie Steyn's farm. The deep shadows of the evening lay heavy across the thorn-bushes, and the furthest of my fence-poles had grown

233

blurred against the sky. It seemed a strange thought to me that my fence-poles were that night for the first time standing upright and in silence, like the trees, awaiting the arrival of the first stars.

Jurie Steyn and I started walking towards the farmhouse, in front of which I had left my mule-cart. The boy Kobus came out to meet us, and I could see from the reddish clay on his knees that he had studied hard at school that day.

"You look tired, Kobus," Jurie Steyn said. And his voice suddenly sounded very soft when he spoke.

And in the dusk I saw the way that Kobus's eyes lit up when he took Jurie Steyn's hand. A singular variety of ideas passed through my mind, then, and I found that I no longer bore Jurie Steyn that same measure of resentment on account of his thoughtless way of acting with my fence-poles. I somehow felt that there were more important things in life than the question of what happened to my roll of barbed wire at Ramoutsa. And more important things than what had happened about the ouderling from near Vleisfontein.

The *Trek* and *On Parade* Years
(1948–51)

Dopper and Papist

It was a cold night (Oom Schalk Lourens said) on which we drove with Gert Bekker in his Cape-cart to Zeerust. I sat in front, next to Gert, who was driving. In the back seat were the predikant, Rev. Vermooten, and his ouderling, Isak Erasmus, who were on their way to Pretoria for the meeting of the synod of the Dutch Reformed Church. The predikant was lean and hawk-faced; the ouderling was fat and had broad shoulders.

Gert Bekker and I did not speak. We had been transport drivers together in our time, and we had learnt that when it is two men alone, travelling over a long distance, it is best to use few words, and those well chosen. Two men, alone in each other's company, understand each other better the less they speak.

The horses kept up a good, steady trot. The lantern, swinging from side to side with the jogging of the cart, lit up stray patches of the uneven road and made bulky shadows rise up among the thorn-trees. In the back seat the predikant and the ouderling were discussing theology.

"You never saw such a lot of brandsiek sheep in your life," the predikant was saying, "as what Chris Haasbroek brought along as tithe."

We then came to a stony part of the road, and so I did not hear the ouderling's reply; but afterwards, above the rattling of the cart-wheels, I caught other snatches of God-fearing conversation, to do with the raising of pew-rents.

From there the predikant started discussing the proselytising activities being carried on among the local Bapedi kaffirs by the Catholic mission at Vleisfontein. The predikant dwelt particularly on the ignorance of the Bapedi tribes and on the idolatrous form of the Papist communion service, which was quite different from the Protestant Nagmaal, the predikant said, although to a Bapedi, walking with his buttocks sticking out, the two services might, perhaps, seem somewhat alike.

Rev. Vermooten was very eloquent when he came to denouncing the heresies of Catholicism. And he spoke loudly, so that we could hear him on the front seat. And I know that both Gert Bekker and I felt very good, then, deep inside us, to think that we were Protestants. The coldness of the night and the pale flickering of the lantern-light among the thorn-trees gave an added solemnity to the predikant's words.

I felt that it might perhaps be all right to be a Catholic if you were walking on the Zeerust sidewalk in broad daylight, say. But it was a different matter to be driving through the middle of the bush on a dark night, with just a swinging lantern fastened to the side of a Cape-cart with baling-wire. If the lantern went out suddenly, and you were left in the loneliest part of the bush, striking matches, then it must be a very frightening thing to be a Catholic, I thought.

This led me to thinking of Piet Reilly and his family, who were Afrikaners, like you and me, except that they were Catholics. Piet Reilly even brought out his vote for General Lemmer at the last Volksraad election, which we thought would make it unlucky for our candidate. But General Lemmer said, no, he didn't mind how many Catholics voted for him. A Catholic's vote was, naturally, not as good as a Dopper's, he said, but the little cross that had to be made behind a candidate's name cast out the evil that was of course otherwise lurking in a Catholic's ballot paper. And General Lemmer must have been right, because he got elected, that time.

While I was thinking on these lines, it suddenly struck me that Piet Reilly was now living on a farm about six miles on the Bushveld side of Sephton's Nek, and that we would be passing his farmhouse, which was near the road, just before daybreak. It was comforting to think that we would have the predikant and the ouderling in the Cape-cart with us, when we passed the homestead of Piet Reilly, a Catholic, in the dark.

I tried to hear what the predikant was saying, in the back seat, to the ouderling. But the predikant was once more dealing with an abstruse point of religion, and had lowered his voice accordingly. I could catch only fragments of the ouderling's replies.

"Yes, dominee," I heard the ouderling affirm, "you are quite right. If he again tries to overlook your son for the job of anthrax inspector, then you must make it clear to the Chairman of the Board that you have all that information about his private life . . ."

I realised then that you could find much useful guidance for your everyday problems in the conversation of holy men.

The night got colder and darker.

The palm of my hand, pressed tight around the bowl of my pipe, was the only part of me that felt warm. My teeth began to chatter. I wished that, next time we stopped to let the horses blow, we could light a fire and boil coffee. But I knew that there was no coffee left in the chest under the back seat.

While I sat silent next to Gert Bekker, I continued to think of Piet Reilly and his wife and children. With Piet, of course, I could understand it. He himself had merely kept up the religion – if you can call what the Catholics believe in a religion – that he had inherited from his father and his grandfather. But there was Piet Reilly's wife, Gertruida, now. She had been brought up a respectable Dopper girl. She was one of the Drogedal Bekkers, and was, in fact, distantly related to Gert Bekker, who was sitting on the Cape-cart next to me. There was something for you to ponder about, I thought to myself, with the cold all the time looking for new places in my skin through which to strike into my bones.

The moment Gertruida met Piet Reilly she forgot all about the sacred truths she had learnt at her mother's knee. And on the day she got married she was saying prayers to the Virgin Mary on a string of beads, and was wearing a silver cross at her throat that was as soft and white as the roses she held pressed against her. Here was now a sweet Dopper girl turned Papist.

As I have said, I knew that there was no coffee left in the box under the back seat; but I did know that under the front seat there was a full bottle of raw peach brandy. In fact, I could see the neck of the bottle protruding from between Gert Bekker's ankles.

I also knew, through all the years of transport driving that we had done together, that Gert Bekker had already, over many miles of road, been thinking how we could get the cork off the bottle without the predikant and the ouderling shaking their heads reprovingly. And the way he managed it in the end was, I thought, highly intelligent.

For, when he stopped the cart again to rest the horses, he alighted beside the road and held out the bottle to our full view.

"There is brandy in this bottle, dominee," Gert Bekker said to the predikant, "that I keep for the sake of the horses on cold nights, like now. It is an old Marico remedy for when the horses are in danger of getting the floute. I take a few mouthfuls of the brandy, which I then blow into the nostrils of the horses, who don't feel the cold so much, after that. The brandy revives them."

Gert commenced blowing brandy into the face of the horse on the near side, to show us.

Then he beckoned to me, and I also alighted and went and stood next to him, taking turns with him in blowing brandy into the eyes and nostrils of the offside horse. We did this several times.

The predikant asked various questions, to show how interested he was in this old-fashioned method of overcoming fatigue in draught-animals. But what the predikant said at the next stop made me perceive that he was more than a match for a dozen men like Gert Bekker in point of astuteness.

When we stopped the cart, the predikant held up his hand.

"Don't you and your friend trouble to get off this time," the predikant called out when Gert Bekker was once more reaching for the bottle. "The ouderling and I have decided to take turns with you in blowing brandy into the horses' faces. We don't want to put all the hard work on to your shoulders."

We made several more halts after that, with the result that daybreak found us still a long way from Sephton's Nek. In the early dawn we saw the thatched roof of Piet Reilly's house through the thorn-trees some distance from the road. When the predikant suggested that we call at the homestead for coffee, we explained to him that the Reillys were Catholics.

"But isn't Piet Reilly's wife a relative of yours?" the predikant asked of Gert Bekker. "Isn't she your second-cousin, or something?"

"They are Catholics," Gert answered.

"Coffee," the predikant insisted.

"Catholics," Gert Bekker repeated stolidly.

The upshot of it was, naturally enough, that we outspanned shortly afterwards in front of the Reilly homestead. That was the kind of man that the predikant was in an argument.

"The coffee will be ready soon," the predikant said as we walked up to the front door. "There is smoke coming out of the chimney."

Almost before we had stopped knocking, Gertruida Reilly had opened both the top and bottom doors. She started slightly when she saw, standing in front of her, a minister of the Dutch Reformed Church. In spite of her look of agitation, Gertruida was still pretty, I thought, after ten years of being married to Piet Reilly.

When she stepped forward to kiss her cousin, Gert Bekker, I saw him turn away, sadly; and I realised something of the shame that she had brought on her whole family through her marriage to a Catholic.

"You looked startled when you saw me, Gertruida," the predikant said, calling her by her first name, as though she was still a member of his congregation.

"Yes," Gertruida answered. "Yes – I was – surprised."

"I suppose it was a Catholic priest that you wanted to come to your front door," Gert Bekker said, sarcastically. Yet there was a tone in his voice that was not altogether unfriendly.

"Indeed, I was expecting a Catholic priest," Gertruida said, leading us into the voorkamer. "But if the Lord has sent the dominee and his ouderling, instead, I am sure it will be well, also."

It was only then, after she had explained to us what had happened, that we understood why Gertruida was looking so troubled. Her eight-year-old daughter had been bitten by a snake: they couldn't tell from the fang-marks if it was a ringhals or a bakkop. Piet Reilly had driven off in the mule-cart to Vleisfontein, the Catholic mission station, for a priest.

They had cut open and cauterised the wound and had applied red permanganate. The rest was a matter for God. And that was why, when she saw the predikant and the ouderling at her front door, Gertruida believed that the Lord had sent them.

I was glad that Gert Bekker did not at that moment think of mentioning that we had really come for coffee.

241

"Certainly, I shall pray for your little girl's recovery," the predikant said to Gertruida. "Take me to her."

Gertruida hesitated.

"Will you – will you pray for her the Catholic way, dominee?" Gertruida asked.

Now it was the predikant's turn to draw back.

"But, Gertruida," he said, "you, you whom I myself confirmed in the Enkel-Gereformeerde Kerk in Zeerust – how can you now ask me such a thing? Did you not learn in the catechism that the Romish ritual is a mockery of the Holy Ghost?"

"I married Piet Reilly," Gertruida answered simply, "and his faith is my faith. Piet has been very good to me, Father. And I love him."

We noticed that Gertruida called the predikant 'Father,' now, and not 'Dominee.' During the silence that followed, I glanced at the candle burning before an image of the Mother Mary in a corner of the voorkamer. I looked away quickly from that unrighteousness.

The predikant's next words took us by complete surprise.

"Have you got some kind of prayer-book," the predikant asked, "that sets out the – the Catholic form for a . . ."

"I'll fetch it from the other room," Gertruida answered.

When she had left, the predikant tried to put our minds at ease.

"I am only doing this to help a mother in distress," he explained to the ouderling. "It is something that the Lord will understand. Gertruida was brought up a Dopper girl. In some ways she is still one of us. She does not understand that I have no authority to conduct this Catholic service for the sick."

The ouderling was going to say something.

But at that moment Gertruida returned with a little black book that you could almost have taken for a Dutch Reformed Church psalm-book. Only, I knew that what was printed inside it was as iniquitous as the candle burning in the corner.

Yet I also began to wonder if, in not knowing the difference, a Bapedi really was so very ignorant, even though he walked with his buttocks sticking out.

"My daughter is in this other room," Gertruida said, and started in the direction of the door. The predikant followed her. Just before entering the bedroom he turned round and faced the ouderling.

"Will you enter with me, Brother Erasmus?" the predikant asked.

The ouderling did not answer. The veins stood out on his forehead. On his face you could read the conflict that went on inside him. For what seemed a very long time he stood quite motionless. Then he stooped down to the rusbank for his hat – which he did not need – and walked after the predikant into the bedroom.

COMETH COMET

Hans Engelbrecht was the first farmer in the Schweizer-Reneke District to trek (Oom Schalk Lourens said). With his wife and daughter and what was left of his cattle, he moved away to the northern slopes of the Dwarsberge, where the drought was less severe. Afterwards he was joined by other farmers from the same area. I can still remember how untidy the veld looked in those days, with rotting carcasses and sun-bleached bones lying about everywhere. Day after day we had stood at the boreholes, pumping an ever-decreasing trickle of brackish water into the cattle troughs. We watched in vain for a sign of a cloud. And it seemed that if anything did fall out of that sky, it wouldn't do us much good: it would be a shower of brimstone, most likely.

Still, it was a fine time for the aasvoëls and the crows. That was at the beginning, of course. Afterwards, when all the carcasses had been picked bare, and the Boers had trekked, most of the birds of prey flew away, also.

We trekked away in different directions. Four or five families eventually came to a halt at the foot of the Dwarsberge, near the place where Hans Engelbrecht was outspanned. In the vast area of the Schweizer-Reneke District only one man had chosen to stay behind. He was Ocker Gieljan, a young bywoner who had worked for Hans Engelbrecht since his boyhood. Ocker Gieljan spoke rarely, and then his words did not always seem to us to make sense.

Hans Engelbrecht was only partly surprised when, on the morning that the ox-wagon was loaded and the long line of oxen that were skin and bone started stumbling along the road to the north, Ocker Gieljan made it clear that he was not leaving the farm. The native voorloper had already gone to the head of the span and Hans Engelbrecht's wife and his eighteen-year-old daughter, Maria, were seated on the wagon, under the tent-sail,

244

when Ocker Gieljan suddenly declared that he had decided to stay behind on the farm "to look after things here."

This was another instance of Ocker Gieljan's saying something that did not make sense. There could be nothing for him to look after, there, since in the whole district hardly a lizard was left alive.

Hans Engelbrecht was in no mood to waste time in arguing with a daft bywoner. Accordingly, he got the kaffirs to unload half a sack of mealie-meal and a quantity of biltong in front of Ocker Gieljan's mud-walled room.

During the past few years it had not rained much in the Marico Bushveld, either. But there was at least water in the Molopo, and the grazing was fair. Several months passed. Every day, from our camp by the Molopo, we studied the skies, which were of an intense blue. There was no longer that yellow tinge in the air that we had got used to in the Schweizer-Reneke District. But there was never a rain-cloud.

The time came, also, when Hans Engelbrecht was brought to understand that the Lord had visited still more trouble on himself and his family. A little while before we had trekked away from our farms, a young insurance agent had left the district suddenly for Cape Town. That was a long distance to run away, especially when you think of how bad the roads were in those days. And in some strange fashion it seemed to me as though that young insurance agent was actually our leader. For he stood, after all, with his light hat and short jacket, at the head of our flight out of the Schweizer-Reneke area.

It became a commonplace, after a while, for Maria Engelbrecht to be seen seated in the grass beside her father's wagon, weeping. Few pitied her. She must have sat in the grass too often, with that insurance agent with the pointed, polished shoes, Lettie Grobler said to some of the women – forgetting that there had been no grass left in the Schweizer-Reneke veld at the time when Hans Engelbrecht's daughter was being courted.

It was easy for Maria to wipe the tears from her face, another woman said. Easier than to wipe away her shame, the woman meant.

Now and again, from some traveller who had passed through Schweizer-Reneke, we who had trekked out of that stricken region would hear a few useless things about it. We learnt nothing that we did not already know. Ocker Gieljan was still on the Engelbrecht farm, we heard. And the only other living creature in the whole district was a solitary crow. A passing traveller had seen Ocker Gieljan at the borehole. He was pumping water into a trough for the crow, the traveller said.

"When his mealie-meal gives out, Ocker will find his way here, right enough," Hans Engelbrecht growled impatiently.

Then the night came when, from our encampment beside the Molopo, we first saw the comet, in the place above the Dwarsberg rante where the sun had gone down. We all began to wonder what that new star with the long tail meant. Would it bring rain? We didn't know. We could see, of course, that the star was an omen. Even an uneducated kaffir would know that. But we did not know what sort of omen it was.

If the bark of the maroelas turned black before the polgras was in seed, we would know that it would be a long winter. And if a wind sprang up suddenly in the evening, blowing away from the sunset, we would next morning send the cattle out later to graze. We knew many things about the veld and the sky and the seasons. But even the oldest Free State farmer among us didn't know what effect a comet had on a mealie-crop.

Hans Engelbrecht said that we should send for Rev. Losper, the missionary who ministered to the Bechuanas at Ramoutsa. But the rest of us ignored his suggestion.

During the following nights the comet became more clearly visible. A young policeman on patrol in these parts called on us one evening. When we spoke to him about the star, he said that he could do nothing about it, himself. It was a matter for the higher authorities, he said, laughing.

Nevertheless, he had made a few calculations, the policeman explained, and he had sent a report to Pretoria. He estimated that the star was twenty-seven and a half miles in length, and that it was travelling faster than a railway train. He would not be surprised if the star reached Pretoria before his report got there. That would spoil his chances of promotion, he added.

We did not take much notice of the policeman's remarks, however. For one thing, he was young. And, for another, we did not have much respect for the police.

"If a policeman doesn't even know how to get on to the spoor of a couple of kaffir oxen that I smuggle across the Bechuanaland border," Thys Bekker said, "how does he expect to be able to follow the footprints of a star across the sky? That is big man's work."

The appearance of the comet caused consternation among the Bechuanas in the village of Ramoutsa, where the mission station was. It did not take long for some of their stories about the star to reach our encampment on the other side of the Molopo. And although, at first, most of us professed to laugh at what we said were just ignorant kaffir superstitions, yet in the end we also began to share something of the Bechuana's fears.

"Have you heard what the kaffirs say about the new star?" Arnoldus Grobler, husband of Lettie Grobler, asked of Thys Bekker. "They say that it is a red beast with a fat belly like a very great chief, and it is going to come to eat up every blade of grass and every living thing."

"In that case, I hope he lands in Schweizer-Reneke," Thys Bekker said. "If that red beast comes down on my farm, all that will happen is that in a short while there will be a whole lot more bones lying around to get white in the sun."

Some of us felt that it was wrong of Thys Bekker to treat the matter so lightly. Moreover, this story only emanated from Ramoutsa, where there were a mission station and a post office. But a number of other stories, that were in every way much better, started soon afterwards to come out of the wilder parts of the Bushveld, travelling on foot. It seemed that the further a tribe of kaffirs lived away from civilisation, the more detailed and dependable was the information they had about the comet.

I know that I began to feel that Hans Engelbrecht had made the right suggestion in the first place, when he had said that we should send for the missionary. And I sensed that a number of others in our camp shared my feelings. But not one of us wanted to make this admission openly.

In the end it was Hans Engelbrecht himself who sent to

247

Ramoutsa for Rev. Losper. By that time the comet was – each night in its rising – higher in the heavens, and it soon got round that the new star portended the end of the world. Lettie Grobler went so far as to declare that she had seen the good Lord Himself riding in the tail of the comet. What convinced us that she had, indeed, seen the Lord, was when she said that He had on a hat of the same shape as the predikant in Zwartruggens wore.

Lettie Grobler also said that the Lord was coming down to punish all of us for the sins of Maria Engelbrecht. This thought disturbed us greatly. We began to resent Maria's presence in our midst.

It was then that Hans Engelbrecht had sent for the missionary.

Meanwhile, Rev. Losper had his hands full with the Bechuanas at Ramoutsa, who seemed on the point of panicking in earnest. The latest story about the comet had just reached them, and because it had come from somewhere out of the deepest part of Africa, where the natives wore arrows tipped with leopard fangs stuck through their nostrils, like moustaches, it was easily the most terrifying story of all. The story had come to the village, thumped out on the tom-toms.

The Bechuana chief at Ramoutsa – so Rev. Losper told us afterwards – fell into such a terror at the message brought by the speaking drums, that he thrust a handful of earth into his mouth, without thinking. He would have swallowed it, too, the missionary said, if one of his indunas hadn't restrained him in time, pointing out to the chief that perhaps the drum-men had got the message wrong. For, since the post office had come to Ramoutsa, the kaffirs whose work in the village it was to receive and send out messages on their tom-toms had got somewhat out of practice.

Consequently, because of the tumult at Ramoutsa, it happened that Ocker Gieljan arrived at the encampment before Rev. Losper got there.

Ocker Gieljan looked very tired and dusty on that afternoon when he walked up to Hans Engelbrecht's wagon. He took off his hat and, smiling somewhat vacantly, sat down without speaking in the shade of the veld-tent, inside which Maria Engelbrecht lay on a mattress. Neither Hans Engelbrecht nor his wife asked Ocker Gieljan any questions about his journey from the Schweizer-Reneke farm. They knew that he could have nothing to tell.

Shortly afterwards, Ocker Gieljan made a communication to Hans Engelbrecht, speaking diffidently. Thereupon Hans Engelbrecht went into the tent and spoke to his wife and daughter. A few minutes later he came out, looking pleased with himself.

"Sit down here on this riempiestoel, Ocker," Hans Engelbrecht said to his prospective son-in-law, "and tell me how you came to leave the farm."

"I got lonely," Ocker Gieljan answered, thoughtfully. "You see, the crow flew away. I was alone, after that. The crow was then already weak. He didn't fly straight, like crows do. His wings wobbled."

When he told me about this, years later, Hans Engelbrecht said that something in Ocker Gieljan's tone brought him a sudden vision of the way his daughter, Maria, had also left the Schweizer-Reneke District. With broken wings.

I thought that Rev. Losper looked relieved to find, on his arrival at the camp, some time later, that all that was required of him, now, was the performance of a marriage ceremony.

On the next night but one, Maria Engelbrecht's child was born. All the adults in our little trekker community came in the night and the rain – which had been falling steadily for many hours – with gifts for Maria and her child.

And when I saw the star again, during the temporary break in the rain-clouds, it seemed to me that it was not such a new star, at all: that it was, indeed, a mighty old star.

GREAT-UNCLE JORIS

For quite a number of Boers in the Transvaal Bushveld the expedition against Majaja's tribe of Bechuanas – we called them the Platkop kaffirs – was unlucky.

There was a young man with us on this expedition who did not finish a story that he started to tell of a bygone war. And for a good while afterwards the relations were considerably strained between the long-established Transvalers living in these parts and the Cape Boers who had trekked in more recently.

I can still remember all the activity that went on north of the Dwarsberge at that time, with veldkornets going from one farmhouse to another to recruit burghers for the expedition, and with provisions and ammunition having to be got together, and with new stories being told every day about how cheeky the Platkop kaffirs were getting.

I must mention that about that time a number of Boers from the Cape had trekked into the Marico Bushveld. In the Drogedal area, indeed, the recently arrived Cape Boers were almost as numerous as the Transvalers who had been settled here for a considerable while. At that time I, too, still regarded myself as a Cape Boer, since I had only a few years before quit the Schweizer-Reneke District for the Western Transvaal. When the veldkornet came to my farm on his recruiting tour, I volunteered my services immediately.

"Of course, we don't want *everybody* to go on commando," the veldkornet said, studying me somewhat dubiously, after I had informed him that I was from the Cape, and that older relatives of mine had taken part in wars against the kaffirs in the Eastern Province. "We need some burghers to stay behind to help guard the farms. We can't leave all that to the women and children."

The veldkornet seemed to have conceived an unreasonable prejudice against people whose forebears had fought against the

Xhosas in the Eastern Province. But I assured him that I was very anxious to join, and so in the end he consented. "A volunteer is, after all, worth more to a fighting force than a man who has to be commandeered against his will," the veldkornet said, stroking his beard. "Usually."

A week later, on my arrival at the big camp by the Steenbok-spruit, where the expedition against the Platkop kaffirs was being assembled, I was agreeably surprised to find many old friends and acquaintances from the Cape Colony among the burghers on commando. There were also a large number of others whom I then met for the first time, who were introduced to me as new immigrants from the Cape.

Indeed, among ourselves we spoke a good deal about this proud circumstance – about the fact that we Cape Boers actually outnumbered the Transvalers in this expedition against Majaja – and we were glad to think that in time of need we had not failed to come to the help of our new fatherland. For this reason the coolness that made itself felt as between Transvaler and Cape Boer, after the expedition was over, was all the more regrettable.

We remained camped for a good number of days beside the Steenbokspruit. During that time I became friendly with Frikkie van Blerk and Jan Bezuidenhout, who were also originally from the Cape. We craved excitement. And when we were seated around the camp-fire, talking of life in the Eastern Province, it was natural enough that we should find ourselves swapping stories of the adventures of our older relatives in the wars against the Xhosas. We were all three young, and so we spoke like veterans, forgetting that our knowledge of frontier fighting was based only on hearsay. Each of us was an authority on the best way of defeating a Xhosa impi without loss of life to anybody except the members of the impi. Frikkie van Blerk took the lead in this kind of talk, and I may say that he was peculiar in his manner of expressing himself, some-times. Unfeeling, you might say. Anyway, as the night wore on, there were in the whole Transvaal, I am sure, no three young men less worried than we were about the different kinds of calamities that, in this uncertain world, would overtake a Xhosa impi.

"Are you married, Schalk?" Jan Bezuidenhout asked me, sud-denly.

"No," I replied, "but Frikkie van Blerk is. Why do you ask?"
Jan Bezuidenhout sighed.

"It is all right for you," he informed me. "But I am also married. And it is for burghers like Frikkie van Blerk and myself that a war can become a most serious thing. Who is looking after your place while you are on commando, Frikkie?"

Frikkie van Blerk said that a friend and neighbour, Gideon Kotze, had made special arrangement with the veldkornet, whereby he was released from service with the commando on condition that he kept an eye on the farms within a twenty-mile radius of his own.

"The thought that Gideon Kotze is looking after things, in that way, makes me feel much happier," Frikkie van Blerk added. "It is nice for me to know that my wife will not be quite alone all the time."

"Gideon Kotze –" Jan Bezuidenhout repeated, and sighed again.

"What do you mean by that sigh?" Frikkie van Blerk demanded, quickly, a nasty tone seeming to creep into his voice.

"Oh, nothing," Jan Bezuidenhout answered, "oh, nothing at all."

As he spoke he kicked at a log on the edge of the fire. The fine sparks rose up very high in the still air and got lost in the leaves of the thorn-tree overhead.

Frikkie van Blerk cleared his throat. "For that matter," he said in a meaningful way to Jan Bezuidenhout, "you are also a married man. Who is looking after *your* farm – and *your* wife – while you are sitting here?"

Jan Bezuidenhout waited for several moments before he answered.

"Who?" he repeated, "who? Why, Gideon Kotze, also."

This time when Jan Bezuidenhout sighed, Frikkie van Blerk joined in, audibly. And I, who had nothing at all to do with any part of this situation, seeing that I was not married, found myself sighing as well. And this time it was Frikkie van Blerk who kicked the log by the side of the fire. The chunk of white wood, which had been hollowed out by the ants, fell into several pieces, sending up a fiery shower so high that, to us, looking up to follow their flight, the yellow sparks became for a few moments almost indistinguishable from the stars.

"It's all rotten," Frikkie van Blerk said, taking another kick at the crumbling log, and missing.

252

"There's something in the Bible about something else being something like sparks flying upwards," Jan Bezuidenhout announced. His words sounded very solemn. They served as an introduction to the following story that he told us:

"It was during my grandfather's time," Jan Bezuidenhout said. "My great-uncle Joris, who had a farm near the Keiskamma, had been commandeered to take the field in the Fifth Kaffir War. Before setting out for the war, my great-uncle Joris arranged for a friend and neighbour to visit his farm regularly, in case his wife needed help. Well, as you know, there is no real danger in a war against kaffirs –"

"Yes, we know that," Frikkie van Blerk and I agreed simultaneously, to sound knowledgeable.

"I mean, there's no danger as long as you don't go so near that a kaffir can reach you with an assegai," Jan Bezuidenhout continued. "And, of course, no white man is as uneducated as all that. But what happened to my great-uncle Joris was that his horse threw him. The commando was retreating just about then –"

"To reload," Frikkie van Blerk and I both said, eager to show how well acquainted we were with the strategy used in kaffir wars.

"Yes," Jan Bezuidenhout went on. "To reload. And there was no time for the commando to stop for my great-uncle Joris. The last his comrades saw of him, he was crawling on his hands and knees towards an aardvark hole. They didn't know whether the Xhosas had seen him. Perhaps the commando had to ride back fast because –"

Jan Bezuidenhout did not finish his story. For, just then, a veldkornet came with orders from Kommandant Pienaar. We had to put out the fire. We had not to make so much noise. We were to hold ourselves in readiness, in case the kaffirs launched a night attack. The veldkornet also instructed Jan Bezuidenhout to get his gun and go on guard duty.

"There was never any nonsense like this in the Cape," Frikkie van Blerk grumbled, "when we were fighting the Xhosas. It seems the Transvalers don't know what a kaffir war is."

By this time Frikkie van Blerk had got to believe that he actually had taken part in the campaigns against the Xhosas.

I have mentioned that there were certain differences between the Transvalers and the Cape Boers. For one thing, we from the Cape had a lightness of heart which the Transvalers lacked – possibly (I thought at the time) because the stubborn Transvaal soil made the conditions of life more harsh for them. And the difference between the two sections was particularly noticeable on the following morning, when Kommandant Pienaar, after having delivered a short speech about how it was our duty to bring book-learning and refinement to the Platkop kaffirs, gave the order to advance. We who were from the Cape cheered lustily. The Transvalers were, as always, subdued. They turned pale, too, some of them. We rode on for the best part of an hour. Frikkie van Blerk, Jan Bezuidenhout and I found ourselves together in a small group on one flank of the commando.

"It's funny," Jan Bezuidenhout said, "but I don't see any kaffirs, anywhere, with assegais. It doesn't seem to be like it was against the Xhosas –"

He stopped abruptly. For we heard what sounded surprisingly like a shot. Afterwards we heard what sounded surprisingly like more shots.

"These Platkop Bechuanas are *not* like the Cape Xhosas," I agreed, then, dismounting.

In no time the whole commando had dismounted. We sought cover in dongas and behind rocks from the fire of an enemy who had concealed himself better than we were doing.

"No, the Xhosas were not at all like this," Frikkie van Blerk announced, tearing off a strip of shirt to bandage a place in his leg from which the blood flowed. "Why didn't the Transvalers let us know it would be like this?"

It was an ambush. Things happened very quickly. It became only too clear to me why the Transvalers had not shared in our enthusiasm earlier on, when we had gone over the rise together, at a canter, through the yellow grass, singing. I was still reflecting on this circumstance, some time later, when our commando remounted and galloped away out of that whole part of the district. To reload, we said, years afterwards, to strangers who asked. The last we saw of Jan Bezuidenhout was after he had had his horse shot down from under him. He was crawling on hands and knees in the direction of an aardvark hole.

254

"Like great-uncle, like nephew," Frikkie van Blerk said, when we were discussing the affair some time later, back in camp beside the Steenbokspruit. Frikkie van Blerk's unfeeling sally was not well received.

Thus ended the expedition against Majaja, which brought little honour to the commando that took part in it. There was not a burgher who retained any sort of a happy memory of the affair. And for a good while afterwards the relations were strained between Transvaler and Cape Boer in the Marico.

It was with a sense of bitterness that, some months later, I had occasion to call to mind the fact that Gideon Kotze, the man appointed to look after the farms of the burghers on commando, was a Transvaler.

And when I saw Gideon Kotze sitting talking to Jan Bezuidenhout's widow, on the front stoep of their house, I wondered what the story was, about his great-uncle Joris, that Jan Bezuidenhout had not been able to finish telling.

TREASURE TROVE

It is queer (Oom Schalk Lourens said), about treasure hunting.
You can actually find the treasure, and through ignorance, or
through forgetting to look, at the moment when you have got it,
you can let it slip through your fingers like sand. Take Namaqualand, for instance. That part where all the diamonds are lying
around, waiting to be picked up. Now they have got it all fenced
in, and there are hundreds of police patrolling what we thought,
in those days, was just a piece of desert. I remember the last time
I trekked through that part of the country, which I took to be an
ungodly stretch of sandy waste. But if I had known that I was
travelling through thousands of miles of diamond mine, I don't
think I would have hurried so much. And that area wouldn't have
seemed so very ungodly, either.

I made the last part of the journey on foot. And you know how
it is when you are walking through the sand; how you have to stop
every so often to sit down and shake out your boots. I get quite a
sick feeling, even now, when I think that I never once looked to see
what I was shaking out. You hear of a person allowing a fortune to
slip through his fingers. But it is much sadder if he lets it trickle
away through the leather of his veldskoens.

Anyway, when the talk comes round to fortunes, and so on, I
always call to mind the somewhat singular search that went on,
for the better part of a Bushveld summer, on Jan Slabbert's farm.
We all said, afterwards, that Jan Slabbert should have known better, at his age and experience, than to have allowed a stranger like
that callow young Hendrik Buys, on the strength of a few lines
drawn on a piece of wrapping paper, to come along and start up
so much foolishness.

Jan Slabbert was very mysterious about the whole thing, at
first. He introduced Hendrik Buys to us as "a young man from the

Cape who is having a look over my farm." These words of Jan Slabbert's did not, however, reveal to us much that we did not already know. Indeed, I had on more than one occasion come across Hendrik Buys, unexpectedly and from behind, when he was quite clearly engaged in looking over Jan Slabbert's farm. He had even got down on his hands and knees to look it over better.

But in the end, after several neighbours had unexpectedly come across Jan Slabbert in the same way, he admitted that they were conducting a search for hidden treasure.

"I suppose, because it's hidden treasure, Jan Slabbert thinks that is has got to be kept hidden from us, also," Jurie Bekker said one day when several of us were sitting in his post office.

"It's a treasure consisting of gold coins and jewels that were buried on Jan Slabbert's farm many years ago," Neels Erasmus, who was a church elder, explained. "I called on Jan Slabbert – not because I was inquisitive about the treasure, of course – but in connection with something of a theological character that happened at the last Nagmaal, and Jan Slabbert and Hendrik Buys were both out. They were on the veld."

"On their hands and knees," Jurie Bekker said.

The ouderling went on to tell us that Jan Slabbert's daughter, Susannah, had said that a piece of the map which that young fellow, Buys, had brought with him from the Cape, was missing, with the result that they were having difficulty in locating the spot marked with a cross.

"It's always like that with a map of a place where there is buried treasure," Jurie Bekker said. "You follow a lot of directions, until you come to an old tree or an old grave or an old forked road with cobwebs on it, and then you have to take a hundred paces to the west, and then there's something missing –"

Neels Erasmus, the ouderling, said *he* was talking to Susannah, and his voice sounded kind of rasping. He always liked to be the first with the news. But Jurie Bekker was able to assure us that he had just guessed those details. Every treasure-hunt map was like that, he repeated.

"Well, you got it pretty right," Neels Erasmus said. "There *is* an old tree in it, and an old forked road and an old grave, I think, and also a pair of men's underpants – the long kind. The underpants seem to have been the oldest clue of the whole lot. And it was the underpants that convinced Jan Slabbert that the map was genuine. He was doubtful about it, until then."

The ouderling went on to say that where this map also differed from the usual run of treasure-trove maps was that you didn't have to pace off one hundred yards to the west in the last stage of trying to locate the spot.

"Instead," he explained, "you've got to crawl on your hands and knees for I don't know how far. You see, the treasure was buried at night. And the men that buried it crawled through the bush on hands and knees for the last part of the way."

We said that from the positions in which we had often seen Jan Slabbert and Hendrik Buys of late, it was clear that they were also on the last part of their search.

Andries Prinsloo, a young man who had all this while been sitting in a corner on a low riempiestoel, and had until then taken no part in the conversation, suddenly remarked to Neels Erasmus (and he cleared his throat nervously as he spoke), that it seemed to him as though the ouderling "and – and Susannah – er – had quite a lot to say to each other." Perhaps it was because he was respectful of our company that Andries Prinsloo spoke so diffidently.

At all events, Andries Prinsloo's remark started us off saying all kinds of things of an improving nature.

"Yes," I said to Neels Erasmus, "I wonder what your wife would say if she knew that you went to call at Jan Slabbert's house when only his daughter, Susannah, was at home."

"You went in the morning, because you knew that Jan Slabbert and Hendrik Buys would be outside, then, creeping through the wag-'n-bietjie thorns," Jurie Bekker said. "The afternoons, of course, they keep free for creeping through the haakdoring thorns."

"And what will your wife say if she knew of the subjects you discussed with Susannah?" I asked.

"Yes, all those intimate things," Jurie Bekker continued. "Like about that pair of old underpants. How could you talk to a young, innocent girl like Susannah about those awful old underp –"

Jurie Bekker spluttered so much that he couldn't get the word out. Then we both broke into loud guffaws. And in the midst of all this laughter, Andries Prinsloo went out very quietly, almost as though he didn't want to disturb us. It seemed that that young fellow had so much respect for our company that he did not wish to take part in anything that might resemble unseemly mirth. And we did not feel like laughing anymore, either, somehow, after he had left.

When we again discussed Jan Slabbert's affairs in the post office, the treasure hunt had reached the stage where a gang of kaffirs, under the supervision of the two white men, went from place to place on the farm, digging holes. In some places they even dug tunnels. They found nothing. We said that it would only be somebody like Jan Slabbert, who was already the richest man in the whole of the Northern Transvaal, that would get all worked up over the prospect of unearthing buried treasure.

"Jan Slabbert has given Hendrik Buys a contract," Neels Erasmus, the ouderling, said. "I learnt about it when I went there in connection with something of an ecclesiastical nature that happened at the Nagmaal before last. They will split whatever treasure they find. Jan Slabbert will get two-thirds and Hendrik Buys one-third."

We said that it sounded a sinful arrangement, somehow. We also spoke much about what it said in the Good Book about treasures in heaven that the moth could not corrupt. That was after Neels Erasmus had said that there was no chance of the treasure having been buried on some neighbour's farm, instead, by mistake.

"Actually, according to the map," the ouderling said, "it would appear that the treasure is buried right in the middle of Jan Slabbert's farm, somewhere. Just about where his house is."

"If Hendrik Buys has got any sense," Jurie Bekker said, "he would drive a tunnel right under Jan Slabbert's house, and as far as under his bedroom. If the tunnel came out under Jan Slabbert's bed, where he keeps that iron chest of his – well, even if Hendrik Buys is allowed to take only one-third of what is in there, it will still be something."

We then said that perhaps that was the treasure that was marked on Hendrik Buys's map with a cross, but that they hadn't guessed it yet.

That gave me an idea. I asked how Jan Slabbert's daughter, Susannah, was taking all those irregular carryings-on on the farm. The ouderling moved the winking muscle of his left eye in a peculiar way.

"The moment Hendrik Buys came into the house I understood it all clearly," he said. "Susannah's face got all lit up as she kind of skipped into the kitchen to make fresh coffee. But Hendrik Buys was too wrapped up in the treasure-hunt business to notice, even. What a pity – a nice girl like that, and all."

It seemed that that well-behaved young fellow, Andries Prinsloo, who always took the same place in the corner, was getting more respect for our company than ever. Because, this time, when he slipped out of the post office – and it was just about at that moment, too – he appeared actually to be walking on tiptoe.

Well, I didn't come across Jan Slabbert and Hendrik Buys again until about the time when they had finally decided to abandon the search. They had quarrelled quite often, too, by then. They would be on quite friendly terms when they showed the kaffirs where to start digging another hole. But by the time the hole was very wide, and about ten foot deep, in blue slate, they would start quarrelling.

The funny part of it all was that Hendrik Buys remained optimistic about the treasure right through, and he wouldn't have given up, either, if in the course of their last quarrel Jan Slabbert had not decided the matter for him, bundling him on to the Government lorry back to Zeerust, after kicking him.

The quarrel had to do with a hole eighteen foot deep, in gneiss.

But on that last occasion on which I saw them together in the voorkamer, Jan Slabbert and his daughter, Susannah, and Hendrik Buys, it seemed to me that Hendrik Buys was still very hopeful.

"There are lots of parts of the farm that I haven't crawled through yet," Hendrik Buys explained. "Likely places, according to the map, such as the pigsty. I have not yet crept through the pigsty. I must remember that for tomorrow. You see, the men who buried the treasure crept for the last part of the way through the bush in the dark." Hendrik Buys paused. It was clear that an idea had struck him. "Do you think it possible," he asked, excitedly, "that they might have crawled through the bush *backwards* – you know, in the dark? That is something that I had not thought of until this moment. What do you say, Oom Jan, tomorrow you and I go and creep backwards, in the direction of the pigsty?"

Jan Slabbert did not answer. And Susannah's efforts at keeping the conversation going made the situation seem all the more awkward. I felt sorry for her. It was a relief to us all when Neels Erasmus, the ouderling, arrived at the front door just then. He had come to see Jan Slabbert in connection with something of an apostolic description that might happen at the forthcoming Nagmaal.

I never saw Hendrik Buys again, but I did think of him quite a number of times afterwards, particularly on the occasion of Susannah Slabbert's wedding. And I wondered, in the course of his treasure hunting, how much Hendrik Buys had possibly let slip through his fingers like sand. That was when the ceremony was over, and a couple of men among the wedding guests were discharging their Mausers into the air – welcoming the bride as she was being lifted down from the Cape-cart by the quiet-mannered young fellow, Andries Prinsloo. He seemed more subdued than ever, now, as a bridegroom.

And so I understood then about the distracted air which Andries Prinsloo had worn throughout that feverish time of the great Bushveld treasure hunt; that it was in reality the half-dazed look of a man who had unearthed a pot of gold at the foot of the rainbow.

Unto Dust

I have noticed that when a young man or woman dies, people get the feeling that there is something beautiful and touching in the event, and that it is different from the death of an old person. In the thought, say, of a girl of twenty sinking into an untimely grave, there is a sweet wistfulness that makes people talk all kinds of romantic words. She died, they say, young, she that was so full of life and so fair. She was a flower that withered before it bloomed, they say, and it all seems so fitting and beautiful that there is a good deal of resentment, at the funeral, over the crude questions that a couple of men in plain clothes from the land-drost's office are asking about cattle-dip.

But when you have grown old, nobody is very much interested in the manner of your dying. Nobody except you yourself, that is. And I think that your past life has got a lot to do with the way you feel when you get near the end of your days. I remember how, when he was lying on his death-bed, Andries Wessels kept on telling us that it was because of the blameless path he had trodden from his earliest years that he could compose himself in peace to lay down his burdens. And I certainly never saw a man breathe his last more tranquilly, seeing that right up to the end he kept on murmuring to us how happy he was, with heavenly hosts and invisible choirs of angels all around him.

Just before he died, he told us that the angels had even become visible. They were medium-sized angels, he said, and they had cloven hoofs and carried forks. It was obvious that Andries Wessels's ideas were getting a bit confused by then, but all the same I never saw a man die in a more hallowed sort of calm.

Once, during the malaria season in the Eastern Transvaal, it seemed to me, when I was in a high fever and like to die, that the whole

262

world was a big burial-ground. I thought it was the earth itself that was a graveyard, and not just those little fenced-in bits of land dotted with tombstones, in the shade of a Western Province oak-tree or by the side of a Transvaal koppie. This was a night-mare that worried me a great deal, and so I was very glad, when I recovered from the fever, to think that we Boers had properly marked-out places on our farms for white people to be laid to rest in, in a civilised Christian way, instead of having to be buried just anyhow, along with a dead wild-cat, maybe, or a Bushman with a clay pot, and things.

When I mentioned this to my friend, Stoffel Oosthuizen, who was in the Low Country with me at the time, he agreed with me wholeheartedly. There were people who talked in a high-flown way of death as the great leveller, he said, and those high-flown people also declared that everyone was made kin by death. He would still like to see those things proved, Stoffel Oosthuizen said. After all, that was one of the reasons why the Boers had trekked away into the Transvaal and the Free State, he said, because the British Government wanted to give the vote to any Cape Coloured person walking about with a kroes head and big cracks in his feet.

The first time he heard that sort of talk about death coming to all of us alike, and making us all equal, Stoffel Oosthuizen's sus-picions were aroused. It sounded like out of a speech made by one of those liberal Cape politicians, he explained.

I found something very comforting in Stoffel Oosthuizen's words.

Then, to illustrate his contention, Stoffel Oosthuizen told me a story of an incident that took place in a bygone Transvaal kaffir war. I don't know whether he told the story incorrectly, or whether it was just that kind of a story, but, by the time he had fin-ished, all my uncertainties had, I discovered, come back to me.

"You can go and look at Hans Welman's tombstone any time you are at Nietverdiend," Stoffel Oosthuizen said. "The slab of red sandstone is weathered by now, of course, seeing how long ago it all happened. But the inscription is still legible. I was with Hans Welman on that morning when he fell. Our commando had been ambushed by the kaffirs and was retreating. I could do nothing for Hans Welman. Once, when I looked round, I saw a tall kaffir bending over him and plunging an assegai into him. Shortly afterwards I saw the kaffir stripping the clothes off Hans Welman. A yellow kaffir dog was yelping excitedly around his black master. Although I was in grave danger myself, with several dozen kaffirs making straight for me on foot through the bush, the fury I felt at the sight of what that tall kaffir was doing made me hazard a last shot. Reining in my horse, and taking what aim I could under the circumstances, I pressed the trigger. My luck was in. I saw the kaffir fall forward beside the naked body of Hans Welman. Then I set spurs to my horse and galloped off at full speed, with the foremost of my pursuers already almost upon me. The last I saw was that yellow dog bounding up to his master – whom I had wounded mortally, as we were to discover later.

"As you know, that kaffir war dragged on for a long time. There were few pitched battles. Mainly, what took place were bush skirmishes, like the one in which Hans Welman lost his life.

"After about six months, quiet of a sort was restored to the Marico and Zoutpansberg Districts. Then the day came when I went out, in company of a handful of other burghers, to fetch in the remains of Hans Welman, at his widow's request, for burial in the little cemetery plot on the farm. We took a coffin with us on a Cape-cart.

"We located the scene of the skirmish without difficulty. Indeed, Hans Welman had been killed not very far from his own farm, which had been temporarily abandoned, together with the other farms in that part, during the time that the trouble with the kaffirs had lasted. We drove up to the spot where I remembered having seen Hans Welman lying dead on the ground, with the tall kaffir next to him. From a distance I again saw that yellow dog. He slipped away into the bush at our approach. I could not help feeling that there was something rather stirring about that beast's fidelity, even though it was bestowed on a dead kaffir.

"We were now confronted with a queer situation. We found that what was left of Hans Welman and the kaffir consisted of little more than pieces of sun-dried flesh and the dismembered fragments of bleached skeletons. The sun and wild animals and birds of prey had done their work. There was a heap of human bones, with here and there leathery strips of blackened flesh. But we could not tell which was the white man and which the kaffir. To make it still more confusing, a lot of bones were missing alto- gether, having no doubt been dragged away by wild animals into their lairs in the bush. Another thing was that Hans Welman and that kaffir had been just about the same size."

Stoffel Oosthuizen paused in his narrative, and I let my imagina- tion dwell for a moment on that situation. And I realised just how those Boers must have felt about it: about the thought of bringing the remains of a Transvaal burgher home to his widow for Chris- tian burial, and perhaps having a lot of kaffir bones mixed up with the burgher – lying with him in the same tomb on which the mauve petals from the oleander overhead would fall.

"I remember one of our party saying that that was the worst of these kaffir wars," Stoffel Oosthuizen continued. "If it had been a war against the English, and part of a dead Englishman had got lifted into that coffin by mistake, it wouldn't have mattered so much," he said.

There seemed to me in this story to be something as strange as the African veld.

Stoffel Oosthuizen said that the little party of Boers spent almost a whole afternoon with the remains in order to try to get the white man sorted out from the kaffir. By the evening they had laid all they could find of what seemed like Hans Welman's bones in the coffin in the Cape-cart. The rest of the bones and flesh they buried on the spot.

Stoffel Oosthuizen added that, no matter what the difference in the colour of their skin had been, it was impossible to say that the kaffir's bones were less white than Hans Welman's. Nor was it possible to say that the kaffir's sun-dried flesh was any blacker than the white man's. Alive, you couldn't go wrong in distinguishing between a white man and a kaffir. Dead, you had great difficulty in telling them apart.

"Naturally, we burghers felt very bitter about this whole affair," Stoffel Oosthuizen said, "and our resentment was something that we couldn't explain, quite. Afterwards, several other men who were there that day told me that they had the same feelings of suppressed anger that I did. They wanted somebody – just once – to make a remark such as 'in death they were not divided.' Then you would have seen an outburst, all right. Nobody did say anything like that, however. We all knew better. Two days later a funeral service was conducted in the little cemetery on the Welman farm, and shortly afterwards the sandstone memorial was erected that you can still see there."

That was the story Stoffel Oosthuizen told me after I had recovered from the fever. It was a story that, as I have said, had in it features as strange as the African veld. But it brought me no peace in my broodings after that attack of malaria. Especially when Stoffel Oosthuizen spoke of how he had occasion, one clear night when the stars shone, to pass that quiet graveyard on the Welman farm. Something leapt up from the mound beside the sandstone slab. It gave him quite a turn, Stoffel Oosthuizen said, for the third time – and in that way – to come across that yellow kaffir dog.

266

GRAVEN IMAGE

Yes, I know those wood-carvings that the kaffirs used to make long ago (Oom Schalk Lourens said). They were very silly things, of course, and I had a good laugh at them myself, more than once. Several of my neighbours, including Karel Nienaber, had a good laugh at them, also, at various times. In fact, when you come to think of it, the one particular thing about those figures that the kaffirs used to carve out of soft wood like kremetart or 'ndubu was that you could always get a good laugh out of them.

And it is singular how into these mirthful incidents there got tangled part of the darker being of Louisa Wessels, a girl who did not laugh. And she seems almost as reluctant now to enter the story as she was then about becoming Karel Nienaber's bride. I can picture Louisa Wessels yet, shy but firm in her withdrawing, and as still as blue water.

It was all right, of course, as long as those wood-carvers stuck to chiselling certain kinds of animals that they knew well. The way they could carve a giraffe, for instance: his long neck, cut out of a piece of mesetla wood with a blunt knife, and the whole of him covered in black spots burnt with a red-hot iron, and his pointed head turned to one side, half upwards – why, you could *see* that giraffe. It was almost as though you could see the leaves of the tree, too, that he was pulling down and eating for his breakfast.

Although we knew that the whole thing was cut out of a piece of Bushveld wood by a lazy Bechuana, who would have been better employed in chopping up that wood and bringing a bundle of it into a farmer's kitchen, nevertheless, we could see that, for all his ignorance, the Bechuana kaffir knew how to carve a giraffe so that it looked really life-like. Because we Marico farmers knew a giraffe when we saw one. And when one of those

267

wood-carvers brought along a model of a giraffe, we would smile to think that that kaffir was so uneducated, but we would also know that the thing he had carved was exactly like a giraffe. Sometimes we could even tell, from the way that the giraffe was standing, as to what particular kind of tree he was eating his breakfast from. Just from the way his head was turned, and the position in which his hind legs were placed, and the manner in which he would droop his shoulders to miss the thorns.

And the wood-carvers would also cut out, joined together on a piece of stick, three wild ducks swimming one behind the other. That was one of their favourite pieces of carving. The way that the ducks sat on the water was very true to life, the front duck swimming with his head high up, since he was naturally proud to be the leader. The only thing that was wrong was that those three wild ducks were held together by a piece of stick. That used to give us a very good laugh. I mean, we had often seen three ducks swimming in a row in that particular way. But they had never been tied together on a piece of stick.

It was when an old Bechuana wood-carver named Radipalong, in Ramoutsa, began carving what he said were the images of various white men living in the Marico, that we really started laughing.

I suppose you know that a kaffir wood-carver will never cut a figure of another kaffir. He's not allowed to. Because, if that kaffir finds out about it, there will be a lot of trouble in the kraal. The kaffirs believe that if you have got an enemy that you want to get rid of, then what you have to do is to make an image of him: it doesn't matter if it is a good likeness or not, as long as you yourself know what is meant by it: and then you hammer something, a strip of brass or an iron nail, into that part of your enemy that you want to get stricken. And the kaffirs say that it always works, when you do that. They say that that is the reason, for instance, why many an unpopular chief has been known to die prematurely, going to his death with a sudden pain in his belly, for which there has been no explanation. And then, later on, in the hut of some enemy of the chief, there has been found a little wooden image with an iron nail driven through its stomach. And how they knew that it was the chief was because something that belonged to him, like a piece of his kaross, was attached to the wooden image . . . And, also, of course, because the chief had died . . .

For this reason a kaffir is not very happy when a wood-carver comes along to him with a piece of wood fashioned in the likeness of a human being, and informs him, "This is you." Even when the image hasn't got a piece of brass driven into its belly, the ordinary ignorant kaffir, confronted with his own likeness cut out of wood, will bid the wood-carver tarry a little while in front of the hut – while he goes round to the back to look for his axe.

All of this brings me to that wood-carver in Ramoutsa, Radipalong, who, because the kaffirs would not allow him to carve likenesses of themselves, took it into his head to cut what he thought were images of white people.

There is no doubt about it that when Radipalong, who was very old and emaciated-looking, confined himself to cutting the figures of animals from soft wood – the softer, the better, because you had merely to look at him to see that he did not like exerting himself too much – then what he carved was quite all right. He could carve a hippopotamus, or a rhinoceros, or an elephant, or a yellow-bellied hyena – the more low sort of hyena – in such a way that you *knew* that animal exactly, through your having seen it grazing under a tree, or drinking at a waterhole, or just leaning against an ant-hill without doing anything in particular.

But it was when Radipalong started carving what he imagined, in his kaffir ignorance, to be the likenesses of Boer farmers in this part of the Marico, that we commenced laughing differently from the way we laughed at his wild ducks. Our laughter now seemed to have more meaning in it.

For instance, Radipalong carved what he said was the image of the Dutch Reformed Church missionary at Ramoutsa, Rev. Kriel. That was one of the first good laughs we had, Rev. Kriel joining in loudly – although I thought that his laughter came from rather too deep down.

"See how silly that kaffir, Radipalong, makes me look," Rev. Kriel said to us, one day, after he had conducted a service in Jurie Bekker's farmhouse. "I brought along this carving that he made of me. I brought it along just for fun. I gave him one shilling and ninepence for it, also just for fun. Look how foolishly he makes my collar stand up, right under my ears. And my eyes – so close together. Have you ever seen such a dishonest-looking pair of eyes before? And the way he makes my chin slope backwards from my bottom teeth. . . You should have heard how my wife laughed when I showed her this carving. In fact, every time she sees me now, she laughs. I suppose she feels how incredible it is that, in these times, you can still find as benighted a heathen as that old Radipalong is. And the funny part of it is that he seems to take his ridiculous wood-carving seriously. As though he is carving out a career for himself, I said to my wife. Ha, ha."

We all laughed at that. Ha, ha, we said.

After that, Radipalong made an image of Karel Nienaber. Once more we laughed a good deal. That was in the Nienaber voorhuis, where we were drinking coffee. Old Piet Nienaber's son, Karel, was engaged to be married to Louisa Wessels, and Louisa and her parents, who stayed at Abjaterskop, were on a visit that afternoon to the Nienaber family. A few neighbours had dropped in as well, and, as I have said, there was much laughter when young Karel produced Radipalong's latest piece of wood-carving. The wood that the image was made of was so soft that it was more like cork. Almost like a piece of sponge, I thought. It seemed that Radipalong was getting lazier than ever.

"Just see how low he makes my forehead," Karel Nienaber said, and we all laughed again, at the idea that that kaffir, who could carve a leopard exactly like it was, should be so ignorant when it came to making the image of a white man.

"And look at my ears," Karel added, "the way they stick out. They look as though they have been made for a person twice my size."

Again we all guffawed. All of us, that is, except Louisa Wessels. I noticed that she was not laughing at all. Naturally, this circumstance did not at first appear singular to me. It was only right, I felt, that a young girl should not laugh at seeing her lover made to look ridiculous – even though that kaffir wood-carver did not mean to poke fun at Karel, of course. Radipalong just didn't know any better.

Nevertheless, there was something in Louisa's manner that disturbed me. She seemed too quiet. And when Karel Nienaber said, "Just look at my ears," she had not looked at the wooden likeness that he was holding in his hand. Instead, her dark eyes went actually to her lover's face. For a few moments she appeared to be studying Karel's ears, which did, somehow, in that instant, seem to be somewhat too large for the rest of him.

"And what do you think of the way he has done the rest of me?" Karel Nienaber asked again, and by this time he could hardly talk, he was laughing so much at the kaffir's absurd misrepresentation of his figure. "Why, he makes my body look all clumsy, like a sort of pumpkin. To move, I would have to go on wheels."

Once again I noticed that Louisa Wessels looked at Karel Nienaber and not at the carving. And this time, too, she did not laugh. And so I remembered that young man who had been courting Louisa in the past, and to whom her parents had objected, because they wanted their daughter to marry Karel Nienaber. And I wondered what thoughts were going on behind Louisa's expressionless features, when Karel came up to her and laughingly placed the image in her lap.

"You can look after this for us," Karel said. "I gave Radipalong a piece of roll-tobacco for it, just for fun. I asked him why he used such a white piece of wood to carve my image out of, and what do you think he said? He said, 'Well, but you are a white man, baas Karel.' And I said, well of course, I was white but I wasn't sick. And then I asked him why he had made me out of such soft wood. And – you know what? – he just didn't answer me at all."

Louisa sat with her eyes lowered. And, as I am talking to you, I can sense how unwillingly she comes into this story, even now.

Anyway, the stupidity of that wood-carver caused a good deal of merriment in the Marico Bushveld for a while. When Radipalong brought me a carving of myself, with a jaw like an aardvark and big, flat feet, I laughed so much that I just pulled the thing away from him roughly, without paying him anything – not even for fun. And when Radipalong gave Hendrik Pretorius *his* likeness, Hendrik was so amused that Radipalong had a lump behind his ear from where Hendrik Pretorius hit him with a piece of wood that was harder than the wood out of which he made the carving.

Shortly afterwards, Radipalong went out of the business of carving images of white men.

The white men laughed too much.

It was some time later that the engagement between Louisa Wessels and Karel Nienaber got broken off. Although nobody knew all the details surrounding the circumstances under which those two young people parted, we had a pretty good general sort of idea. And we were not surprised when, shortly afterwards, Karel Nienaber left the Marico Bushveld to go and work for a blacksmith in Zeerust. He said he felt it wasn't healthy living in the Bushveld, among all those dark trees.

But what we never understood clearly was how Karel Nienaber had come to open the tamboetie kist in which Louisa Wessels was collecting her trousseau. We did know, however, that Karel found, lying on top of the bridal silks and ribbons, the wooden image that Radipalong had carved of him. And, driven into the place where the heart was, were several rusty nails.

THE PICTURE OF GYSBERT JONKER

This tobacco-bag, now (Oom Schalk Lourens said, producing a four-ounce linen bag with the picture on it of a leaping bles-buck – the trademark of a well-known tobacco company), well, it is very unusual, the way this tobacco-bag picture fits into the life-story of Gysbert Jonker. I had occasion to think of that only the other day, when at the Zeerust bioscope during the last Nagmaal they showed a film about an English lord who had his portrait painted. And it seemed that after that only the portrait changed, with the years, as the lord grew older and more sinful.

Some of the young people, when they got back from the bio-scope, came and called on me, on the kerkplein, and told me what a good film it was. A few of them hinted that I ought also to go to the bioscope, now and again – say, once in two years, or so – to get new ideas for my stories.

Koos Steyn's younger son, Frikkie, even went so far as to say, straight out, that I should go oftener than just once every two years. A good deal oftener. And that I shouldn't see the same film through more than once, either.

"Important things are happening in the world, Oom Schalk," young Frikkie said. "You know, culture and all that. That's why you should go to a film like the one we have just seen. A film with artists in it, and all."

"Yes, artists," another young fellow said. "Like an artist that got pointed out to me last time I was in Johannesburg. With his wide hat and his corduroy trousers, he looked just like a Marico farmer, except that his beard was too wild. We don't grow our beards so long in these parts, anymore, since that new threshing machine with the wide hopper came in. That machine is so quick."

"That is the trouble with your stories, Oom Schalk," Frikkie Steyn continued. "The Boers in them all grow their beards too

273

long. And the uppers of their veldskoens have got an old-fashioned look. Why can't you bring into your next story a young man with a pair of brown shop boots on, and" – hitching his pants up and looking down – "yellow-and-pink striped socks with a –"

"And a waistcoat with long points coming over the top part of the trousers," another young man interrupted him. "And braces with clips that you can make longer or shorter, just as you like."

Anyway, after Theunis Malan had demonstrated to me the difference between a loose and an attached collar, and then couldn't find his stud, and after an ouderling had come past just when another young man was using bad language because he couldn't get his head out through his shirt again – through somebody else having thoughtfully tied the shirt-tails together while the young man was explaining about a new kind of underwear – well, there wasn't much about their new Nagmaal clothes that these young men wanted me to leave out of my next story. And the ouderling, without knowing what was going on, and without trying to find out, even, merely shook his head solemnly as he went past.

And, of course, Frikkie Steyn, just to make sure that I had it right, told the bioscope story of the English lord all over again – all the time that I was filling my pipe from a quarter-pound bag of Magaliesberg tobacco; the sort with the picture of the high-bounding blesbuck on it.

So I thought, well, maybe Gysbert was not an English lord. But I could remember the time when his portrait, painted in the most beautiful colours, hung in his voorkamer. And I also thought of the way in which Gysbert's portrait was on display on every railway platform and in every Indian shop in the country. And almost until the very end the portrait remained unchanged. It was only Gysbert Jonker who, despite all his efforts, altered with the years. But when the portrait did eventually change, it was a much more incredible transformation than anything that could have happened to the portrait of that lord in the bioscope story.

It was while we were sitting in the Indian store at Ramoutsa, drinking coffee and waiting for the afternoon to get cool enough

274

for us to be able to drive back home by mule- and donkey-cart, that we first noticed the resemblance.

Our conversation was, as usual, of an edifying character. We spoke about how sensible we were to go on sitting in the Indian store, hour after hour, like that, and drinking coffee, instead of driving out in the hot sun, and running the risk of getting sunstroke. Later on, when some clouds came up, we were even more glad that we had not ventured out in our open carts, because everybody knows that the worst kind of sunstroke is what you get when the sun shines on to the back of your head through the clouds.

Of course, there were other forms of conveyance, such as Cape-carts, we said. But that sort of thing only undermined you. Naturally, we did not wish to be undermined. We spoke about how the younger generation was losing its self-reliance through – and we started naming some of the things we saw on the shelves around us. Gramophones, we said. And paraffin candles in packets, we said, instead of making our own. And tubes with white grease that you squeeze at the end to polish your plates and spoons with, one of us said. No, it was to brush your teeth with, somebody else interrupted him. And we said that, well, whatever it was for, it was undermining. And we said that our own generation was being sapped, also.

After we had asked the Indian behind the counter to stand to one side, so that we could see better how we were being undermined, Hans Bekker pointed to a shelf holding tins of coffee. "Formerly we burnt and ground our own coffee," Hans Bekker said. "Today –"

"Before I could walk," Andries Claassens said, "I used to shred my own tobacco from a black roll. I could cut up plug tobacco for my pipe before I could sharpen a slate-pencil. But now I have to sit with this little bag –"

I don't know who made the following observation, but we laughed at it for a long time. We looked back from Andries Claassens's tobacco-bag to the shelf on which dozens of similar bags were displayed. On each was the picture of a farmer with a black beard and a red-and-yellow checked shirt; and in his right hand, which was raised level with his shoulders, he held, elegantly if somewhat stiffly, a pipe. Perhaps you remember that picture, which did not appear only on the tobacco-bags, but was reproduced, also, in the newspapers, and stood on oblong metal sheets, enamelled in bright colours, in front of every store.

When our attention had been drawn to it, we saw the resemblance very clearly. In respect of both his features and his expression, the farmer on the tobacco-bag was almost the exact image of Gysbert Jonker. Gysbert's beard was not so neatly trimmed, and his eyebrows were straighter; also, his mouth considerably larger than the man's on the picture. But in every other way – taking into consideration the difference in their dress – the likeness was astonishing.

Gysbert Jonker was there, in the Indian store, with us, when we made the discovery. He seemed very much interested.

"You will now have to push your ears in under the sweatband of your hat, in the city fashion," Hans Bekker said to Gysbert. "You can't have them bent anymore."

"And you will now have to hold your pipe up in the air, next to your shoulder, when you walk behind the plough," Andries Claassens added, "in your riding-breeches and leggings."

We were more than a little surprised at Gysbert's answer.

"It is absurd to think that I could do farm-work in that rig-out," he replied. "But on Sundays, and some evenings after work, I shall wear riding-pants and top-boots. And it's a queer thing, but I have always wanted a shirt with red-and-yellow checks. In any case, it's the least I can do, in view of the fact that this tobacco company has honoured the Marico by making use of the portrait of the district's most progressive cattle farmer in this way. I suppose the tobacco firm selected me for this purpose because of the improvements I made to my cement-dip last year."

Gysbert Jonker added that next year he intended erecting another barbed-wire camp on the other side of the dam, and that he could bring this to the notice of the tobacco company as well.

We suddenly found that we had nothing more to say. And we were so taken aback at the way Gysbert responded to the purely accidental circumstance of his resembling the man in the picture that we were quite unable to laugh about it, even.

And I am sure that I was not the only Marico farmer, driving back home later that afternoon over the dusty road through the

276

camel-thorns, who reflected earnestly on the nature (and dangers) of sunstroke.

After a while, however, we got used to the change that had taken place in Gysbert Jonker's soul.

Consequently, with the passage of time, there was less and less said about the gorgeously coloured shirts that Gysbert Jonker wore on Sundays, when he strolled about the front part of his homestead in riding breeches and gaiters, apparently carefree and at ease, except that he held his pipe high up near his shoulder, somewhat stiffly. In time, too, the ouderling ceased calling on Gysbert in order to dissuade him from going about dressed as a tobacco advertisement on Sundays – a practice that the ouderling regarded as a desecration of the Sabbath.

In spite of everything, we had to admit that Gysbert Jonker had succeeded to a remarkable degree in imitating his portrait – especially when he started shaving the sides of his eyebrows to make them look more curved, and when he had cultivated a smile that wrinkled up his left cheek, halfway to his ear. And he used to smile carefully, almost as though he was afraid that some of the enamel would chip off him.

277

Jonker on one occasion announced to a number of acquaintances at a meeting of the Dwarsberg debating society: "Look at
this shirt I have got on, for instance. Just feel the quality of it, and
then compare it with the shirt on your tobacco-bag. I had my
photo taken last month in Zeerust, in these clothes. I sent the
photograph to the head office of the tobacco company in Johannesburg – and would you believe it? The tobacco people sent me
by the following railway-lorry, one of those life-sized enamelled
pictures of myself painted on a sheet of iron. You know, the kind
that you see on stations and in front of shops. I nailed it to the
wall of my voorkamer."

Gysbert kept up this foolishness for a number of years. And it
was, of course, this particular characteristic of his that we admired. We could see from this that he was a real Afrikaner, as
obstinate as the Transvaal turf-soil. Even when, with the years, it
became difficult for him to compete successfully with his portrait
that did not age, so that he had to resort to artificial aids to keep
his hair and beard black – then we did not laugh about it. We even
sympathised with him in his hopeless struggle against the
onslaughts of time. And we noticed that, the older Gysbert Jonker
got, the more youthful his shirt seemed.

In the end, Gysbert Jonker had had to hands-up, of course. But he
gave in only after his portrait had changed. And it was so stupen-
dous a change that it was beyond the capacity even of Gysbert to
try to follow suit. One day suddenly – without any kind of warn-
ing from the tobacco firm – we noticed, when we were again in
the Indian store at Ramoutsa, that the picture of the farmer in riding pants had disappeared from the tobacco-bags. Just like that.
The farmer was replaced with the picture of the leaping blesbuck
that you see on this bag, here. Afterwards, the blesbuck took the
place of the riding-pants farmer on the enamelled iron sheets as
well.

Meanwhile, however, when it dawned on us that the tobacco
company was busy changing its advertisement, we made many
carefully considered remarks about Gysbert Jonker. We said that
he would now, in his old age, have to start practising the high-
jump, in order to be able to resemble his new portrait. We also

278

THE PICTURE OF GYSBERT JONKER

said that he would now have to paint his belly white, like the bles-buck's. We also expressed the hope that a leopard wouldn't catch Gysbert Jonker when he walked about the veld on a Sunday morning, dressed up like his new portrait.

Nevertheless, I had the feeling that Gysbert Jonker did not altogether regret the fact that his portrait had been unrecognis-ably changed. For one thing, he was now relieved of the strain of having all the time to live up to the opinion that the tobacco com-pany had formed of him.

And although he removed the enamelled portrait from the wall of his voorkamer, and used it to repair a hole in the pigsty, and although he wore his gaudily coloured shirts every day, now, and while doing the roughest kind of work, just so as to get rid of them – yet there were times, when I looked at Gysbert Jonker, that my thoughts were carried right back to the past. Most often this would happen when he was smoking. To the end, he retained something of his enamelled way of holding his pipe – his hand raised almost level with his shoulder, elegantly, but just a shade stiffly.

Some years later, when Gysbert Jonker was engaged in wear-ing out the last of his red-and-yellow checked shirts, I came across him at the back of his pigsty. He was standing near the spot where he had replaced a damaged sheet of corrugated iron with his tobacco-advertisement portrait.

And it struck me that in some mysterious way, Gysbert Jonker had again caught up with his portrait. For they looked equally shabby and dilapidated, then, the portrait and Gysbert Jonker. They seemed to have become equally sullied – through the years and through sin. And so I turned away quickly from that rusted sheet of iron, with the picture on it of that farmer with his battered pipe, and his beard that was now greying and unkempt. And his shirt that looked as patched as Gysbert Jonker's own. And his eyes that had grown as wistful.

The Homecoming

Laughter (Oom Schalk Lourens said). Well, there's a queer thing for you, now, and something not so easy to understand. And the older you get, the more things you seem to find to laugh at. Take old Frans Els, for instance. I can still remember the way he laughed, that time at Zeerust, when we were coming around the church building and we saw one of the tents from the Nagmaal camping-ground being carried away by a sudden gust of wind.

"It must be the ouderling's tent," Frans Els called out. "Well, he never was any good at fixing the ground-pegs. Look, kêrels, there it goes right across the road." And he laughed so much that his beard, which was turning white in places, flapped about almost like that tent in the wind.

Shortly afterwards, what was left of the tent got caught round the wooden poles of somebody's veranda, and several adults and a lot of children came running out of the house, shouting. By that time Frans Els was standing bent almost double over a fence. The tears were streaming down his cheeks and he had difficulty in get-

BERRY

280

ting his breath. I don't think I ever saw a man laugh so much in my life.

I don't think I ever saw a man stop laughing as quickly, either, as what Frans Els did when some people from the camping-ground came up and spoke to him. They had to say it over twice before he could get the full purport of the message, which was to the effect that it was not the ouderling's tent at all that had got blown away, but his.

I suppose you could describe the way in which Frans Els carried on that day while he still thought that it was the ouderling's tent, as one kind of laughter. The fact is that there are more kinds of laughter than just that one sort, and it seems to me that this is the cause of a lot of regrettable awkwardness in the world.

Another thing I have noticed is that when a woman laughs it usually means a good deal of trouble for a man. Not at that very moment, maybe, but afterwards. And more especially when it is a musical sort of laugh.

There is still another kind of laughter that you have also come across in your time, I am sure. That is the way we laugh when there are a number of us together in the Indian store at Ramoutsa, and Hendrik Moolman tells a funny story that he has read in the *Goede Hoop*. What is so entertaining about his way of telling these stories is that Hendrik Moolman always forgets what the point is. Then when we ask, "But what's so funny about it?" he tries to make up another story as he goes along. And because he's so weak at that, it makes us laugh more than ever.

So when we talk about Hendrik Moolman's funny stories, it is not the stories themselves that we find amusing, but his lack of skill in telling them. But I suppose it's all the same to Hendrik Moolman. He joins heartily in our laughter and waves his crutch about. Sometimes he even gets so excited that you almost expect him to rise up out of his chair without help.

It all happened very long ago, the first part of this story of Hendrik Moolman and his wife Malie. And in those days, when they had just married, you would not, if the idea of laughter had come into your mind, have thought first of Hendrik Moolman telling jokes in the Indian store.

They were just of an age, the young Moolman couple, and they were both good to look at. And when they arrived back from Zeerust after the wedding, Hendrik made a stirring show of the way he lifted Malie from the mule-cart, to carry her across the threshold of the little farmhouse in which their future life was to be cast. Needless to say, that was many years before Hendrik Moolman was to acquire the nickname of Crippled Hendrik, as the result of a fall into a diamond claim when he was drunk. Some said that his fall was an accident. Others saw in the occurrence the hand of the Lord.

What I remember most vividly about Malie, as she was in those early days of her marriage, were her eyes, and her laughter that was in such strange contrast to her eyes. Her laughter was free and clear and ringing. Each time you heard it, it was like a sudden bright light. Her laughter was like a summer's morning. But her eyes were dark and did not seem to belong with any part of the day at all.

It was the women who by and by started to say about the marriage of Hendrik and Malie this thing, that Malie's love for Hendrik was greater than his love for her. You could see it all, they said, by that look that came on her face when Hendrik entered the voorkamer, called in from the lands because there were visitors. You could tell it too, they declared, by that unnatural stillness that would possess her when she was left alone on the farm for a few days, as would happen each time her husband went with cattle or mealies to the market town.

With the years, also, that gay laugh of Malie Moolman's was heard more seldom, until in the end she seemed to have forgotten how to laugh at all. But there was never any suggestion of Malie having been unhappy. That was the queerest part of it – that part of the marriage of Malie and Hendrik that confuted all the busy-bodies. For it proved that Malie's devotion to Hendrik had not been just one-sided.

They had been married a good many years before that day when it became known to Malie – as a good while before that it had become known to the rest of the white people living on this side of the Dwarsberge – that Hendrik's return from the market town of Zeerust would be indefinitely delayed.

Those were prosperous times, and it was said that Hendrik had taken a considerable sum with him in gold coins for his journey to the Elandsputte diamond diggings, whither he had gone in the company of the Woman of Zeerust. Malie went on staying on the farm, and saw to it that the day-to-day activities in the kraal and on the lands and in the homestead went on just as though Hendrik were still there. Instead of in the arms of the Woman of Zeerust.

This went on for a good while, with Hendrik Moolman throwing away, on the diggings, real gold after visionary diamonds.

There were many curious features about this thing that had happened with Hendrik Moolman. For instance, it was known that he had written to his wife quite a number of times. Jurie Steyn, who kept the post office at Drogedal, had taken the trouble on one occasion to deliver into Malie's hands personally a letter addressed to her in her husband's handwriting. He had taken over the letter himself, instead of waiting for Malie to send for it. And Jurie Steyn said that Malie had thanked him very warmly for the letter, and had torn open the envelope in a state of agitation, and had wept over the contents of the letter, and had then informed Jurie Steyn that it was from her sister in Kuruman, who wrote about the drought there.

"It seemed to be a pretty long drought," Jurie Steyn said to us afterwards in the post office, "judging from the number of pages."

It was known, however, that when a woman visitor had made open reference to the state of affairs on the Elandsputte diggings, Malie had said that her husband was suffering from a temporary infatuation for the Woman of Zeerust, of whom she spoke without bitterness. Malie said she was certain that Hendrik would grow tired of that woman, and return to her.

Meanwhile, many rumours of what was happening with Hendrik Moolman on the Elandsputte diggings were conveyed to this part of the Marico by one means and another – mainly by donkey-cart. Later on it became known that Hendrik had sold the wagon and the oxen with which he had trekked from his farm to the diggings. Still later it became known why Malie was sending so many head of cattle to market. Finally, when a man with a waxed moustache and a notebook appeared in the neighbourhood, the farmers hereabouts, betokening no surprise, were able to direct him to the Moolman farm, where he went to take an inventory of the stock.

By that time the Woman of Zeerust must have discovered that Hendrik Moolman was about at the end of his resources. But nobody knew for sure when she deserted him – whether it was before or after that thing had happened to him which paralysed the left side of his body.

And that was how it came about that in the end Hendrik Moolman did return to his wife, Malie, just as she had during all that time maintained that he would. In reply to a message from Elandsputte diggings she had sent a kaffir in the mule-cart to fetch Baas Hendrik Moolman back to his farm.

Hendrik Moolman was seated in a half-reclining posture against the kaffir who held the reins, that evening when the mule-cart drew up in front of the home into which, many years before, on the day of their wedding, he had carried his wife, Malie. There was something not unfitting about his own homecoming in the evening, in the thought that Malie would be helping to lift him off the mule-cart, now.

Some such thought must have been uppermost in Malie's mind also. At all events, she came forward to greet her errant husband. Apparently she now comprehended for the first time the true extent of his incapacitation. Malie had not laughed for many years. Now the sound of her laughter, gay and silvery, sent its infectious echoes ringing through the farmyard.

SUSANNAH AND THE PLAY-ACTOR

I see a company of professional actors is going to stage a performance in the schoolroom at Drogedal (Oom Schalk Lourens
said). There is a poster about it nailed to a kremetart tree in front
of the building. I wonder what Henri le Valois thinks of it. His
name is actually Hendrik de Waal, of course. But we still call him
Le Valois in the Marico. And I wonder what his wife, Susannah,
thinks of it also.

It's many years now since Henri le Valois quit the stage to go
to work on his father-in-law's farm. But there seem to be more
play-actors about than ever. The Agricultural Department has got
rid of the worst of the locust plagues in these parts. But I suppose
it will take more than Cooper's dip to thin out the professional
actors.

The play presented by Henri le Valois in Zeerust – where I saw
him on the stage for the first and last time – was about men who
wore hats with ostrich-feathers and carried swords and had blankets slung over their shoulders, not striped, like the Basuto's, but
black; and about women who had their hair put high up and wore
jewels on their silk dresses but all the same did not look as grand
as the men. Henri le Valois played the role of a young captain who
falls in love with the king's wife and then leaves her in the end
because of his loyalty to the king.

Henri le Valois was very fine in that last farewell scene. From
my seat near the back of the hall I very much admired the way he
walked out backwards, with his arms extended towards the
queen, and saying, I must away adieu adieu for ever. Only a great
actor, I felt, could walk out backwards like that and not trip over
his sword or get the lower part of the blanket mixed up with his
spurs.

The girls all fell in love with Henri le Valois, of course. Among them was Susannah Bekker, daughter of Petrus Bekker of Droge-dal.

I wondered whether the girls would still feel attracted to him in the same way if they could have met him off-stage. I started wondering like that when I came across Henri le Valois in the bar of the Transvaal Hotel, one evening after the show, and most of the paint was washed off his face, and he was dressed just like me or At Naudé when we go into town and wear our shop clothes.

286

I hardly ever enter a bar, of course. I just happened to drop in on that evening because I thought I might find At Naudé there, and I wanted to talk to him about fetching some milk-cans for me from Ramoutsa. Strangely enough, At Naudé said that he had just dropped in on the off-chance of finding *me* there. And because this was such a peculiar coincidence, we thought it would be a good idea to reflect further on it over a glass of brandy. There were more coincidences like that as the evening wore on and other farmers from the Groot Marico came into the bar, also just on the off-chance.

When the coincidences had reached the stage where the bar was so full of farmers that you couldn't walk – then it was that Henri le Valois came in. He was accompanied by Alwyn Klopper who acted the part of the king in the play.

But before the arrival in the bar of these two actors, a great deal of talk had been going on about them. Somebody mentioned that Henri le Valois's real name was Hendrik de Waal, and that he had taken that foreign-sounding name so that he could move about better on the stage. The name helped him particularly in the showy farewell scene at the end, that person added. You couldn't believe then that he was actually just an ordinary farmer's son, who had once herded cattle over rough veld with polgras, when you saw how gracefully he went off the stage – as though he was pedalling a push-bike backwards. We also said that it was quite clear why Alwyn Klopper didn't also change his name to something French. The size of his feet were against him.

Henri le Valois seemed surprised to find the bar so crowded when he came in, accompanied by the king. He explained that his play-acting company was concerned with improving the minds of the people living in the backveld and with bringing culture to the Boers, and so he naturally did not frequent tap rooms. He had only dropped in there for some purpose which he had forgotten now. It had gone clean out of his mind, he said, through the shock of finding so many members of his audience in a public bar. He drank a couple of quick double brandies to get over the shock.

When it was explained to him that most of the farmers in that bar room were not members of his audience, or likely to be, he seemed to feel better about it, at first. Afterwards he didn't seem so sure.

A little later, when he had had a few more double brandies, Henri le Valois, standing against the crowded counter with a cigarette in the side of his mouth, gave us an interesting talk on what he referred to as the higher ideals of his art.

"Why, do you know," he said, "tonight I counted no less than nine people in the half-crown seats."

He had put on the play about himself and the king in every dorp from Zwartruggens to Zeerust, he said, and it had everywhere been a great cultural success. The biggest cultural success had been at Rysmierbult, where he had cleared over eleven pounds, after paying for the hall and the hotel bills of the touring company.

"Strictly speaking, Slurry was still more of a cultural success," he added. "I mean, we left Slurry with even more money. Only, we had a little misunderstanding with the hotel proprietor, who kept a couple of suitcases behind. Fortunately, they were suitcases belonging to the minor members of our company and whom we could replace. Yes, you have no idea how much we artists have to suffer."

Henri le Valois grew more and more sad. He turned to Alwyn Klopper, the king, who during all this time had been standing next to him, silent and not drinking much.

"That pigskin suitcase with the gold monogram, who did it belong to?" Henri le Valois asked him.

"To a school-teacher at Krugersdorp," the king answered, shortly. "But don't worry about her. She got a lift back home on a lorry."

"And that black-and-white portmanteau with the wavy initials –" Le Valois began again. By this time he was so sad that if he hadn't held tight on to the edge of the counter he would have fallen.

"Wolmaransstad," the king snapped. "He was a former income-tax official. Nobody would give *him* a lift back home."

So Henri le Valois went on drinking large quantities of brandy. In the end he was crying into his glass. And all the time the king stood watching him, smiling and drinking scarcely at all.

288

Suddenly Henri le Valois thrust the glass away from him and drew himself up to look very tall and imposing.

"All those beautiful suitcases," he cried.

Then he stood back a couple of paces from the king.

"I quit," he said to Alwyn Klopper. "You take over. I shall not be unfaithful further. Farewell I must away adieu adieu for ever."

And he started back-pedalling out of the bar.

There were those present in the bar that night who said of Henri le Valois that he had never acted more grandly, more magnificently, in his life than in that scene in which he took final leave of the stage. I also thought that it was most impressive, the way he made his way out through the curtains at the bar entrance, turning his feet half outwards, as though he still had spurs on them, and making a wide sweep with his left arm as though from his waist there hung a sword.

When he bared his hat in a farewell bow, I could almost have believed that there was a painted ostrich plume decorating his grey felt hat.

And that was the moment in which Susannah Bekker, passing the hotel on her way back to the boarding-house where she was staying for the Nagmaal week with her parents, encountered Henri le Valois. She had before seen him only on the stage, dressed as a gallant. And so she recognised him immediately, then, in front of the bar, not from his clothing but from his bearing. They got talking, Susannah told me about it long afterwards, and she was thrilled by how human he was. This was a greater thrill than anything she had felt about him when she had seen him on the stage, even. Especially when he talked about how he was being bullied all the time by the king, who had no soul and no feelings.

"I realised that Henri le Valois was not only a very fine human being," Susannah said, finally, "but also a very great actor. He was play-acting drunk. What do you think of that?"

There was no call for me to tell her that that part of it hadn't been play-acting.

Peaches Ripening in the Sun

The way Ben Myburg lost his memory (Oom Schalk Lourens said) made a deep impression on all of us. We reasoned that that was the sort of thing that a sudden shock could do to you. There were those in our small section of General du Toit's commando who could recall similar stories of how people in a moment could forget everything about the past, just because of a single dreadful happening.

A shock like that can have the same effect on you even if you are prepared for it. Maybe it can be worse, even. And in this connection I often think of what it says in the Good Book, about that which you most feared having now at last caught up with you.

Our commando went as far as the border by train. And when the engine came to a stop on a piece of open veld, and it wasn't for water, this time, and the engine-driver and fireman didn't step down with a spanner and use bad language, then we understood that the train stopping there was the beginning of the Second Boer War.

We were wearing new clothes and we had new equipment, and the sun was shining on the barrels of our Mausers. Our new clothes had been requisitioned for us by our veldkornet at stores along the way. All the veldkornet had to do was to sign his name on a piece of paper for whatever his men purchased.

In most cases, after we had patronised a store in that manner, the shopkeeper would put up his shutters for the day. And three years would pass and the Boer War would be over before the shopkeeper would display any sort of inclination to take the shutters down again.

Maybe he should have put them up before we came.

Only one seksie of General du Toit's commando entered Natal looking considerably dilapidated. This seksie looked as though it was already the end of the Boer War, and not just the beginning. Afterwards we found out that their veldkornet had never learnt to write his name. We were glad that in the first big battle these men kept well to the rear, apparently conscious of how sinful they looked. For, to make matters worse, a regiment of Indian troops was fighting on that front, and we were not anxious that an Eastern race should see white men at such a disadvantage.

"You don't seem to remember me, Schalk," a young fellow came up and said to me. I admitted that I didn't recognise him, straight away, as Ben Myburg. He did look different in those smart light-green riding pants and that new hat with the ostrich feather stuck in it. You could see that he had patronised some mine concession store before the owner got his shutters down.

"But I would know you anywhere, Schalk," Ben Myburg went on. "Just from the quick way you hid that soap under your saddle a couple of minutes ago. I remembered where I had last seen something so quick. It was two years ago, at the Nagmaal in Nylstroom."

I told Ben Myburg that if it was that jar of brandy he meant, then he must realise that there had also been a good deal of misunderstanding about it. Moreover, it was not even a full jar, I said.

But I congratulated him on his powers of memory, which I said I was sure would yet stand the Republic in good stead.

And I was right. For afterwards, when the war of the big commandos was over, and we were in constant retreat, it would be Ben Myburg who, next day, would lead us back to the donga in which we had hidden some mealie-meal and a tin of cooking fat. And if the tin of cooking fat was empty, he would be able to tell us right away if it was kaffirs or baboons. A kaffir had a different way of eating cooking fat out of a tin from what a baboon had, Ben Myburg said.

Ben Myburg had been recently married to Mimi van Blerk, who came from Schweizer-Reneke, a district that was known as far as the Limpopo for its attractive girls. I remembered Mimi van Blerk well. She had full red lips and thick yellow hair. Ben Myburg always looked forward very eagerly to getting letters from his pretty young wife. He would also read out to us extracts from her letters, in which she encouraged us to drive the English into the blue grass – which was the name we gave to the sea in those days. For the English we had other names.

One of Mimi's letters was accompanied by a wooden candle-box filled with dried peaches. Ben Myburg was most proud to share out the dried fruit among our company, for he had several times spoken of the orchard of yellow cling peaches that he had laid out at the side of his house.

"We've already got dried peaches," Jurie Bekker said. Then he added, making free with our projected invasion of Natal: "In a few weeks' time we will be picking bananas."

It was in this spirit, as I have said, that we set out to meet the enemy. But nobody knew better than ourselves how much of this fine talk was to hide what we really felt. And I know, speaking for myself, that when we got the command "Opsaal", and we were crossing the border between the Transvaal and Natal, I was less happy at the thought that my horse was such a mettlesome animal. For it seemed to me that my horse was far more anxious to invade Natal than I was. I had to rein him in a good deal on the way to Spioenkop and Colenso. And I told myself that it was because I did not want him to go too fast downhill.

Eighteen months later saw the armed forces of the Republic in a worse case than I should imagine any army has ever been in, and that army still fighting. We were spread all over the country in small groups. We were in rags.

Many burghers had been taken prisoner. Others had yielded themselves up to British magistrates, holding not their rifles in their hands but their hats. There were a number of Boers, also, who had gone and joined the English.

For the Transvaal Republic it was near the end of a tale that you tell, sitting around the kitchen fire on a cold night. The story of the Transvaal Republic was at that place where you clear your throat before saying which of the two men the girl finally married. Or whether it was the cattle-smuggler or the Sunday school superintendent who stole the money. Or whether it was a real ghost or just her uncle with a sheet round him that Lettie van Zyl saw at the drift.

One night, when we were camped just outside Nietverdiend, and it was Ben Myburg's and my turn to go on guard, he told me that he knew that part well.

"You see that rant there, Schalk?" he asked. "Well, I have often stood on the other side of it, under the stars, just like now. You know, I've got a lot of peach trees on my farm. Well, I have stood there, under the ripening peaches, just after dark, with Mimi at my side. There is no smell like the smell of young peach trees in the evening, Schalk, when the fruit is ripening. I can almost imagine I am back there now. And it is just the time for it, too."

I tried to explain to Ben Myburg, in a roundabout way, that although everything might be exactly the same on this side of the rant, he would have to be prepared for certain changes on the other side, seeing that it was war.

Ben Myburg agreed that I was probably right. Nevertheless, he began to talk to me at length about his courtship days. He spoke of Mimi with her full red lips and her yellow hair.

"I can still remember the evening when Mimi promised that she would marry me, Schalk," Ben Myburg said. "It was in Zeerust. We were there for the Nagmaal. When I walked back to my tent on the kerkplein I was so happy that I just kicked the first three kaffirs I saw."

I could see that, talking to me while we stood on guard, Ben Myburg was living through that time all over again. I was glad, for their sakes, that no kaffirs came past at that moment. For Ben Myburg was again very happy.

I was pleased, too, for Ben Myburg's own sake, that he did at least have that hour of deep joy in which he could recall the past so vividly. For it was after that that his memory went.

By the following evening we had crossed the rant and had arrived at Ben Myburg's farm. We camped among the smoke-blackened walls of his former homestead, erecting a rough shelter with some sheets of corrugated iron that we could still use. And although he must have known only too well what to expect, yet what Ben Myburg saw there came as so much of a shock to his senses that from that moment all he could remember from the past vanished for ever.

It was pitiful to see the change that had come over him. If his farm had been laid to ruins, the devastation that had taken place in Ben Myburg's mind was no less dreadful.

Perhaps it was that, in truth, there was nothing more left in the past to remember.

We noticed, also, that in singular ways, certain fragments of the bygone would come into Ben Myburg's mind; and that he would almost – but not quite – succeed in fitting these pieces together.

We observed that almost immediately. For instance, we remained camped on his farm for several days. And one morning, when the fire for our mealie-pap was crackling under one of the few remaining fruit trees that had once been an orchard, Ben Myburg reached up and picked a peach that was, in advance of its season, ripe and yellow.

"It's funny," Ben Myburg said, "but I seem to remember, from long ago, reaching up and picking a yellow peach, just like this one. I don't quite remember where."

We did not tell him that he was picking one of his own peaches.

Some time later our seksie was captured in a night attack.

For us the Boer War was over. We were going to St. Helena. We were driven to Nylstroom, the nearest railhead, in a mule-wagon. It was a strange experience for us to be driving along the main road, in broad daylight, for all the world to see us. From years of war-time habit, our eyes still went to the horizon. A bitter thing about our captivity was that among our guards were men of our own people.

Outside Nylstroom we alighted from the mule-wagon and the English sergeant in charge of our escort got us to form fours by the roadside. It was queer – our having to learn to be soldiers at the end of a war instead of at the beginning.

Eventually we got into some sort of formation, the veldkornet, Jurie Bekker, Ben Myburg and I making up the first four. It was already evening. From a distance we could see the lights in the town. The way to the main street of Nylstroom led by the cemetery. Although it was dark, we could yet distinguish several rows of newly made mounds. We did not need to be told that they were concentration camp graves. We took off our battered hats and tramped on in a great silence.

Soon we were in the main street. We saw, then, what those lights were. There was a dance at the hotel. Paraffin lamps were hanging under the hotel's low, wide veranda. There was much laughter. We saw girls and English officers. In our unaccustomed fours we slouched past in the dark.

Several of the girls went inside, then. But a few of the women-folk remained on the veranda, not looking in our direction. Among them I noticed particularly a girl leaning on an English officer's shoulder. She looked very pretty, with the light from a paraffin lamp shining on her full lips and yellow hair.

When we had turned the corner, and the darkness was wrapping us round again, I heard Ben Myburg speak.

"It's funny," I heard Ben Myburg say, "but I seem to remember, from long ago, a girl with yellow hair, just like that one. I don't quite remember where."

And this time, too, we did not tell him.

Last Stories

(1948–51)

Romaunt of the Smuggler's Daughter

Long ago, there was more money (Oom Schalk Lourens said, wistfully) to be made out of cattle-smuggling that there is in these times. The Government knows that, of course. But the Government thinks that why we Marico farmers don't bring such large herds of native cattle across the Bechuanaland border anymore, on moonless nights, is because the mounted police are more efficient than they used to be.

That isn't the reason, of course.

You still get as good a sort of night as ever – a night when there is only the light of the stars shining on the barbed wire that separates the Transvaal from the Protectorate. But why my wire-cutters are rusting in the buitekamer from disuse is not because the border is better patrolled than it was in the old days. For it is not the mounted police, with their polished boots and clicking spurs, but the barefoot Bechuana kaffirs that have grown more cunning.

We all said that it was the fault of the mission school at Ramoutsa, of course. Afterwards, when more schools were opened, deeper into the Protectorate, we gave those schools a share of the blame as well . . . Naturally, it wasn't a thing that happened suddenly. Only, we found, as the years went by, that the kaffirs in the Bechuanaland Protectorate wanted more and more for their cattle. And later on they would traffic with us only when we paid them in hard cash; they frowned on the idea of barter.

I can still remember the look of grieved wonderment on Jurie Prinsloo's face when he told us about his encounter with the Bapedi chief near Malopolole. Jurie came across the Bapedi chief in front of his hut. And the Bapedi chief was not squatting on an animal skin spread on the ground; instead, he was sitting on a real chair, and looking quite comfortable sitting in it, too.

"Here's a nice, useful roll of copper wire for you," Jurie

Prinsloo said to the Bapedi chief, who was lazily scratching the back of his instep against the lower cross-piece of the chair. "You can give me an ox for it. That red ox, there, with the long horns and the loose dewlap will be all right. They don't know any better about an ox on the Johannesburg market."

"But what can I do with the copper wire?" the Bapedi chief asked. "I have not got a telephone."

This was a real problem for Jurie Prinsloo, of course. For many years he had been trading rolls of copper wire for kaffir cattle, and it had never occurred to him to think out what the kaffirs used the wire for.

"Well," Jurie Prinsloo said, weakly, "you can make it into a ring to put through your nose, and you can also –"

But even as Jurie Prinsloo spoke, he realised that the old times had passed away for ever.

And we all said, yes, it was these missionaries, with the schools they were opening up all over the place, who were ruining the kaffirs. As if the kaffirs weren't uncivilised enough in the first place, we said. And now the missionaries had to come along and educate them on top of it.

Anyway, the superior sort of smile that came across the left side of the chief's face, at the suggestion that he should wear a copper ring in his nose, made Jurie Prinsloo feel that he had to educate the Bapedi chief some more. What was left of the chair, after Jurie Prinsloo had finished educating the Bapedi chief, was produced in the magistrate's court in Gaborone, where Jurie Prinsloo was fined ten pounds for assault with intent to do grievous bodily harm. In those days you could buy quite a few head of cattle for ten pounds.

And, in spite of his schooling, the Bapedi chief remained as ignorant as ever. For, during the rest of the time that he remained head of the tribe, he would not allow a white man to enter his stat again.

But, as I have said, it was different, long ago. Then the Bechuanaland kaffirs would still take an interest in their appearance, and they would be glad to exchange their cattle for brass and beads and old whale-bone corsets and tins of axle-grease (to make the skin on their chests shine) and cheap watches. They would even come and help us drive the cattle across the line, just for the excitement of it, and to show off their new finery, in the way of umbrellas and top-hats and pieces of pink underwear, at the kraals through which we passed.

Easily the most enterprising cattle-smuggler in the Marico Bushveld at the time of which I am talking was Gerrit Oost-huizen. He had a farm right next to the Protectorate border. So that the barbed wire that he cut at night, when he brought over a herd of cattle, was also the fence of his own farm. Within a few years Gerrit Oosthuizen had made so much money out of smuggled cattle that he was able to introduce a large number of improvements on his farm, including a new type of concrete cattle dip with iron steps, and a piano for which he had a special kind of stand built into the floor of his voorkamer, so as to keep the white ants away.

Gerrit Oosthuizen's daughter, Jemima, who was then sixteen years of age and very pretty, with dark hair and a red mouth and a soft shadow at the side of her throat, started learning to play the piano. Farmers and their wives from many miles away came to visit Gerrit Oosthuizen. They came to look at the piano stand, which had been specially designed by a Pretoria engineer, and had an aluminium tank underneath that you kept filled with water, so that it was impossible for the white ants to effect much damage – if you wiped them off from the underneath part of the piano with a paraffin rag every morning.

The visitors would come to the farm, and they would drink coffee in the voorkamer, and they would listen to Jemima Oost-huizen playing a long piece out of a music book with one finger, and they would nod their heads solemnly, at the end of it, when Jemima sat very still, with her dark hair falling forward over her eyes, and they would say, well, if that Pretoria engineer thought that, in the long run, the white ants would not be able to find a way of beating his aluminium invention, and of eating up all the inside of the piano, then they didn't know the Marico white ant, that's all.

We who were visitors to the Oosthuizen farm spoke almost with pride of the cleverness of the white ant. We felt, somehow, that the white ants belonged to the Marico Bushveld, just like we did, and we didn't like the idea of a Pretoria engineer, who was an uitlander, almost, thinking that with his invention – which consisted just of bits of shiny tin – he would be able to outwit the cunning of a Marico white ant.

Through his conducting his cattle-smuggling operations on so large and successful a scale, Gerrit Oosthuizen soon got rich. He was respected – and even envied – throughout the Marico. They say that when the Volksraad member came to Gerrit Oosthuizen's farm, and he saw around him so many unmistakable signs of great wealth, including green window-blinds that rolled up by themselves when you jerked the sashcord – they say that even the Volksraad member was very much impressed, and that he seemed to be deep in thought for a long time. It almost seemed as though he was wondering whether, in having taken up politics, he had chosen the right career, after all.

If that was how the Volksraad member really did feel about the matter, then it must have been a sad thing for him, when the debates in the Raadsaal at Pretoria dragged far into the night, and he had to remain seated on his back bench, without having much heart in the proceedings, since he would be dreaming all the time of a herd of red cattle being driven towards a fence in the starlight. And when the Chairman of the Committee called another member to order, it might almost have sounded to this Volksraad member as though it was a voice coming out of the shadows of the maroelas and demanding, suddenly, "Who goes there?"

To this question – which he had heard more than once, of course, during the years in which he had smuggled cattle – Gerrit Oosthuizen nearly always had the right answer. It was always more difficult for Gerrit Oosthuizen if it was a youthful-sounding voice shouting out that challenge. Because it usually meant, then, that the uniformed man on horseback, half hidden in the shadow of a withaak, was a young recruit, anxious to get promotion. Gerrit Oosthuizen could not handle him in the same way as he could an elderly mounted police sergeant, who was a married man with a number of children, and who had learnt, through long years of service, a deeper kind of wisdom about life on this old earth.

It was, each time, through mistaken zeal on the part of a young recruit – who nearly always got a transfer, shortly afterwards –

302

that Gerrit Oosthuizen had to stand his trial in the Zeerust court-house. He was several times acquitted. On a few occasions he was fined quite heavily. Once he was sentenced to six months' impris-onment without the option of a fine. Consequently, while Gerrit Oosthuizen was known to entertain a warm regard for almost any middle-aged mounted policeman with a fat stomach, he invari-ably displayed a certain measure of impatience towards a raw recruit. It was said that on more than one occasion, in the past, Gerrit Oosthuizen had given expression to his impatience by dis-charging a couple of Mauser bullets – aimed high – into the sha-dows from which an adolescent voice had spoken out of turn.

Needless to say, all these stories that went the rounds of the Marico about Gerrit Oosthuizen only added to his popularity with the farmers. Even when the predikant shook his head, on being informed of Gerrit Oosthuizen's latest escapade, you could see that he regarded it as being but little more than a rather risky sort of prank, and that, if anything, he admired Gerrit Oost-huizen, the Marico's champion cattle-smuggler, for the careless way in which he defied the law. Whatever he did, Gerrit Oost-huizen always seemed to act in the right way. And it seems to me that, if he adheres to such a kind of rule, the man who goes against the law gets as much respect from the people around him as does the law-giver. More, even.

"The law stops on the south side of the Dwarsberge," Gerrit Oosthuizen said to a couple of his neighbours, in a sudden burst of pride, on the day that the piano arrived and was placed on top of the patent aluminium stand. "And north of the Dwarsberge I am the law."

But soon after that Gerrit Oosthuizen did something that the Marico farmers did not understand, and that they did not forgive him for so easily. Just at the time when his daughter, Jemima, was most attractive, and was beginning to play herself in on the piano, using two fingers of each hand – and when quite a number of the young men of the district were beginning to pay court to her – Gerrit Oosthuizen sent her away to the seminary for young ladies that had just been opened in Zeerust.

We expressed our surprise to Gerrit Oosthuizen in various ways. After all, we all liked Jemima, and it didn't seem right that an attractive Bushveld girl should be sent away like that to get spoilt. She would come back with city affectations and foreign ways. She would no longer be able to make a good, simple wife for an honest Boer lad. It was, of course, the young men who expressed this view with the greatest measure of indignation – even those who were not so particularly honest, either, perhaps.

But Gerrit Oosthuizen said, no, he believed in his daughter having the best opportunities. There were all sorts of arts and graces of life that she would learn at the finishing-school, he said. Among the Marico's young men, however, were some who thought that there was very little that any young ladies' seminary would be able to teach Jemima that she did not already know.

We lost confidence in Gerrit Oosthuizen after that, of course. And when next we got up a deputation to the Government to protest about the money being spent on native education – because there were already signs of a falling-off in the cattle trade with the Bechuanas – then we did not elect Gerrit Oosthuizen as a delegate. We felt that his ideas on education, generally, were becoming unsound.

It is true, however, that, during the time that Jemima was at the seminary, Gerrit Oosthuizen did once or twice express doubts about his wisdom in having sent her there.

"Jemima writes to say that she is reading a lot of poetry," Gerrit Oosthuizen said to me, once. "I wonder if that isn't per-haps, sort of . . . you know . . ."

I agreed with Gerrit that it seemed as if his daughter was embarking on something dangerous. But she was still very young, I added. She might yet grow out of that sort of foolishness. I said that when the right young man for her came along she would close that book of poetry quick enough, without even bothering to mark the place that she had got up to. Nevertheless, I was glad to think that Gerrit Oosthuizen was not so happy, any-more, about his daughter's higher education.

"Still, she gets very good reports from her teachers," Gerrit Oosthuizen said, but without any real enthusiasm. "Especially from her poetry teacher."

Meanwhile, the cattle-smuggling business was going from bad to worse, and by the time Jemima returned from her stay at the seminary, Gerrit Oosthuizen had his hands full with his personal affairs. He had made a few singularly unsuccessful cattle-smuggling trips into the Protectorate. By that time the kaffirs had got so educated that one squint-eyed Mtosa even tried to fall back on barter – but the other way around. He wanted Gerrit Oosthuizen to trade his mules and cart for a piece of glass that the Mtosa claimed was a Namaqualand diamond. And, on top of everything else, when Gerrit Oosthuizen did on a few occasions get back into the Transvaal with a likely herd of cattle, it was with Daniel Malan, a new recruit to the border patrol, hot on his trail.

It was under these circumstances that Jemima Oosthuizen returned to the Bushveld farm from the young ladies' seminary in Zeerust. Just to look at her, it seemed that the time she had spent at the finishing-school had not changed her very much. If anything, she was even prettier than she had been before she left. Her lips were still curved and red. There was still that soft shadow at the side of her throat. Only, it seemed to me that in her dark eyes there was now a dreamy look that wouldn't fit in too readily with the everyday life of a Bushveld farm.

And I was right. And it didn't take the young fellows of the neighbourhood very long to find out, either, that Jemima Oosthuizen had, indeed, changed. It saddened them to realise that they could do very little about it.

Jemima Oosthuizen was, as always, friendly to each young man who called. But it was easy for these young men to detect that it was a general sort of friendliness – which she felt for them all equally and alike. She would read poetry to them, reading and explaining to them passages out of the many books of verse that she had brought back with her. And while they were very ready to be thrilled – even when they knew that it was a foolish waste of time – yet they felt that there was no way in which they could make any progress with her. No matter what any young man might feel about her, Jemima's feelings for him remained impersonal.

"What's wrong with me?" Andries Steyn asked of a number of young men, once. "She can go on reading that poetry to me as long as she likes. I don't mind. I don't understand anything about it, in any case. But the moment I start holding her hand, I know that she isn't thinking of me at all. It's like she wants me to come to her out of one of those books."

"Yes, like that fellow by the dam, looking all pale and upset about something," Fritz Pretorius interrupted him. "Yes, I know all that nonsense. And there am I sitting on the rusbank next to her, wearing my best clothes and my veldskoens rubbed smooth with sheep's fat. And she doesn't seem to see me, at all. I don't mind her explaining all about that stuff she reads. I like the sound of her voice. But she doesn't make me feel that I am even a human being to her."

They went on to say that perhaps Jemima didn't want a man who was a human being. Maybe she wanted a lover who reminded her of one of those young men in the poetry books. A young man who wore shining armour. Or jet-black armour. Or even rusty armour. They had all kinds in the different poems that Jemima Oosthuizen explained to her suitors. But where did a young man of the Marico Bushveld come in, in all that?

Lovers came and went. Jemima was never long without a suitor. But she never favoured one above the other – never warming noticeably to anyone. Whatever the qualities were that she sought in a lover – going by the romantic heroes that she read about in old poetry – Jemima never found a Marico lover who fitted in with the things that she read about.

Yes, Gerrit Oosthuizen certainly had a lot of trouble. We even began to feel slightly sorry for him. Here was his daughter who, at a marriageable age, was driving all the young men away from her because of some fantastic ideas that they had put into her head at the finishing-school. Then there were the kaffirs in the Protectorate, who were daily getting more difficult to deal with. And then, finally, there was that new police recruit who was putting in all his time trying to trap Gerrit.

And those who sympathised with Gerrit Oosthuizen also thought it right to blame his daughter on the score of ingratitude. After all, it had cost her father a good deal of money to see Jemima through the finishing-school. He had sent her to the young ladies' seminary in Zeerust in order that she should gain refinement and culture: instead, she had come back talking poetry. Others, again, said that it was her father's lawlessness – which was also, after a fashion, romantic – that had come out in Jemima in that way.

It was on an afternoon when a horseman came riding from over the veld up to her front gate, that Jemima saw the young man that she had read about in olden poems. And she recognised him instantly as her lover. She did not take great note of what he looked like. Nor did she even observe, at first glance, that he was wearing a uniform. All that Jemima Oosthuizen saw very clearly was that, when he came riding up to her from the highway, he was seated on a white horse.

And when she had gone hastily into her bedroom – and had come out again, wearing a pink frock – Jemima hardly understood, at first, the meaning of the young policeman's words when she heard him say, to her father, that he had a warrant for his arrest.

THE FERREIRA MILLIONS

Marthinus Taljaard lived in a house that his grandfather had built on the slope of a koppie in the Dwarsberge (Oom Schalk Lourens said). It was a big, rambling house with more rooms than what Marthinus Taljaard needed for just his daughter, Rosina, and himself. Marthinus Taljaard was known as the richest man in the whole of the Dwarsberge. It was these two circumstances that led to the koppie around his house becoming hollowed out with tunnels like the nest of a white ant.

Only a man who, like Marthinus Taljaard, already had more possessions in cattle and money than he knew what to do with, would still want more. That was why he listened to the story that Giel Bothma came all the way from Johannesburg to tell him about the Ferreira millions.

Of course, any Marico farmer would have been interested to hear what a young man in city clothes had to say, talking fast, about the meaning of a piece of yellow paper with lines and words on it, that he held in his hand. If Giel Bothma had come to me in that way, I would have listened to him, also. We would have sat on the stoep, drinking coffee. And I would have told him that it was a good story. I would also have shown him, if he was a young man willing to learn, how he could improve on it. Furthermore, I would have told him a few stories of my own, by way of guidance to him as to how to tell a story.

But towards milking time I would have to leave that young man sitting on the stoep, the while I went out to see what was happening in the cattle-kraal.

That was where Marthinus Taljaard, because he was the wealthiest man in the Dwarsberge, was different. He listened to Giel Bothma's story about the Ferreira millions from the early part of the forenoon onwards. He listened with his mouth open.

308

And when it came to milking time, he invited Giel Bothma over to the kraal with him, with Giel Bothma still talking. And when it came to the time for feeding the pigs, Giel Bothma helped to carry a heavy bucket of swill to the troughs, without seeming to notice the looks of surprise on the faces of the Bechuana farm labourers.

A little later, when Giel Bothma saw what the leaking bucket of swill had done to the legs of his smoothly pressed trousers, he spoke a lot more. And what he used were not just all city words, either.

Anyway, the result of Giel Bothma's visit from Johannesburg was that he convinced Marthinus Taljaard, by means of the words and lines on that bit of yellow paper, that the Ferreira millions, a treasure comprised of gold and diamonds and elephant tusks, was buried on his farm.

We in the Marico had, needless to say, never heard of the Ferreira millions before. We knew only that Ferreira was a good Afrikaner name. And we often sang that old song, "Vat Jou Goed en Trek, Ferreira" – meaning to journey northwards out of the Cape to get away from English rule. Moreover, there was the Hans Ferreira family. They were Doppers and lived near Enzelsberg. But when you saw Hans Ferreira at the Indian store at Ramoutsa, lifting a few sheep-skins out of his donkey-cart and trying to exchange them for coffee and sugar, then you could not help greeting with a certain measure of amusement the idea conveyed by the words, 'Ferreira millions.'

These were the matters that we discussed one midday while we were sitting around in Jurie Steyn's post office, waiting for our letters from Zeerust.

Marthinus Taljaard and his daughter, Rosina, had come to the post office, leaving Giel Bothma alone on the farm to work out, with the help of his yellowed map and the kaffirs, the place where to dig the tunnel.

"This map with the Ferreira millions in gold and diamonds and elephant tusks," Marthinus Taljaard said, pompously, sitting forward on Jurie Steyn's riempiestoel, "was made many years ago – before my grandfather's time, even. That's why it is so yellow. Giel Bothma got hold of it just by accident. And the map shows clearly that the Portuguese explorer, Ferreira, buried his treasure somewhere in that koppie in the middle of my farm."

"Anyway, that piece of paper is yellow enough," Jurie Steyn said with a slight sneer. "That paper is yellower than the iron pyrites that a prospector found at Witfontein, so it must be gold, all right. And I can also see that it is gold, from the way you hang on to it."

Several of us laughed, then.

"But I can't imagine there being such a thing as the Ferreira millions," Stephanus van Tonder said, expressing what we all felt. "Not if you think that Hans Ferreira's wife went to the last Nagmaal with a mimosa thorn holding up her skirt because they didn't have a safety-pin in the house."

Marthinus Taljaard explained to us where we were wrong.

"The treasure was buried on my farm very long ago," Marthinus Taljaard said, "long before there were any white people in the Transvaal. It was the treasure that the Portuguese explorer, Ferreira, stole from the Mtosas. Maybe that Portuguese explorer was the ancestor of Hans Ferreira. I don't know. But I am talking about very long ago, before the Ferreiras were Afrikaners, but were just Portuguese. I am talking of *very* long ago."

We told Marthinus Taljaard that he had better not make wild statements like that in Hans Ferreira's hearing. Hans Ferreira was a Dopper and quick-tempered. And even though he had to trade sheep-skins for coffee and sugar, we said, not being able to wait to change the skins into money first, he would nevertheless go many miles out of his way with a sjambok to look for a man who spoke of him as a Portuguese.

And no matter how long ago, either, we added.

Marthinus Taljaard sat up even straighter on the riempiestoel then.

By way of changing the conversation, Jurie Steyn asked Marthinus how he knew for certain that it was his farm on which the treasure was buried.

Marthinus Taljaard said that that part of the map was very clear.

"The site of the treasure, marked with a cross, is twelve thousand Cape feet north of Abjaterskop, in a straight line," he said, "so that's almost in the exact middle of my farm."

He went on to explain, wistfully, that that was about the only part of the map that was in a straight line.

"It's all in Cape roods and Cape ells, like it has on the back of the school exercise books," Marthinus Taljaard's daughter, Rosina, went on to tell us. "That's what makes it so hard for Mr Bothma to work out the Ferreira map. We sometimes sit up quite late at night, working out sums."

After Marthinus Taljaard and Rosina had left, we said that young Giel Bothma must be pretty slow for a young man. Sitting up late at night with an attractive girl like Rosina Taljaard, and being able to think of nothing better to do than working out sums.

We also said it was funny that that first Ferreira should have filled up his treasure map with Cape measurements, when the later Ferreiras were in so much of a hurry to trek away from anything that even looked like the Cape.

In the months that followed there was a great deal of activity on Marthinus Taljaard's farm. I didn't go over there myself, but other farmers had passed that way, driving slowly in their mule-carts down the Government Road and trying to see all they could without appearing inquisitive. From them I learnt that a large number of tunnels had been dug into the side of a hill on which the Taljaard farmhouse stood.

During those months, also, several of Marthinus Taljaard's Bechuanas left him and came to work for me. That new kind of work on Baas Taljaard's farm was too hard, one of them told me, brushing red soil off his elbow. He also said that Baas Taljaard was unappreciative of their best efforts at digging holes into the side of the koppie. And each time a hole came to an end, and there was no gold in it, or diamonds or elephant teeth, then Baas Taljaard would take a kick at whatever native was nearest.

"He kicked me as though it was my fault that there was no gold there," another Bechuana said to me with a grin, "instead of blaming it on that yellow paper with the writing on it."

The Bechuana said that on a subsequent occasion, when there was no gold at the end of a tunnel that was particularly wide and

311

long, Marthinus Taljaard ran a few yards (Cape yards, I supposed), and took a kick at Giel Bothma.

No doubt Baas Taljaard did that by mistake, the Bechuana added, his grin almost as wide as one of those tunnels.

More months passed before I again saw Marthinus Taljaard and his daughter in Jurie Steyn's post office. Marthinus was saying that they were now digging a tunnel that he was sure was the right one.

"It points straight at my house," he said, "and where it comes up, there we'll find the treasure. We have now worked out from the map that the tunnel should go up, at the end. That wasn't clear before, because there is something missing –"

"Yes, the treasure," Jurie Steyn said, winking at Stephanus van Tonder.

"No," Rosina interjected, flushing. "There is a corner missing from the map. That bit of the map remained between the thumb and forefinger of the man in the bar when he gave it to Giel Bothma."

"We only found out afterwards that Giel Bothma had that map given to him by crooks in a bar," Marthinus Taljaard said. "If I had

known about that from the start, I don't know if I would have
been so keen about it. Why I listened was because Giel Bothma
was so well dressed, in city clothes, and all."

Marthinus Taljaard stirred his coffee.

"But he isn't anymore," he resumed, reflectively. "Not well
dressed, I mean. You should have seen how his suit looked after
the first week of tunnelling."

We had quite a lot to say after Marthinus Taljaard and Rosina
left.

"Crooks in a bar," Stephanus van Tonder snorted. "It's all clear
to me, now. That tunnel is going to come up right under Marthinus Taljaard's bed, where he keeps his money in that tamboetie
chest. I am sure that map has got nothing to do with the Ferreira
treasure at all. But it seems a pretty good map of the Taljaard
treasure."

We also said that it was a very peculiar way that that crook had
of *giving* Giel Bothma the map. With one corner of it remaining in
his hand. It certainly looked as though Giel Bothma must have
pulled on it, a little.

We never found out how much truth there was in our specula-
tions. For we learnt some time later that Giel Bothma did get hold
of the Taljaard fortune, after all. He got it by marrying Rosina.
And that last tunnel did come up under a part of Marthinus
Taljaard's rambling old house, built on the side of the koppie. It
came up at the end of a long passage, right in front of the door of
Rosina Taljaard's bedroom.

SOLD DOWN THE RIVER

W e had, of course, heard of André Maritz's play and his company of play-actors long before they got to Zeerust (Oom Schalk Lourens said).

For they had travelled a long road. Some of the distance they went by train. Other parts of the way they travelled by mule-cart or ox-wagon. They visited all the dorps from the Cape – where they had started from – to Zeerust in the Transvaal, where Hannekie Roodt left the company. She had an important part in the play, as we knew even before we saw her name in big letters on the posters.

André Maritz had been somewhat thoughtless, that time, in his choice of a play for his company to act in. The result was that there were some places that he had to go away from at a pace rather faster than could be made by even a good mule-team. Naturally, this sort of thing led to André Maritz's name getting pretty well known throughout the country – and without his having to stick up posters, either.

The trouble did not lie with the acting. There was not very much wrong with that. But anybody could have told André Maritz that he should never have toured the country with that kind of a play. There was a negro in it, called Uncle Tom, who was supposed to be very good and kind-hearted. André Maritz, with his face blackened, took that part. And there was also a white man in the play, named Simon Legree. He was the kind of white man who, if he was your neighbour, would think it funny to lead the Government tax-collector to the aardvark-hole that you were hiding in.

It seems that André Maritz had come across a play that had been popular on the other side of the sea; and he translated it into Afrikaans and adapted it to fit in with South African traditions. André Maritz's fault was that he hadn't adapted the play enough.

314

The company made this discovery in the very first Free State dorp they got to. For, when they left that town, André Maritz had one of his eyes blackened, and not just with burnt cork.

André Maritz adapted his play a good deal more, immediately after that. He made Uncle Tom into a much less kind-hearted negro. And he also made him steal chickens.

The only member of the company that the public of the backveld seemed to have any time for was the young man who acted Simon Legree.

Thus it came about that we heard of André Maritz's company when they were still far away, touring the highveld. Winding their play-actors' road northwards, past koppies and through vlaktes, and by bluegums and willows.

After a few more misunderstandings with the public, André Maritz so far adapted the play to South African conditions as to make Uncle Tom threaten to hit Topsy with a brandy bottle.

The result was that, by the time the company came to Zeerust, even the church elder, Theunis van Zyl, said that there was much in the story of Uncle Tom that could be considered instructive.

True, there were still one or two little things, Elder van Zyl declared, that did not perhaps altogether accord with what was best in our outlook. For instance, it was not right that we should be made to feel so sentimental about the slave-girl as played by Hannekie Roodt. The elder was referring to that powerful scene in which Hannekie Roodt got sold down the river by Simon Legree. We couldn't understand very clearly what it meant to be sold down the river. But from Hannekie Roodt's acting we could see that it must be the most awful fate that could overtake anybody.

She was so quiet. She did not speak in that scene. She just picked up the small bundle containing her belongings. Then she put her hand up to her coat collar and closed over the lapel in front, even though the weather was not cold.

Yet there were still some people in Zeerust who, after they had attended the play on the first night, thought that that scene could be improved on. They said that when Hannekie Roodt walked off the stage for the last time, sold down the river, and carrying the bundle of her poor possessions tied up in a red-spotted rag, a few

315

of her mistress's knives and forks could have been made to drop out of the bundle.

As I have said, André Maritz's company eventually arrived in Zeerust. They came by mule-cart from Slurry, where the railway ended in those days. They stayed at the Marico Hotel, which was a few doors from Elder van Zyl's house. It was thus that André Maritz met Deborah, the daughter of the elder. That was one thing that occasioned a good deal of talk. Especially as we believed that even if Hannekie Roodt was not actually married to André Maritz in the eyes of the law, the two of them were nevertheless as nearly husband and wife as it is possible for play-actors to be, since they are known to be very unenlightened in such matters.

The other things that gave rise to much talk had to do with what happened on the first night of the staging of the play in Zeerust. André Maritz hired the old hall adjoining the mill. The hall had last been used two years before.

The result was that, after the curtain had gone up for the first act of André Maritz's play, it was discovered that a wooden platform above the stage was piled high with fine flour that had sifted through the ceiling from the mill next door. The platform had been erected by the stage company that had given a performance in the hall two years previously. That other company had used the platform to throw down bits of paper from to look like snow, in a scene in which a girl gets thrust out into the world with her baby in her arms.

At the end of the first act, when the curtain was lowered, André Maritz had the platform swept. But until then, with all that flour coming down, it looked as though he and his company were moving about the stage in a Cape mist. Each time an actor took a step forward or spoke too loudly – down would come a shower of fine meal. Afterwards the players took to standing in one place as much as possible, to avoid shaking down the flour – and in fear of losing their way in the mist, too, by the look of things.

Naturally, all this confused the audience a good deal. For, with the flour sifting down on to the faces of the actors, it became difficult, after a little while, to tell which were the white people and which the negroes. Towards the end of the first act Uncle Tom, with a layer of flour covering his make-up, looked just as white as Simon Legree.

During the time when the curtain was lowered, however, the flour was swept from the platform and the actors repaired their faces very neatly, so that when the next act began there was nothing anymore to remind us of that first unhappy incident.

Later on I was to think that it was a pity that the consequences of that *second* unhappy incident, that of André Maritz's meeting with the daughter of Elder van Zyl, could not also have been brushed away so tidily.

The play was nevertheless very successful. And I am sure that in the crowded hall that night there were very few dry eyes when Hannekie Roodt played her great farewell scene. When she picked up her bundle and got ready to leave, having been sold down the river, you could see by her stillness that her parting from her lover and her people would be for ever. No one who saw her act that night would ever forget the tragic moment when she put her hand up to her coat collar and closed over the lapels in front, even though – as I have said – the weather was not cold.

The applause at the end lasted for many minutes.

The play got the same enthusiastic reception night after night. Meanwhile, off the stage, there were many stories linking Deborah van Zyl's name with André Maritz's.

"They say that Deborah van Zyl is going to be an actress now," Flip Welman said when several of us were standing smoking in the hardware store. "She is supposed to be getting Hannekie Roodt's part."

"We all know that Deborah van Zyl has been talking for a long while about going on the stage," Koos Steyn said. "And maybe this is the chance she was been waiting for. But I can't see her in Hannekie Roodt's part for very long. I think she will rather be like the girl in that other play we saw here a few years ago – the one with the baby."

Knowing what play-actors were, I could readily picture Deborah van Zyl being pushed out into the world, carrying a child in her arms, and with the white-paper snow fluttering about her.

As for Hannekie Roodt, she shortly afterwards left André Maritz's company of play-actors. She arranged with Koos Steyn to drive her, with her suitcases, to Slurry station. Koos explained to me that he was a married man and so he could not allow it to be said of him, afterwards, that he had driven alone in a cart with a play-actress. That was how it came about that I rode with them.

But Koos Steyn need have had no fears of the kind that he hinted at. Hannekie Roodt spoke hardly a word. At close hand she looked different from what she had done on the stage. Her hair was scraggy. I also noticed that her teeth were uneven and that there was loose skin at her throat.

Yet, there was something about her looks that was not without a strange sort of beauty. And in her presence there was that which made me think of great cities. There were also marks on her face from which you could tell that she had travelled a long road. A road that was longer than just the thousand miles from the Cape to the Marico.

Hannekie Roodt was going away from André Maritz. And during the whole of that long journey by mule-cart she did not once weep. I could not help but think that it was true what people said about play-actors. They had no real human feelings. They could act on the stage and bring tears to your eyes, but they themselves had no emotions.

We arrived at Slurry station. Hannekie Roodt thanked Koos Steyn and paid him. There was no platform there in those days. So Hannekie had to climb up several steps to get on to the balcony of the carriage. It was almost as though she were getting on to the stage. We lifted up her suitcases for her.

Koos Steyn and I returned to the mule-cart. Something made me look back over my shoulder. That was my last glimpse of Hannekie Roodt. I saw her put her hand up to her coat collar. She closed over the lapels in front. The weather was not cold.

THE LOVER WHO CAME BACK

It caused no small stir in the Marico (Oom Schalk Lourens said) when Piet Human came back after an absence of twenty years. His return was as unexpected as his departure had been sudden.

It was quite a story, the manner of his leaving the farm his father had bought for him at Gemsbokvlei, and also the reasons for his leaving. Since it was a story of young love, the women took pleasure in discussing it in much detail.

The result was that with the years the events surrounding Piet Human's sudden decision to move out of the Marico remained fresh in people's memories. More, the affair grew into something like a folk-tale, almost, with the passage of time.

Indeed, I heard one version of the story of Piet Human and the girl Wanda Rossouw as far away as Schweizer-Reneke, where I had trekked with my cattle during a season of drought. It was told me by one of the daughters in the house of a farmer with whom I had made arrangements for grazing my cattle.

The main feature of the story was the wooden stile between the two farms – Piet Human's farm and the farm of Wanda Rossouw's parents. If you brought that stile into it, you could not go wrong in the telling of the story, whatever else you added to it or left out.

And so the farmer's daughter in Schweizer-Reneke, because she mentioned the stile at the beginning, related the story very pleasantly.

Piet Human had been courting Wanda Rossouw for some time. And they had met often by the white-painted wooden fence that stood at the boundary of the two farms. And Wanda Rossouw had dark eyes and a wild heart.

Now, it had been well known that, before Piet Human came to

319

live at Gemsbokvlei, there had been another young man who had called very regularly at the Rossouw homestead. This young man was Gerhard Oelofse. He was somewhat of a braggart. But he had dashing ways. In his stride there was a kind of freedom that you could not help noticing. It was said that there were few girls in the Groot Marico that Gerhard Oelofse could not have for the asking.

One day Gerhard Oelofse rode off to join Van Pittius's free-booters in Stellaland. Later on he left for the Caprivi Strip. From then onwards we would receive, at long intervals, vague accounts of his activities in those distant parts. And in those fragmentary items of news about Gerhard Oelofse that reached us, there was little that did him credit.

Anyway, to return to Wanda Rossouw and Piet Human. There was an afternoon near to the twilight when they again met at the stile on the boundary between the two farms. It was a low stile, with only two cross-pieces. And the moment came inevitably when Piet Human, standing on his side of the fence, stooped forward to take Wanda Rossouw in his arms and lift her over to him. And in that moment Wanda Rossouw told him of what had happened, two years before, between Gerhard Oelofse and herself.

Piet Human had Wanda Rossouw in his arms. He put her down again, awkwardly, on her own side of the fence; and without a word walked away from her, into the deepening twilight.

Soon afterwards he sold his farm and left the Marico.

Because of the prominence she gave to that wooden stile, the daughter of the farmer in Schweizer-Reneke told the story of Piet Human and Wanda Rossouw remarkably well. True, she introduced into her narrative a few variations that were unfamiliar to us in the Groot Marico, but that made no difference to the quality of the story itself.

When she came to the end of the tale, I mentioned to her that I actually knew that wooden fence – low, with two cross-rails, and painted white. I had seen that stile very often, I said.

The farmer's daughter looked at me with a new sort of interest. She looked at me in such a way that for a little while I felt almost as though I was handsome. On the spur of the moment I went so far as to make up a lie. I told her that I had even carved my initials on that stile. On one of the lower cross-rails, I said. I felt it would have been too presumptuous if I had said one of the upper rails.

But even as I spoke I realised, by the far-off look in her eyes, that the farmer's daughter had already lost interest in me.

Ah, well, the story of Piet Human and Wanda Rossouw was a good love story and I had no right to try to chop a piece of it out for myself, cutting – in imagination – 'Schalk Lourens' into a strip of painted wood with a pocket knife.

"If Piet Human had really loved Wanda Rossouw, he would have forgiven her for what had happened with Gerhard Oelofse," the daughter of the Schweizer-Reneke farmer said, dreamily. "At least, I think so. But I suppose you can never tell . . ."

And so, when Piet Human came back to the Marico, the story of his sudden departure, twenty years earlier, was still fresh in people's memories – and with sundry additions.

I heard of Piet Human's return several weeks before I met him. Indeed, everyone north of the Dwarsberge knew he had come back. We talked of nothing else.

Where I again met him, after twenty years, was in Jurie Bekker's post office. He was staying with Jurie Bekker. I must admit that there were some unhappy aspects of that meeting for me; and I have reason to believe that there were those of the older farmers in Jurie Bekker's post office that day – men who had also known Piet Human long before – who felt as I did. For when Piet Human left us he was a young man of five-and-twenty summers. We saw him again now as a man of mature years. There were wrinkles under his eyes, there were grey hairs at his temples and – with our sudden awareness that Piet Human had indeed grown twenty years older since we had seen him came the knowledge that we, too, each of us, had also aged.

How I knew that others felt as I did was that, when I glanced across at Jurie Bekker, he was sitting back in his chair with his eyes cast down to his stomach. He gazed at his fat stomach with a certain intentness for some moments, and then shook his head sadly.

But it did not last long, this sense of melancholy. We soon

321

shook from our spirits the first stirrings of gloom. Those interven-
ing years that the locusts had eaten were no more than a quick sigh.
We drank our coffee and listened to what Piet Human had to tell
and in a little while it was as though he had never gone away.

Piet Human told us that he had entered the Marico from the
Bechuanaland side and had journeyed through Ramoutsa. He
had decided to stay with Jurie Bekker for a time and had not yet,
in his visits to familiar scenes of twenty years before, gone farther
to the west along the Government Road.

I thought this statement of Piet Human's significant. Farther to
the west lay the farm that had once been his, Gemsbokvlei; and
adjoining it was the Rossouw farm, where Wanda Rossouw still
lived with her widowed mother. For all those years Wanda Rossouw, though attractive and sought after, had remained unmarried.

Piet Human said that in some ways the Marico had changed a
great deal since he had been there last. In other respects there had
been no changes at all. Some of the people he had known had
died; others had trekked away. And children in arms had grown
into young men and women.

But there were just as many features of life in the Marico that
had not changed.

"I came here through Rooigrond," Piet Human said. "That big
white house that used to be the headquarters of the Van Pittius
freebooter gang is still there. But it is today a coach station."

He had asked how much he would have to pay for a coach
ticket to Ottoshoop, and when they told him, he realised that the
place had not changed at all; that big white house was still the
headquarters of robbers.

Then there were those Mtosa huts on the way to Ramoutsa.

Thus Piet Human entertained us. But I noticed that all his stories related only to places on the Ramoutsa side of the Marico. He
made no reference to that other side where his old farm was, and
where the Rossouws dwelt.

We were naturally very curious to know what his plans were, but
there was nobody in the post office that afternoon so coarse-
grained as even to hint at the past. We all felt that the story of Piet

Human and Wanda Rossouw stood for something in our community; there was a fineness about it that we meant to respect.

Even Fritz van Tonder, who was known as a pretty rough character, waited until Piet Human had gone out of the voorkamer before he said anything. And all he said then was, "Well, if Piet Human has decided to forgive Wanda Rossouw for that Gerhard Oelofse business he'll find she's still pretty. And she has waited long enough."

We ignored his remarks.

But the day did come when Piet Human paid a visit to that other part of the Marico where his old farm was. The white-painted wooden stile stood there still. The uprights, before being put into the ground, had been dipped in a Stockholm tar of a kind that you do not get today. And it was when the twilight was beginning to fall that Piet Human again saw Wanda Rossouw by the stile. She wore a pale frock. And although her face had perhaps grown thinner with the years, the look in her dark eyes had not changed. The grass was heavy with the scents of a dying summer's day.

Piet Human spoke urgent, burning words in a low voice. He leaned forward over the fence and took Wanda Rossouw in his arms.

She struggled in his arms, thrusting him from her fiercely when he tried to lift her over the stile.

Then at last Piet Human understood – that it was that other, worthless lover, who had forgotten her years ago, for whom, down the years, vainly, Wanda Rossouw waited.

For the second time Piet Human walked into the gathering dusk alone.

WHEN THE HEART IS EAGER

It was a visit that I remembered for the rest of my life (Oom Schalk Lourens said).

I was a small child, then. My father and his brother took me along in the back seat of the Cape-cart when they went to see an old man with a white beard. And when this old man stooped down to shake hands with me they told me to say, "Goeie dag, Oom Gysbert." I thought Oom Gysbert had something to do with God. I thought so from his voice and from Bible pictures I had seen of holy men, like prophets, who wore the same kind of beards.

My father and uncle went to see Oom Gysbert about pigs, which it seemed that he bred. And afterwards, when we drove home again, and my father and uncle spoke of Oom Gysbert, they both said he was a real old Pharisee. From that I was satisfied that I had been right in thinking of Oom Gysbert as a Bible person.

"Saying that those measled animals he sent us were the same prize pigs we had bought and paid for," my uncle went on, while we were riding back in the Cape-cart. "Does he not know how Ananias was smitten by the Lord?"

But that was not the reason why I remembered our visit to Oom Gysbert. For while I was on his farm I saw no pigs, measled or otherwise. And later in life I was to come across many more people that I have heard compared to Bible characters. To Judas, for instance.

After I had shaken hands with Oom Gysbert, the three men walked off together in the direction of the pigsties. I was left alone there, at the side of the house, where there was a stream of brown water flowing over rounded stones. This in itself was a sufficiently strange circumstance. You know how dry it is in these parts. I had until then seen water only in a dam or being pumped out of a

324

borehole into a cattle-trough. I had never before in my life seen a stream of water flowing away over stones.

I learnt afterwards that Oom Gysbert's farm was near the Molopo, and that he was thus enabled to lead off furrows of water, except in the times of most severe drought, to irrigate his tilled lands. My father and uncle had left me by one of those water-furrows.

That was something I did not know then, of course.

I walked for some little distance downstream, paddling in the water, since I was bare-footed. Then it was that I came across a sight that I have never since forgotten. I had, of course, before then seen flowers. Veld flowers. And the moepel and the maroela in bloom. But that was the first time in my life that I had seen such pink and white flowers, growing in such amazing profusion, climbing over and covering a fence of wire-netting that seemed very high and that stretched away as far as I could see.

I could not explain then, any more than I can now, the feelings of joy that came to me when I stood by that fence where rambling roses clustered.

At intervals, from the direction of the pigsties, came the voices of my father and my uncle and Oom Gysbert, who were conversing. They were quite far away, for I could not see them. But they were conversing to each other very clearly, as though each thought that the other could perhaps not hear very well. Oom Gysbert was saying mostly, "Prize Large Whites," and my father and uncle were saying mostly, "Measled walking rubbish."

Afterwards it seemed that Oom Gysbert's wife had gone across to the pigsties, too. For I could hear a woman's voice starting to converse as well. She conversed even more distinctly than the men. So much so, that when a native passed where I was standing by the roses, he shook his head at me. For Oom Gysbert's wife had likewise begun by saying mostly, "Prize Large Whites." But she also ended up by saying, "Measled walking rubbish." And from the way the native shook his head it appeared that she wasn't talking about the pigs that Oom Gysbert had sold to my father and my uncle.

Meanwhile, I stood there by the fence, in childhood wonderment at all that loveliness. It was getting on towards evening.

And all the air was filled with the fragrance of the roses. And there was the feeling that goes with wet earth. And a few pink and white petals floated in the brown water that rippled about my feet.

I was thrilled at this new strangeness and freshness of the world. And I thought that I would often again know the same kind of thrill.

But I never did.

Perhaps it is that as we grow older our senses do not get swayed by the perfume of flowers as much as they did when we were young. Or maybe it is that flowers just haven't got the same perfume anymore.

I realised that when I met Magda Burgers.

I should explain that my father gave up farming in that part of the Marico a few years after his conversation with Oom Gysbert. My father said that the Bushveld was suited only for pigs. Hypocritical pigs with long white beards, my father took pains to make clear. So we went to the Highveld. Afterwards we trekked back to the Marico.

For in the meantime my father had found that the Highveld was good only for snakes. Snakes in the grass, who said one thing to you when they meant another, my father pointed out.

And years later I went to settle north of the Dwarsberge. Everything had changed a great deal, however, from when I had lived there as a child. People had died or trekked away. Strangers had come in and taken their places. Landmarks had grown unrecognisable.

Then, one day, I met Magda Burgers. I had gone over to Willem Burgers's farm with the intention of staying only long enough to borrow some mealie sacks. When I saw his daughter, Magda, I forgot what I had come about. This was all the more remarkable since the colour of Magda's hair kept on reminding me over and over again of ripe mealies. I stayed until quite late, and before leaving I had promised Willem Burgers that I would vote for him at the next Dwarsberg school committee elections.

I went to call on Willem Burgers often after that. My pretext was that I wanted to know still better why I should not vote for the other school committee candidates.

326

He told me. And I thought it was a pity that my father was not still alive to hear Willem Burgers talk. It would have done my father's heart good for him to know that he had been quite right when he said of the bush country that it was fit only for pigs with white beards. Willem Burgers also brought in pigs with brown beards and black beards, as well as a sprinkling of pigs that were clean-shaven. Willem Burgers also compared several of his rival candidates with persons in the Bible. I felt glad, then, that I had not also allowed my name to go forward the time they were taking nominations for the school committee.

Magda Burgers was in her early twenties. She was gay. There was something in her prettiness that in a strange way eluded me, also. And for this reason, I suppose, I was attracted to her more than ever.

But my real trouble was that I had little opportunity of talking to Magda alone.

I felt that she was not completely indifferent to me. I could tell that in a number of ways. There was, for instance, the afternoon when she allowed me to turn the handle of the cream separator for her in the milk-shed. That was very pleasant. The only difficulty was that I had to stand sideways. For it was a small shed. And Willem Burgers took up most of the room, sitting on an upturned bucket. He was busy telling me that Gerhardus Oosthuizen was like a hyena.

Another time, Magda allowed me to dry the cups for her in the kitchen when she washed up after we had had coffee. But the kitchen was also small, and her father took up a lot of space, sitting on an upturned paraffin box. He was then engaged in explaining to me that Flip Welman was like a green tree-snake with black spots on his behind. Nevertheless, each time Magda Burgers passed me a spoon to dry, I was able to hold her hand for a few moments. Once she was so absent-minded as to pass me her hand even when there wasn't a spoon in it.

But during all these weeks I was never able to speak to Magda Burgers on her own. And always there was something in her prettiness that eluded me.

Then, one afternoon, when Magda's father was telling me that 'Rooi' Francois Hanekom was like a crocodile with laced-up

327

top-boots and a gold chain on his belly, two men came to the
door. They were strangers to me. I could not remember Willem
Burgers having mentioned them to me, either, as resembling
some of the more unsatisfactory sort of Bushveld animal. From
this I concluded that they were not candidates for the school
committee.

Magda told me that the visitors were the Van Breda brothers.

"The tall one with the cleft in his chin is Joost van Breda," she
said.

Willem Burgers walked off with the two men along a footpath
that led to the back of the house.

That was how, for the first time, I came to find myself alone
with Magda. And because she looked so beautiful to me, then,
with a light in her eyes that I thought not to have seen there
before, I told her of my visit to a farm, long ago, in the company
of my father and my uncle. I told her of how I stood by a fence
covered in roses, where there was a stream of brown water. I
spoke of the rose perfume that had enchanted me as a child, and
that I had not known since. It seems queer to me, now, that I was
able to say so much to her, all in a few minutes.

I also said a few more words to her in a voice that I could not
keep steady.

"Oom Gysbert?" Magda asked. "Why, it must be this same
farm. Years ago this farm belonged to an old Gysbert Steenkamp.
Come, I will show you."

Magda led me out of the house along a path which was different from the footpath her father and the Van Breda brothers had
taken, and which was not the way, either, to the milk-shed.

It was getting on towards sunset. In the west the sky was
gaudy with stripes like a native blanket. In the distance we could
hear the voices of Magda's father and the Van Breda brothers
raised in conversation. It was all just like long ago. Before I
realised it I found I had taken Magda's hand.

"I suppose they are talking about pigs," I said to Magda. And
I laughed, remembering that other day, which did not seem so far
off, then, when I was a child.

"Yes," Magda answered. "Joost van Breda – the one with the
cleft in his chin – bought some pigs from my father last month."

328

Even before we got there, I knew it was the same place. I could sense it all in a single moment, and without knowing how.

A few yards further on I came across that fence. It did not look at all high, anymore. But it was clustered about with pink and white roses that grew in great profusion, climbing over and covering the netting for almost as far as I could see.

Before I reached the fence, however, Magda Burgers had left me. She had slipped her small white hand out of mine and had sped off through the trees into the gathering dusk – and in the direction from which came the voices of her father and the two Van Breda brothers. The three men were conversing very clearly, by then, as though each thought the other was deaf. The Van Breda brothers were also laughing very distinctly. They laughed every time Magda's father said, "Prize Large Whites." And after they laughed they used rough language.

A little later a girl's voice started joining in the conversation. And I did not need a native to come by and shake his head at me. It was a sad enough thing for me, in any case, to have to listen to a young girl taking the part of two strangers against her father. She sided particularly with one of the two strangers. I knew, without having to be told, that the stranger was tall and had a cleft in his chin.

I stood for a long time watching the brown water flowing along the furrow. And I thought of how much water had flowed down all the rivers and under all the bridges of the world since I had last stood on that spot, as a child.

The roses clambering over the wire-netting shed no heady perfumes.

THE BROTHERS

It is true saying that man may scheme, but that God has the last word (Oom Schalk Lourens said).

And it was no different with Krisjan Lategan. He had one aim, and that was to make sure that his farm should remain the home of the Lategans from one generation to the next until the end of the world. This would be in about two hundred years, according to the way in which a church elder, who was skilled in Biblical prophecy, had worked it out. It would be on a Sunday morning.

Krisjan Lategan wanted his whole family around him, so that they could all stand up together on the Last Day. There was to be none of that rushing around to look for Lategans who had wandered off into distant parts. Especially with the Last Day being a Sunday and all. Krisjan Lategan was particular that a solemn occasion should not be spoilt by the bad language that always went with searching for stray cattle on a morning when you had to trek.

Afterwards, when they brought the telegraph up as far as Nietverdiend, and they showed the church elder how it worked, the elder said that he did not give the world a full two hundred years anymore. And when in Zeerust he heard a talking machine that could sing songs and speak words just through your turning a handle, the elder said that the end of the world was now quite near.

And he said it almost as though he was glad.

It was then that old Krisjan Lategan set about the construction of the family vault at the end of his farm. It was the kind of vault that you see on some farms in the Cape. There was a low wall round it, like for a sheep fold, and the vault was only a few feet below the level of the ground, and you walked down steps to a wooden door fastened with a chain. Inside were tamboetie-wood

330

trestles for the coffins to go on. The trestles were painted with tar, to keep away the white ants.

It was a fine vault. Farmers came from many miles away to admire it. And, as always happens in such cases, after their first feelings of awe had worn off, the visitors would make remarks which, in the parts of the Marico near the Bechuanaland border, regularly aroused guffaws.

They said, yes, it was quite a nice house, but where was the chimney? They also said that if you got up in the middle of the night and reached your hand under the bed – well, the vault wasn't a properly fixed-up kind of vault at all.

The remark Hans van Tonder made was also regarded as having a lot of class to it. Referring to the tar on the trestles, he said he couldn't understand why old Krisjan Lategan should be so fussy about keeping the white ants out. "When you lie in your coffin, it's not by *ants* that you get eaten up," Hans van Tonder said.

Krisjan Lategan's neighbours had a lot of things of this nature to say about his vault when it was newly constructed. All the same, not one of them would have been anxious to go to the vault alone at night after Krisjan Lategan had been laid to rest in it.

And yet all Krisjan Lategan's plans came to nothing. Shortly after his death certain unusual events occurred on his farm, as a result of which one of his two sons came to an untimely end, and his corpse was placed in the vault in a coffin that was much too long. And the other son fled so far out of the Marico that it would certainly not be possible to find him again before the Last Day. And even then, on the Day of Judgement, he would not be likely to push himself to the front to any extent.

Everybody in the Bushveld knew of the bitterness that there was between old Krisjan Lategan's two sons, Doors and Lodewyk, who were in all things so unlike each other. At their father's death the two brothers were in their twenties. Neither was married. Doors was a few years older than Lodewyk. For a long time the only bond between them seemed to have been their mutual enmity.

Lodewyk, the younger one, was tall and good-looking, and his nature was adventurous. The elder brother, Doors, was a hunchback. He had short legs and unnaturally broad shoulders. He was credited with great strength. Because of his grotesque shape, the natives told stories about him that had to do with witchcraft, and that could not be true.

At his father's funeral Doors, with his short stature and the shapeless hump on his back, looked particularly ungainly among the other pall-bearers, all straight and upstanding men. During the simple service before the open doors of the vault a child burst out crying. It was something of a scandal that the child wept out of terror of Doors Lategan's hunched figure, and not out of sorrow for the departed.

Soon afterwards Lodewyk Lategan left the farm for the diamond diggings at Doornpan. Before that the brothers had quarrelled violently in the mealie-lands. The natives said that the quarrel had been about what cattle Lodewyk could take with him to the diggings. When Lodewyk went it was with the new wagon and the best span of oxen. And Doors said that if he ever returned to the farm he would kill him.

"I will yet make you remember those words," Lodewyk answered.

In this spirit Doors and Lodewyk parted. Tant Alie, old Krisjan Lategan's widow, remained on at the farm with her elder son, Doors. She was an ageing woman with no force of character. Tant Alie had always been considered a bit soft in the head. She came of a Cape family of which quite a few members were known to be 'simpel', although nobody, of course, thought any the less of them on that account. They belonged to a sheep district, Tant Alie's family, and we of the Marico, who were cattle farmers, said that for a sheep farmer it was even a help if his brain was not too sound.

But whatever Tant Alie might have thought and felt about the estrangement that was between her sons, she did not ever discuss the matter. Moreover it is certain that they would have taken no notice of any efforts on her part at reconciling them.

Lodewyk left for the diamond fields in the company of Flippie Geel, who had a piece of Government land at Koedoesrand that he was supposed to improve. Flippie Geel was a good deal older than Lodewyk Lategan. For that reason it seems all the more surprising that he should have helped Lodewyk in his subsequent foolish actions. Perhaps it was because Flippie Geel found that easier than work.

From what came out afterwards, it would appear that Lode-wyk Lategan and Flippie Geel did not dig much on their claim. But they put in a lot of time drinking brandy, which they bought with the money Lodewyk got from selling his trek-oxen, a pair at a time.

And when he was in his cups, Lodewyk would devise elaborate schemes, each more absurd than the last, for getting even with his brother Doors, who, he said, had defrauded him of his share of the inheritance.

After he had rejected a number of ideas, one after the other, as impracticable, Lodewyk got hold of a plan that he decided to carry out. From this you can get some sort of conception as to how crack-brained those plans must have been that he didn't act on. Anyway, he got Flippie Geel to write to Doors to tell him that his brother Lodewyk had been killed in an accident on the diggings, and that his body was being sent home in a coffin by transport wagon. And a few days later a coffin, which Lodewyk had had made to his size, was on its way to the Lategan farm. Inside the coffin, instead of a corpse, was a mealie-sack that Lodewyk and Flippie Geel had filled with gravel. I suppose that was the only time, too, that they had a spade in their hands during their stay on the diggings.

Now, I have often tried to puzzle out – and so have many other people: for although it all happened long ago this story is still well known hereabouts – what idea Lodewyk Lategan had with that coffin. For one thing, he was drunk very often during that period. And he no doubt also inherited a good deal of his mother's weakness of mind. But he must surely have expected Doors to unscrew the lid of the coffin, if for no other reason than just to make certain that Lodewyk really was dead.

He could surely not have foreseen Doors acting the way he did when the coffin was delivered on the front stoep of the Lategan homestead. Without getting up from the riempies chair on which he was sitting – well forward because of his hump – Doors shouted for the farm natives to come and fetch away the coffin.

"The key of the vault is hanging on the wall of the voorkamer,"

Doors said. "Unlock the vault and put this box on one of the trestles. Close the doors but don't put the lock on the chain again."

Doors silenced his mother roughly when she tried to speak. Tant Alie had wanted to be allowed to gaze for the last time on the face of her dead son.

The transport driver, who had helped to carry the coffin on to the stoep and had stood bare-headed beside it in reverence for the dead, walked back to his team a very amazed man.

There were some, however, who say that Doors Lategan had second sight. Or if it wasn't second sight it was a depth of cunning that was even better than second sight. And that he had guessed that his brother Lodewyk's body was not in the coffin.

The farmers of the neighbourhood had naturally no suspicions of this nature, however. Many of them sent wreaths.

A few weeks later it was known that Lodewyk's ghost was haunting the Lategan farm. Several natives testified to having seen the ghost of Baas Lodewyk on a couple of moonlight nights. They had seen Baas Lodewyk's ghost by the vault, they said. Baas Lodewyk's ghost was sitting on the low wall and there was what looked like a black bottle in his hand. One man also said that he thought Baas Lodewyk's ghost was singing. But he couldn't be certain on that point. He didn't want to make sure, the native said.

But what were even better authenticated were the times when Lodewyk's ghost was seen driving along the high road in the back of Flippie Geel's mule-cart that had a half-hood over the back seat. Even white people had seen Lodewyk's ghost riding in the back seat of Flippie Geel's mule-cart. It was known that Flippie Geel had recently returned to the Marico to improve his Government land some more. He had already sold the mealie-planter that he had got on loan from the Government. He was now trying to sell the disc-plough with green handles.

Because in life Lodewyk Lategan had been Flippie Geel's bosom friend, it was not surprising, people said, that Lodewyk's ghost should have been seen in the back of Flippie Geel's mule-cart. But they were glad for Flippie's sake that Flippie hadn't turned round. Lodewyk's ghost looked too awful, the people said who saw it. It was almost as though it was trying to hide itself away against the half-hood of the cart.

It was when an inquisitive farmer crept up on the window of Flippie Geel's rondavel, one evening, and saw Lodewyk's ghost sitting with its feet on the table, eating biltong, that the truth came out. Next day everybody in the Marico knew that Lodewyk Lategan was not dead.

Shortly afterwards came the night when Doors's natives reported to him that they had seen Baas Lodewyk climbing through the barbed wire with a gun in his hands. Doors took down his Mauser from the wall and strode out into the veld.

Except for the few shots during the night, everything on the farm the next day seemed as it had been before. The only difference was that in the Lategan family vault a sack of gravel in a coffin had been replaced by a body, and the lid of the coffin had been screwed on again. During the night one brother had been murdered. And the other had fled. He was never caught.

Several days passed before the veldkornet came to the Lategan farm. And then Tant Alie would not give him permission to open the coffin.

"One of my sons is in the vault and the other is a fugitive over the face of the earth," Tant Alie said. "I don't want to know which is which."

Nevertheless, the veldkornet had his way. He came back with an official paper and unscrewed the lid. In the coffin that was much too long for him – although it was cramped for breadth – lay Doors, the hunchback brother, with a bullet in his heart.

But even before the veldkornet opened the coffin it was known in the Marico that it was Doors that had been murdered. For when Lodewyk Lategan fled from the Marico he drove off in Flippie Geel's mule-cart. Several people had seen Lodewyk driving along the highway in the night. And those people said that for Lodewyk's own sake they were glad that Lodewyk did not look round.

It was as well for Lodewyk Lategan, they said, that he should drive off and not know that there was a passenger in the back seat. The passenger had broad shoulders and the starlight shone through his ungainly hump.

335

OOM PIET'S PARTY

All the young people of the Dwarsberge were at Piet van Zyl's party, that night. Also some people that weren't perhaps so very young. And they had come, some of them, from even further than the Dwarsberge. They explained, a couple of what you can call the more elderly guests, that it was not the thought of Piet van Zyl's moepel brandy that had brought them all that way. For that matter, as Willem Pretorius said, he for his part had not been invited, even. And then Bart Lemmer said that for his part, he had not been invited either, but he had come along there, to Piet van Zyl's farmhouse, in the evening, because Piet van Zyl's farmhouse stood so high up, against Tsalala's Kop, and it would be good for his asthma, to be so high up, for a change. Then Willem Pretorius said that it was something in some part of his spine that was being done good. But he didn't say what with.

Piet van Zyl had taken a lot of trouble over that party. He had cleared all the furniture out of the voorhuis except two chairs for the Bester brothers to sit on with their concertina and guitar, and a tall tamboetie kist that a guest who wasn't dancing could stand and rest his elbows on. In the kitchen there were bottles and jars on a long table.

Wynand Smit was explaining what the exact kind of illness was that had brought him along to the dance, when Willem Pretorius interrupted him.

"Look, kêrels," Willem Pretorius said. "This is, after all, a dance. Let us not be so unsociable as to remain standing here talking on the stoep on our own about our sicknesses."

Bart Lemmer and Wynand Smit agreed with him. He had also been thinking of going into the kitchen, Bart Lemmer said.

On the way to the kitchen they had to pass through the voorkamer where there were young men in shirt-sleeves and young girls in pretty coloured dresses dancing in lively fashion.

"I think I will come back a little later here, and dance," Willem Pretorius said, on the way to the kitchen.

Bart Lemmer said he thought he would, too, when it was a bit cooler, and he didn't need to take his jacket off. It would appear that he had dressed somewhat hurriedly for the dance and had neglected to change the shirt in which he had climbed through a barbed-wire fence a week before, a few yards ahead of a bull.

These smart young men of today, with their striped shirts and their ties with big yellow flowers on, were much too fussy, Wynand Smit acknowledged.

They reached the kitchen just at the moment when the outside door was being opened and Lettie van Zyl, the wife of the host, came in, followed by two Mtosas, who carried between them a dish that was almost the size of a small bath. From the remarks the one Mtosa was making about the way the other Mtosa was not looking where he was going, one gathered that the dish was hot.

"I always say that's the best way to cook, Nig Lettie," Willem Pretorius said to Piet van Zyl's wife in a friendly fashion. "You can't beat the old bakoond of sun-dried brick. That's what I say. And I can see, from what's inside the dish, that you have still got ribbokke under those rante."

By that time both Mtosas were making remarks. They wanted to get the dish on to the kitchen table, and Bart Lemmer was standing in the way. Wynand Smit saw what the difficulty was and stepped forward to help the Mtosas. The dish nearly fell on the floor, then, from the sudden way Wynand Smit jumped when he let go.

"If I had known it was so hot I would have got a rag," he said in sombre tones, looking at his hands.

"All the same, I am surprised," Lettie van Zyl said to Willem Pretorius.

"Ag, think nothing of it, Niggie," Willem Pretorius replied. "We are all Bushveld farmers. And for some special time, like this dance, ah, well, even if ribbok *is* royal game, nobody will think anything –"

"That wasn't what I was talking about," Lettie said quickly, coming to the point. "I am surprised to see you here at the dance.

Not that you aren't very welcome, of course, Neef Willem. Don't think that. You and Neef Bart and Neef Wynand – Piet and I are naturally glad to have you. But I mean, after what happened last time –"

"Oh, that?" Willem Pretorius asked, affecting surprise. "But how was I to know that that man with the black beard was an ouderling? He wasn't wearing a manel. All I saw was a man wearing a black beard. And even if he wore a manel, I don't think it was the right sort of a place for an ouderling to be. With dancing – and – and singing – and – and *drinking* –"

"But the ouderling did not dance," Lettie van Zyl replied. "And all he drank was coffee."

Willem Pretorius looked sceptical.

"Well, all can say," he said, "is that if he wasn't drunk, how did he come to fall into the dam?"

Lettie van Zyl started going out of the kitchen to find out whether her guests would like to eat now or a little later. When she got to the door she turned round and faced Willem Pretorius with a look conveying a sort of finality.

"It wasn't the ouderling that fell into the dam, Neef Willem," she said. "It was you that fell in."

Willem Pretorius kept on insisting, but not very loudly, that a Bushveld party was *still* no place for an ouderling to come dancing and singing and – and *swearing* in.

"Royal game," Piet van Zyl, the host, said. Piet van Zyl was leaning against the tall tamboetie kist in the corner, talking to a small group standing around him with plates. "Royal game is about all we got left to shoot for the bakoond, these days. That's all since the time the game got protected by law. I am not allowed to shoot a ribbok here on my own farm, anymore, because of the law. So that's about all we've got to eat here, today, in the way of wildevleis. And not too much of that, either. And yet I can remember the time when game swarmed around Tsalala's Kop almost like in the Kruger Park. That was before a lot of Volksraad members who just sit and talk and call each other names got hold of the idea that they had to protect the game in the Bushveld by law. Protect them against what? That's what I want to know."

Several members of the little group said he was quite right. Yes, they said, also against what?

"And what's the result today?" Piet van Zyl demanded. "Why, today, about all the game that's left are a few ribbokke in the rante. And all that's just *since* these game laws. They say they've got the game laws for protecting the animals in the Kruger Park, also. Well, if that's so, I won't give much for the chances of the Kruger Park, that's all."

Piet van Zyl's logic made a strong appeal to most of the members of his small audience. Young Dawie Gouws started telling a story that his grandfather told him out of his own mouth about the time Dawie Gouws's grandfather shot a whole herd of elephants that had got knee-deep into the swampy ground by the Molopo.

"And where are those herds of elephants today?" Dawie Gouws asked. "It's all these politicians with their game laws. Why, there is hardly a single elephant left by the Molopo, today."

Piet van Zyl said that, everything considered, it wasn't surprising.

"I got this ribbok at about four hundred yards," Piet van Zyl went on, "just as he was disappearing into a clump of kameeldorings. About a mile from there, on my way home, when I put the ribbok down to rest again, I got an aardvark just as he was disappearing into his hole. I got him at about two hundred yards."

Meneer Strydom, the new schoolmaster, asked Piet van Zyl what he wanted to do that sort of thing for. We called him Meneer Strydom because he called everyone else Meneer, instead of Neef or Oom or Swaer. The schoolmaster was from the city.

"I have read all about the aardvark in a book on natural history," Meneer Strydom went on. "Did you know that the aardvark is the friend of man? I can't understand this senseless lust for destruction – just so that you can say afterwards that you got an animal at so many hundred yards. I mean, nobody has got a greater admiration for a big game hunter than I have – at a suitable distance, and with the wind blowing in the wrong direction, so that he can't smell me. And I would like to be among trees, the trunks of which at a distance you would confuse my flannel trousers with."

Piet van Zyl said he had thought of that before today. The schoolmaster must not think he had not thought of that before today. But if it was an early winter morning and there was a slight breeze blowing, and there was mist on the rante, then he wouldn't mind if he shot a rhinoceros, on such a morning. And if he couldn't get a rhinoceros, then a baboon would do, perhaps. He didn't say that he would feel like that later in the day, now. He had hardly ever gone out hunting later in the day – just mornings and evenings. It wasn't as though he hadn't thought of such things, but that was how it was. It must be some sort of instinct.

"Well, I am glad I haven't got that sort of instinct," Meneer Strydom said. And when Lettie van Zyl came to offer him another thick slice of roast ribbok he declined quite pointedly. He might have a little afterwards, though, he said, with bread and butter.

It was queer how, for a spell, Piet van Zyl's talk of hunting got everybody interested in the subject to the exclusion of the dancing and even of the mampoer. A young man would forget the girl dancing in his arms to the vastrap tune of "Die Wilde Weduwee van Windhoek" and would start demonstrating to another young man how he shot that tree-full of sleeping tarentale.

At one stage the elder Bester brother put down his concertina and started kneeling on the floor, bending forward. It looked as though a piece of his concertina had got lost and he was looking for it on the floor.

But it was only when the younger Bester brother also stopped playing for a bit, and the elder Bester took up the guitar that his younger brother had put down and, still kneeling, pointed with it, that you knew what he was saying.

You didn't have to hear the words.

Meneer Strydom slipped through into the kitchen. In the kitchen Willem Pretorius was kneeling half under the table. Having already heard the elder Bester brother, Meneer Strydom knew what was coming.

"And there was the lion crouching," Willem Pretorius was saying, "ready to –"

While helping himself to a drink, Meneer Strydom took the

340

opportunity of explaining to Bart Lemmer that the despised earthworm was in reality the friend of man. Because Meneer Strydom was a school-teacher, Bart Lemmer took it in good part.

"What I say," Bart Lemmer said to Wynand Smit, however, after Meneer Strydom had gone back into the voorkamer, "is that that schoolmaster must have pretty queer friends. Next thing he'll be saying that the boomslang and the Klipkop Mshangaan are also the friend of man."

"On with the dance," the younger Bester brother called out, taking his guitar away from his elder brother, who was getting ready to reload, to the impairment of the G-string. Soon afterwards the interlude of the huntsman was forgotten. Dust from the swift feet of the dancers rose up once more to the ceiling. Outside there shone the moon that in the past had seen great herds making their way to the water. Old vanished herds.

There was a shot. The music and the dancing ceased. Two more shots in quick succession.

"Poachers from the city," Piet van Zyl declared, his face pale with fury in the candlelight. "Coming here with motor cars. And we can't do anything about it. By the time we get there they will be gone. Bloodthirsty savages from the city coming here to exterminate our wildlife."

We agreed with Piet van Zyl that it was no good going after those poachers. They were sure to be gone. There was also the possibility – although we did not say that to each other openly – that those savages with their senseless bloodlust, and so quick on the trigger in the dark, and all, just might not *be* gone.

Only Willem Pretorius went out to see. Bart Lemmer and Wynand Smit followed him, staggering slightly. A little later we heard evil sounds. But it was not an encounter with poachers. When Bart and Wynand came back they said it was enough they had done in pulling Willem Pretorius out. His hat they would go and look for in the dam in the morning.

FUNERAL EARTH

We had a difficult task, that time (Oom Schalk Lourens said), teaching Sijefu's tribe of Mtosas to become civilised. But they did not show any appreciation. Even after we had set fire to their huts in a long row round the slopes of Abjaterskop, so that you could see the smoke almost as far as Nietverdiend, the Mtosas remained just about as unenlightened as ever. They would retreat into the mountains, where it was almost impossible for our commando to follow them on horseback. They remained hidden in the thick bush.

"I can sense these kaffirs all around us," Veldkornet Andries Joubert said to our seksie of about a dozen burghers when we had come to a halt in a clearing amid the tall withaaks. "I have been in so many kaffir wars that I can almost *smell* when there are kaffirs lying in wait for us with assegais. And yet all day long you never see a single Mtosa that you can put a lead bullet through."

He also said that if this war went on much longer we would forget altogether how to handle a gun. And what would we do then, when we again had to fight England?

Young Fanie Louw, who liked saying funny things, threw back his head and pretended to be sniffing the air with discrimination. "I can smell a whole row of assegais with broad blades and short handles," Fanie Louw said. "The stabbing assegai has got more of a selon's rose sort of smell about it than a throwing spear. The selon's rose that you come across in graveyards."

The veldkornet did not think Fanie Louw's remark very funny, however. And he said we all knew that this was the first time Fanie Louw had ever been on commando. He also said that if a crowd of Mtosas were to leap out of the bush on to us suddenly, then you wouldn't be able to smell Fanie Louw for dust. The veldkornet also said another thing that was even better.

342

Our group of burghers laughed heartily. Maybe Veldkornet Joubert could not think out a lot of nonsense to say just on the spur of the moment, in the way that Fanie Louw could, but give our veldkornet a chance to reflect, first, and he would come out with the kind of remark that you just had to admire.

Indeed, from the very next thing Veldkornet Joubert said, you could see how deep was his insight. And he did not have to think much, either, then.

"Let us get out of here as quick as hell, men," he said, speaking very distinctly. "Perhaps the kaffirs are hiding out in the open turf-lands, where there are no trees. And none of this long tamboekie grass, either."

When we emerged from that stretch of bush we were glad to discover that our veldkornet had been right, like always.

For another group of Transvaal burghers had hit on the same strategy.

"We were in the middle of the bush," their leader, Combrinck, said to us, after we had exchanged greetings. "A very thick part of the bush, with withaaks standing up like skeletons. And we suddenly thought the Mtosas might have gone into hiding out here in the open."

You could see that Veldkornet Joubert was pleased to think that he had, on his own, worked out the same tactics as Combrinck, who was known as a skilful kaffir-fighter. All the same, it seemed as though this was going to be a long war.

It was then that, again speaking out of his turn, Fanie Louw said that all we needed now was for the kommandant himself to arrive there in the middle of the turf-lands with the main body of burghers. "Maybe we should even go back to Pretoria to see if the Mtosas aren't perhaps hiding in the Volksraad," he said. "Passing laws and things. You know how cheeky a Mtosa is."

"It can't be worse than some of the laws that the Volksraad is already passing now," Combrinck said, gruffly. From that we could see that why he had not himself been appointed kommandant was because he had voted against the President in the last elections.

By that time the sun was sitting not more than about two Cape feet above a tall koppie on the horizon. Accordingly, we started looking about for a place to camp. It was muddy in the turf-lands,

343

and there was no firewood there, but we all said that we did not mind. We would not pamper ourselves by going to sleep in the thick bush, we told one another. It was war-time, and we were on commando, and the mud of the turf-lands was good enough for *us*, we said.

It was then that an unusual thing happened.

For we suddenly did see Mtosas. We saw them from a long way off. They came out of the bush and marched right out into the open. They made no attempt to hide. We saw in amazement that they were coming straight in our direction, advancing in single file. And we observed, even from that distance, that they were unarmed. Instead of assegais and shields they carried burdens on their heads. And almost in that same moment we realised, from the heavy look of those burdens, that the carriers must be women.

For that reason we took our guns in our hands and stood waiting. Since it was women, we were naturally prepared for the lowest form of treachery.

As the column drew nearer we saw that at the head of it was Ndambe, an old native whom we knew well. For years he had been Sijefu's chief counsellor. Ndambe held up his hand. The line of women halted. Ndambe spoke. He declared that we white men were kings among kings and elephants among elephants. He also said that we were rinkhals snakes more poisonous and generally disgusting than any rinkhals snake in the country.

We knew, of course, that Ndambe was only paying us compliments in his ignorant Mtosa fashion. And so we naturally felt highly gratified. I can still remember the way Jurie Bekker nudged me in the ribs and said, "Did you hear that?"

When Ndambe went on, however, to say that we were filthier than the spittle of a green tree-toad, several burghers grew restive. They felt that there was perhaps such a thing as carrying these tribal courtesies a bit too far.

It was then that Veldkornet Joubert, slipping his finger inside the trigger guard of his gun, requested Ndambe to come to the point. By the expression on our veldkornet's face, you could see that he had had enough of compliments for one day.

They had come to offer peace, Ndambe told us then.

What the women carried on their heads were presents.

344

At a sign from Ndambe the column knelt in the mud of the turf-land. They brought lion and zebra skins and elephant tusks, and beads and brass bangles and, on a long grass mat, the whole haunch of a red Afrikaner ox, hide and hoof and all. And several pigs cut in half. And clay pots filled to the brim with white beer, and also – and this we prized most – witch-doctor medicines that protected you against goël spirits at night and the evil eye.

Ndambe gave another signal. A woman with a clay pot on her head rose up from the kneeling column and advanced towards us. We saw then that what she had in the pot was black earth. It was wet and almost like turf-soil. We couldn't understand what they wanted to bring us that for. As though we didn't have enough of it, right there where we were standing, and sticking to our veldskoens, and all. And yet Ndambe acted as though that was the most precious part of the peace offerings that his chief, Sijefu, had sent us.

It was when Ndambe spoke again that we saw how ignorant he and his chief and the whole Mtosa tribe were, really.

He took a handful of soil out of the pot and pressed it together between his fingers. Then he told us how honoured the Mtosa tribe was because we were waging war against them. In the past they had only had flat-faced Mshangaans with spiked knobkerries to fight against, he said, but now it was different. Our veldkornet took half a step forward, then, in case Ndambe was going to start flattering us again. So Ndambe said, simply, that the Mtosas would be glad if we came and made war against them later on, when the harvests had been gathered in. But in the meantime the tribe did not wish to continue fighting.

It was the time for sowing.

Ndambe let the soil run through his fingers, to show us how good it was. He also invited us to taste it. We declined.

We accepted the presents and peace was made. And I can still remember how Veldkornet Joubert shook his head and said, "Can you beat the Mtosas for ignorance?"

And I can still remember what Jurie Bekker said, also. That was when something made him examine the haunch of beef more closely, and he found his own brand mark on it.

It was not long afterwards that the war came against England.

345

By the end of the second year of the war the Boer forces were in a very bad way. But we would not make peace. Veldkornet Joubert was now promoted to kommandant. Combrinck fell in the battle before Dalmanutha. Jurie Bekker was still with us. And so was Fanie Louw. And it was strange how attached we had grown to Fanie Louw during the years of hardship that we went through together in the field. But up to the end we had to admit that, while we had got used to his jokes, and we knew there was no harm in them, we would have preferred it that he should stop making them.

He did stop, and for ever, in a skirmish near a blockhouse. We buried him in the shade of a thorn-tree. We got ready to fill in his grave, after which the kommandant would say a few words and we would bare our heads and sing a psalm. As you know, it was customary at a funeral for each mourner to take up a handful of earth and fling it in the grave.

When Kommandant Joubert stooped down and picked up his handful of earth, a strange thing happened. And I remembered that other war, against the Mtosas. And we knew – although we would not say it – what was now that longing in the hearts of each of us. For Kommandant Joubert did not straightway drop the soil into Fanie Louw's grave. Instead, he kneaded the damp ground between his fingers. It was as though he had forgotten that it was funeral earth. He seemed to be thinking not of death, then, but of life.

We patterned after him, picking up handfuls of soil and pressing it together. We felt the deep loam in it, and saw how springy it was, and we let it trickle through our fingers. And we could remember only that it was the time for sowing.

I understood then how, in an earlier war, the Mtosas had felt, they who were also farmers.

THE MISSIONARY

That kaffir carving on the wall of my voorkamer (Oom Schalk Lourens said), it's been there for many years. It was found in the loft of the pastorie at Ramoutsa after the death of the Dutch Reformed missionary there, Reverend Keet.

To look at, it's just one of those figures that a kaffir wood-carver cuts out of soft wood, like mdubu or mesetla. But because I knew him quite well, I can still see a rough sort of resemblance to Reverend Keet in that carving, even though it is now discoloured with age and the white ants have eaten away parts of it. I first saw this figure in the study of the pastorie at Ramoutsa when I went to call on Reverend Keet. And when, after his death, the carving was found in the loft of the pastorie, I brought it here. I kept it in memory of a man who had strange ideas about what he was pleased to call Darkest Africa.

Reverend Keet had not been at Ramoutsa very long. Before that he had worked at a mission station in the Cape. But, as he told us, ever since he had paid a visit to the Marico District, some years before, he had wanted to come to the Western Transvaal. He said he had obtained, in the Bushveld along the Molopo River, a feeling that here was the real Africa. He said there was a spirit of evil in these parts that he believed it was his mission to overcome.

We who had lived in the Marico for the greater part of our lives wondered what we had done to him.

On his previous visit here Reverend Keet had stayed long enough to meet Elsiba Grobler, the daughter of Thys Grobler of Drogedal. Afterwards he had sent for Elsiba to come down to the Cape to be his bride.

And so we thought that the missionary had remembered with affection the scenes that were the setting for his courtship. And that was why he came back here. So you can imagine how disappointed we were in learning the truth.

Nevertheless, I found it interesting to listen to him, just because he had such outlandish views. And so I called on him quite regularly when I passed the mission station on my way back from the Indian store at Ramoutsa.

Reverend Keet and I used to sit in his study, where the curtains were half drawn, as they were in the whole pastorie. I supposed it was to keep out the bright sunshine that Darkest Africa is so full of.

"Only yesterday a kaffir child hurt his leg falling out of a withaak tree," Reverend Keet said to me on one occasion. "And the parents didn't bring the child here so that Elsiba or I could bandage him up. Instead, they said there was a devil in the withaak. And so they got the witch-doctor to fasten a piece of crocodile skin to the child's leg, to drive away the devil."

So I said that that just showed you how ignorant a kaffir was. They should have fastened the crocodile skin to the withaak, instead, like the old people used to do. That would drive the devil away quick enough, I said.

Reverend Keet did not answer. He just shook his head and looked at me in a pitying sort of way, so that I felt sorry I had spoken.

To change the subject I pointed to a kaffir wood-carving standing on a table in the corner of the study. That same wood-carving you see today hanging on the wall of my voorkamer.

"Here's now something that we want to encourage," Reverend Keet said in answer to my question. "Through art we can perhaps bring enlightenment to these parts. The kaffirs here seem to have a natural talent for wood-carving. I have asked Willem Terreblanche to write to the Education Department for a text-book on the subject. It will be another craft that we can teach to the children at the school."

Willem Terreblanche was the assistant teacher at the mission station.

"Anyway, it will be more useful than that last text-book we got on how to make paper serviettes with tassels," Reverend Keet went on, half to himself. Then it was as though an idea struck him. "Oh, by the way," he asked, "would you perhaps like, say, a few dozen paper serviettes with tassels to take home with you?"

I declined his offer in some haste.

Reverend Keet started talking about that carving again.

"You wouldn't think it was meant for me, now, would you?" he asked.

And because I am always polite, that way, I said no, certainly not.

"I mean, just look at the top of my body," he said. "It's like a sack of potatoes. Does the top part of my body look like a sack of potatoes?"

And once again I said no, oh no.

Reverend Keet laughed, then – rather loudly I thought – at the idea of the wood-carver's ignorance. I laughed quite loudly, also, to make it clear that I, too, thought that the kaffir wood-carver was very ignorant.

"All the same, for a raw kaffir who has had no training," the missionary continued, "it's not bad. But take that self-satisfied sort of smile, now, that he put on my face. It only came out that way because the kaffir who made the carving lacks the skill to carve my features as they really are. He hasn't got technique."

I thought, well, maybe that ignorant Bechuana didn't know any more what technique was than I did. But I did think he had a pretty shrewd idea how to carve a wooden figure of Reverend Keet.

"If a kaffir had the impudence to make a likeness like that of me, with such big ears and all," I said to Reverend Keet, "I would kick him in the ribs. I would kick him for being so ignorant, I mean."

It was then that Elsiba brought us in our coffee. Although she was now the missionary's wife, I still thought of her as Elsiba, a Bushveld girl whom I had seen grow up.

"You've still got that thing there," Elsiba said to her husband, after she had greeted me. "I won't have you making a fool of yourself. Every visitor to the pastorie who sees this carving goes away laughing at you."

349

"They laugh at the kaffir who made it, Elsiba, because of his poor technique," Reverend Keet said, drawing himself up in his chair.

"Anyway, I'm taking it out of here," Elsiba answered.

I have since then often thought of that scene. Of the way Elsiba Keet walked from the room, with the carving standing upright on the tray that she had carried the coffee-cups on. Because of its big feet that wooden figure did not fall over when Elsiba flounced out with the tray. And in its stiff, wooden bearing the figure seemed to be expressing the same disdain of the kaffir wood-carver's technique as what Reverend Keet had.

I remained in the study a long time. And all the while the missionary talked of the spirit of evil that hung over the Marico like a heavy blanket. It was something brooding and oppressive, he said, and it did something to the souls of men. He asked me whether I hadn't noticed it myself.

So I told him that I had. I said that he had taken the very words out of my mouth. And I proceeded to tell him about the time Jurie Bekker had impounded some of my cattle that he claimed had strayed into his mealie-lands.

350

"You should have seen Jurie Bekker the morning that he drove off my cattle along the Government Road," I said. "An evil blanket hung over him, all right. You could almost see it. A striped kaffir blanket."

I also told the missionary about the sinful way in which Niklaas Prinsloo had filled in those compensation forms for losses which he had never suffered, even. And about the time Gert Haasbroek sold me what he said was a pedigree Afrikaner bull, and that was just an animal he had smuggled through from the Protectorate one night, with a whole herd of other beasts, and that died afterwards of grass-belly.

I said that the whole of the Marico District was just bristling with evil, and I could give him many more examples, if he would care to listen.

But Reverend Keet said that was not what he meant. He said he was talking of the unnatural influences that hovered over this part of the country. He had felt those things particularly at the swamps by the Molopo, he said, with the green bubbles coming up out of the mud and with those trees that were like shapes oppressing your mind when it is fevered. But it was like that everywhere in the Bushveld, he said. With the sun pouring down at midday, for instance, and the whole veld very still, it was yet as though there was a high black wind, somewhere, an old lost wind. And he felt a chill in all his bones, he said, and it was something unearthly.

It was interesting for me to hear the Reverend Keet talk like that. I had heard the same sort of thing before from strangers. I wondered what he could take for it.

"Even here in this study, where I am sitting talking to you," he added, "I can sense a baleful influence. It is some form of – of something skulking, somehow."

I knew, of course, that Reverend Keet was not making any underhanded allusion to my being there in his study. He was too religious to do a thing like that. Nevertheless, I felt uncomfortable. Shortly afterwards I left.

On my way back in the mule-cart I passed the mission school. And I thought then that it was funny that Elsiba was so concerned that a kaffir should not make a fool of her husband with a wood-

carving of him. Because she did not seem to mind making a fool
of him in another way. From the mule-cart I saw Elsiba and Willem Terreblanche in the doorway of the schoolroom. And from the
way they were holding hands I could see that they were not discussing paper serviettes with tassels, or any similar school subjects.

Still, as it turned out, it never came to any scandal in the district. For Willem Terreblanche left some time later to take up a
teaching post in the Free State. And after Reverend Keet's death
Elsiba allowed a respectable interval to elapse before she went to
the Free State to marry Willem Terreblanche.

Some distance beyond the mission school I came across the
Ramoutsa witch-doctor that Reverend Keet had spoken about.
The witch-doctor was busy digging up roots on the veld for medicine. I reined in the mules and the witch-doctor came up to me.
He had on a pair of brown leggings and a woman's corset. And
he carried an umbrella. Around his neck he wore a few feet of
light-green tree-snake that didn't look as though it had been dead
very long. I could see that the witch-doctor was particular about
how he dressed when he went out.

I spoke to him in Sechuana about Reverend Keet. I told him that Reverend Keet said the Marico was a bad place. I also told him that the missionary did not believe in the cure of fastening a piece of crocodile skin to the leg of a child who had fallen out of a withaak tree. And I said that he did not seem to think, either, that if you fastened crocodile skin to the withaak it would drive the devil out of it.

The witch-doctor stood thinking for some while. And when he spoke again it seemed to me that in his answer there was a measure of wisdom.

"The best thing," he said, "would be to fasten a piece of crocodile skin on to the baas missionary."

It seemed quite possible that the devils were not all just in the Marico Bushveld. There might be one or two inside Reverend Keet himself, also.

Nevertheless, I have often since then thought of how almost inspired Reverend Keet was when he said that there was evil going on around him, right here in the Marico. In his very home – he could have said. With the curtains half drawn and all. Only, of course, he didn't mean it that way.

Yet I have also wondered if, in the way he did mean it – when he spoke of those darker things that he claimed were at work in Africa – I wonder if there, too, Reverend Keet was as wide of the mark as one might lightly suppose.

That thought first occurred to me after Reverend Keet's death and Elsiba's departure. In fact, it was when the new missionary took over the pastorie at Ramoutsa and this wood-carving was found in the loft.

But before I hung up the carving where you see it now, I first took the trouble to pluck off the lock of Reverend Keet's hair that had been glued to it. And I also plucked out the nails that had been driven – by Elsiba's hands, I could not but think – into the head and heart.

THE TRAITOR'S WIFE

We did not like the sound of the wind that morning, as we cantered over a veld trail that we had made much use of, during the past year, when there were English forces in the neighbourhood.

The wind blew short wisps of yellow grass in quick flurries over the veld and the smoke from the fire in front of a row of kaffir huts hung low in the air. From that we knew that the third winter of the Boer War was at hand. Our small group of burghers dismounted at the edge of a clump of camel-thorns to rest our horses.

"It's going to be an early winter," Jan Vermeulen said, and from force of habit he put his hand up to his throat in order to close his jacket collar over in front. We all laughed, then. We realised that Jan Vermeulen had forgotten how he had come to leave his jacket behind when the English had surprised us at the spruit a few days before. And instead of a jacket, he was now wearing a mealie sack with holes cut in it for his head and arms. You could not just close over in front of your throat, airily, the lapels cut in a grain bag.

"Anyway, Jan, you're all right for clothes," Kobus Ferreira said, "but look at me."

Kobus Ferreira was wearing a missionary's frock-coat that he had found outside Kronendal, where it had been hung on a clothes-line to air.

"This frock-coat is cut so tight across my middle and shoulders that I have to sit very stiff and awkward in my saddle, just like the missionary sits on a chair when he is visiting at a farmhouse," Kobus Ferreira added. "Several times my horse has taken me for an Englishman, in consequence of the way I sit. I am only afraid that when a bugle blows my horse will carry me over the rant into the English camp."

At Kobus Ferreira's remark the early winter wind seemed to take on a keener edge.

For our thoughts went immediately to Leendert Roux, who had been with us on commando a long while and who had been spoken of as a likely man to be veldkornet – and who had gone scouting, one night, and did not come back with a report.

There were, of course, other Boers who had also joined the English. But there was not one of them that we had respected as much as we had done Leendert Roux.

Shortly afterwards we were on the move again.

In the late afternoon we emerged through the Crocodile Poort that brought us in sight of Leendert Roux's farmhouse. Next to the dam was a patch of mealies that Leendert Roux's wife had got the kaffirs to cultivate.

"Anyway, we'll camp on Leendert Roux's farm and eat roast mealies tonight," our veldkornet, Apie Theron, observed.

"Let us first rather burn his house down," Kobus Ferreira said. And in a strange way it seemed as though his violent language was not out of place in a missionary's frock-coat. "I would like to roast mealies in the thatch of Leendert Roux's house."

Many of us were in agreement with Kobus.

But our veldkornet, Apie Theron, counselled us against that form of vengeance.

"Leendert Roux's having his wife and farmstead here will yet lead to his undoing," the veldkornet said. "One day he will risk coming out here on a visit, when he hasn't got Kitchener's whole army at his back. That will be when we will settle our reckoning with him."

We did not guess that that day would be soon.

The road we were following led past Leendert Roux's homestead. The noise of our horses' hooves brought Leendert Roux's wife, Serfina, to the door. She stood in the open doorway and watched us riding by. Serfina was pretty, taller than most women, and slender, and there was no expression in her eyes that you could read, and her face was very white.

It was strange, I thought, as we rode past the homestead, that the sight of Serfina Roux did not fill us with bitterness.

Afterwards, when we had dismounted in the mealie-lands, Jan Vermeulen made a remark at which we laughed.

"For me it was the worst moment in the Boer War," Jan Vermeulen said. "Having to ride past a pretty girl, and me wearing just a sack. I was glad there was Kobus Ferreira's frock-coat for me to hide behind."

Jurie Bekker said there was something about Serfina Roux that reminded him of the Transvaal. He did not know how it was, but he repeated that, with the wind of early winter fluttering her skirts about her ankles, that was how it seemed to him.

Then Kobus Ferreira said that he had wanted to shout out something to her when we rode past the door, to let Serfina know how we, who were fighting in the last ditch – and in unsuitable clothing – felt about the wife of a traitor. "But she stood there so still," Kobus Ferreira said, "that I just couldn't say anything. I felt I would like to visit her, even."

That remark of Kobus Ferreira's fitted in with his frock-coat, also. It would not be the first time a man in ecclesiastical dress called on a woman while her husband was away.

Then, once again, a remark of Jan Vermeulen's made us realise that there was a war on. Jan Vermeulen had taken the mealie sack off his body and had threaded a length of baling-wire above the places where the holes were. He was now restoring the grain bag to the use it had been meant for, and I suppose that, in consequence, his views generally also got sensible.

"Just because Serfina Roux is pretty," Jan Vermeulen said, flinging mealie heads into the sack, "let us not forget who and what she is. Perhaps it is not safe for us to camp tonight on this farm. She is sure to be in touch with the English. She may tell them where we are. Especially now that we have taken her mealies."

But our veldkornet said that it wasn't important if the English knew where we were. Indeed, any kaffir in the neighbourhood

could go and report our position to them.
But what did matter was that we should know
where the English were. And he reminded us that in two years he
had never made a serious mistake that way.

"What about the affair at the spruit, though?" Jan Vermeulen
asked him. "And my pipe and tinder-box were in the jacket, too."

By sunset the wind had gone down. But there was a chill in the
air. We had pitched our camp in the tamboekie grass on the far
side of Leendert Roux's farm. And I was glad, lying in my blankets, to think that it was the turn of the veldkornet and Jurie
Bekker to stand guard.

Far away a jackal howled. Then there was silence again. A little later the stillness was disturbed by sterner sounds of the veld
at night. And those sounds did not come from very far away,
either. They were sounds Jurie Bekker made – first, when he fell
over a beacon, and then when he gave his opinion of Leendert
Roux for setting up a beacon in the middle of a stretch of

357

dubbeltjie thorns. The blankets felt very snug, pulled over my shoulders, when I reflected on those thorns.

And because I was young, there came into my thoughts, at Jurie Bekker's mention of Leendert Roux, the picture of Serfina as she had stood in front of her door.

The dream I had of Serfina Roux was that she came to me, tall and graceful, beside a white beacon on her husband's farm. It was that haunting kind of dream, in which you half know all the time that you are dreaming. And she was very beautiful in my dream. And it was as though her hair was hanging half out of my dream and reaching down into the wind when she came closer to me. And I knew what she wanted to tell me. But I did not wish to hear it. I knew that if Serfina spoke that thing I would wake up from my dream. And in that moment, like it always happens in a dream, Serfina did speak.

"Opskud, kêrels!" I heard.

But it was not Serfina who gave that command. It was Apie Theron, the veldkornet. He came running into the camp with his rifle at the trail. And Serfina was gone. In a few minutes we had saddled our horses and were ready to gallop away. Many times during the past couple of years our scouts had roused us thus when an English column was approaching.

We were already in the saddle when Apie Theron let us know what was toward. He had received information, he said, that Leendert Roux had that very night ventured back to his homestead. If we hurried we might trap him in his own house. The veldkornet warned us to take no chances, reminding us that when Leendert Roux had still stood on our side he had been a fearless and resourceful fighter.

So we rode back during the night along the same way we had come in the afternoon. We tethered our horses in a clump of trees near the mealie-land and started to surround the farmhouse. When we saw a figure running for the stable at the side of the house, we realised that Leendert Roux had been almost too quick for us.

In the cold, thin wind that springs up just before the dawn we surprised Leendert Roux at the door of his stable. But when he made no resistance it was almost as though it was Leendert Roux who had taken us by surprise. Leendert Roux's calm acceptance of his fate made it seem almost as though he had never turned traitor, but that he was laying down his life for the Transvaal.

In answer to the veldkornet's question, Leendert Roux said that he would be glad if Kobus Ferreira – he having noticed that Kobus was wearing the frock-coat of a man of religion – would read Psalm 110 over his grave. He also said that he did not want his eyes bandaged. And he asked to be allowed to say goodbye to his wife.

Serfina was sent for. At the side of the stable, in the wind of early morning, Leendert and Serfina Roux, husband and wife, bade each other farewell.

Serfina looked even more shadowy than she had done in my dream when she set off back to the homestead along the footpath through the thorns. The sun was just beginning to rise. And I understood how right Jurie Bekker had been when he said that she was just like the Transvaal, with the dawn wind fluttering her skirts about her ankles as it rippled the grass. And I remembered that it was the Boer women that kept on when their menfolk re-coiled before the steepness of the Drakensberge and spoke of turning back.

I also thought of how strange it was that Serfina should have come walking over to our camp, in the middle of the night, just as she had done in my dream. But where my dream was different was that she had reported not to me but to our veldkornet where Leendert Roux was.

Unpublished
in His Lifetime

THE RED COAT

I have spoken before of some of the queer things that happen to your mind through fever (Oom Schalk Lourens said). In the past there was a good deal more fever in the Marico and Waterberg Districts than there is today. And you got it in a more severe form, too. Today you still get malaria in these parts, of course. But your temperature doesn't go so high anymore before the fever breaks. And you are not left as weak after an attack of malaria as you were in the old days. Nor do you often get illusions of the sort that afterwards came to trouble the mind of Andries Visagie.

They say that this improvement is due to civilisation.

Well, I suppose that must be right. For one thing, we now have a Government lorry from Zeerust every week with letters and newspapers and catalogues from Johannesburg shopkeepers. And only three years ago Jurie Bekker bought a wooden stand with a glass for measuring how much rain he gets on his farm. Jurie Bekker is very proud of his rain-gauge, too, and will accompany any white visitor to the back of his house to show him how well it works. "We have had no rain for the last three years," Jurie Bekker will explain, "and that is exactly what the rain-gauge records, also. Look, you can see for yourself – nil!"

Jurie Bekker also tried to explain the rain instrument to the kaffirs on his farm. But he gave it up. "A kaffir with a blanket on hasn't got the brain to understand a white man's inventions," Jurie Bekker said about it, afterwards. "When I showed my kaffirs what this rain-gauge was all about, they just stood in a long row and laughed."

Nevertheless, I must admit that, with all this civilisation we are getting here, the malaria fever has not of recent years been the scourge it was in the old days.

The story of Andries Visagie and his fever begins at the battle of Bronkhorstspruit. It was at the battle of Bronkhorstspruit that Andries Visagie had his life saved by Piet Niemand, according to all accounts. And yet it was also arising out of that incident that many people in this part of the Marico in later years came to the conclusion that Andries Visagie was somebody whose word you could not take seriously, because of the suffering that he had undergone.

You know, of course, that the Bronkhorstspruit battle was fought very long ago. In those days we still called the English 'redcoats.' For the English soldiers wore red jackets that we could see against the khaki colour of the tamboekie grass for almost as far as the bullets from our Martini-Henry rifles could carry. That shows you how uncivilised those times were.

I often heard Piet Niemand relate the story of how he found Andries Visagie lying unconscious in a donga on the battlefield, and of how he revived him with brandy that he had in his water-bottle.

Piet Niemand explained that, from the number of redcoats that were lined up at Bronkhorstspruit that morning, he could see it was going to be a serious engagement, and so he had thoughtfully emptied all the water out of his bottle and had replaced it with Magaliesberg peach brandy of the rawest kind he could get. Piet Niemand said that he was advancing against the English when he came across that donga. He was advancing very fast and was looking neither to right nor left of him, he said. And he would draw lines on any piece of paper that was handy to show you the direction he took.

I can still remember how annoyed we all were when a young school-teacher, looking intently at that piece of paper, said that if that was the direction in which Piet Niemand was advancing, then it must have meant that the English had got right to behind the Boer lines, which was contrary to what he had read in the history books. Shortly afterwards Hannes Potgieter, who was chairman of our school committee, got that young school-teacher transferred.

As Hannes Potgieter said, that young school-teacher with his history-book ideas had never been in a battle and didn't know what real fighting was. In the confusion of a fight, with guns going off all round you, Hannes Potgieter declared, it was not

364

unusual for a burgher to find himself advancing away from the enemy – and quite fast, too.

He was not ashamed to admit that a very similar thing had happened to him at one stage of the battle of Majuba Hill. He had run back a long way, because he had suddenly felt that he wanted to make sure that the kaffir agterryers were taking proper care of the horses. But he need have had no fears on that score, Hannes Potgieter added. Because when he reached the sheltered spot among the thorn-trees where the horses were tethered, he found that three kommandants and a veldkornet had arrived there before him, on the same errand. The veldkornet was so anxious to reassure himself that the horses were all right, that he was even trying to mount one of them.

When Hannes Potgieter said that, he winked. And we all laughed. For we knew that he had fought bravely at Majuba Hill. But he was also ready always to acknowledge that he had been very frightened at Majuba Hill. And because he had been in several wars, he did not like to hear the courage of Piet Niemand called in question. What Hannes Potgieter meant us to understand was that if, at the battle of Bronkhorstspruit, Piet Niemand did perhaps run at one stage, it was the sort of thing that could happen to any man; and for which any man could be forgiven, too.

And, in any case, Piet Niemand's story was interesting enough. He said that in the course of his advance he came across a donga, on the edge of which a thorn-bush was growing. The donga was about ten foot deep. He descended into the donga to light his pipe. He couldn't light his pipe out there on the open veld, because it was too windy, he said. When he reached the bottom of the donga, he also found that he had brought most of that thorn-bush along with him.

Then, in a bend of the donga, Piet Niemand saw what he thought was an English soldier, lying face downwards. He thought, at first, that the English soldier had come down there to light his pipe, also, and had decided to stay longer. He couldn't see too clearly, Piet Niemand said, because the smoke of the battle of Bronkhorstspruit had got into his eyes. Maybe the smoke from his pipe, too, I thought. That is, if what he was lighting up there in the donga was Piet Retief roll tobacco.

365

Why Piet Niemand thought that the man lying at the bend of the donga was an Englishman was because he was wearing a red coat. But in the next moment Piet Niemand realised that the man was not an Englishman. For the man's neck was not also red.

Immediately there flashed into Piet Niemand's mind the suspicion that the man was a Boer in English uniform – a Transvaal Boer fighting against his own people. If it had been an Englishman lying there, he would have called on him to surrender, Piet Niemand said, but a Boer traitor he was going to shoot without giving him a chance to get up.

He was in the act of raising his Martini-Henry to fire, when the truth came to him. And that was how he first met Andries Visagie and how he came to save his life. He saw that while Andries Visagie's coat was indeed red, it was not with dye, but with the blood from his wound. Piet Niemand said that he was so overcome at the thought of the sin he had been about to commit that when he unstrapped his water-bottle his knees trembled as much as did his fingers. But when Piet Niemand told this part of his story, Hannes Potgieter said that he need not make any excuses for himself, especially as no harm had come of it. If it had been a Boer traitor instead of Piet Niemand who had found himself in that same situation, Hannes Potgieter said, then the Boer traitor would have fired in any case, without bothering very much as to whether it was a Boer or an Englishman that he was shooting.

Piet Niemand knelt down beside Andries Visagie and turned him round and succeeded in pouring a quantity of brandy down his throat. Andries Visagie was not seriously wounded, but he had a high fever, from the sun and through loss of blood, and he spoke strange words.

That was the story that Piet Niemand had to tell.

Afterwards Andries Visagie made a good recovery in the mill at Bronkhorstspruit, that the kommandant had turned into a hospital. And they say it was very touching to observe Andries Visagie's gratitude when Piet Niemand came to visit him.

Andries Visagie lay on the floor, on a rough mattress filled with grass and dried mealie-leaves. Piet Niemand went and sat on the floor beside him. They conversed. By that time Andries Visagie had recovered sufficiently to remember that he had shot three redcoats for sure. He added, however, that as a result of the weakness caused by his wound, his mind was not very clear, at times. But when he got quite well and strong again, he would remember better. And then he would not be at all surprised if he remembered that he had also shot a general, he said.

Piet Niemand then related some of his own acts of bravery. And because they were both young men it gave them much pleasure to pass themselves off as heroes in each other's company.

Piet Niemand had already stood up to go when Andries Visagie reached his hand underneath the mattress and pulled out a watch with a heavy gold chain. The watch was shaped like an egg and on the case were pictures of angels, painted in enamel. Even without those angels, it would have been a very magnificent watch. But with those angels painted on the case, you would not care much if the watch did not go, even, and you still had to tell the time from the sun, holding your hand cupped over your eyes.

"I inherited this watch from my grandfather," Andries Visagie said. "He brought it with him on the Great Trek. You saved my life in the donga. You must take this watch as a keepsake."

Those who were present at this incident in the temporary hospital at Bronkhorstspruit said that Piet Niemand reached over to receive the gift. He almost had his hand on the watch, they say. And then he changed his mind and stood up straight.

"What I did was nothing," Piet Niemand said. "It was something anybody would have done. Anybody that was brave enough, I mean. But I want no reward for it. Maybe I'll some day buy myself a watch like that."

Andries Visagie kept his father's father's egg-shaped watch, after all. But in his having offered Piet Niemand his most treasured possession, and in Piet Niemand having declined to accept it, there was set the seal on the friendship of those two young men. This friendship was guarded, maybe, by the wings of the angels painted in enamel on the watch-case. Afterwards people were to say that it was a pity Andries Visagie should have turned so queer in the head. It must have been that he had suffered too much, these people said.

In gratitude for their services in the First Boer War, the Government of the Transvaal Republic made grants of farming land in

367

the Waterberg District to those Boers on commando who had no ground of their own. The Government of the Transvaal Republic did not think it necessary to explain that the area in question was already occupied – by lions and malaria mosquitoes and hostile kaffirs. Nevertheless, many Boers knew the facts about that part of the Waterberg pretty well. So only a handful of burghers were prepared to accept Government farms. Most of the others felt that, seeing they had just come out of one war, there was not much point in going straight back into another.

All the same, a number of burghers did go and take up land in that area, and to everybody's surprise – not least to the surprise of the Government, I suppose – they fared reasonably well. And among those new settlers in the Waterberg were Piet Niemand and Andries Visagie. Their farms were not more than two days' journey apart. So you could almost say they were neighbours. They visited each other regularly.

The years went by, and then in a certain wet season Andries Visagie lay stricken with malaria. And in his delirium he said strange things. Fancying himself back again at Bronkhorstspruit, Andries Visagie said he could remember the long line of English generals he was shooting. He was shooting them full of medals, he said.

But there was another thing that Andries Visagie said he remembered then. And after he recovered from the malaria he still insisted that the circumstance he had recalled during his illness was the truth. He said that through that second bout of fever he was able to remember what had happened years before, in the donga, when he was also delirious.

And it was then that many of the farmers in the Waterberg began to say what a pity it was that Andries Visagie's illness should so far have affected his mind.

For Andries Visagie said that he could remember distinctly, now, that time when he was lying in the donga. And he would never, of course, know who shot him. But what he did remember was that when Piet Niemand was bending over him, holding a water-bottle in his hand, Piet Niemand was wearing a red coat.

THE QUESTION

Stefanus Malherbe had difficulty in getting access to the president, to put to him the question of which we were all anxious to learn the answer.

It was at Waterval Onder and President Kruger was making preparations to leave for Europe to enlist the help of foreign countries in the Transvaal's struggle against England. General Louis Botha had just been defeated at Dalmanutha. Accordingly, we who were the last of the Boer commandos in the field found ourselves hemmed in against the Portuguese border by the British forces, the few miles of railway-line from Nelspruit to Komatipoort being all that still remained to us of Transvaal soil. The Boer War had hardly begun, and it already looked like the end.

But when we had occasion to watch, from a considerable distance, a column of British dragoons advancing through a half-mile stretch of bush country, there were those of us who realised that the Boer War might, after all, not be over yet. It took the column two hours to get through that bush.

Although we who served under Veldkornet Stefanus Malherbe were appointed to the duty of guarding President Kruger during those last days, we had neither the opportunity nor the temerity to talk to him in that house at Waterval Onder. For one thing, there were those men with big stomachs and heavy gold watch-chains all crowding around the president with papers they wanted him to sign. Nevertheless, when the news came that the English had broken through at Dalmanutha, we overheard some of those men say, not raising their voices unduly, that something or other was no longer worth the paper it was written on. Next morning, when President Kruger again came on the front stoep of the house, alone this time, we were for the first time able to see him

THE COMPLETE OOM SCHALK LOURENS STORIES

clearly, instead of through the thick screen of grey smoke being blown into his face from imported cigars.

"Well," Thys Haasbroek said, "I hope the president when he gets to Europe enlists the right kind of foreigners to come and fight for the Republic. It would be too bad if he came back with another crowd of uitlanders with big stomachs and watch-chains, waving papers for concessions."

I mention this remark made by one of the burghers then at Waterval Onder with the president to show you that there was not a uniform spirit of bitter-end loyalty animating the three thousand men who saw day by day the net of the enemy getting more tightly drawn around them. Indeed, speaking for myself, I must confess that the enthusiasm of those of our leaders who at intervals addressed us, exhorting us to courage, had but a restricted influence on my mind.

Especially when the orders came for the rolling stock to be dynamited.

For we had brought with us, in our retreat from Magersfontein, practically all the carriages and engines and trucks of the Transvaal and Orange Free State railways. At first we were much saddened by the necessity for destroying the property of our country. But afterwards something got into our blood which made it all seem like a good joke.

I know that our own little group that was under the leadership of Veldkornet Stefanus Malherbe really derived a considerable amount of enjoyment, towards the end, out of blowing railway engines and whole trains into the air. A couple of former shunters who were on commando with us would say things like, "There goes the Cape mail via Fourteen Streams." And we would fling ourselves into a ditch to escape the flying fragments of wood and steel. One of them also used to shout, "All seats for Bloemfontein," or "First stop Elandsfontein," after the fuse was lit and he would blow his whistle and wave a green flag. For several days it seemed that between Nelspruit and Hectorspruit you couldn't look up at any part of the sky without seeing wheels in it.

And during all this time we treated the whole affair as fun, and the former shunters had got to calling out, "There goes the 9.20 to De Aar against the signals" and, "There's a girl with fair hair

370

travelling by herself in the end compartment." Being railwaymen, they couldn't think of anything else to say.

Because the war of the big commandos, and of men like Generals Joubert and Cronje, was over, it seemed to us that all the fighting was just about done. We did not know that the Boer War of General de Wet and Ben Viljoen and General Muller was then only about to begin.

The next order that our veldkornet, Stefanus Malherbe, brought us from the kommandant was for the destruction of our stores and field guns and ammunition dumps as well. All we had to retain were our Mausers and horses, the order said. That did not give us much cause for hope. At the same time the first of General Louis Botha's burghers from the Dalmanutha fight began to arrive in our camp. They were worn out from their long retreat and many of them had acquired the singular habit of looking round over their shoulders very quickly, every so often, right in the middle of a conversation. Their presence did not help to inspire us with military ardour. One of these burghers was very upset at our having blown up all the trains. He had been born and bred in the gramadoelas and had been looking forward to his first journey by rail.

"I just wanted to feel how the thing rides," he said in disappointed tones, in between trying to wipe off stray patches of yellow lyddite stains he had got at Dalmanutha. "But even if there *was* still another train left, I suppose it would be too late, now."

"Yes, I am sure it would be too late," I said, also looking quickly over my shoulder. There was something infectious about this habit that Louis Botha's burghers had brought with them.

Actually, of course, it was not yet too late, for there was still a train, with the engine and carriages intact, waiting to take the president out of the Transvaal into Portuguese territory. There were also in the Boer ranks men whose loyalty to the Republic never wavered even in the darkest times. It had been a very long retreat from the northern Cape Province through the Orange Free State and the Transvaal to where we were now shut in near the Komati River. And it had all happened so quickly.

The Boer withdrawal, when once it got under way, had been very fast and very complete. I found it not a little disconcerting to

371

think that on one day I had seen the president seated in a spider just outside Paardeberg drinking buttermilk and then on another day, only a few months later, I had seen him sitting on the front stoep of a house at Waterval Onder a thousand miles away, drinking brandy. Moreover, he was getting ready to move again.

"If it is only to Europe that he is going, then it is not too bad," said an old farmer with a long beard who was an ignorant man in many ways, but whose faith had not faltered throughout the retreat. "I would not have liked our beloved president to have to travel all that way back to the northern Cape where we started from. He hasn't the strength for so long a journey. I am glad that it is only to Russia that he is going."

Because he was not demoralised by defeat, as so many of us were, we who listened to this old farmer's words were touched by his simple loyalty. Indeed, the example set by men of his sort had a far greater influence on the course of the war during the difficult period ahead than the speeches that our leaders came round and made to us from time to time.

Certainly we did not feel that the veldkornet, Stefanus Malherbe, was a tower of strength. We did not dislike him nor did we distrust him. We only felt, after a peculiar fashion, that he was too much the same kind of man that we ourselves were. So we did not have overmuch respect for him.

I have said that we ordinary burghers did not have the temerity to approach the president and to talk to him as man to man of the matter that we wanted to know about. And so we hung back a little while Stefanus Malherbe, an officer on whom many weighty responsibilities reposed, put out his chest and strode toward the house to interview the president. "Put out your stomach," one of the burghers called out. He was of course thinking of those men who until lately had surrounded the president with their papers and watch-chains and cigars.

And then, when Stefanus Malherbe was moving in the direction of the voorkamer, where he knew the president to be, and when the rest of the members of our veldkornetskap had drawn ourselves together in a little knot that stood nervously waiting just off the stoep for the president's reply – I suppose it had to happen that just then a newly appointed general should have decided to treat us to a patriotic talk. Under other circumstances we would have been impressed, perhaps, but at that point in time, when we had already blown up our trains and stores and ammunition dumps, and had sunk the pieces that remained of the Staat's Artillerie in the Komati River – along with some papers we had captured in earlier battle – we were not an ideal audience.

We stood still, out of politeness, and listened. But all the time we were wondering if the veldkornet would perhaps be able to slip away at the end of the speech and manage to get in a few words with President Kruger after all. Anyway, I am sure that we took in very little of what the newly appointed general had to say.

In the end the general realised the position too. We gathered that he had known he was going to get the appointment that day, and that he had prepared a speech for the occasion, to deliver before the president and the State Council, but that he had been unable to have his say in the house because of the bustle attendant upon the president's impending departure. Consequently, the general delivered his set speech to us, the first group of burghers he encountered on his way out. After he had got us to sing Psalm 83 and had adjured each one of us to humble himself before the Lord, the general explained at great length that if we could perhaps not hope for victory, since victory might be beyond our capacity, we could still hope for a more worthy kind of defeat.

We made no response to his eloquence. We did not sweep our hats upward in a cheer. We did not call out, "Ou perd!" We were only concerned with the veldkornet's chances of getting in a word with the president before it was too late. The general understood, eventually, that our hearts were not in his address and so he concluded his speech rather abruptly. "Some defeats are greater than victories," he said, and he paused for a little while to survey us before adding, "but not this one, I don't think."

The meeting having ended suddenly like that, Veldkornet Stefanus Malherbe did, after all, manage to get into the voorkamer to speak to President Kruger alone. That much we knew. But when he came out of the house, the veldkornet was silent about his conversation with the president. He did not tell us what the president had said in answer to his question. And in the next advance of the English, which was made within that same week, and which took them right into Komatipoort, Veldkornet Stefanus Malherbe was killed. So he never told us what the president had said in answer to his question about the Kruger millions.

THE OLD POTCHEFSTROOM GAOL

You can always get people to listen to a story with a murder and a hanging in it (Oom Schalk Lourens said). And it does-n't matter, then, if it is even quite an ordinary sort of murder. Nor are people particular if the hanging is not so very up-to-date, either. They can stand it.

The authorities ordered the old gaol in Potchefstroom to be rebuilt because it was damp; and neither light nor air could get into it. And it was very unhealthy. Many people considered that this was a foolish step on the part of the authorities, rebuilding the place. After all, what was the good of a prison if it *wasn't* unhealthy?

The prisoners from behind the bars of their cells saw the outer walls of the prison being pulled down. And they started getting hopeful. But the look of expectancy went from their faces when they were shortly afterwards moved to another prison. With the walls down, the gallows in the courtyard stood revealed. And so the story of Karel Malan and Thys Burkhardt – and of Wiesie van Breda – was recalled as clearly as though the gallows had been erected only yesterday, and not half a century before.

You might think, perhaps, that an old gaol is a strange setting for the story of a courtship. But when it is young love, in the springtime – why, the gates of a prison can help a good deal to make it impressive. Young hearts and an old gaol. I've seen it hap-pen here, in the Marico Bushveld. And I have seen the same thing in the bioscope in Zeerust. Maybe the best kind of love story *is* when it's round a prison.

Wiesie van Breda had been betrothed to Karel Malan, the young Sunday school-teacher, a good while before she attracted the attention of Thys Burkhardt, who was not like a Sunday school-teacher at all. For when Thys Burkhardt laughed in the bar you could hear him as far as Suid Street.

Then one Sunday morning Thys Burkhardt was found lying in the vlei with a Mauser bullet in his heart. And for Karel Malan a class sat waiting, on the hard benches of a Sunday school, a long while, in vain.

Karel Malan was tried for the murder of Thys Burkhardt and was sentenced to be hanged.

That was why Karel Malan would not one day be coming out of the church with Wiesie van Breda's hand tucked under his arm, the members of the congregation throwing rice. It was all just because what Karel Malan carried in the bend of his arm was not his hymn-book – on that Sunday morning when he went through the vlei looking for Thys Burkhardt.

And the story that got spread about Karel Malan, later on, was that he was never hanged. He had family – and church – influence, it was said. And on the night preceding the morning set down for his execution he was smuggled out of the prison in time to get on the mail-coach for the Cape, the hangman walking in front, carrying Karel Malan's portmanteau as far as the coach station for him.

There was not much evidence in support of this story – as there never is, in such matters, I have noticed. But then, it was not likely that a condemned man would be smuggled out of a prison at night in such a way that everybody could see it being done. The authorities would not have moved Karel Malan out of the prison as openly as they were, fifty years later, to move all the convicts to another place of confinement – the authorities even allowing the Salvation Army to distribute tracts to the prisoners as they came out of the front gate. The municipal refuse span used very bad language, that time, about all the religious leaflets they had to sweep up that the more hardened convicts threw away in the street.

About all there was to go by, with regard to Karel Malan having been smuggled out of gaol, was the statement made by the driver of the Cape stage-coach. The driver said that he had a passenger aboard from the Transvaal who sang Sunday school hymns right as far into the Karoo as Matjesfontein, at which place the passenger got hoarse.

When a responsible citizen in the Potchefstroom saloon bar put him the question, the driver of the stage-coach said, yes, he did notice that the passenger had a portmanteau. But he wouldn't know whether a hangman had carried it for some distance. He hadn't taken a proper look at the handle of the portmanteau, the stage-coach driver said.

The other piece of evidence was that Warder Visagie – who had not been at the Potchefstroom gaol above a month or two – was suddenly transferred to Pretoria. And people said it was because he talked too much.

Well, it was true enough that Warder Visagie was talking quite a lot about then. But his talk was mostly about a girl with ringlets, who lived next door to the boarding-house in which he was staying, and with whom he had fallen in love, having seen her a few times on the other side of the galvanised-iron fence; and who didn't seem to want him; and whose name he didn't know, even, he being too shy to ask – contenting himself, instead, with throwing her an orange.

"I honestly don't know anything about a hanging in the gaol just lately," Warder Visagie announced in the saloon bar. "I mean, if there was a hanging I would have known, wouldn't I? Especially if it was a white man, as you say . . . What? Oh, *him*. Well, I mean, I never worried much about Karel Malan. With nothing more on his mind than a hanging, Karel Malan couldn't know what real trouble was. I tell you, her hair is all in ringlets. And I could never work up enough courage to talk to her, even. And then I threw her that ripe orange for a present. And it had to be my luck that it should hit her on her left ear, just as she was walking back into the kitchen. And she said to me, 'Why don't you —' And she slammed the kitchen door shut behind her."

Warder Visagie sighed deeply, then, in that old saloon bar in which a shining paraffin lamp had a few months earlier taken the place of a row of candles.

"She's got dark eyes," Warder Visagie said after a pause, "as far as I can see from my side of the fence. And she's got ringlets. And her eyes turn up at the corners when she laughs."

"I should think she must laugh a good deal," the bartender said, drily, "looking at what's on the other side of the fence."

Because he didn't catch on, the patrons of the saloon bar

understood that Warder Visagie really was in love. His face that was flushed with brandy was also strangely shadowed under the paraffin lamp.

All those stories were remembered, in great detail, fifty years later, at the rebuilding of the old gaol. The Potchefstroom public walked about the prison terrain, after the front walls had been demolished, with a freedom that even a prison governor of long standing would never have dared assume and that even the oldest convict would not have permitted himself, as long as he had any appearance to keep up.

The first thing that struck visitors from the town about the prison was the fine state of preservation of the gallows. Riem Pienaar summed it up in these words: "They don't make gallows like that these days. Today, they would never use that class of wood anymore."

But it was just like Riem Pienaar to talk that way, of course, as though he knew everything: in this case, he was talking as an authority on being hanged. The truth was, however, that with the years Riem Pienaar had gained an ascendancy with the citizens of Potchefstroom, just through making statements that nobody thought of questioning.

"All the same," Riem Pienaar asserted, "if Karel Malan really had been hanged, the gallows wouldn't have looked nearly so new. You've got no idea how old a gallows gets to look, suddenly, just from having had a white man hanged from it."

Nobody tried to argue with Riem Pienaar. From past experience they knew it was useless.

Now, it was just at this time, too, that the Sunday school building had to be extended and repaired. The thatched roof had to be replaced by galvanised iron. And it so happened that the contract for the work on the Sunday school building was given to the same builder who was renovating the gaol. The price he had quoted the church was so low.

There was some dissatisfaction among a section of churchgoers, however, when they discovered why the builder could make the extensions to the Sunday school so cheaply. They found he was using the building materials from the gaol.

378

When the matter was put to him the builder affected surprise.

"Why, there's no better timber in the country for the rafters than what I'm taking out of the gaol," he said. "It's real stinkwood. And as good as when it was put up. Where can you get timber like that today?"

He said he would also have used the windows of the gaol for the Sunday school. Only, he added, the gaol had no windows. It was not the sort of gaol that went in for fresh air.

Nevertheless, the protests began again when the builder had the gallows cut down, as well, and got the kaffirs to carry the gallows timber across the way to the Sunday school.

"Why, it's real oak," he said. "This wood is as solid as the day they hanged Karel Malan on it. It's also seasoned."

The builder seemed surprised that his arguments did not silence the protests.

It was in the midst of this unpleasantness that it became known that the Sunday school was being haunted by Karel Malan's ghost. You could understand that, with his gallows gone, the murderer of Thys Burkhardt would not be able to rest in peace. Karel Malan had got used to his gallows standing there for over half a century. That was what some people said. Others said again that why Karel Malan was haunting the Sunday school building was because he himself had been a Sunday school teacher. His spirit was unhappy at the builder's desecration of the place of worship in which he had worked earnestly in the old days.

Those who had seen the ghost of Karel Malan all described it in the same way. It was the ghost of an old man with a long white beard. This was a sufficiently singular circumstance. How could Karel Malan's ghost grow old like that, if he had been hanged in his early manhood?

A few days later the builder's kaffirs found a very old man with a white beard walking about the Sunday school building where they were busy extending a wall. And they were in deadly fear, the kaffirs said. For they thought that the old man with the white beard was from the Works Department, and that he would discover that the mortar they were mixing consisted of six wheelbarrow-loads of river sand to one shovelful of cement.

In a few minutes a small band had gathered about the old man. He was plied with questions. "Are you really Karel Malan?" "Did you murder Thys Burkhardt?" "Is it true that you escaped the night before you were going to be hanged?"

The old man could answer only falteringly. He had forgotten most of the early years of his life, he said. But he knew he had lived in Potchefstroom as a young man. Certain scenes were still familiar to him.

The builder tapped his forehead.

"The old Oom is clearly in his second childhood," the builder said. "But maybe he is after all Karel Malan. And there is one person alone who can prove it – Tant Wiesie van Breda."

It was quite a procession that moved off shortly, with the white-bearded old man and the builder at the front, in the direction of Wiesie van Breda's cottage.

Riem Pienaar thoughtfully went on ahead to prepare Wiesie van Breda's mind beforehand. She mustn't faint, but her dead lover was at that moment coming up the street, some people with him, Riem Pienaar warned Wiesie van Breda.

It took quite a lot of rooi laventel and a cup of water to bring Wiesie van Breda round again, because of Riem Pienaar's tactful words. And when the elderly stranger came in at the front gate, the crowd around him having grown quite considerably, Wiesie van Breda was able to take a good look at him and to assure the bystanders that he wasn't Karel Malan.

Riem Pienaar looked a very disappointed man.

"Could he –" Riem Pienaar asked after a pause, "could he perhaps be the other one? Thys Burkhardt, that is?" His voice did not sound very hopeful.

In the meantime, although the stranger was not Karel Malan come back from the past, Wiesie van Breda nevertheless falteringly held out her hand to him.

The elderly stranger was the first to talk.

"What did you mean when you said to me, 'Why don't you —?'" the old man asked. "You've still got ringlets . . ."

"I meant, 'Why don't you come round to the front door and knock?'" Wiesie van Breda answered. "Where's that funny blue uniform you used to wear, with the flat cap?"

"Your eyes still turn up like that at the corners when you laugh," the old man said. "I'm on pension and I've come to settle down here," ex-Warder Visagie added, during all that time not letting go of Wiesie van Breda's hand.

THE GHOST AT THE DRIFT

Ghost stories that I have heard people tell (Oom Schalk Lou-rens said), are always about the same sort of thing. You must have heard this kind of story often. A traveller is on his way some-where, and he has to cross a drift after nightfall. People in the neighbourhood warn him that no man has ever been able to ride his horse past the drift in the dark. But the stranger proceeds on his way until he reaches a spot where his horse suddenly rears up in terror. Thereupon the traveller returns to the people who warned him about the drift; and he spends the night with them, and they enlighten him at considerable length about the circum-stances of the murder that was committed there long ago, and about the ghost that haunts the place near the drift where the grass does not grow.

This is quite a good story, of course, if it is properly told, without too much detail. You spoil the story if you describe too fully how the ghost looks, and if you try to imitate the noises it makes – as I have heard some storytellers do.

Anyway, I have heard this story so often that I have almost come to the conclusion that there is only one ghost in the Transvaal. And that there has been only one murder.

All this reminds me of the time when Gert Bekker and I were driving by mule-cart to the Kalahari. We went through Rooikrans. Because this was my first visit to the Molopo area, and because Gert Bekker had been on that road before, a singular thing hap-pened to Gert Bekker. He felt that he had to take the lead in every-thing, and he gave me a lot of instructions and good counsel. Although I had grown up in the Bushveld, Gert Bekker treated me as though I was some newcomer from an overseas city, just because I had not been in that small part of the Groot Marico before – whereas I knew the rest of the district as well as I knew my own farm.

"There are many ways in which a stranger to these parts can deceive himself, Schalk," Gert Bekker was saying. "That kwê-bird that you heard calling now. You thought that sound came from in front, didn't you?"

"I *saw* the kwê-bird when we passed him a few moments ago," I answered. "He was perched on a bough of one of those withaaks to the left there."

"It's a good thing you saw him, then," Gert Bekker continued. "Otherwise you might have got startled. I've seen strangers to these parts –"

"Kwê – ê – ê!" we heard the bird call again.

And so Gert Bekker went on talking, with the mule-cart bumping over the dusty road in the heat of the afternoon. Gert Bekker's voice sounded as empty as the mule-cart's rattling: his conversation was as dusty as the road: I only thought that his words couldn't take a turn as neatly as the cart-wheels did in the sand.

Afterwards, in treating me as a foreigner in the Marico, Gert Bekker even went so far as to begin thinking out lies to tell me. The kind of lies that Marico farmers make up for a stranger from the city, so that they can laugh about it afterwards when they think of how the stranger's jaw fell.

Among other things, Gert Bekker told me of a farmer near the Molopo who had trained a team of green mambas to form themselves into a long chain to draw water from the well in a bucket. "A mamba-chain is no stronger than its weakest link," Gert Bekker said, making up more lies as we went along. And he looked at me sideways, at intervals, to see if my mouth was also beginning to open in astonishment.

Later in the afternoon we outspanned at the farmhouse of Jurie Snyman, whom I had met once or twice in Zeerust at the Nagmaal. I was glad that I could shake hands with Jurie Snyman and say, "Middag, Neef Jurie," quickly, before Gert Bekker could introduce me as "Schalk Lourens, a stranger to these parts" – as he had done at other farmhouses where we had called along the road.

Jurie Snyman's wife brought us coffee into the voorkamer, and we sat and spoke about the new kind of bot-fly pest that was invading the Marico from the Kalahari side.

"Do you know what a bot-fly is, Schalk?" Gert Bekker had the impudence to ask me, still keeping on with his role of being a mentor to a new arrival in that region.

"Yes," I answered, shortly, "and I also know what a pest is."

Jurie Snyman laughed, thinking that I was referring to our Volksraad member who was sitting in Pretoria and had done nothing to get government assistance for the farmers in our struggle against the bot-fly plague. The result was that we spent several hours in discussing our Volksraad member, whom we ended up by talking about as our bot-fly member, so that it was quite late in the afternoon when we again stood beside the mule-cart, which Jurie Snyman's kaffirs were busy inspanning. Jurie Snyman came out with us. His farmhouse faced on to the road. Opposite the farmhouse was a rondavel that was used as a post office. Further down the road, partly hidden by the thorn-trees, was the thatched roof of a schoolroom.

"Your farm is growing into a fair-sized town," Gert Bekker said to Jurie Snyman.

"Yes, indeed," Jurie Snyman answered, proudly. "About half a mile beyond the school building there is also Ouma Theron's house: she's the local midwife. And just behind the bult is the new Indian store. That means five buildings by the road – two on the other side of the road, and three on this side – in a distance of a little more than a mile. There are seventeen pupils in the school. The teacher boards with Haasbroek near the Molopo drift and comes in every day by the donkey-wagon that the Education Department provides for the schoolchildren. My farm is actually the biggest town in the Marico, north of the Dwarsberge, when the school is in session."

Gert Bekker looked at me significantly. He meant that here was something else of which I, a stranger to these parts, had until that moment been ignorant.

We were already seated on the mule-cart when it seemed as though Jurie Snyman had suddenly remembered something. He looked at the sun, which was within an hour of setting.

384

"You may as well spend the night with me," he said to Gert Bekker. "No man can drive his trek-animals past a certain spot near the Molopo drift after dark. The Molopo is nearly eight miles from here. You won't make it before nightfall."

Gert Bekker, unlike myself, did not guess what was coming. So he said, no, while he was grateful for Jurie Snyman's offer of hospitality, we had arranged to stay over with Faan Cronje, who lived just across the drift. Faan was his wife's sister-in-law's second cousin on the Liebenberg side, Gert Bekker explained, and he dared not be neglectful of the social obligations when it came to the more intimate kind of family ties.

"But after your mules get a fright there, just before the drift, and they won't go any further," Jurie Snyman said, "then don't sleep out on the veld, but come back here. I'll be expecting you in any case."

Gert Bekker, not guessing what it was all about, looked at Jurie Snyman in some surprise. So I was glad that I was at last presented with an opportunity for enlightening Gert Bekker, instead of having had, until now, to receive all kinds of unwanted information and advice from him. For although I might be a stranger to that small part of the Marico around the Molopo, I was not a foreigner when it came to recognising a story, and in the few remarks that Jurie Snyman had made I detected all the signs of the Transvaal's oldest and most worn kind of ghost story.

"The ghost of a tall woman dressed all in white haunts a spot near the drift," I announced, "and no horse will go past that spot at night."

"And she carries a baby at her breast, and the baby cries," Jurie Snyman added.

"And no grass grows there," I said.

"And around the woman's waist is a long black girdle whose ends reach almost to the ground," Jurie Snyman said again.

At last Gert Bekker was able to find words.

"But how do you know all these things?" he called out to me in astonishment. "I thought you were a strange –"

"It's all to do with a murder of long ago," I replied airily. "Shake the reins."

Before he realised that he was taking instructions from me,

Gert Bekker had cracked his whip and the mule-cart began to move off along the road. He waved goodbye to Jurie Snyman.

"You'll be back here this same night," was the last thing we heard Jurie Snyman shout.

There was something in Jurie Snyman's tones that made the afternoon seem later than it already was.

We had driven past the school building and the thatched roof, and past the house of Ouma Theron, the midwife, and past the new Indian store that was about half a mile around the bend, before Gert Bekker again spoke to me. And then I thought that I noticed in his voice a certain measure of respect that had not been there before.

"I suppose it is – it's all just nonsense, Schalk, about – about that woman in the white dress?" Gert Bekker asked me. "And do you think it really is a white dress, or is it just that all ghosts look white?"

"I am sure I don't know," I answered. "I don't know these parts around the Molopo at all. You know what it is when one is a stranger to a place. I thought you were familiar with –"

"I didn't know *all that*," Gert Bekker answered. "And do you think that a murder really was committed there?"

I told him that I didn't know about that, either. I had merely guessed.

"We should have asked Jurie Snyman more about it," Gert Bekker said, "before we drove off in such a hurry. We can't just go by guesswork in a thing like this. When it comes to ghosts you've got to have hard facts. Like how the ghost looks, and everything."

Afterwards, when the shadows began to lengthen, I also started feeling that it would perhaps have been as well if we had asked Jurie Snyman a few more questions . . .

A little further on Gert Bekker again broke the silence.

"Perhaps we don't need to go all that way, across the drift, to spend the night with my wife's relatives," he said. "We can call on them in the morning. I sometimes think that we Afrikaners lay too much stress on family attachments. It is something that becomes unhealthy if it gets overdone. We can perhaps just camp out next to the road, this side of the drift."

"Even a good distance this side of the drift will do," I answered.

"I've got some mealie-meal and coffee and boerewors in the back of the cart," Gert Bekker said again.

"And we can scoop up water out of the next jackal-hole we come to," I said.

We also said that it would be a good idea to pitch camp while there was still plenty of daylight. We would be able to get together a large quantity of dry branches for the fire.

"And a couple of dead tree-trunks," Gert Bekker supplemented. "A dead tree-trunk, if it's a good one, keeps burning all night."

I did not care for the thoughtless way in which Gert Bekker kept on repeating the word 'dead.'

After we had eaten the boerewors and drunk our coffee, and had tethered the mules, we crept in under our blankets beside the fire. I wanted to talk about the thing that was uppermost in my mind, but I could sense that Gert Bekker was afraid to talk about it, and that made me also afraid to broach the subject. It is a peculiar thing that when you are alone at night in the company of a person with an ignorant mind, your own sensible outlook becomes clouded by the other person's superstitions. That was what I felt was happening to me, lying there in the night with Gert Bekker only a few yards away from me.

And, of course – as I learnt afterwards – when Gert Bekker spoke about that night, he always said that if it hadn't been for my absurd kaffir beliefs, which gradually undermined his own sound understanding and education, he would not have been afraid to sleep right next to the drift, on that very spot, even, where the grass did not grow. He didn't mind sleeping on the hard ground, he said.

I mention all this so that you can see from it what an impossible sort of person Gert Bekker always was.

Anyway, we couldn't sleep. We talked about things in which neither of us was at all interested. And we did not speak much above a whisper.

I can't remember when it was that I first sensed something. I turned my head to one side and what I saw then made me dart one swift glance at Gert Bekker, to find out if he had also seen it. I concluded that he had. Because in a single wild movement he pulled the blankets right over his head. I didn't see what he did after that, because at almost the same time I pulled the blankets over my head as well. After all – as Gert Bekker had taken so much care to point out to me – I was a stranger, comparatively speaking, to the Molopo area, and I could therefore do no better, in an emergency of this nature, than to follow his example. He had been on the road to the Molopo before, and he would naturally know that the right thing to do, when you get a sudden glimpse of a spectral shape a few feet away from you – a woman all in white and with the fire-light flickering on her ghostly features, and on the child held in her arms – is to pull the blankets over your head very quickly.

I lay a long time in the dark, too frightened to move. The blankets pressed close around my face, but I knew that I wouldn't suffocate: I was afraid to breathe much, in any case. And I knew only one thing, and that was that nothing on earth would induce me to gaze voluntarily upon that ghostly shape again.

I hadn't looked, either, to see if she was wearing a black sash reaching to her feet . . .

I only felt that we had pitched our camp much too near to the drift, after all.

For a long time I heard nothing but the beating of my own heart. I lay like that for hours, it seemed. Then, through the padding of the blankets, I thought I heard – laughter. I listened. No, I couldn't be mistaken. It was, indeed, laughter of a sort. I would know the sound of Gert Bekker's empty guffaws anywhere.

The explanation was simple enough. The wife of Piet Haasbroek was in labour. Piet Haasbroek had left for Rustenburg a few days before by donkey-cart, the family's only form of conveyance. And since there was no one else to send, Rena van Dam, the young school-teacher who boarded with the Haasbroeks, had set out in the dark to call on Ouma Theron, the midwife, whose house we had passed in the afternoon. Rena van Dam had seen the camp-fire and had walked up to get our help.

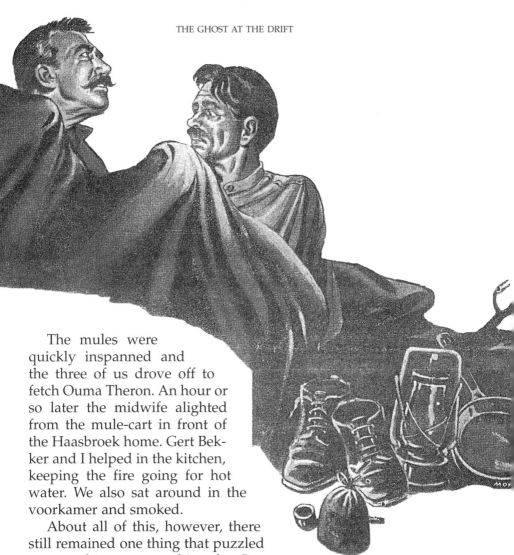

The mules were quickly inspanned and the three of us drove off to fetch Ouma Theron. An hour or so later the midwife alighted from the mule-cart in front of the Haasbroek home. Gert Bekker and I helped in the kitchen, keeping the fire going for hot water. We also sat around in the voorkamer and smoked.

About all of this, however, there still remained one thing that puzzled me – and it was something that I was shy to ask about. I was on the point of mentioning the matter to Gert Bekker on a few occasions, when we were alone together in the voorkamer and the three women were in the bedroom. And for the reasons I have already given you – to do with Gert Bekker's gross superstitions – I each time restrained myself. And I had the peculiar feeling that Gert Bekker wanted to ask the same question of me, but that something that was almost like fear was holding him back, also.

Round about midnight Mevrou Haasbroek's child was born. Of course, Gert Bekker and I asked to be allowed to see the baby. And, somehow, it seemed to me that the birth of a child in that house, a little while before, and the murder at the drift, long ago, were in that moment equally lonely and solemn things.

We heard voices in the bedroom, and few minutes later Rena van Dam came out, carrying the child wrapped in swaddling-clothes.

And this shows you what a strange thing the imagination is.

For when Gert Bekker spoke then, he uttered the very words that I wanted to say. And he brought up just that thing that I had been worrying about all night.

"That's like the child you had in your arms when I first saw you by the camp-fire," Gert Bekker exclaimed, "before I pulled the blankets over my head."

From her answer, it appeared to me that Rena van Dam had been a school-teacher in the Molopo area somewhat too long. It must be the influence of the neighbourhood that affected her, I decided. And I felt sad to think that an educated girl should suffer like that from self-delusions.

"When I got to the camp-fire," Rena van Dam said, "you were both of you already lying with your heads under the blankets. I saw the two of you by the light of the fire when I was still a long way off."

BUSH TELEGRAPH

Boom – boom – boom – *boom* – boom – boom – those kaffir drums (Oom Schalk Lourens said). There they go again. There must be a big beer drink being held in those Mtosa huts in the vlakte. Boom – *boom* – boom – boom. Yes, it sounds like a good party, all right.

Of course, that's about all the kaffirs use their drums for, these days – to summon the neighbours to a dance. But there was a time when the sound of the drums travelled from one end of Africa to the other.

In the old days the drum-men would receive and send messages that went from village to village and across thick bush and by deserts, and it made no difference what languages were spoken by the various tribes, either. The drum-men would know what a message meant, no matter where it came from.

The drum-man was taught his work from boyhood. And sometimes when a drum-man got a message to say that a cattle-raiding impi sent out by the chief was on its way back without cattle, and running quite fast – some of the fatter indunas throwing away their spears as they were running – then the chief would as likely as not be ungrateful about the message, and would have the drum-man taken around the corner and stoned, as though it was the drum-man's fault.

Afterwards, however, when we white men brought the telegraph up through these parts on the copper wires, there wasn't any more need for the kaffir drums.

I remember the last drum-man they had at the Mtosa huts outside Ramoutsa. His name was Mosigo. He was very old and his face was wrinkled. I often thought that those wrinkles looked like the kaffir footpaths that go twisting across the length and breadth of Africa, and that you can follow for mile after mile and day after day, and that never come to an end. And I would think how the messages that Mosigo received on his drum would come from somewhere along the furthest paths that the kaffirs followed across Africa, getting foot-sore on the way, and that were like the wrinkles on Mosigo's face.

"The drum is better than the copper wire that you white men bring up on long poles across the veld," Mosigo said to me on one occasion.

He was sitting in front of his hut and was tapping on his drum that went *boom* – boom – boom – boom – *boom* – boom. (Just like the way you hear that drum going down there in the vlakte, now.)

Far away it seemed as though other drums were taking up and repeating Mosigo's pattern of drum-sounds. Or it may be that what you heard, coming from the distant koppies, were only echoes.

"I don't need copper wires for my drum's messages," Mosigo went on. "Or long poles with rows of little white medicine bottles on them, either."

Now, this talk that I had with Mosigo took place very long ago. It happened soon after the first telegraph office was opened at Nietverdiend. And so when I went to Nietverdiend a few days later, it was natural that I should have mentioned to a few of my Bushveld neighbours at the post office what Mosigo had said.

I was not surprised to find that those farmers were in the main in agreement with Mosigo's remarks. Gysbert van Tonder said it was well known how ignorant the kaffirs were, but there were also some things that the kaffirs did have more understanding of than white men.

Then Gysbert van Tonder told us about the time when he had gone with his brother, 'Rooi', to hunt elephants far up into Portuguese territory. And wherever they went, he and his brother 'Rooi', the kaffirs knew beforehand of their coming, by means of the drums.

"I tried to get some of the drum-men to explain to me what the different sounds they made on the drums meant," Gysbert van Tonder said. "But that again shows you the really ignorant side of the kaffir. Those drum-men just couldn't get me to understand the first thing of what they were wanting to teach me. And it wasn't that they didn't try, mind you. Indeed, some of the drum-men were very patient about it. They would explain over and over again. But I just couldn't grasp it. They were so ignorant, I mean."

Gysbert van Tonder went on to say that afterwards, through having heard that same message tapped out so often, he grew to recognise the kind of taps that meant that his brother, 'Rooi', had killed an elephant. And then the day came when an elephant killed his brother, 'Rooi.' And Gysbert van Tonder listened carefully to the drums. And it was the same message as always, he said. Only, it was the other way around.

As I have told you, the telegraph had only recently come up as far as Nietverdiend. And because we had no newspaper here in those days, the telegraph-operator, who was a young fellow without much sense, had arranged with a friend in the Pretoria head office to send him short items of news which he pinned on the wall inside the post office.

"Look what it says there, now," Org Smit said, spelling out the words of one of the telegrams on the wall. "'President Kruger visits Johannesburg stop Miners' procession throws bottles stop.' Now, is there anything *in* that? And what's the idea of all those 'stops'?"

"Why, I remember the time when the only news we *had* was the sort the drum-men got over their drums," Johnny Welman said. "And it made sense, that sort of news. I am not ashamed to say that I brought up a family of six sons and three daughters on nothing else *but* that sort of news. And it was useful news to know. I can still remember the day when the message came over the drums about the three tax-collectors that had got eaten by crocodiles when their canoe capsized in the Limpopo. I don't mean that we were *glad* to hear that three tax-collectors had been eaten by crocodiles –"

And we all laughed and said, no, of course not.

Then Org Smit started spelling out another telegraph message pinned on the wall.

"'Fanatic shoots at King of Spain,'" he read. "'King unharmed stop. This enrages crowd which flings fanatic in royal fish-pond stop.'"

"What's the good of news like that to white farmers living in the Bushveld?" we asked of each other.

And when the telegraph-operator came from behind the counter to pin up another little bit of news we told him straight out what we thought. It was just a waste of money, we said, bringing the telegraph all that way up to Nietverdiend.

The telegraphist looked us up and down for a few moments in silence.

"Yes, I think it was a waste," he said, finally.

Boom – boom – boom – boom – boom – *boom*. Getting louder, do you notice? The whole village down there must be pretty drunk

394

by now. Of course, why we can hear it so clearly is because of the direction of the wind.

Anyway, there was that other time when I again went to Mosigo and I told him about the King of Spain. And Mosigo said to me that he did not think much of that kind of news, and that if that was the best the white man could do with his telegraph wires, then the white man still had a lot to learn. The telegraph people could come right down to his hut and learn. Even though he did not have a yellow rod – like they had shown him on the roof of the post office – to keep the lightning away, but only a piece of python skin, he said.

Although I did not myself have a high opinion of the telegraph, I was not altogether pleased that an old kaffir like Mosigo should speak lightly of an invention that came out of the white man's brain. And so I said that the telegraph was still quite a new thing and that it would no doubt improve in time. Perhaps how it would improve quite a lot would be if they sacked that young telegraph-operator at Nietverdiend for a start, I said.

That young telegraph-operator was too impertinent, I said.

Mosigo agreed that it would help. It was a very important thing, he said, that for such work you should have the right sort of person. And then Mosigo asked if I could not perhaps put in a word for him in Pretoria for the telegraph-operator's job. He would one day – soon, even – show me how good he really was. It was no good, he explained, having news told to you by a man who was not suited to that kind of work. And Mosigo spat contemptuously on the ground beside the drum. You could see, then, how much he resented the competition that the telegraph-operator at Nietverdiend was introducing. Much as he would resent the spectacular achievements of a rival drum-man, I suppose.

"Another thing that is important is having the right person to tell the news to," Mosigo went on. "And you must also consider well as to whom the news is about. Take that king, now, of whom you have told me, that you heard of at Nietverdiend through the telegraph. He is a great chief, that king, is he not?"

I said to Mosigo that I should imagine that he must be a great chief, the King of Spain. I couldn't know for sure, of course. You can't, really, with foreigners.

"Has he many herds of cattle and many wives hoeing in the bean-fields?" Mosigo asked. "Has he many huts and does he drink much beer and is his stomach very fat? Do you know him well, this great chief?"

I told Mosigo that I did not know the King of Spain to speak to, since I had never met him. But if I did meet him – if the King of Spain came to the Dwarsberge, say – I would go up to him and say I was Schalk Lourens and he would say he was the King of Spain, and we would shake hands and talk about the crops and the drought and the Government – and perhaps about the new telegraph, even. We would talk together like any two white men would talk, I said.

But Mosigo explained that that was not what he meant. "What is the good of hearing about a man," he asked, "unless you know who that man *is*? When the telegraph-operator told you about that big chief, he told it to the wrong man."

Mosigo fell to beating his drum again. Boom – boom – boom – *boom* – boom – *boom* it went. Just like that drum down there in the village. Sounds wild, in the night, doesn't it? And did you hear that other sound? That one there, that shrill sound? I expected something like it. Yes, that shrill sound is a police whistle.

Some time later I was again at Nietverdiend. On the wall of the post office there were some more messages that Org Smit spelt out for us. Org Smit was on his way to Zeerust by ox-wagon with a load of mealies.

"Fanatic fires at Shah of Persia" – Org Smit read – "stop Misses stop Infuriated crowd throws fanatic in royal horse-trough stop."

On the way back from Nietverdiend I again called round at Mosigo's hut. I started telling him about the message that Org Smit had read out, but Mosigo interrupted me. Boom – boom – boom – *boom*, Mosigo's drum was going . . . By the way, do you hear how loud those drums are beating in the village? And the police whistle has stopped. I mean, it stopped suddenly. I hope it isn't serious trouble . . .

"Baas Org Smit?" Mosigo said to me. "Baas Org Smit is dead. A wagon with mealies went over him."

I did not wait to hear more. I climbed back on to my mule-cart and drove away fast along the road I had come. When I was almost halfway back to Nietverdiend I could still hear Mosigo's drum throbbing.

I had travelled a good distance along the Zeerust road and it was late afternoon when I saw a wagon that I recognised as Org Smit's and that was loaded high with mealies. The wagon was proceeding slowly down the dusty road. I made haste to overtake it. I drew close enough to see the driver. He was sitting on the seat and brandishing his long whip. From the back I recognised the driver as Org Smit. When I was almost abreast of the wagon I shouted. In the moment of Org Smit's turning round on the seat his whip caught in one of the wheels.

When I saw Org Smit fall from the wagon, I turned my face away.

TRYST BY THE VAAL

"Three is no company."

It was the landdrost's man who spoke these words (Oom Schalk Lourens said). The landdrost's man made that comment when three people kept a tryst by the willows on the Vaal.

I was on my way to the town with a load of mealies, that time when the Vaal was in flood. It was not a big load, because of the stalk-borer. A short distance away Nicolaas Vermeulen was standing with his trek. His wagon had been outspanned there for several days. He, too, had been making his way to the dorp and had been held up by floodwaters. Nicolaas Vermeulen was on a visit to relatives and had brought his wife and family with him. Along with his family, Nicolaas Vermeulen had with him, on his wagon, Miemie Retief, who was about nineteen years of age. Miemie Retief was the daughter of a neighbour. She was supposed to be accompanying the Vermeulens to town also in order to visit relatives.

Still further away Gerrit Huyser was camped. He had arrived at the drift a little while before Nicolaas Vermeulen. He had a kaffir to help with the oxen. But otherwise he was travelling alone. Gerrit Huyser's farm was some distance further up along the Vaal River.

He was now camped on the same outspan with Nicolaas Vermeulen and myself, but had drawn his wagon up nearer the drift, so that when the river went down he would be the first to cross.

I learnt from Nicolaas Vermeulen and his wife that Gerrit Huyser was on his way to the diamond diggings. Well, the mealie crop had been a failure in most parts of the Transvaal that year, and Gerrit Huyser was not the only farmer from that area who had decided to try his luck on the diggings for a while. And because of what had happened with the mealies, I suppose that

398

more than one farmer, in turning up a diamond on the sorting table, would first look to see if there wasn't a stalk-borer in it.

What was singular about Gerrit Huyser's trek, however, was the kind of load he had on his wagon. It looked to be mostly household furniture. We could see that from where the bucksails did not fit properly.

One evening Nicolaas Vermeulen and his wife and I sat in front of their family tent after supper, drinking coffee.

Nicolaas Vermeulen's children played around the camp-fire while we talked and Miemie Retief, the daughter of their neighbour, sat on a riempies stool some distance from us. She had threaded a red ribbon into her black hair. And I was glad of it. Here on a lonely part of the veld, next to a river in flood, where there was nobody to see her – as you would think – she still wanted to appear at her best.

I regretted that I hadn't thought of wearing my new veldskoens.

After Nicolaas Vermeulen and I had, each in turn, said that it would probably take another two days for the river to go down enough for us to be able to cross, the conversation turned to Gerrit Huyser.

"It's not as though he has sold up," Nicolaas Vermeulen said, "and no farmer goes and stays on the diggings for more than a few months. When I first saw his wagon loaded up so high I thought it was with tree-trunks that he had fished out of the flooded river. I thought it was firewood –"

"If he's brought along that big tamboetie-wood cupboard in which his wife keeps those plates with the blue twigs painted on them," Nicolaas Vermeulen's wife, Martha, interrupted him, "then it might perhaps not be so foolish, after all. That's about all that cupboard is any good for – to light the fire with . . . The airs she gives herself over that piece of junk."

I mentioned that I had that very morning also seen Gerrit Huyser's rusbank on the wagon. I had seen it while I was talking to Gerrit Huyser, I explained, and a gust of wind had raised a corner of the wagon-sail. Later in the day I had seen him fasten down that flap with an ox-riem.

So we said that it looked as though Gerrit Huyser intended taking things in rather too easy a way on the diggings.

"I suppose he thinks he can sit back on that rusbank and watch the kaffirs work," Nicolaas Vermeulen said. "Just as though he's still at home on his farm."

We said that with all that furniture in his tent on the diggings, it looked as though Gerrit Huyser was expecting company. We started to wonder if he would have the coloured portrait of the president hanging on the inside of his tent, opposite his family tree in its gold frame – just like in his voorkamer at home.

It was then that Martha Vermeulen asked what Gerrit Huyser's wife would be doing all that time on the farm, alone and without any furniture in the house.

"Anyway," I said, "she'll find it easy to keep the place tidy."

I said this several times. But Nicolaas Vermeulen and his wife did not laugh. I looked quickly in the direction of Miemie Retief. The light from the fire made pictures on her cheeks and forehead.

That was the moment when Gerrit Huyser arrived in our midst. He came out of the veld, where a dark wind was, and he moved slowly and ponderously. For a moment he stood between us and the fire, his shoulders high against the night. Then he took off his hat in a way that seemed to hold in it a kind of challenge.

Nicolaas Vermeulen invited him to sit down. Gerrit Huyser found a place for himself that was furthest away from where Miemie Retief was seated.

We spoke first in general terms, and then I mentioned to Gerrit Huyser that he would find quite a number of farmers from our area on the diggings. There were Stoffel Lange and his cousin Maans and Oupa Snyman and almost all the Bekkers, not even to mention the farmers from the Kromberg section.

"Anyway, if they all come to visit you at the same time in your tent on the diggings," Nicolaas Vermeulen said, playfully, "you'll have chairs for them all."

I was surprised at the way Nicolaas Vermeulen was talking.

"And if you find a big diamond you'll be able to buy yourself a new span of red Afrikaner oxen, with their coats all shining," Nicolaas Vermeulen chuckled. "And you'll be able to get perhaps even a new wife."

I looked down at the ground and felt uncomfortable. When I glanced up again I could see that Martha Vermeulen had nudged her husband. She had nudged him almost off the upturned candle-box he was sitting on. The Vermeulens, at all events – I realised – had not brought many chairs with them.

I suddenly thought of looking at Miemie Retief. She was sitting with her head bent slightly forward and with her eyes cast on the ground, as mine had been. Then she raised her head again, and in the swift look that passed between herself and Gerrit Huyser I understood that it would have made no difference if I had thought of wearing my new veldskoens that evening.

The little party in front of the Vermeulens' tent broke up shortly afterwards.

But the things Nicolaas Vermeulen had to tell me next morning did not come as a surprise to me. He told me of Miemie Retief's meeting with Gerrit Huyser under the stars. He said that his wife, Martha, had watched those two from behind the flap of the tent.

"Miemie's coming with my wife and me was just a trick of hers to get away from home," Nicolaas Vermeulen said. "It is clear that she and Gerrit Huyser had an appointment to meet here by the Vaal. How it will all end, the good Lord only knows."

You can imagine for yourself the strain that was in the situation after that. When we were all five of us together, we spoke nervously about unimportant things. When I was with Nicolaas Vermeulen and his wife we spoke of Miemie Retief and Gerrit Huyser. But what Miemie Retief and Gerrit Huyser spoke about at those times when they were alone together, I suppose no one can tell.

Hour after hour we waited for the river to go down. But nobody scanned the floodwaters more anxiously than did Gerrit Huyser.

Nicolaas Vermeulen's wife said she was convinced that Gerrit Huyser would yet murder us all in our sleep. She was also sure that he had murdered his wife and had brought her along on the wagon, lying in that tall cupboard. Every murder story had a chest or something like that in it, for the body.

"And how she used to polish that cupboard with olieblaar," Martha Vermeulen added. "I can't bear to think of it. The poor thing – lying there, in amongst those plates with all the blue twigs painted on them."

I tried to comfort her by saying that Gerrit Huyser would at least have had the forethought to take the plates out first.

Martha Vermeulen's agitation had an unhappy effect on both Nicolaas and myself.

Meanwhile, it seemed to me that Gerrit Huyser's wagon wore a doomed look, somehow, with all that furniture piled on it. And it was at the wagon that Gerrit Huyser and Miemie Retief were standing when two men called on Gerrit Huyser. Even at a distance we could tell, from their official air, that the visitors were landdrost's men. Gerrit did not take some chairs down from the wagon for his guests to sit on.

And, as always seems to happen in such cases, it was at about that time, also, that the third person in this affair arrived. She came there, to the trysting place, under the willows by the Vaal, where wild birds sang.

The landdrost's men lifted her out of the water and loosened the ox-riems that had bound her feet over the long distance that the flooded river had carried her. And it was after they had laid the body of Gerrit Huyser's wife in the tall tamboetie cupboard that one of the landdrost's men made the remark that, earlier on, I told you of. – "Three," the landdrost's man said, "is no company."

THE SELON'S ROSE

A ny story (Oom Schalk Lourens said) about that half-red flower, the selon's rose, must be an old story. It is the flower that a Marico girl most often pins in her hair to attract a lover. The selon's rose is also the flower that here, in the Marico, we customarily plant upon a grave.

One thing that certain thoughtless people sometimes hint at about my stories is that nothing ever seems to happen in them. Then there is another kind of person who goes even further, and *he* says that the stories I tell are all stories that he has heard before, somewhere, long ago – he can't remember when, exactly, but somewhere at the back of his mind he knows that it is not a new story.

I have heard that remark passed quite often – which is not surprising, seeing that I really don't know any new stories. But the funny part of it is that these very people will come around, say, ten years later, and ask me to tell them another story. And they will say, then, because of what they have learnt of life in between, that the older the better.

Anyway, I have come to the conclusion that with an old story it is like with an old song. People tire of a new song readily. I remember how it was when Marie Dupreez came back to the Bushveld after her parents had sent her overseas to learn singing, because they had found diamonds on their farm, and because Marie's teacher said she had a nice singing voice. Then, when Marie came back from Europe – through the diamonds on the Dupreez farm having given out suddenly – we on this side of the Dwarsberge were keen to have Marie sing for us.

There was a large attendance, that night, when Marie Dupreez gave a concert in the Drogedal schoolroom. She sang what she called arias from Italian opera. And at first things didn't go at all well. We didn't care much for those new songs in Italian. One song was about the dawn being near, goodbye beloved and about being under somebody's window – that was what Marie's mother told us it was.

Marie Dupreez's mother came from the Cape and had studied at the Wellington seminary. Another song was about mother see these tears. The Hollander schoolmaster told me the meaning of that one. But I didn't know if it was Marie's mother that was meant.

We didn't actually dislike those songs that Marie Dupreez sang. It was only that we weren't moved by them.

Accordingly, after the interval, when Marie was again stepping up on to the low platform before the blackboard on which the teacher wrote sums on school days, Philippus Bonthuys, a farmer who had come all the way from Nietverdiend to attend the concert, got up and stood beside Marie Dupreez. And because he was so tall and broad it seemed almost as though he stood half in front of her, elbowing her a little, even.

Philippus Bonthuys said that he was just a plain Dopper. And we all cheered. Then Philippus Bonthuys said that his grandfather was also just a plain Dopper, who wore his pipe and his tobacco-bag on a piece of string fastened at the side of his trousers. We cheered a lot more, then. Philippus Bonthuys went on to say that he liked the old songs best. They could keep those new songs about laugh because somebody has stolen your clown. We gathered from this that Marie's mother had been explaining to Philippus Bonthuys, also, in quick whispers, the meanings of some of Marie's songs.

And before we knew where we were, the whole crowd in the schoolroom was singing, with Philippus Bonthuys beating time, "My Oupa was 'n Dopper, en 'n Dopper was Hy." You've got no idea how stirring that old song sounded, with Philippus Bonthuys beating time, in the night, under the thatch of that Marico schoolroom, and with Marie Dupreez looking slightly bewildered but joining in all the same – since it was her concert, after all – and not singing in Italian, either.

We sang many songs, after that, and they were all old songs. We sang "Die Vaal Hare en die Blou Oge" and "Daar Waar die

Son en die Maan Ondergaan" and "Vat Jou Goed en Trek, Ferreira" and "Met My Rooi Rok Voor Jou Deur." It was very beautiful.

We sang until late into the night. Afterwards, when we congratulated Marie Dupreez's mother, who had arranged it all, on the success of her daughter's concert, Mevrou Dupreez said it was nothing, and she smiled. But it was a peculiar sort of smile.

I felt that she must have smiled very much the same way when she was informed that the diamond mine on the Dupreez farm was only an alluvial gravel-bed, and not a pipe, like in Kimberley.

Now, Marie Dupreez had not been out of the Marico very long. All told, I don't suppose she had been in Europe for more than six months before the last shovelful of diamondiferous gravel went through Dupreez's sieve. By the time she got back, her father was so desperate that he was even trying to sift ordinary Transvaal red clay. But Marie's visit overseas had made her restive.

That, of course, is something that I can't understand. I have also been to foreign parts. During the Boer War I was a prisoner on St. Helena. And I was twice in Johannesburg. And one thing about St. Helena is that there were no Uitlanders on it. There were just Boers and English and Coloureds and Indians, like you come across here in the Marico. There were none of those all-sorts that you've got to push past on Johannesburg pavements. And each time I got back to my own farm, and I could sit on my stoep and fill my pipe with honest Magaliesberg tobacco, I was pleased to think I was away from all that sin that you read about in the Bible.

But with Marie Dupreez it was different.

Marie Dupreez, after she came back from Europe, spoke a great deal about how unhappy a person with a sensitive nature could be over certain aspects of life in the Marico.

We were not unwilling to agree with her.

"When I woke up that morning at Nietverdiend," Willie Prinsloo said to Marie during a party at the Dupreez homestead, "and I found that I couldn't inspan my oxen because during the night the Mlapi kaffirs had stolen my trek-chain – well, to a person with a sensitive nature, I can't tell you how unhappy I felt about the Marico."

Marie said that was the sort of thing that made her ill, almost.

"It's always the same kind of conversation that you have to listen to, day in and day out," Marie Dupreez said. "A farmer out-spans his oxen for the night. And next morning, when he has to move on, the kaffirs have stolen his trek-chain. I don't know how often I have heard that same story. Why can't something different ever happen? Why can't a kaffir think of stealing something else, for a change?"

"Yes," Jurie Bekker interjected, quickly, "why can't they steal a clown, say?"

Thereupon Marie explained that it was not a clown that had got stolen in that Italian song that she sang in the schoolroom, but a girl who had belonged to a clown. And so several of us said, speaking at the same time, that she couldn't have been much of a girl, anyway, belonging to a clown. We said we might be behind the times and so forth, here in the Bushveld, but we had seen clowns in the circus in Zeerust, and we could imagine what a clown's girl must be like, with her nose painted all red.

I must admit, however, that we men enjoyed Marie's wild talk. We preferred it to her singing, anyway. And the women also listened quite indulgently.

Shortly afterwards Marie Dupreez made a remark that hurt me, a little.

"People here in the Marico say all the same things over and over again," Marie announced. "Nobody ever says anything new. You all talk just like the people in Oom Schalk Lourens's stories. Whenever we have visitors it's always the same thing. If it's a husband and wife, it will be the man who first starts talking. And he'll say that his Afrikaner cattle are in a bad way with the heart-water. Even though he drives his cattle straight out on to the veld with the first frost, and he keeps to regular seven-day dipping, he just can't get rid of the heart-water ticks."

Marie Dupreez paused. None of us said anything, at first. I only know that for myself I thought this much: I thought that, even though I dip my cattle only when the Government inspector from Onderstepoort is in the neighbourhood, I still lose just as many Afrikaner beasts from the heart-water as any of the farmers hereabouts who go in for the seven-day dipping.

"They should dip the Onderstepoort inspector every seven

days," Jurie Bekker called out suddenly, expressing all our feelings.

"And they should drive the Onderstepoort inspector straight out on to the veld first with the first frost," Willie Prinsloo added.

We got pretty worked up, I can tell you.

"And it's the same with the women," Marie Dupreez went on. "Do they ever discuss books or fashion or music? No. They also talk just like those simple Boer women that Oom Schalk Lourens's head is so full of. They talk about the amount of Kalahari sand that the Indian in the store at Ramoutsa mixed with the last bag of yellow sugar they bought off him. You know, I have heard that same thing so often, I am surprised that there is any sand at all left in the Kalahari desert, the way that Indian uses it all up."

Those of us who were in the Dupreez voorkamer that evening, in spite of our amusement, also felt sad at the thought of how Marie Dupreez had altered from her natural self, like a seedling that has been transplanted too often in different kinds of soil.

But we felt that Marie should not be blamed too much. For one thing, her mother had been taught at that women's college at the Cape. And her father had also got his native knowledge of the soil pretty mixed up, in his own way. It was said that he was by now even trying to find diamonds in the turfgrond on his farm. I could just imagine how *that* must be clogging up his sieves.

"One thing I am glad about, though," Marie said after a pause, "is that since my return from Europe I have not yet come across a Marico girl who wears a selon's rose in her hair to make herself look more attractive to a young man – as happens time after time in Oom Schalk's stories."

This remark of Marie's gave a new turn to the conversation, and I felt relieved. For a moment I had feared that Marie Dupreez was also becoming addicted to the kind of Bushveld conversation that she complained about, and that she, too, was beginning to say the same thing over and over again.

Several women started talking, after that, about how hard it was to get flowers to grow in the Marico, on account of the prolonged droughts. The most they could hope for was to keep a bush of selon's roses alive near the kitchen door. It was a flower that seemed, if anything, to thrive on harsh sunlight and soapy dishwater and Marico earth, the women said.

Some time later we learnt that Theunis Dupreez, Marie's father, was giving up active farming, because of his rheumatics. We said, of course, that we knew how he had got his rheumatics. Through having spent so much time in all kinds of weather, we said, walking about the vlei in search of a new kind of sticky soil to put through his sieves.

Consequently, Theunis Dupreez engaged a young fellow, Joachem Bonthuys, to come and work on his farm as a bywoner. Joachem was a nephew of Philippus Bonthuys, and I was at the post office when he arrived at Drogedal, on the lorry from Zeerust, with Theunis Dupreez and his daughter, Marie, there to meet him.

Joachem Bonthuys's appearance was not very prepossessing, I thought. He shook hands somewhat awkwardly with the farmers who had come to meet the lorry to collect their milk-cans. Joachem did not seem to have much to say for himself, either, until Theunis Dupreez, his new employer, asked him what his journey up from Zeerust had been like.

"The veld is dry all the way," he replied. "And I've never seen so much heart-water in Afrikaner herds. They should dip their cattle every seven days."

Joachem Bonthuys spoke at great length, then, and I could not help smiling to myself when I saw Marie Dupreez turn away. In that moment my feelings also grew warmer towards Joachem. I felt that, at all events, he was not the kind of young man who would go and sing foreign songs under a respectable Boer girl's window.

All this brings me back to what I was saying about an old song and an old story. For it was quite a while before I again had occasion to visit the Dupreez farm. And when I sat smoking on the stoep with Theunis Dupreez it was just like an old story to hear him talk about his rheumatics.

Marie came out on to the stoep with a tray to bring us our coffee. – Yes, you've heard all that before, the same sort of thing. The same stoep. The same tray. – And for that reason, when she held the glass bowl out towards me, Marie Dupreez apologised for the yellow sugar.

"It's full of Kalahari sand, Oom Schalk," she said. "It's that Indian at Ramoutsa."

And when she turned to go back into the kitchen, leaving the two old men to their stories, it was not difficult for me to guess who the young man was for whom she was wearing a selon's rose pinned in her dark hair.

BOSMAN'S ILLUSTRATORS

ABE BERRY (1911–1992) was a distinguished cartoonist and a life-long friend of Herman Charles Bosman. A staunch opponent of the National Party regime, he did many satirical cartoons of prominent members of the party, but also found time to depict life in South Africa's rural areas, and often undertook considerable research before attempting to draw cartoons that had a strong historical resonance. His 'Canterberry Tales' (after Chaucer) and 'Berry Tapestry' (after the Bayeux Tapestry) illustrations are examples of this. Some of his satirical cartoons were collected in *Abe Berry's South Africa and How It Works* (1980). A skilled watercolourist, his drawings and paintings of 'old Johannesburg' appeared in *Abe Berry's Johannesburg* (1982). He also has the distinction of having been featured in *Punch* magazine no fewer than ten times. His illustrations of Bosman's stories appeared in *On Parade* (1948–1951) and *Trek* (1949), and one of his cartoons of Bosman addressing a riotous meeting on the City Hall steps has been preserved.

WILFRID L. W. CROSS emerged as a political cartoonist in the late 1930s. Having trained as a civil engineer and architectural draughtsman, he moved into the world of commercial art and broadcasting. He worked chiefly for *The Rand Daily Mail* and later for *The Forum*. When Bosman returned from London in 1940 the two both contributed to *The Forum*, and also worked together on *The Sunday Express* – Bosman as a chief sub and Cross as the paper's weekly political cartoonist. He is the most prolific illustrator of Bosman's Oom Schalk Lourens stories, contributing a dozen works to *The South African Opinion* between 1935 and 1945. His iconic, cubist-influenced image of two men sitting around a camp-fire on the veld (for "Starlight on the Veld", *The South*

African Opinion, January 1946) was to feature on the dust-jacket of the first edition of *Mafeking Road* in 1947. Of his work Bosman wrote in one of his art criticism columns: "He is charged with individuality, with the underlying bitterness of one who, clutching at a star, has found in the end fantasy."

DONALD HARRIS (b. 1924) studied art during World War Two at the Witwatersrand Technical College under Van Essche, where he met Ella Manson, Bosman's second wife. After Bosman divorced Ella in 1944, Harris married her, and she became Harris's chief artistic subject for the short period that the two were together. After Ella's sudden death in 1945, Harris held an exhibition in Johannesburg at the Gallerie des Beaux Arts devoted almost entirely to drawings and paintings of her. Some years later, Harris remarried and left for Madeira. He illustrated the reprinted version of Bosman's famous "Mafeking Road" for the December 1944 issue of *The South African Opinion*, and provided two pen-and-ink drawings for "The Wind in the Tree" (*The South African Opinion*, January 1945). Bosman wrote in a review column of a Harris show at Herman Wald's studio in March 1946, "I am fairly certain that Mr Harris does his best work only when he retains and not when he suppresses his sense of humour."

JOHN HALKETT JACKSON (1919–1981) grew up near Naboomspruit in the former Northern Transvaal and began drawing scenes on his parents' farm at an early age. He had no formal education, but demonstrated his artistic talent very early on, his political cartoons first appearing in the late 1930s. He served in North and East Africa during World War Two, providing humorous sketches of army life for *The Nongqai*. From 1945 he worked as a freelance artist, mainly for *The Outspan*, *Lantern*, *Spotlight* and *Personality*, the last of which featured his illustrations of some of Bosman's posthumously published stories in the late 1960s.

ALBERT EDWARD MASON (1895–1950) was born in Britain and trained as an artist at St. Martin's Lane Academy and Birkbeck College, University of London. Apart from a period of service during the First World War in France, he lived in South Africa from 1914 onwards. He spent time on the diamond diggings in Kimberley between 1918 and 1920, but thereafter resided in Johannesburg. A retiring person by nature, he was chiefly a portrait and landscape painter, but also painted oils of Johannesburg's mining activities in the 1930s and 40s. He was appointed to the staff of the newly established Witwatersrand Technical School of Art, where he taught Commercial Art and Poster design. His work was exhibited as part of the Royal Academy Summer Exhibitions in London both in 1939 and 1948. He provided striking illustrations of "The Rooinek", which was originally published in two parts in *The Touleier* (January–February and March 1931). When he exhibited at Bothner's Gallery in Johannesburg in 1945, Bosman wrote of him that "there is a lot about his work that entitles him to be regarded as one of the great painters of his time."

RENÉ SHAPSHAK (1899–1988) was born in France and trained at the École des Beaux Arts in Paris. He came to South Africa in the mid-1930s and was one of the founding members of the Transvaal Art Society. A well-known decorator, he is remembered primarily for his sculptures that were designed to give the mid-century SABC building in Commissioner Street, Johannesburg, its progressive art deco look. He was considered as one of the alternative artists to those sanctioned by the South African Association of Arts, together with other contributors to the post-war *South African Opinion*, on which he was a regular. He illustrated "Concertinas and Confetti" for the April 1944 issue of *The South African Opinion*. In the 1940s and early 50s he provided training to a number of emerging black artists at his home in Yeoville, Johannesburg. In 1953, with South Africa's political situation worsening, he left the country for New York.

RICHARD JOHN TEMPLETON SMITH (b. 1947) was something of a teenage prodigy, his sharp-edged satirical caricatures first appearing in 1966. Born in Scotland, he came to South Africa with his parents in 1958, and was educated at Queen's College and Witwatersrand Technical College, where his cartoons appeared in the student publication *Wits-Wits*. He did freelance work in the late 1960s for *The Sunday Express* and *The Star*, before moving to

London in 1970. Returning to South Africa in 1972, he produced cartoons for *The Rand Daily Mail, The Sunday Tribune, The Financial Mail* and *The Sunday Express,* where his illustrations for a series of republished Bosman stories appeared in 1979.

REGINALD TURVEY (1882–1968) was born on a farm in Ladybrand near the border of Lesotho (then Basutoland), the descendent of an original 1820 settler. His schooling at Grey College in Bloemfontein was interrupted when he was sent to London for art training in 1903, where he attended the Slade School of Art. He excelled early on at portrait painting, but also did striking landscapes in oils. After a short trip to Japan, he returned to South Africa in 1910 to work on the family farm. When his father died, Turvey went back to England, settling in St. Ives in 1917, where he worked successfully as an artist for the next twenty-three years. He joined the Bahá'í faith in 1935, a belief that he was to hold to (and that influenced his art) for the rest of his life. In 1940 he left war-time England once more for South Africa, where he exhibited and sold his work, his reputation as an artist growing steadily with the passing years. When he exhibited at the Constantia Gallery in 1947 Bosman commented that the "aspect of his work that interests me very strongly at the moment is related to his incursions into a fascinating world of his own, that is midway between fantasy and reality." His numerous illustrations of Bosman's stories appeared in *The South African Opinion* in 1946, and a posthumous selection of his work, entitled *Life and Art,* was published in 1986.

MAURICE VAN ESSCHE (1906–1977) was born in Antwerp and trained under Henri Matisse. He lived in South Africa from 1940 to 1971. He was a versatile painter of portraits, landscapes and still lifes, working in oil, gouache and watercolour. He lectured at the Witwatersrand Technical College between 1943 and 1945, where he occasionally employed Bosman's second wife, Ella Manson, as a model, and in this way came to know of her husband's work. He also taught at the Michaelis School of Fine Arts (University of Cape Town) between 1964 and 1970. From 1971 until his death he lived in Thonon, on Lake Geneva, France. His illustration of one of Bosman's most famous stories, "In the Withaak's Shade", appeared in *The South African Opinion* in March 1945. He also illustrated "Camp-fires at Nagmaal" (*The South African Opinion*, June 1945), "Brown Mamba" (*The South African Opinion*, August 1945) and some of Bosman's poetry. When Van Essche exhibited at Gerrit Bakker's Constantia Gallery, Bosman enthused that he was "in a class considerably above the general run of painters who hold exhibitions."

HENRY EDWARD WINDER (1897–1982) was born in London. He served in the Home Counties Brigades in the First World War, but was badly wounded in 1916 and spent nearly three years in hospital. He later attended the Slade School of Art before moving to South Africa in 1920, where he worked on *The Rand Daily Mail* and *The Sunday Times*. In the 1930s he freelanced for *The Outspan*, *The Nongqai* and *The Tatler*. It was at this time that he was approached by Bosman and Jean Blignaut (co-editors of the newly launched *The Touleier*) to provide illustrations for their literary monthly. He duly provided a striking cover for the first issue, and also has the distinction of illustrating Bosman's first Oom Schalk Lourens story, "Makapan's Caves", for the same issue of the magazine (December 1930). He went on to have a long and distinguished career, which included being commissioned to do anatomical drawings for Professor Raymond Dart, the famous anatomist and paleontologist based at the University of the Witwatersrand.

415

NOTES ON THE STORIES

1. The *Touleier* Years (1930–31)

When Bosman emerged from prison in September 1930 he recuperated for a month on his uncle's farm at Bronkhorstspruit, east of Pretoria. Thereafter he moved back to Johannesburg, where he teamed up with John Webb and Aegidius Jean Blignaut to launch the monthly literary journal *The Touleier*. The first three issues of the periodical (December 1930, January–February 1931 and March 1931) contained Bosman's first two Schalk Lourens stories, "Makapan's Caves" and "The Rooinek" (in two instalments). Grandly conceived as a successor to the famous Campbell–Plomer–Van der Post *Voorslag* of 1926, *The Touleier* was very much a showcase for Bosman's burgeoning talent, and the first issue also contained reviews and a poem by him. After just five numbers, however, the periodical sank under the weight of its overheads and debts, but not before it had published another Oom Schalk classic, "The Gramophone" (in May 1931). Webb attempted to resuscitate the venture under the name *The African Magazine*, which duly carried Bosman's "Karel Flysman" in its first and only number (in June 1931). In between *The Touleier* and *The African Magazine*, Bosman and Blignaut seized the opportunity occasioned by the demise of Stephen Black's *The Sjambok* (and shortly thereafter of the man himself) to launch their *New L. S. D.* ('Life, Sport and Drama'), named after another ill-fated Black periodical of 1913–14. *The New L. S. D.* carried two little-known Schalk Lourens stories, "Francina Malherbe" and "The Ramoutsa Road", as well as the very sketchy "Veld Fire", omitted here as it is not certain that Oom Schalk is the narrator.

2. London Stories – *The South African Opinion* (1934–37)

The Bosman–Blignaut partnership regularly landed the pair in gaol, and in early 1934, in what was clearly a bold attempt to break with his past and his gaolbird cronies, Bosman left South Africa for London with his second wife, Ella Manson. In November of that year, Bosman's old school-friend Bernard Sachs launched *The South African Opinion*, a periodical professedly 'non-political', but clearly Left-leaning in orientation. It was to provide Bosman with perhaps his finest creative platform. With the sharpness of vision that distance brings, tinged with rich nostalgia for the country he left behind, Bosman was to write his best-known Oom Schalks at a rate of more than one every two months between December 1934 and July 1937. Indeed, the first fourteen, from "Veld Maiden" to "Starlight on the Veld", were produced on a monthly basis – a spurt of creativity not to be matched until 1950–51, when Bosman wrote his weekly 'Voorkamer' pieces for *The Forum*.

3. Back Home – *The South African Opinion* (new series) (1944–46)

By late 1939, with war having been declared in Europe and down on their luck, the Bosmans took advantage of an offer by the South African High Commissioner in London to repatriate them to South Africa. They were back in January 1940, and Bosman returned to the world of journalism, eventually taking up the editorship of the Pietersburg-based *Zoutpansberg Review and Mining Journal* in March 1943. The period between July 1937, when "On to Freedom" appeared, and March 1944, when the revived *South African Opinion* started reappearing as a monthly (and in which the signature-piece "Starlight on the Veld" was reprinted), was a particularly lean period for Oom Schalk stories. The only one to appear was "Martha and the Snake", which was printed (probably without Bosman's knowledge) in October 1939 in another of Jean Blignaut's ephemeral ventures, *The Ringhals* (again borrowed from a short-lived Stephen Black periodical of the same name of early 1931). After what was an effective seven-year silence, the new *S. A. Opinion* provided Bosman with a welcome opportunity to reacquaint post-war South Africa with his master storyteller. He reprinted ten of the earlier Oom Schalks here, but this was no mere act of 'recycling', as several of them were significantly edited down by Bosman himself before being deemed fit for publication. Interspersed with these republished pieces were seven new ones, including the powerful anti-racist statement "The Prophet" (significant, given the pro-Nazi sentiments of many Afrikaners during and immediately after the war) and the subtle masterpiece "Seed-time and Harvest."

4. The *Trek* and *On Parade* Years (1948–51)

Following a disastrous six-month business venture in Cape Town, in which he was contracted to translate literary classics into Afrikaans and then find a market for them, Bosman and third wife Helena returned to Johannesburg penniless. Bernard Sachs had amalgamated the now-defunct *S. A. Opinion* with *Trek* (formerly the Cape Town-based *Independent*), which also shifted its operations to Johannesburg, and he invited Bosman to join him. *Trek* was a monthly review that had attracted some notable Leftist intellectuals to its pages, including Dora Taylor, Eddie Roux and Jack Cope. Lily Rabkin, who would become a staunch supporter of Bosman's work, joined the team as assistant editor on cultural matters. Along with several 'Talk of the Town' columns that he contributed over the years, Bosman provided five new Oom Schalk stories, among them "Dopper and Papist" (which originally appeared in *Trek* under the mystifying title "Dopper and Baptist"), and perhaps his most famous story, "Unto Dust."

On Parade was a different sort of venture, although it also had as its purpose the unification of what was becoming, after 1948 with the National Party victory, a society increasingly divided along ethnic and, of course, language lines. Former school-teacher and non-conformist freelance contributor to the press over the years, Ehrhardt Planjé, after two earlier failed efforts in this vein, launched the bilingual *On Parade / Op Parade* in August 1948, with "Graven Image" prominently featured (it was to be re-used by Planjé after Bosman's death). Four other Oom Schalks would follow, including the Boer War classic "Peaches Ripening in the Sun", the penultimate Oom Schalk to appear in Bosman's lifetime. As an independent fortnightly paper launched at a fateful time in South African history, *On Parade* aimed to promote goodwill and understanding among all sectors of South African society and to combat racism. With the sturdy support of the Afrikaans-speaking Helena, Bosman was to publish several Afrikaans Oom Schalks in *On Parade*, including "Tot Stof" (which first appeared in Afrikaans in 1948, significantly) and "Die Storie van die Rooibaadjie" (published only posthumously in English).

5. Last Stories (1948–51)

The 1948–51 period saw Bosman placing stories in a variety of publications, as the occasion arose. The three Oom Schalks that *The Forum* carried in late 1949 and early 1950, however, were perhaps more purposefully placed: they were Bosman's entrée to his 'In die Voorkamer' sequence, which ran to eighty items in *The Forum* between April 1950 and October 1951. This liberal-Left weekly, which would go on to support the new Liberal Party (formed in 1953), attempted to articulate a broad, inclusive 'South Africanism.' It had J. H. Hofmeyr (nephew of the famous 'Onze Jan' Hofmeyr) as chair of its board of directors, J. P. (John) Cope as editor, and Lily Rabkin, who had defected from the faltering *Trek*, in charge of the cultural pages.

In June 1950, the secretary of the University of the Witwatersrand's Council of Cultural Committees asked Bosman to provide a story of around 3 600 words – adding, however, that the Council wasn't able to pay him. Bosman nonetheless provided one of his most memorable Oom Schalks, "Funeral Earth", for *Vista* and was duly paid in the form of two complimentary tickets for the university Arts Festival film evening.

The Cape Town-based large-format pictorial magazine *Spotlight* had earlier honoured Bosman by reprinting his "The

Rooinek" in December 1946. It now took up two sterling late Oom Schalks in January and February 1951 – "The Missionary" and "The Traitor's Wife" – with Bosman pleased to remark in his contributor's note to the January edition that his stories were being broadcast by the BBC, no less.

6. Unpublished in His Lifetime

Although all of these stories had to wait some years before finally being published in English, it is significant that Bosman managed to see five of the seven into press in Afrikaans versions: "Dit Spook by die Drif" (April 1948); "Die Kaffer-tamboer" ("Bush Telegraph", February 1949); "Ontmoetingsplek aan die Vaal" (May 1949); "Ou Liedjies en Ou Stories" ("The Selon's Rose", September 1949); and "Die Storie van die Rooibaadjie" (February 1950). These were among the total of sixteen Afrikaans stories Bosman published in his lifetime, all but one of them in *On Parade* between August 1948 and February 1950.

Bosman probably allowed the English versions included here to languish because during 1948–51 he consciously set out to establish himself as a bilingual writer. His renown in the English language was well established, but his stature as an Afrikaans writer was just beginning to emerge and was what clearly preoccupied him in this period.

The English versions were to lie unpublished in the Harry Ransom Humanities Research Center at the University of Texas at Austin – in some cases for decades. In 1969 *Personality* published a set of six previously unpublished Bosman stories, one of them the Oom Schalk story "The Question." The others appeared in later posthumous collections of Bosman's work, four of them ("The Old Potchefstroom Gaol", "The Ghost at the Drift", "Bush Telegraph", and "Tryst by the Vaal") seeing print for the first time only in 2001 and 2002, in the Anniversary Edition of Bosman's works. It is likely that Bosman wanted to polish them a little more before releasing them for publication, but his premature death prevented this.

420

Sources of the texts and illustrations

The following were used as source texts, with later versions being followed (where applicable). Details about the illustrations are provided at the end of each entry; in some cases the original artists have proved untraceable.

1. "Makapan's Caves." *The Touleier* 1.1 (Dec 1930): 15–20. (Illustrator: H. E. Winder, 19.)
2. "The Rooinek" (Parts 1 and 2). *The Touleier* 1.2 (Jan–Feb 1931): 8–13; and 1.3 (Mar 1931): 126–32. (Illustrator: A. E. Mason, *The Touleier* 1.2 (Jan–Feb 1931): 8–9, 11; second illustration repeated *The Touleier* 1.3 (Mar 1931): 126.)
3. "Francina Malherbe." *The New LSD* 1.6 (1 May 1931): 5. (Illustrator: unknown, *The Sunday Express* 17 May 1979: 25.)
4. "The Ramoutsa Road." *The New LSD* 1.8 (16 May 1931): 11–12. (Illustrator: Richard Smith, *The Sunday Express* 9 Sept 1979: 8.)
5. "The Gramophone." *The Touleier* 1.5 (May 1931): 310–13.
6. "Karel Flysman." *The African Magazine* 1.1 (June 1931): 379–81. (Illustrator: Richard Smith, *The Sunday Express* 3 June 1979: 5.)
7. "Veld Maiden." *The South African Opinion* (*SAO*) 1.4 (14 Dec 1934): 9–10.
8. "Yellow Moepels." *SAO* 1.7 (25 Jan 1935): 7–8; reprinted *SAO* 2.2 (Apr 1945): 14–15.
9. "The Love Potion." *SAO* 1.9 (22 Feb 1935): 8–9.
10. "In the Withaak's Shade." *SAO* 1.11 (22 Mar 1935): 4–5; reprinted *SAO* 2.1 (Mar 1945): 18–19, 30. (Illustrator: Maurice van Essche, *SAO* 2.1 (Mar 1945): 19.)
11. "The Widow." *SAO* 1.13 (19 Apr 1935): 10–11; reprinted *SAO* 3.7 (Sept 1946): 14–15, 20. (Illustrator: Reginald Turvey, *SAO* 3.7 (Sept 1946): 15.)
12. "Willem Prinsloo's Peach Brandy." *SAO* 1.15 (17 May 1935): 5–6.
13. "Ox-wagons on Trek." *SAO* 1.16 (31 May 1935): 6–7; reprinted *SAO* 2.12 (Feb 1946): 20–21, 30. (Illustrator: Reginald Turvey, *SAO* 2.12 (Feb 1946): 21.)

14. "The Music Maker." *SAO* 1.20 (26 July 1935): 6–7; reprinted *SAO* 2.7 (Sept 1945): 18–19.
15. "Drieka and the Moon." *SAO* 1.21 (9 Aug 1935): 8–9; reprinted *SAO* 3.2 (Apr 1946): 18–19, 21. (Illustrator: Reginald Turvey, *SAO* 3.2 (Apr 1946): 19.)
16. "The Mafeking Road." *SAO* 1.22 (23 Aug 1935): 6–7; reprinted *SAO* 1.10 (Dec 1944): 12–13, 28. (Illustrators: 'R. L.', *SAO* 1.22 (23 Aug 1935): 7; Donald Harris, *SAO* 1.10 (Dec 1944): 13.)
17. "Marico Scandal." *SAO* 1.25 (4 Oct 1935): 8–10; reprinted *SAO* 1.7 (Sept 1944): 18–19. (Illustrator: Wilfrid Cross, *SAO* 1.25 (4 Oct 1935): 8, 9; first illustration repeated *SAO* 1.7 (Sept 1944): 19.)
18. "Bechuana Interlude." *SAO* 1.26 (18 Oct 1935): 11–13. (Illustrator: Wilfrid Cross, 11, 12.)
19. "Visitors to Platrand." *SAO* 2.1 (1 Nov 1935): 10–12. (Illustrator: Wilfrid Cross, 10, 11.)
20. "Starlight on the Veld." *SAO* 2.6 (10 Jan 1936): 9–11; reprinted *SAO* 1.1 (Mar 1944): 20–21, 31. (Illustrator: Wilfrid Cross, *SAO* 2.6 (10 Jan 1936): 9, 10; repeated *SAO* 1.1 (Mar 1944): 21.)
21. "Marico Moon." *SAO* 3.3 (28 Nov 1936): 13–14, as "Thorn Trees in the Wind"; reprinted *Trek* 13.4 (Apr 1949): 14–15.
22. "Splendours from Ramoutsa." *SAO* 3.9 (20 Feb 1937): 9–10.
23. "Bushveld Romance." *SAO* 3.13 (17 Apr 1937): 9–10. (Illustrator: Richard Smith, *The Sunday Express* 24 June 1979: 8.)
24. "Dream by the Bluegums." *SAO* 3.18 (26 June 1937): 12–13.
25. "On to Freedom." *SAO* 3.20 (24 July 1937): 8–9. (Illustrator: Richard Smith, *The Sunday Express* 6 May 1979: 24.)
26. "Martha and the Snake." *The Ringhals* 3.3 (13 Oct 1939): 8–9. (Illustrator: Richard Smith, *The Sunday Express* 1 July 1979: 11.)
27. "Concertinas and Confetti." *SAO* 1.2 (Apr 1944): 20–21, 32. (Illustrator: René Shapshak, 21.)
28. "The Story of Hester van Wyk." *SAO* 1.4 (June 1944): 9–11. (Illustrator: Wilfrid Cross, 10.)
29. "The Wind in the Tree." *SAO* 1.11 (Jan 1945): 18–19, 28. (Illustrator: Donald Harris, 18, 19.)
30. "Camp-fires at Nagmaal." *SAO* 2.4 (June 1945): 14–15, 31. (Illustrator: Maurice van Essche, 15.)
31. "The Prophet." *SAO* 2.10 (Dec 1945): 10–11, 31. (Illustrator: Wilfrid Cross, 11.)

32. "Mampoer." *SAO* 2.11 (Jan 1946): 14–15, 27. (Illustrator: Reginald Turvey, 15.)
33. "Seed-time and Harvest." *SAO* 3.10 (Dec 1946): 18–19, 27; reprinted *On Parade* (1 Oct 1948): 8. (Illustrators: Reginald Turvey, *SAO* 3.10 (Dec 1946): 19; Abe Berry, *On Parade* (1 Oct 1948).)
34. "Dopper and Papist." *Trek* 12.3 (Mar 1948): 22–23, 31.
35. "Cometh Comet." *Trek* 12.6 (June 1948): 16–17. (Illustrator: unknown, 17.)
36. "Great-uncle Joris." *Trek* 12.10 (Dec 1948): 14–15, 29. (Illustrator: Richard Smith, *The Sunday Express* 12 Aug 1979: 9.)
37. "Treasure Trove." *Trek* 12.10 (Oct 1948): 18–19. (Illustrator: Richard Smith, *The Sunday Express* 5 Aug 1979: 7.)
38. "Unto Dust." *Trek* 13.2 (Feb 1949): 18–19. (Illustrator: Abe Berry, 19.)
39. "Graven Image." *On Parade* (6 Aug 1948): 8.
40. "The Picture of Gysbert Jonker." *On Parade* 22 Oct 1948: 4–5. (Illustrator: Abe Berry, 4.)
41. "The Homecoming." *On Parade* 16 Mar 1949: 10. (Illustrator: Abe Berry.)
42. "Susannah and the Play-actor." *On Parade* 14 Apr 1949: 10. (Illustrator: unknown.)
43. "Peaches Ripening in the Sun." *On Parade* 27 Feb 1951: 12–13.
44. "Romaunt of the Smuggler's Daughter." Undated typescript, Harry Ransom Humanities Research Center (HRHRC). First published as "The Romance of the Smuggler's Daughter" in *The Sunday Tribune* 19 Sept 1948: 22, 25. (Illustrator: unknown, 22.)
45. "The Ferreira Millions." *The Forum* 13.1 (1 Apr 1950): 24–25. (Illustrator: Richard Smith, *The Sunday Express* 19 August 1979: 10.)
46. "Sold Down the River." *The South African Jewish Times* Sept 1949: 25.
47. "The Lover Who Came Back." *The Star* 23 July 1949: 7; reprinted *The Sunday Tribune* 18 Sept 1949: 20.
48. "When the Heart is Eager." *The Forum* 12.26 (1 Oct 1949): 20–21.
49. "The Brothers." *The Forum* 12.44 (4 Feb 1950): 24–25.

50. "Oom Piet's Party." *The Sunday Express Supplement* 28 May 1950: 14–15.

51. "Funeral Earth." *Vista*. Johannesburg: Council of Cultural Societies, University of the Witwatersrand, 1950: 62–65.

52. "The Missionary." *Spotlight* Jan 1951: 14–15. (Illustrators: 'ADI', 14; Richard Smith, *The Sunday Express* 26 August 1979: 12.)

53. "The Traitor's Wife." *Spotlight* Feb 1951: 6–7, 57. (Illustrator: 'Flip', 6–7.)

54. "The Red Coat." Undated typescript, HRHRC.

55. "The Question." Undated typescript, HRHRC. (Illustrator: John Jackson, *Personality* 14 Aug 1969: 139.)

56. "The Old Potchefstroom Gaol." Undated typescript, HRHRC; title supplied.

57. "The Ghost at the Drift." Undated typescript, HRHRC. (Published in Afrikaans as "Dit Spook by die Drif", *Die Brandwag* 11.550 (16 Apr 1948): 9, 38, 40–41. Illustrator: 'Monté', 9.)

58. "Bush Telegraph." Undated typescript, HRHRC. (Published in Afrikaans as "Die Kaffer-tamboer", *On Parade* 3.9 (24 Aug 1949): 9. Illustrator: Abe Berry.)

59. "Tryst by the Vaal." Undated typescript, HRHRC.

60. "The Selon's Rose." Undated typescript, HRHRC.